Here Lies Memory

A Pittsburgh Novel

Here Lies Memory

A Pittsburgh Novel

by

Doug Rice

BLACK SCAT BOOKS

2016

Here Lies Memory
A Pittsburgh Novel
by Doug Rice

ISBN-13 978-0-997-77711-6

Cover & book design by Norman Conquest
Cover and interior photographs by the author

ACKNOWLEDGMENTS: Excerpts from this novel first appeared in radically different forms in *Western Humanities Review*, *Gargoyle*, *Black Scat Review*, *Entropy*, *Black Rabbit*, *Prapositio*, *The Collagist*, *580 Split* and *The Akademie Schloss Solitude Blog*.

This novel could not have been written without the generous support of the Akademie Schloss Solitude, Stuttgart, Germany.

Black Scat Books
P.O. Box 684
Guerneville, CA 95446-0684
BlackScatBooks.com

For Amber

And, as always, for my children:
Cory Douglas, Anna Livia and Quentin Joyce

The purest of all enigmas is that of memory, of time that seemed to have gone away and taken people, homes, and desires with it, time that seemed to have become past, to have murdered itself. The most direct, most intimate, form of suicide is the loss of memory. Such a suicide becomes a death that keeps a man living while all that is of what that man has become dies.

CHAPTER 1

Fred and Jim called what they did with words "mirrortalk." Night after night, Fred's words reflected Jim's and Jim's reflected Fred's. Neither of the men knew where their own words began or where the words of the other ended. Every night, they stood on Fred's back porch, drinking bottle after bottle of Iron City Beer, wishing their pain would disappear.

Beer bottles lined the railing, glass soldiers protecting the two men from their fears. Fred thought about counting each one, as if numbers could make sense of anything. Like so many other nights over the years, this night quickly faded into one more late night of either Jim or Fred nearly saying what needed to be said and, then, at the last second, gracefully avoiding saying any of it. Their friendship rested in these quiet moments. Waiting but not wanting, no longer even hoping.

A light flared on in the kitchen, and both men flinched and quickly turned away from the screen door, and stared out past Fred's backyard into the alley, where two teenagers were walking and kicking at loose gravel. They locked their gazes on the boy and girl and kept their mouths closed tight. Fred and Jim held their breath, waiting, wanting the world to be safe. In the kitchen, Debra, Fred's wife, opened the refrigerator door. They sensed her standing at the door staring into the nearly barren refrigerator, deliberately holding the door open in order to warm their beer, trying as best she could to destroy its usefulness.

"Don't expect me to pick up those bottles." She spoke directly into the cold mist of the refrigerator. "They're your problems. Yours, not mine." Most nights, Debra strolled into the kitchen, circled the table, stopped and stared through the screen door at Fred's and Jim's backs, then walked to the fridge, opened the door, mumbled incoherent litanies. Eventually, she turned off the light and returned to wherever she had come from. "There's no turning back," she yelled out at her husband. "Nope. No turning. This happens, that happens. Your skin changes. You get wrinkled up beyond recognition. Your mouth goes dry. Promises are broken. You'll see. You forget you ever believed in one damned thing. You forget words. One day," Debra said. "One day. Love becomes as useless as yesterday's *Post-Gazette*."

Fred and Jim quit staring at the teenagers and looked at each other. "I told you not to marry her," Jim whispered. "We could have been sitting in the bleachers at a Pirates' game that day instead of standing inside that damned church." Fred kicked at a loose board on the porch. "How many times I tell you that madness ran all through that woman's family. Brothers and sisters doing God knows what. Unspeakable madness. Ruined blood. I've been telling you that since high school, since before you met her, warning you to be careful around her and her brother." He held his beer bottle up to the light of the moon, hoping to discover some deep truth floating in it. "And what do you do? You marry her."

"Yeah, yeah. I know."

"You know?" Jim let out a light, muffled chuckle. "You say that like you believe it." He tried to look over at Fred without turning his head too much. "Those weren't dreadlocks in that woman's hair, bud. They were snakes crawling out of her thoughts. Waiting. A woman's patience is more frightening than her fury. The way they carry the memory of the tiniest indiscretion."

"You're the one true wise man, aren't you?" Fred said. "You know all this, and yet, you're the one who's divorced."

"Got that right. Wise enough to know when to find the door. And, here you are, out on the porch, not going anywhere, keeping your back to the kitchen door, whispering, drinking beer to give your heart the courage to go back in there and fall asleep in that bed and pray for morning."

Debra moved a chair in the kitchen, scraped it across the floor.

"There's no difference between what's happened and what never happened in the first place," Debra shouted softly. Then she paused. Fred and Jim waited, quiet, not even daring to look at each other. "It's just the things we remember and the way we remember them. It does not change anything. What we say. What we did. What happened to our flesh and blood." The light in the kitchen died away. "Fred?" Debra's voice softened. The night sky, for a moment, became lighter, the moon slipped out from behind the clouds. The kitchen returned to a quiet stillness. Jim and Fred relaxed their shoulders.

Their beers were empty. They took turns faking that they were still drinking, pretending that beer, or at least the hope for beer, still remained in their bottles. They both knew the other one was faking, but each of them feared going into that silent kitchen, afraid of what it might mean, afraid of what their steps might awaken.

"Fake swallowing?" Jim smiled.

"Yeah." They both laughed. "We have to get a cooler set up out here." The night grew darker, stars straining to shine, the moon had found its way around to the other side of the house, but the dense, humid heat, the kind that destroyed a man's heart, stayed, refused to let up.

Silence took over the night. All the talking they had done in their lives had nearly emptied their bodies of words. More than anything else, these nights were little more than their private ritual for drinking beer. Maybe they were afraid that they could not drink beer alone, that they would not know how. One night, one of them said, "Our silence speaks volumes." The other nodded, said, "Yes. Yes, it does." Neither knew for certain who had said what or why they had said what they had said. Then they went back into their solitude together, back to their beers, back to the kind of waiting that cracked ice on frozen lakes in early spring.

Flies stuck to their skin and to the window screens. Flies, lightning bugs, gnats, even bats were floating more than flying in the humid night air. Mosquitoes settled on veins, lethargically sucking at blood, because it was their fate to do so. Lightning bugs barely bothered to light up. The Pirates had a day off, so the radio was silent. Every blade of grass, every leaf on the tree longed for a breeze, no matter how slight.

"You have to do something about Lucas' bicycle." Jim lifted his chin to point at it, as if Fred did not know what he was talking about.

"It's rusted," Fred said, without bothering to look over at the bicycle. "Rusted clean through. I never thought anything could get so rusted." Fred believed it would be best for everyone if he hid that bicycle away in the garage, or buried it in the yard, but, more than anything, he prayed that Lucas' bicycle would disappear into the thin air. He looked at the deflated tires, the faded seat, the wild tangle of blackberry bushes and poison ivy weaving through the spokes. "Rust never sleeps," he said.

"What?" Jim asked.

"I'm in bed dreaming, and that rust still goes at it. I stand at the screen door in the morning with my coffee, and the rust is still at work. Destroying metal. Sun. Rain. Snow." Fred took another pull from his beer, wiped his lips with the back of his hand. "Rust never gives up, Jim. I wish I had that kind of devotion in me. I wish I had whatever it is that rust got in it that gives rust all that passion." He looked at Jim. "I wish I was rust."

"We all have our dreams," Jim said. He kept his stare locked on the bicycle. "It's not right, though. You know it isn't. You can't just ignore it. Leaving that bicycle there doesn't change anything. Not a damn thing. It doesn't make anything true. You do know that, right?" He glanced over at Fred. "Lucas still isn't here. Never was. And just because you lean a bicycle against a tree doesn't make a story true."

"I'm thinking the rust will take care of it." Fred looked at his empty beer bottle. "I got faith in that. It's all the faith I got left in me."

The bicycle had been leaning against the tree for years. The grass had grown high and wild. The blackberry bushes had taken over most of the yard. Truth be told, Fred wanted the whole yard to disappear, the bicycle to be stolen, the tree to be returned to its native soil; he wanted to forget all those nights of his past: that night in April he made love with Debra, that night Debra said she had gotten pregnant, and that day they had gotten married, and then that rainy morning they had had a son– Lucas– and the morning that this only begotten son, disappeared. Fred wanted to forget all of it, but some memories are not meant to be forgotten. Some are meant to stay in your skin, even if you forget the words that make the memory a memory.

Eleven years or so after the story of that child's birth, Debra changed the story, and Lucas disappeared. It just happened. Fred, groggy from nights of drinking beer, and Debra, groggy from years of misplaced dreams, woke up, and Debra whispered, "Lucas is gone." They looked everywhere. First, under the covers of his bed, then under his bed and in his closet, then under the cushion to the rocking chair, then in his toy chest. They called out his name a few times as they wandered through the hallways. They looked out onto the front porch from beneath the blinds in the living room, then Debra stepped out into the early August morning heat and crawled under the front porch, but no Lucas. Wet with morning perspiration and dew from the fog, and covered by spider webs, she found her way back into their house, back up the steps to their own bedroom, and began, once again, to rummage around for a child who could not truly be missing.

Debra stripped the bed of its blankets and sheets. She lifted each pillow, looked under each one, but no Lucas. She placed her finger-tips gently on her stomach and looked down, thinking that Lucas had escaped into her womb. She said, "There should be a map for missing children." Fred glanced over his shoulder at his wife; he shook his head, then returned to his quest. He opened the drawers to both dressers and stared inside. He searched beneath t-shirts and underwear. He opened the closet doors, lifted shoes, looked under them and looked inside them. Nothing. Even faced with all this clear evidence that this child no longer existed, both Fred and Debra remained commited to the story that Lucas had to be somewhere nearby, perhaps in the yard, trapped in the tree, or lost in the garage, or locked in some delightful story so childish that adults were the ones who had truly become lost. All either one of them had to do was place their son into the right sentence, and he would reappear.

Fred clearly remembered the night before this fateful morning. The Pirates had lost again. Jim had less beer than normal. Debra was in bed sleeping—or something like that—when he finally made his way inside the house from the porch and up the stairs to their bed. He remembered thinking for a moment that it would be nice to kiss Debra, even though she was fast asleep, snoring. He held a vague sensation that he did kiss Debra, actually bit her on the back of her neck, and she said, "Now is no longer the time for this to be done." He remembered falling asleep and waking up.

Debra walked out of their bedroom, away from Fred, calling for Lucas, her voice barely above a whisper, in the process of accepting that Lucas had left or had been taken away to some other land or that they had perhaps forgotten him somewhere. She walked down the steps one by one. Her throat tight. Her mouth dry. She thought, so this is what it feels like to lose faith.

The day before Lucas' disappearance, Debra had driven to the grocery store, stopped at church, and visited her brother, Bob. She remembered that, at the grocery store, she put three boxes of Lucky Charms into their cart. She laughed and imagined telling Lucas she was going to hide all of the marshmallows, so he could only dream about how a cereal could be so magically delicious. "You are silly to believe that the marshmallows in Lucky Charms were like anything else in the world," she said aloud. "They have special powers." She smiled, until she realized she was blushing, and that other shoppers were staring at her.

Debra remembered walking down the aisle at church and re-minding herself to stare at the floor, to keep her eyes on the floor, not to look up at the crucifix. The almost-naked body of Christ, on display in front of the church, disturbed her. Even the most innocent child could see Christ's muscular thighs, his thin torso, his sculpted ribs openly displayed. Debra had tasted the body and blood of Christ many times, and she had experienced seeing the body of Christ many more times in her daily thoughts, on the crucifix in church, on the crucifix above her bed, in photographs, carved in marble, beneath her eyelids when she lay flat on her back with Fred on top of her, but yesterday the nearly naked body of Christ unnerved her.

She remembered Bob saying that, any day now, something was going to happen. He kept saying, "Any day now," but Debra could not remember what he said was going to happen. She only remembered that he said he was not here to forgive her sins or to forget all she had done. She never quite understood what her brother meant by that, but she had been confessing to him since the day of his birth. She never held anything back, telling him stories of what her body had done and what had been done to her soul. Telling Bob what she saw in the darkness. Telling him that shadows destroyed the light. Telling him shadows were stronger than light and that she could prove it, but there was nothing to fear. Shadows were only shadows. In a whisper, she told Bob she had her suspicions about their father.

Debra became lightheaded thinking of these desires, and she leaned her shoulder against the wall. She inhaled slowly, tentatively, uncertain, about whether or not she still had God's permission to breathe, before continuing to walk down the hallway toward Lucas' room. She called his name, careful not to let the neighbors overhear her pleading, her longing for Lucas to call back to her.

Fred listened to her voice and footsteps fade, then he climbed the ladder into the attic. Even though he knew Lucas could not possibly be in the attic, stranger things have happened. Men had walked on the moon. Men had crucified the Son of God and the New York Mets had won a World Series. So Fred believed the incredible could still happen. Mostly, he simply wanted to sit down, away from Debra, maybe go back to sleep, or try to figure out what day of the week it was. He thought that if he were absolutely certain what day it was, he would be able to come up with an idea about why Debra had lost faith in Lucas. He was certain that this day, like every other day, had to be one of the days of the week. Something like Thursday, maybe, or Tuesday. Fred picked up a shoebox full of blurry Polaroid photographs, mostly black and white, some color. Perhaps Lucas was trapped inside one of them. Perhaps he had fallen into a memory. But his son was not in any of the photographs. Fred put the box back on the shelf, then climbed down the ladder.

Debra stood in the kitchen running water, doing dishes, making coffee. Doing things that people do everyday of their natural lives before they die. Doing these things because, by doing them over and over everyday, people are made to feel that their lives have meaning.

Fred called out for Lucas, but nothing happened. He stopped at the bathroom, looked in the shower, then stared into the mirror. He remembered a girl falling into a mirror and another one falling down a well. Falling. Being trapped in a mirror, with things getting bigger, then smaller. He looked into the corners of the mirror and picked at something gooey. Then he looked into his own face. Explored the color of his eyes, the strange pimples that just might be cancer. His body seemed to be getting angry at him as he grew older. Fred's doctor told him that when a man lives long enough, or too long, his body was bound to do some "crazy shit." He asked the doctor if "crazy shit" was a medical term, and the doctor said that it was in remote villages in France, but not so much in the states. Fred opened the medicine cabinet and peered inside. He moved bottles of prescriptions around, medicines saving Fred and Debra from death and madness. But no Lucas. He opened a few of the bottles, poured the little capsules out into the palm of his hand. Still no Lucas.

The phone rang. Debra answered it and called up to Fred, saying it was work wanting to know why he wasn't there. Her voice sounded calm, calmer than he had ever heard her voice before in his entire life.

"What day is it?"

"Tuesday."

"Are you sure?"

"Yes."

"Do you see Lucas?"

"No," Debra replied, her voice, even calmer than it was moments ago when she called to him.

Fred walked into the kitchen. Lucky Charms soaked in a bowl of milk. Imagining that today was like yesterday and like the day before that and like any other day that ever was or ever will be, Debra had set the breakfast table believing Lucas would appear.

When they were children, Bob told Debra that it was a sin to eat a spoonful of Lucky Charms before the milk turned pink. One day, their mother yelled at Bob to hurry, told him that he would miss the bus if he did not eat his cereal this very second. He replied, "I can't go any faster. None of this is up to us." Bob said it with such tenderness toward his mother, that she stopped moving and stood in the kitchen watching him sitting, perfectly still, beautifully still, with hands resting on his lap, never taking his eyes off the bowl of Lucky Charms, longing for the precise moment when the milk changed color, longing for that one mystical moment when milk became something more than it had ever been before.

The first day that their mother brought home Lucky Charms, she told Bob and Debra it was good for them, that Lucky Charms was fortified with vitamins and minerals; it would make them grow up to be strong and desirable; eating it would change their lives, that boys and girls would see the difference. "They will notice you," she whispered. The first time the milk turned pinkish-red, Bob became terrified. Even at seven years old, he knew that anything possessing the power to change milk into that color was dangerous and would do unspeakable harm to the insides of his body, so he pushed the contaminated cereal bowl as far away from him as possible with his white scrawny arms and his tiny boy hands. Their mother smacked Bob on the back of his head, smacked him three or four times until he gave up and ate and ate. The cereal disappeared into him, and there was no turning back. Nothing would ever be the same again.

Cereal can do that to a child. Change everything. Bob still eats Lucky Charms every morning. Debra stockpiles boxes of Lucky Charms. Row upon row in the kitchen cabinets. Bob's teeth fall out on a regular basis, and he cannot concentrate for more than a minute or two, but his life is filled with leprechauns and marshmallow stars. He sees them everywhere. He has sudden bursts of wild energy for no apparent reason, then he collapses into complete exhaustion for even less reason. He suffers from migraines. He stares out windows. Still, he loves his Lucky Charms.

"You want coffee?"

Fred looked at Debra as if she had asked him something far too impossible for him to ever understand, far too complicated to answer truthfully. Debra turned away from Fred. He took two or three steps across the quiet linoleum floor that no longer seemed familiar to him, toward her silent body. He lifted Debra's hair off the back of her neck. In the old days, he would kiss her on the spot where he had bitten her the night before, but those days were gone. Today, he lifted her hair, searching.

Nothing. Debra's hair fell back over her shoulders, and he walked to the sink, bent down, and opened the cabinet doors and took a quick look, calling out Lucas' name into that tiny space. Nothing. Not even the smallest of voices called back to him. He reached his hand into the cabinet. Again, nothing. Space. Time. Silence. Fred stood, straightened his tie, grabbed his suit coat from the back of a chair, and told Debra he did not have time for coffee, that time seemed to be running out or running away from them, then he headed out the kitchen door. He would go to work, and, when he returned from work, his wife would tell him that their son was playing in his bedroom or in the yard. Everything would be as it once was, as it was before this day began. The door closed behind Fred. He stopped for one brief moment on the porch. He needed to say something to Debra, but he could only turn silently away from her and walk into the day.

Debra remained standing at the sink. The water running. The sun breaking through the clouds. The day started like any other day of her life. She said Lucas' name. She did not call out his name. She simply said it as if she were saying her son's name for the very last time.

CHAPTER 2

Elgin, Johnny's grandfather, said he had no choice but to go blind. The world had been turning more and more blue to him, drifting in and out of focus, and he was tired of seeing, anyway. He had seen enough with his eyes and had done enough harm with his looking over the years, and all he had seen had done more damage to his soul than a lifetime of sins. He knew the time had come for him to forget, to forgive and to move on.

Elgin had seen the war in Vietnam. He had been a part of it. Had done his duty. Had killed men, had been told by Sergeant Joseph Anthony Badalamenti that "every man in all of America had the God-given and atheist-given right to kill gooks, to hunt them down and to kill them without thinking about it." Elgin and every other soldier in the platoon were told they had been given all the right they needed to burn down the trees of those heathens, to toss grenades into their tunnels, to reduce their villages to cinders, and to not lose sleep over any of it. And to never ask for forgiveness. "We are not doing anything wrong," Sergeant Badalamanti told them. "We do not need to be forgiven."

Young Elgin could not reconcile the beauty of Sergeant Badalamenti's name with the orders that came out of his mouth. The sergeant's sweet name was as close to a song as a man could get in those humid jungles. Any time Elgin said Badalamente's name, even when he screamed it out in anger or in fear, he had to hold himself back from bursting into song, from singing that sergeant's name up to the heavens. Elgin asked him what he was doing out there in the jungle with mere humans. "You should be in Carnegie Hall," Elgin told him. "You wouldn't even have to sing. You could just stand on stage and say your name, slow and subtle, and people would swoon."

Badalamente looked at Elgin with a quiet desperation, a kind of shy fear. "Just kill them, Private. Kill as many of them as you can," he told Elgin. "Keep your life simple." Sergeant Badalamenti looked down into the mud like he was only then seeing mud for the first time in his life. "Kill every single one of them, and then we'll go home, and we'll never see each other again, and we'll believe none of this really happened, and no one will know. We'll keep all we do here between us, between us and our nightmares and our maker."

In Vietnam, the enemy was anything that moved. Elgin shot leaves off trees; he shot birds in mid-flight. Only the stars and the moon survived in the night. And they survived because they moved too slowly for anyone to consider them to be enemies. One night, he watched a man shooting at ripples in a creek. Emptying round after round and that man saying, over and over: "They keep coming. I shoot them and I shoot them, but they keep coming." The point was to destroy anything that even slightly resembled life and to leave Vietnam uninhabitable, to make Vietnam an impossible place. Elgin had seen all of this and still sees it in his dreams, in his coffee, in streetlamps, in raindrops, in the whites of the eyes of people who wished he did not exist, people who never thanked him, not even once. He still coughs dirt from that war out of his mouth. Dirt from that many years ago continues to fill his lungs and to choke his breathing; occasionally, he spits blood, but thinks nothing of it. "Man lives long enough," he once told Johnny, "he's bound to spit blood or worse. Blood is bound to get angry at a man for the life he's been living. Blood done with you, before you done with it, and it just wants to escape. Skin can't hold a body back from bleeding."

After all the American bombs had carpeted the earth, Elgin moved in, humped down the trails between the trees in the tall grasses, doing clean-up, following orders, lifting wooden doors to underground shelters and, without looking, being told, "Never look, never ever look," then being ordered to drop grenades into those shelters and being told, "Never listen for their screams," being told to remember, always remember: "They're not people, they're not even human, they're gooks." Day and night, Elgin being told it was dangerous to forget that. Even as he lived through all that, he still believed in something that he could not name. At least he could not name it back then. He had seen all this fire and all this blood, still sees it everywhere he looks. He sees it in those places where he refuses to look; even with his eyes closed to the world, he sees it. And now he has grown tired of seeing anything at all.

Still, inside all those flames and inside all that noise, inside all the chaos of boots caked with mud and of corpses in bags waiting to go home, somehow, inside all that, Elgin was able to see the beauty of Johnny's grandmother, Thuy. Her beauty set his skin on fire, a slow blaze, burning his flesh and his muscle. It awakened him and reminded him that there still was still a place beyond all that fire and smoke. She rescued Elgin as much as he rescued her. He stole Thuy away from the fire and rain and mud, and brought her back to his home in America, to Pittsburgh, brought her to a wood-frame house in the Hill District, where they would live, and they would listen to R&B on WAMO late into the night, resting in each other's arms, drifting into sleep on that swing on their front porch, until, one cool autumn morning, she would give birth to Lehuong, a girl so beautiful speech got stupid around her, and Thuy would love Elgin and be loved by him, then, after all that, Thuy would die. Too young and too soon. She would be taken from this world, from Pittsburgh, from Lehuong, from Johnny, from Elgin, from that quiet wood-frame house on the hill, too soon.

Thuy's death tired Elgin out, exhausted him of seeing. What was left for him to see, anyway? An actor, against any form of logical thought, had become president of the United States of America. A man had walked on the moon for no apparent reason. One of the only experiences he lived through that made sense to him after Thuy died was that of his cherished Pirates becoming family, and those boys of Pittsburgh beating those Orioles from Baltimore, the ones who thought they were so high and mighty going up against those simple working-class boys from Pittsburgh. Those Pirates won that World Series, taught the world a lesson that the world did not want to believe, taught the world that money did not matter, that spirit and faith still mattered more than all the money in the world, that simply playing the game as they did in the old days mattered more than riches. Elgin was just sad that Clemente missed it, and sad that Thuy and Lehuoung missed it, too.

Elgin saw beauty so deep in the eyes of his wife, in the shape of her smile, and saw the wonder of a different kind of beauty in their daughter, who also died so very young, but Lehuong's beauty was in so many ways not of this world. She could never quite fit into the rhythms of daily life. She was constantly tripping, bumping into people. The world could not understand a beauty so complex, a beauty so strong, a beauty that limped. And when they died, their deaths emptied the world of truth. Losing such love did something to Elgin, to his eyes. Having seen such beauty, he lived the rest of his days in simple terror.

Not even a year after his mother's death, Johnny started running with the worst of the bad on the North Side, mostly along East North Avenue near Federal Street, and lately he had begun staying out all night, sleeping along the banks of the Monongahela River, living the life of one of those lost boys from Peter Pan. Elgin saw the marks in Johnny's eyes. He saw more in the boy's eyes than Johnny himself was able to understand. He knew what waited for Johnny, even though Johnny could not know, would never know, until he could not stop it from becoming true. Elgin knew all he could do was try to lift those marks from his eyes before they formed scars and blinded the boy.

So this night, this very last night of Elgin being able to see before going blind, was in some ways long overdue. For years, he looked forward to day after day of seeing nothing of what the world wanted to force him to see. But Elgin was no fool. He knew simply willing himself to go blind would not stop his memories or his visions or his night terrors. He knew those visions were inscribed on the insides of his eyelids, burned deep, napalm-orange deep into his muscles, carved into the grey lines that covered the palms of his hands. He knew those visions would stay with him and maybe even become stronger. He had been living with them for so long that they had become the biggest part of him. Elgin simply did not want to add to those old memories by seeing anymore of the goings-on of the outside world, any more of what was no longer there, of all that was being torn down and being celebrated as progress.

Johnny walked into his grandfather's bedroom. Elgin was sitting, silent and still, in his rocking chair, reading the very last book he would ever read. Most of the letters on the pages seemed to have taken on a life of their own. Moving in uncertain ways, trying to find their passage to the end of the sentence or trying to escape the page, trying to find a different life, a better story, a safer place, trying to be left alone, to say no more than what they had to say.

Elgin lifted his eyes, but he could not bring up the courage to look directly at his grandson. He stared off to the side of his face, close enough to make him believe he was still capable of looking at Johnny if he ever desired to do so. Elgin survived Vietnam without blinking one single time. But looking at his grandson was different. He saw too much of Lehuong in Johnny's eyes, in his cheekbones, in his olive-stained dark skin. And Thuy haunted his expressions, struggling to remind him of his past, of his ancestors, so Elgin forced himself to look to the side of Johnny's face. Maybe the real reason he wanted to go blind was to no longer see the ghosts that attached themselves to his grandson's face.

"What are you reading?"

"Words," Elgin said softly and closed the book, holding his place with his thumb. "Words on empty pages," he smiled. "Words that want to tell stories, but I can't make much sense of them." Elgin began to push himself out of the rocking chair, but decided to remain sitting a bit longer. Johnny took a step forward to help his grandfather, but he stopped. He and his grandfather were both forever on the edge of moving back into each other's lives, but each time they moved toward each other something stopped them. They were trapped inside a perpetual hesitation.

"You sure it happens this way? You just go to sleep like any night, but you wake up blind?" He looked down at his grandfather's weathered hands.

"Yes." Elgin placed the book on the table beside his rocking chair. He pulled his thumb out, losing his place in the book. He would never finish reading it. He would never know what happened next or why all that had happened earlier in the book had happened. He would never know why any of it mattered, where any of it was leading. He would only know that middle passage, that moment of stopping before arriving, before reaching the end. Like drowning. Not a drowning that puts an end to something, but one that remembers. Until that point, the book had been about another heartbroken saint lost in the forest, a man looking for a river in a dry pasture and wanting to grow roses in a soil that God had meant for something else. A man fighting demons, resisting the temptations of his wife, a man drifting in the vast desert of loneliness, living with hopeless memories of a time when he was not so alone, not so adrift. But all Elgin clearly remembered from his distracted reading was some woman named Ruth, or some other Biblical name, saying, "They're not savages. They're salvages." He had no idea what the woman meant. What she intended for the man, her husband, to understand, or what the woman hoped Elgin would understand by reading it. And there was some boy in the book, pressed into the sentences, a boy missing since dawn, and a girl, a young girl, forgotten. And the man in the book, the husband, Elgin couldn't remember his name, saying something about every woman's head or thoughts crawling with snakes. There was no trusting them. Women or snakes. They were all caught in the evil mysteries.

But Elgin refused to believe what that man said. He did not trust him. He felt the man was only saying things so that he could go on living his life the way he wanted to live it. Dead of truly seeing into that woman.

Johnny looked around the room, looked at everything he could look at in order to avoid looking at his grandfather. He was never one to hold his eyes still. "Impatient eyes move too fast." Elgin often lectured the boy. "Impatient eyes are blind. Too busy looking instead of seeing. Your eyes will always be disappointed. It's a sin the way you move your eyes. Butterfly eyes. You got to be patient." Johnny continued searching the room, seeking out a place to look without seeing too much of what even he feared he needed to see.

"How can you know for certain you're going to wake up blind?" Johnny asked. He stared at the slippers covering his grandfather's feet, doing all he could not to look into his grandfather's face—his mouth, his eyes, those wrinkles. He did not want to get too close to his grandfather's thoughts. He knew from his grandfather that any man who looks too long into one place is bound to see more than he bargained for.

"You get old like this, and you know things. Your eyes end up wanting a life of their own," his grandfather said. "They get tired of your life."

Johnny shook his head. He wanted to walk over to his grandfather, but he stood still, remained frozen. Elgin looked at Johnny's uncertain hesitation, his feet almost lifting off the carpet, his hands, restless, at his side. He looked at his grandson struggling not to cross his arms or to shove his hands into his pockets. "You got places to go, you go," Elgin said. "I can manage." He pushed his war-torn flesh out of the rocking chair. "I don't want you standing around here, pacing the floors, if you got some other place you'd rather to be. Ain't right for no one to be standing in one place when they want to be in some other place. Boys in school, they want to be graduated and off living their lives. They get a job, they want to be retired." Elgin rubbed his tired eyes. "Maybe that's what they mean when they say 'life after death.' Maybe that's where life is hiding away. Life is waiting for us after death. You got to kill this life before you can come to understand you ain't never lived this life."

Elgin walked over to the window, each step more broken than the last one. "The afterlife. What's that even mean? Gives people an excuse not to live this life, but this life is the only one you truly got." Elgin placed a hand on the windowsill and pressed another against the windowpane. "You don't see your grandma or your mother on these streets no more, do you, Johnny? You only hear about them in stories. Afterlife ain't no life; afterlife is just an excuse. This is your life, boy. Ain't no grand reward waiting for you. The reward's here. You've been given a life to live. God didn't want no one to be waiting for no afterlife. This life is the gift. Go do something with it. You're killing too much time, Johnny. Imagine if you could hear time screaming in agony with all the killing of time people do?" Elgin looked over his shoulder toward Johnny. "It ain't right to hurt time, let alone to kill it."

Elgin slowly turned back to the window and stared out into the night. "It don't feel so much like it's the last time that I'm seeing Dinwiddie Street as it feels like it's the first time I'm seeing it." He wiped at his eyes with the back of his hand. "It's the edges that are gone.

Everything just blends and turns blue. Most of the street has already disappeared." Elgin stopped himself. Some sentences need to end; others should end before they begin. Suicide sentences that never say what needs to be said, sentences that kill themselves in the act of being spoken. Old shadows appeared, reflected, more against the window than in it. The shadows seemed to be both outside and inside, tired but patient with years of waiting. The shadows brought with them a light wisp of Thuy's beauty, a moment of Elgin seeing her eyes once again. "The street's just rags and bones and whispers," Elgin said, "and when winter comes, it's just cold and empty and wanting."

Johnny remained standing at that distance, a truce of sorts that he and his grandfather had silently agreed upon the moment that Johnny's mother died. He stood, safely away from his grandfather, looking at his back. His shoulders had shrunk; the old man's ribs seemed to be caving in. He was collapsing in on himself. His body was getting tired all at once, like all those years were finally falling down on his shoulders and resting there.

"You could have fixed this, stopped it. You had that choice." Johnny's words came out angrier than he had meant them to be.

Elgin kept his back to Johnny, kept looking out through the shadowed window into this last night of seeing. "We all have choices. We're making choices now, Johnny. Each word is a choice. Silence wants to be left alone, but we can't leave it be, so we crowd it with talk. Word after word killing the silence," Elgin said. "Each time we look at something, we're choosing to look. We only see any damn thing because we make choices."

Johnny stood his ground, refused what he felt was his grandfather's invitation to start yet another argument about the way he was living his life, about all that he was throwing away. "But," Johnny shot gently at his grandfather's back, "how are you ever going to be able to find your way down to Jack's Uptown or to the river? To Grandma's grave? To Red's?" Johnny kept his voice soft and low. "How are you going to be able to walk down to Red's and back up the hill, when you're blind?"

"Man wants a beer, Johnny, a man finds his way to it. That doesn't change. I know men who climb out of their graves and stumble all over the city, most never find their way home, but they always find a beer." He let out a laugh. Johnny smiled. "I still know where there's beer, and I will know how to get there. Beer memory is ingrained. You know that. In this city, we're all born knowing where beer hides. Even you got that in you. Man don't need to see to find beer. You have faith. It's what it means to be a man in this city."

Elgin smiled in the direction of his grandson. He knew that what he said was no longer all that true. Pittsburgh was changing, had been changing, destroying itself to become something Elgin wanted nothing to do with. A decaying city trying to save itself by being something in the eyes of people not born in it. "I know how to feel my way through the streets," Elgin continued, "It's a miracle these streets are still here." He placed his hands flat on the windowsill, leaned heavy on that old, wooden windowsill, and he took a deep breath. He pressed his forehead against the window. That window seemed to hold as much pain in it as was in Elgin's memories. Years of people looking out that window, wanting something that could not be touched, or people looking up from the streets at the window, wanting to find their way in. Years of Elgin's ancestors looking out that window and hoping.

"It's dangerous," Johnny said. He stepped forward, toward his grandfather, then sideways, then he took a step backwards. His body confused by what it needed to do, what it wanted to do, what it was required to do. "They're not just streets anymore."

"They're no more dangerous for a blind man than for a man who thinks he can see. Half of what you think you see, you don't see at all." Elgin lifted his forehead from the window, nearly went so far as to turn around toward Johnny, but he kept peering out the window. "This is something I need, Johnny. You need to respect my wanting it." Elgin nearly let out some kind of breath from his past. He leaned back in closer to the window again and squinted, looking for something he longed to see one last time. He wiped dust from the glass. "I need this. You needn't worry. I won't burden you. Blindness normally gets thrust on a man, gives him no choice. It's better to choose blindness. Those kids in Vietnam screaming for their sight to come back, and God just ignoring them, and part of me being grateful it wasn't happening to me, grateful I could see your grandmother, see the footprints, find a way to get back home. Another part of me thought they were the lucky ones to be done with seeing all that I was seeing there, knowing everything I saw was becoming a part of me."

"What if you change your mind?"

"I'll have you see for me. How's that?" Elgin took another breath, a deeper breath that Elgin often called on to reach into his soul, down into the man he was before the war, into the place of his ancestors. "And my hands. I know the kinds of things my hands can see. It won't be the first time my hands guided me."

Only a few hours remained before midnight. Johnny didn't know if his grandfather would become blind at the strike of midnight or if a bolt of lightning would kill off the last of his grandfather's seeing. He didn't know if it happened slowly, while his grandfather slept. "How are you going to be able to watch baseball, or how are you ever going to dream or even know that you're dreaming?"

"I've been watching baseball inside my head all my life. All those summers I lost fighting for whatever it was we were dying for, and missing baseball game after baseball game. I made it through that damn war by watching ball games inside my head. Imagining Clemente gunning down some fool crazy enough to try to score from third. Test the Great One's arm. Or Clendenon stretching out at first. I got enough of them images inside my head. Once you seen what you've seen, you've seen it. No erasing it. No place to hide from what you've seen. Even when you think what you saw is gone from you, it's still in you."

Elgin stood up straight, stretched. He turned around to look toward his grandson. Their eyes met for a moment, but they both quickly looked away. He stared down at Johnny's feet. Too often Elgin could only see all there was that was no longer here, Lehuoung's dream of love or Thuy's eyes, all that was dead and departed. Elgin only saw the haunting. He could not rest his memory and see the young boy standing in front of him. "Tomorrow will be no different for you, Johnny. You'll have a blind grandfather. That's all. Maybe a new story or two to tell. You close your eyes for a minute, then you open them. The world is still there. You close your eyes for years, then you open them. The world is still there. I'm just going to close my eyes until death parts me from this. The world don't go nowhere. Your mother stopped seeing. She's dead now. We're still here, even without her seeing us. The world goes on."

Elgin returned his gaze to the rapidly darkening world outside the window. Johnny found enough courage to take a true step closer to his grandfather. "A final moment of seeing, before the blue turns into darkness," Elgin said. Johnny's grandfather looked more like he was waiting to hear a sound, a cricket from his childhood, perhaps, than waiting to see some final miracle, some final magic. "In the morning, all this will be over."

Johnny tried to touch his grandfather's shoulder. His hand thinking back to some lost moment of innocence, remembering who he was when he was still a boy. "Seeing is nothing more than a hoax," Elgin said. "There's not much good to it." He turned away from the window and looked over at a photograph of Thuy and him on their wedding day. Johnny followed his grandfather's gaze. "It's why I first fell in love with your grandmother, though. It's God's truth. Seeing is." He lowered his eyes as if to pray with his eyes instead of with his voice, then he slowly lifted his eyes and looked one final time at the photograph before going back to staring out the window. He peered into the night, away from everything that was inside, peered at the empty, useless street.

"Maybe God should have made it that all men be born blind, so a man have to learn how to see, same way a man got to learn how to eat," Elgin said. "Man learns to eat slow and careful, he learns to be grateful, attentive, with his eating, with all he's putting into his body. Same with seeing. A man got to take his time with whatever it is that he's looking at, so he sees what he's seeing instead of what he wants to see."

Elgin wiped at dust clinging to the windowpane, rubbed his thumb into that glass. "Imagine a world where a man got to learn to sit and listen to a woman's voice to guide him out of his blindness. Create a world so that listening to a woman makes a man want to be near her. Make a man long to touch a woman's soul, because he listens to her stories." He leaned his forehead against the windowpane. "Imagine a world where seeing comes to a man slow, real slow. A man can't even see a woman until her storytelling makes her become visible to him. Until then, any woman is invisible. Imagine a world where seeing starts out unfocused, then a woman's voice focuses his seeing. A woman coaxing a man's seeing out of him. Maybe that'll fix what's wrong everywhere." Elgin let out a tiny laugh. "Man wanders the streets, longing for a woman to give him sight. Such a world takes longer than seven days to create, takes more patience than even God had. Maybe that's the flaw with seeing. It speeds up desire too much, turns desire into lust."

Elgin closed his eyes. He kept them closed for a long while. He seemed to be practicing for his blindness. Held the darkness down below. After breathing with the dark, he opened his eyes and looked out that window again, kept staring out into the night, like Johnny was not even there. He looked out the window like he was trying to see if anything, if any tiny detail, had changed while he had his eyes closed.

Johnny remained quiet, even though he was tempted to remind his grandfather about the story Elgin's father, Clarence, had told him about the sins of the Garden of Eden and how Eve's storytelling and her desire for riches beyond her own sense of her self, about her desire for knowledge that would make her different than the woman God meant her to be, about how Eve's storytelling had dirtied up seeing for all mankind for good. "Once that kind of dirt happened, there weren't no turning back." Clarence told Johnny's grandfather that story to keep Elgin from falling prey to a woman's desires. "A woman telling you stories makes you want to know what you should never want to know," he told him. And Elgin told Johnny that story, but never told him why he needed to know it.

Elgin cleared his dry throat. "Your mother wanted to keep you blindfolded from the time you were born. She feared you'd be see-ing and wanting too soon. But the way God created it, a man sees a woman before he talks to her. It's seeing that makes him do the wanting, but what a man truly needs to see ain't there for him to see. A man cries he loves a woman, body and soul. But all he wants is the body."

Elgin shook his head. "It's what I did, it's all I knew to do. I sat and looked at your grandmother until day turned to night and turned back to day. It's all we seemed able to do when we first met. Sit with each other in the quiet. But seeing your grandmother wasn't why I married her or why I stayed and wanted the staying to last until every human being on the planet took their last breath. It's not why I lived with her through her memories of those fires, all those bombs falling from the skies, all that flesh falling into the mud. Those nights of your grandmother whispering, 'Fuck you, America, and your war', in her sleep. Her feet kicking at phantoms, at me, at the blankets. I wished I could have stayed awake all night and held her ankles. Helped her find peace. And her fists, so small and confused. Her fists waking me out of dreams. Bruising my tired shoulders. She suffered night terrors more than I did. Voices she heard more true than the ones I heard. Her dreams were never dreams. Sleep never sleep. And me wanting to do just one thing for her that made sense. If I could have just done one thing for her. Just one."

Elgin stopped to catch his breath, stopped to try to forget the pain that kept Thuy's body captive. "And no one in this neighborhood knew any of it; they just looked at your grandmother," Elgin went on. "That's all they could do. Looking is why every man in this neighborhood knocked on our kitchen door at all hours of the day, every day, even Sundays, year after year. It's why they waited behind trees for your grandmother and for your mother, too. It's why they chased your mother everywhere. Looking with eyes blinder than my eyes ever will be. It's what looking does. It turns you. It decays your eyes and makes you want . . ." Elgin looked back out the window, shook his head. "I can't say in words. There's words. I just don't have them. They're gone."

Johnny touched his grandfather's shoulder in the same way that people tap a burner on the stove with their fingertips, testing to see if the burner was hot. Then he rested his hand there. "But if it weren't for seeing, it would be something else, I guess. There's no stopping what gets inside a man's head once it gets inside there," Elgin said.

Johnny looked over his grandfather's shoulder, out the window onto Dinwiddie Street, out over the buildings to the city. There were more and more darkened houses on the street, abandoned and dilapidated houses that, at one time, had been homes. Broken doorways. Boarded-up windows. Broken glass in what little yellowed and burned grass survived the humidity of the dry summers in Pittsburgh. There were fewer and fewer streetlights, a sputtering one here or there. Cars with shattered windshields or sitting up on cinder blocks. Cars frozen in place by a boot. The few people who walked the streets at night did all they could to avoid being seen, darting from shadow to shadow.

"The streets," Elgin said, still looking out the window. "All these streets have gone precious on me."

CHAPTER 3

With Lucas gone, Fred and Debra continued to live their lives in their two-storey, wood-frame house with a front porch and a back porch, a tiny postage-stamp-sized backyard, and an empty bedroom that never made sense to anyone. They lived inside the rooms of this house on Center Street in the small village of West View on the outskirts of Pittsburgh.

Debra no longer knew the day or the month or the year that their child evaporated, leaving behind only small traces of his former self in words and stories. With each passing sunset and each coming sunrise, Debra came closer and closer to believing they never had a son.

Lucas, so the story goes, must have walked out the kitchen door one early morning when his parents were not looking. Perhaps they were only dreaming or had always been dreaming. Some parents tend to do that. Dream away lives that they never seem to live. Everything that belonged to Lucas remained in the house. His rusted bicycle leaned against the maple tree. His clothes remained on the floor of his bedroom or were jammed into overflowing drawers. His toys cluttered the house, waiting for him to return from some distant land that only existed in fairy tales. And if Debra knew anything, she knew where fairy tales took little boys and girls. And she also knew that fairy tales demanded patient waiting by parents in the midst of disordered desire and hope.

The last time Debra thought she might have seen Lucas, he was standing against a blank wall in his bedroom. She thought that he most likely had blended into the wall in some sort of perfect union.

A few times she ran her hand over the wall and whispered his name. Before going to bed, she placed a doughnut on a plate and a glass of milk on the kitchen table. She insisted that Fred leave the porch light on, a beacon of disappointment, and she also turned on a nightlight in the hallway. By morning, the milk had turned sour. The doughnut had gone stale. Occasionally, ants covered the doughnut. Debra imagined the ants lifting the doughnut and carrying it off to Lucas in his secret world. Fred called all of it a waste, a waste of time, a waste of food, but Debra told him that she believed even boys who had disappeared into the invisible world enjoyed doughnuts.

Little by little, days grew darker, more humid, became quieter, and a touch more desperate. Neighbors said it was the changing of the season, late summer into early autumn. But Fred knew better. He knew that he and Debra were coming closer and closer to some kind of an end. The kind of end that no one ever returned from. The simple disappearance of Lucas made the sun grow tired. It gave up earlier and earlier each day and fell down behind the hills to make way for the darkness.

One night, a wedding photograph of Fred and Debra, laughing as they ran out of Saint Mary's church into the rapidly disappearing daylight, fell off the hallway wall onto the floor. The frame broke, the glass cut into the flesh of the photograph. "One less memory of a memory," Fred mumbled as he swept up the tiny shards of glass. He was sure that some people would call such an accident an omen, but he knew better than to pay attention to such thoughts.

And Fred knew that Jim—an English major in college—would give that broken photograph all kinds of meaning. Fear in a carpet full of broken glass. Jim would ask Fred, or anyone within hearing distance, when lilacs last in some disappointed dooryard bloomed, when rain last fell on a red wheelbarrow—crazy talk about abbeys and lonely blonde-haired women too beautiful for the world of the common man. Jim would go on and on, until he himself had had enough with it, or until someone threatened him. Drunk or sober, at ballgames or in churches, Jim liked seeking out meaning where things were best left unsaid or unknown; he liked playing the detective, looking under the surface, lifting carpets, staring into white spaces, licking his lips like he saw things the rest of the world should be jealous of him for seeing. Fred could hear Jim saying that so much, so very much, depended on that glass in the carpet. Then he imagined Jim winding down, saying something about it being the best of times and the worst of times, like saying that meant something more than it could say.

Fred liked it simple. He liked the true to be true, not hidden. He liked the false to be false, not hidden. Life. Love. Loss. Desire. Words. Touch. Beer. Pure and simple. He still loved Debra, even in this awkward silence that had now grown into the only intimacy holding them together. There was a time, years back, when either Fred or Debra would break the silence. Sometimes one word spoken just above a whisper would be enough to pull them into each other's arms. Now, they seemed to have forgotten how to speak to each other.

Fred drank, slow and casual, with the tender joy of a man in love with his cold beer, and never said anything. His beer, itself, became a weapon that protected him from talking and from listening. He knew people around him were talking. He saw their lips moving, but he only nodded or mumbled a barely audible, "Yeah." The silence never felt all that lonely to him when he held his beer in his weak hand. The silence, in fact, seemed downright musical, as long as Fred had his beer. In one of his more poetic moments—a rare moment— he called the silence a symphony. He just blurted it out one day. He told Jim they were musicians in a symphony of silence. Jim looked at him and said, "The hell we are." Then they both went back to being silent.

Fred also knew that all this silence crowding his life with Debra was caused by more than just the fact that she said Lucas was missing. He knew deep down it had something to do with something he did or didn't do years ago. Something that broke Debra's heart and that then festered there, and that whatever it was that he had done or not done had grown into this dark, vast silence that now existed between them. He knew in his own heart that this silence must have grown out of a look he gave some woman, most likely the way he looked at their neighbor Gabriela's cheekbones, all high and mighty, reaching to the heavens and pulling men down into the depths of hell, but more likely it was the way Debra saw him looking into Gabriela's eyes. Her eyes had a criminal beauty about them.

The only day any living soul in the neighborhood could recall Gabriela removing her sunglasses, Fred wrecked his car, drove it up over the curb. She simply took her sunglasses off like doing so was not going to change the entire world. Those dazed and mystified eyes of that woman, who had journeyed up to Pittsburgh from Chile, made men go blind. And Debra never did forgive Fred for that simple, innocent act of looking.

Now Debra rests her chin in the palm of her hand and quietly waits for her tea to cool. She remembers the bill for the repair of the car to the exact penny. $786.23. Because Gabriela has green eyes. Because she removed her sunglasses. Because she exposed herself to the gaze of just anyone and everyone in the entire neighborhood. Because Debra's husband could not refrain from looking. "What sort of neighbor does that to other women's husbands?" But Debra wasn't asking Fred a question; she was letting him know that nothing would ever be the same again and that she hoped he enjoyed seeing Gabriela's eyes that one time.

Ever since the day he watched Gabriella take off her sunglasses and saw her eyes—and he did not even say hello to her, he only looked into her eyes—ever since then, Debra seemed to look at Fred with the kind of soft stare that a child gives to their mother when they can no longer trust her. That very first moment a child experiences and knows doubt. There was no way to look back at such a stare. The best he could ever do was look down at his shoes, kick at an invisible pebble, and wait for Debra to look away.

And now Lucas is missing, has been missing; the police say he will be missing for the rest of their lives. Some mysteries, they say, are not meant to be solved. There are days when Fred and Debra cannot remember his birthday. They only remember waking one morning in the long ago, to some indistinct disappointment mixed with a vague longing and to a house that had become quiet.

In this drawn-out silence, they glanced at each other only on the rarest of occasions. Usually by accident. One or the other might step into the other's line of vision, and the other would quickly look as far away as either of them could look. Still, they loved each other. A lingering sweetness from the day when that broken, injured photograph was taken and from all those years before that day. From so many nights, in each other's arms. That kind of love never really goes away, even in the worst of times; it might disappear for a while, but it stays, even in silence.

When Fred came home that night of the first day that Lucas had disappeared, Debra was still standing at the kitchen sink, staring out the window. She looked like she had forgotten about God. It wasn't that she had lost her faith in God or was angry with Him; it was more like she had somehow, through the day, forgotten He ever existed. She stood, staring, as close to naked as a woman could get while still wearing clothes, stood there without God, exposed, twisting a dishrag in her white hands, waiting. Maybe it wasn't so much waiting, since waiting meant that something would be coming sooner or later. She just stood. Rigid, but not cold. Frightened, but not afraid. And when Fred walked into the kitchen and saw her, she did not move, nor did she turn around.

And that was the moment when the deeper silence began. The silence that turned dark, that became a cave, the silence that destroyed whatever remained of their trust in each other. Fred had called home throughout the day, but the phone only rang and rang. Sometimes he thought that Debra had forgotten how to answer a telephone. She never answered when he called. Or maybe there was something in the way the phone rang, so that Debra knew not to pick up, that it would be him, that it could only be her husband, the man who had looked into those green eyes of that Chilean woman and lost control of their car. And they must have been the only family in America that did not own an answering machine.

"Either we are home or we are not home," Debra said whenever Fred brought up the possibility of buying an answering machine. "What kind of person wants to talk to a machine? Leave their voice on it?" she said. "Who is possessed by that kind of madness? I'll tell you. People I do not want to know, not even to say 'Hello' to in passing." She looked at the phone, helpless on the wall, daring it to ring. "I would never leave my voice on a machine. It's worse than leaving a thumbprint on a bed frame. Who knows what those people with their answering machines will do with my voice once I leave it on their machine?"

Fred walked up behind Debra. He wanted to say something, had so much to say, but could not find words. He went looking for words, knowing that once words had been there on the inside of him, somewhere, and that usually it was not so difficult to find them. Now there was only silence. A hole.

"Lucas?"

"I called."

"Is he here?"

"I looked. He's not here."

"I shouldn't have gone to work."

"They would've fired you."

"What do you mean, you called?"

"For Lucas. In the rooms. In the yard. In the garage. Everywhere we looked this morning, and then everywhere we did not look. Lucas is nowhere."

"Did you tell anyone else that you think Lucas is missing?"

"The police. I called them. They could not find him. They think Lucas might be somewhere we have not looked."

"You should have called me."

Debra finally turned away from the window. She stared straight into the center of Fred's eyes. "The police said that would not be necessary. They said not to call you. They warned me. They said under no circumstances should I call my husband. There are procedures to follow. Sometimes people take children from their home. A policewoman sat beside me, and she held my hand between her hands and said something to me. Her hands were soft and warm. I looked up into the eyes of a very tall officer who wrote down every word I said. He even wrote down my breathing. I liked what I saw when I looked up at him. I liked how he made me feel. Sometimes any wife forgets herself or her husband. And I felt that at any moment something could happen." She reached her hand out toward her husband and lightly touched his cheek. "Nothing did. But something could have. You need to know that something could have happened. I called for Lucas, but only in my tiny voice, and the officer squeezed my hand, but that did not change anything either."

Debra looked down at the dishrag in her hands. She looked at Fred's feet, then back up at the eyes of her husband. She knew she needed to tell him more, to tell him everything, even though so much of it seemed like it had not happened, and so much of it seemed like it would harm him, hurt him somewhere inside.

"The police," she continued, "said sometimes the people you least suspect take children. They steal their own children and take them into the forest or factories or basements or shopping malls. The police said there are candy stores everywhere. They said sometimes there are money problems or not enough food. Sometimes the wife is the last to know. Parents become bored and need something that they cannot say to anyone. The police are looking into it. Into everything. Our lives. The basement. The attic. The garbage cans. They will come to know more than we bargained for. I am certain of this." Debra dropped the dishrag to the floor, then rubbed her hands together so hard that Fred thought they would start bleeding or go up in flames. She rubbed her thumb into the palm of her hand, rubbed it and rubbed it. "Sometimes skin is not thick enough," she said. She bent over to pick up the dishrag. Before standing back up, she told Fred they were going to check him out at work, that they had a sense about these things.

Fred tried to ask why, but he could not find the words. Debra twisted the dishrag and waited. "Lucas," he started and ended. "Lucas," he repeated the name they had given their son and waited for any word to follow that name, but saying his son's name erased every other word that he had ever known.

Debra looked back into his eyes. "The police want to make sure everything is the way it should be. They said they knew things that I would never know. Things I would not want to know. Things that would never go away. The police said they would keep an eye on me, too, watch me for signs, just like they are going to watch you. They said for me not to think I was in the clear. They asked me if I felt threatened. They asked me if they were scaring me. Sometimes a mother feels threatened by the truth. Sometimes children abandon their homes. One day a child is in the house, at the kitchen table eating a cookie, and the next day the child is no longer there. They said things like that happen every day, even if no one wants to believe it. And there are other things, worse things that happen to children that no one ever wants to believe. They told me the man in the moon is a man, has always been a man, not a woman. That it will always be that way. Forever. That there will never be a woman in the moon to watch over children at night. I wanted to hurt the police officer who said that, but he had his hand on his gun, and I asked them what they did to the other officer, the tall one who said he would watch over me."

Debra's shoulders relaxed, but the muscles in her neck tightened. She nearly cried, but held the tears inside her, held the pain down in her chest. Choked. The loss caught in her throat. "I want," Debra said. She brought her lips together, closed her eyes. "We need." Her sentences stayed simple. Incomplete. "This. We need this. A woman." She looked around the kitchen for that woman, the one they needed. Debra nearly looked outside the window and into the world that seemed to be vanishing. "There must be someplace where there is a woman on the moon. There must be." She placed the dishrag on the kitchen counter. It fell to the floor. She looked down at it, but left it there.

The police did not give up. They promised they would never give up. They returned again that night with flashlights and dogs and sus-picions. And they returned again the next morning with coffee and more dogs. And they whispered. They blew across their coffee to cool it down, and whispered again. They whispered all they feared or hoped was true of Fred and Debra. And they did follow Fred. And they questioned every person he worked with. They questioned people who Fred did not even know existed. The police also ques-tioned the neighbors. They even questioned Gabriela. They wanted to know if she had noticed anything strange. If Fred had made prom-ises to her that no husband should ever make to some other woman. They made it clear to her that they knew everything there was to know about that accident. They told her that she was safe, that no one could harm her.

One young officer sat on the steps of their back porch and smoked a cigarette. Debra shouted through the screen door at him. She said smoking would kill him, that he would die before he got old. The officer said that he hoped he did and laughed a laugh Debra thought was too soft for a man with so much power. She felt something wake inside her, but she turned away from the screen door and washed her face with a cool washrag. Outside, she heard the police officer singing something about being gone and not being able to come back. She wanted to ask the police officer to come inside, to follow her.

And the police did not stop with all that. They questioned their relatives. And in the evening they followed Fred to the grocery store and to the beer distributor. And the police watched their house, stared at it like they were waiting for the house to lift off its foundation and fly into outer space. And the police came again and again, day after day after day. They came for years. Knocked on Fred and Debra's doors. Tapped on their windows. Fred half-expected them to come down the chimney. And then the police tapped their phone. For safety reasons. They said that it's best that way. And they questioned Debra. And they had her evaluated by doctors. And these doctors prescribed pills. The police said there have been women who have done things, terrible things, without wanting to do them. But, once those kinds of things were done, they were done and there was nothing anyone could do about it. "What's done is done," they told her. Then the woman officer asked Debra if she remembered anything, if, perhaps, there was something she did that she did not mean to do. Perhaps it was a misunderstanding? An accident? But she could not say what the police needed her to say.

And the police watched for strange cars and vans in the neighborhood. And they asked more questions. Sometimes they asked the same questions over and over, trying to trip Fred or Debra and make them contradict each other or themselves, and sometimes they became angry, so very angry and frustrated, when they asked their questions; sometimes the police wanted Fred or Debra to admit something, anything. Tell us, they demanded. Tell us. You can trust us. Just say what you need to say, they whispered. Their lips close to Debra's ear, so very close.

One morning, Fred did almost say something. He nearly told them a story. But nothing of what he wanted to say seemed true. He thought what he had to say was a dream or a fairy tale. The police were interested, wanted to know more, but Fred only could say that it was a dream or a fear of something his wife had buried. So the police asked again for Fred and Debra to say something, anything. To say whatever came into their minds and not worry about any sort of punishment. But Fred and Debra had nothing to say, nothing they could say.

And when the police finally found Bob, Debra's brother, who had been damaged by a war that made no sense to anyone in Pittsburgh and by far too many days alone in the forest with his sister during his childhood, they did not just question him. They went at him. The police did more than was necessary. They crossed lines. They did things to what Bob said that would make even an immoral man blush. Turned Bob's words against him. They twisted his sentences into knots and tied his wrists and ankles and tongue together with his stories. Those police made assumptions. They pressed their fingers into his chest. They laughed. They told him there was nothing he could do about any of it. But Bob was never one to be intimidated. He entered every Ed McMahon sweepstakes, thinking that he would win, if not this time then the next time. He wore a suit almost every day and sat on his sofa waiting for Ed McMahon to knock on his front door with an over-sized check. He hoped that Johnny Carson would come along with him. Bob wanted to say, "Here's, Johnny." He wanted to shake his hand, and he wanted to pose with Ed holding that over-sized check, and he hoped that perhaps Johnny would ask him to appear on *The Tonight Show* and say a thing or two about what he knew. Bob, like other mortals, had dreams. He had desires. And Bob knew a thing or two.

Bob kept his home tidy, perhaps too tidy for a man from Pittsburgh. He used potpourri, even though he had trouble pronouncing the word. He disliked words that even slightly resembled French words. Words with letters that he never knew what to do about. He didn't know if he should say them or leave them alone. Letters falling off the ends of words or disappearing in the middle of words. Bob felt harassed by all of it. He often threatened to force French people either to say every letter or to not be permitted to have a language of their own.

But, for all his obsessive tidiness, Bob did write on all the walls of his house. He covered the walls with stories of all that happened and all that only was rumored to have happened. The police read what he had written. They brought in anthropologists. They had their suspicions; they thought Bob had a motive. They worried about his nightmares, about how the voices he heard spoke languages that were no longer spoken. But Bob feared no one. Not anymore. Not since childhood. He told the police as much, told them he was not afraid. Bob was a man who perhaps wrote one too many letters to the editor of the local newspaper, about purple rain caused by politicians who should know better, a rain caused by a war that should never have been fought, a war that nearly killed him and did kill his only son, a war that they said was not a war but a conflict, the same war that made his wife, Mary, drink so much whiskey that she eventually lost the ability to speak, until one day she never came home. "You don't hear me complaining about her being gone, do you? I make my own breakfast. You learn to do that, and you manage," he told the police. "They're still looking for her. The helicopters. You hear them? I see Mary, but I can't get to her. Not yet, anyway. You live with the sound of helicopters inside your head, and not much of anything will ever scare you."

Everyone in the family made fun of Bob's war stories, as if he had never gone over there. And when he started asking the police more questions, the police decided Bob was not a viable suspect after all. They felt they had heard enough. One officer became so uncomfortable with his questions that he placed his hand on the handle of his gun, rested his hand there, like he was about to do something. He looked at Bob, as if to say, sometimes choices have to be made. But such a look did not frighten him. A hand on a gun never worried Bob.

Then one day they stopped. The police. They just stopped. They had asked their questions. They had looked for Lucas. They had forced Fred and Debra to go on the local news. They stapled fliers to telephone poles. They put his picture on milk cartons. Debra asked if they could put Lucas' picture on boxes of Lucky Charms. She told them that Lucas would like that. Then, like Lucas, the police disappeared.

Fred and Debra stared into each other's eyes, where desire, like despair, lingered a bit longer than it should. They wanted to see something that could no longer be seen, and they knew that this would be the last time that they would truly be able to look directly into each other's eyes. They were simply saying goodbye to such a way for looking at each other. Still, they hoped to see something that refused to appear, but they saw how this would end, the slow movement toward departure and all that they would leave behind. The hardwood floors. Mason jars abandoned in the cellar. Confused spiders hoping to capture flies in webs they spun in abandoned rooms. Desperate, starving field mice. A few forgotten photographs on the floor of the attic, covered in dust. An imprint or two pressed into the carpet of the living room from where furniture once rested.

Debra opened her mouth. She tried to speak, but no sound came out. Nothing. Not even a lie.

CHAPTER 4

Uncertain dreams, powerful as thunderstorms, woke Elgin the morning after he slipped into blindness. For one fleeting moment, he thought he might have become immortal. The world around him had gone slow and easy, a lazy opening to his new life. He lay in his bed, as the last tiny fragments of his blind dreams drifted out the window; then, and only then, did he open his eyes. The old man, battered by that jungle war, and by losing all that he ever loved, strained to see if he could see. He knew, even without seeing it, that the stain in the far corner of the ceiling still had to be there. He looked over at the place where he had stood the night before with his back turned away from his grandson. He still saw that—the memory—but he could not see the morning sunlight. Elgin wondered if what he was doing could still be called looking, if he no longer saw anything of the present when he looked. He wondered if plantation owners punished blind slaves for looking in the same ways that they punished the slaves who could see.

Elgin's grandmother told him to look at her whenever she spoke to him. "You got to see me when I'm talking." Her stare strong and steady, like it came direct out of the earth and still had the mud of the riverbank in it. Blood of her ancestors. "Always be looking at your elders. We be gone one day, then our staying be up to you. You got to keep us here."

"Everything happens in a man's eyes," she said. "It don't happen nowhere else. Nothing ain't never happened in the world but that what happened before your eyes." He wondered where everything would happen for him, to him, now that he was done with seeing. His grandmother warned him not to look at those who looked at him. "Look at your feet. Your feet is safe," she said. "The soles of your feet do more than those white people let you do with your eyes. Those people think you blind with fearing them when you look down at your feet. Let them think that. They think what they don't know ain't worth the pain of knowing it. Fact is, that's all there is that's worth the knowing."

Before Vietnam, Elgin's feet were too soft, his eyes too gentle, like his past had not yet found its way out of his soul and onto his skin. "Best that way," his grandmother told him. "Let them think your eyes ain't seeing. Ain't remembering. Let those people think your eyes have forgot what there was to know. And the earth will mark up the soles of your feet with what you need to know. You walk with that." Elgin rubbed his feet together, letting them tell their silent stories to each other. When he rubbed his grandmother's tired old feet at the end of her days, she smiled and told him to listen, feel the stories traveling into his hands. "They the true ones," she said. "Secret skin." Calloused stories of loving Thuy, of running over hot asphalt that burned in the rain to see Thuy breathing one final breath, of walking over mud and bones, through the hills of Vietnam. Feet know when to pray.

Elgin knew nothing in the outside world had changed. He grabbed his blanket, felt it with his fingers. The gentle morning sun warmed him, but he did not see it on his skin or on the night table. He no longer saw shadows; he only felt them. Elgin woke as blind as he had been dreaming he would one day be. He woke feeling protected, cared for. God had finally descended and taken him by his hand. In this way, he began the first day of his blind life.

The surface of his skin made less sense to him now, or perhaps it made more sense. Skin changes when seeing stops, he knew that much. He thought the end of Thuy's life would have been easier for her had she gone blind. In those final days, she screamed at the sight of his tattoos, wanting them to go away. She screamed at his scar left by a bullet that nearly crippled him, screamed until her throat was raw from her rage. "They. Those people," she closed her eyes. "They did this, Elgin. Those ones did it." She kept her eyes closed. Her fists balled tight.

Elgin started wearing long-sleeve shirts, no matter how hot and humid the day got. He loved Thuy that much. He wore shirts to bed. Just to calm her. He loved her that deeply, and, in Pittsburgh, in September, in that humidity with no air conditioning, wearing a shirt to bed was true love, physical love, the kind of love from deep down in the heart, that rose up all through you. The kind of love you can see inside each drop of sweat. Not an expression of love, but love itself. The kind of strong love a young boy carved into the bark of a tree back when such ways for loving were still possible. Elgin thought of each bead of sweat as a word, a whispering in a new language. Every action Elgin put into the world made him sweat, and his muscle-strained sweating made his love for Thuy that much more visible and immediate, that much more a part of his day. She called him crazy. The jungle made him mad, she said, and now the city fed that madness. Fueled it. But she smiled when she called him crazy. She smiled. Until the scars came back. Until the burning in her skin, in her eyes, came back. Then her eyes weakened and her throat contracted. And all Elgin seemed capable of saying was her name. Soft and slow, the gentle breath of Thuy's name in his mouth. And all he seemed capable of doing was holding her hand, having her rest her hand in his, while her eyes burned and her mouth dried up. "We had families," Thuy whispered against Elgin's skin. "It was our blood, not rain, mixing with the dirt, making that dry dirt into mud, the mud that all of you stepped in, walked over."

Before pulling his body out of bed, he took one of those deep breaths of his. Thuy loved his deep breaths, loved being in his arms when he pulled such a breath into his body. The breath of roots. The breath of trees. The story of the world was in his breath. This morning, when he released that breath back into the world, all he experienced in his mouth was the aftertaste of ashes. The war stayed on his tongue, in his throat, even more than in his muscle and joint pain, even more than in the shrapnel wounds. It clogged his breathing. He thought going blind would give him a new birth, but something about this morning felt like a death. He felt something lifting out of him. He found it funny, after spending a night dreaming the dreams of an immortal, that he would wake feeling something fleeing his body. Not a feeling of death, but of renewal. Rising from the ashes. A blind prophet. He remembered being told that most prophets could not see. Every man has to sacrifice something, if he is ever going to learn what he never wanted to learn in the first place, and that he wished he could forget. But ancient prophets were punished by blindness, because their way of seeing frightened the gods. Those prophets had no choice. Blindness descended on them.

He made his way down the steps by sound and by touch, and he shuffled into the kitchen, afraid to lift his feet too high off the floor, afraid he would fall through some crack in the hardwood floor into a bottomless pit.

Johnny leaned against the kitchen sink, watching his grandfather. He wanted with all his heart to help him. He tried to move his feet, get them to obey, get them to carry his body over to his grandfather. He felt that urge, almost a demand, deep inside, to push himself away from the sink and help his grandfather to his chair, but he also knew more deeply than that urge to help, that his newly blind grandfather needed to be the same old man he was the night before, just one without eyes. Elgin pulled out his chair and sat his body down into it. He seemed tired already, like those dreams, and his walk to the kitchen had worn him out before the day even had a chance to begin.

Johnny watched his grandfather's eyes, looked to see what they were looking at, what they might be looking for, but his eyes did not seem to be looking anywhere. "You blind?" Johnny surprised even himself with the question. It just lifted itself from his thoughts, floated out of his mouth and came about as close to sarcasm as you could get without it becoming truly sarcastic. In fact, the way he said it was tender, filled with care and kindness and a touch of hope. Johnny smiled. His grandfather remained silent. Every morning his grandfather sat in that chair, sat and ate his breakfast and never had much to say since his wife and young daughter died. Since death had taken most of his life away. "You still eat eggs? Drink coffee?" For a moment Johnny thought maybe his grandfather had gone deaf or dumb as well as blind, but he still could not tell if his grandfather had actually gone blind. "Blind men eat, right?" Johnny continued to surprise himself with his tone. Elgin's eyes looked the same as they had last

50

night. Two eyes staring off away from Johnny. He seemed to have fixed them on the kitchen window. At least his grandfather's eyes still knew where to safely rest. Johnny took a final bite of an apple he was eating.

"You're too careless when you eat, Johnny. You weren't always this way. You weren't born careless." Elgin looked away from the window and down at the table, as if he were still able to see and was searching for something that was no longer there. "You think fruit will be waiting for you every time you reach for it? Like you don't have to do anything? Fruit just sits and waits for little Johnny to come along. That's right. You eat that apple like you're believing, since apples were here yesterday, they're going to be here tomorrow. That kind of faith is plain stupid. There's good faith and there's stupid faith."

Johnny stopped in the middle of his chewing. His grandfather had not moved his eyes from that empty stare at the table. "I'm just eating," he said.

"That's right. That's all you're doing. Eating." Elgin reached forward to grab the table to steady his old bones, straighten out his thoughts. At times, like this one, Elgin talked the way most people yawned. Words simply dropped from his mouth into the world. No anger, no spite, only a sense that these words needed to be in the world. "You got no reverence for what you put into your body. You eat that apple like it's something that came from a bin in the produce section of a grocery store."

He stopped talking, rolled his shoulders back a bit. Stretching. Johnny thought his grandfather was waiting for him to say something, but he had nothing to say. "Apples aren't from the grocers. When you eat whatever you eat, you need to be thankful, son. You need to know what you are eating." Elgin stopped, put his hands flat on the table. "When you bite into that apple, you're biting into sunshine, you're biting into rain. You're swallowing dirt and roots. Some man or woman pulled that apple off a tree. You're eating their touch. When you bite into that apple, you remember this; you're biting into God. And you think on that. You're eating a little bit of God's imagination with each bite. You got to cherish that apple. You don't know when it's not going to be here anymore."

Johnny's grandfather stopped. Johnny did not know the world

could be so quiet, so still. He waited for a siren from a police car, a blaring horn, a cursing drunk; he longed for anything to break the silence. He wished Emmanuel's dog would let out some vicious wild barking. "Day will come when there ain't no apples no more. Just like that day came for the dinosaurs. You don't see no dinosaur walking the streets now, do you?" his grandfather asked. "You need to be thankful that you're living at the time of apples, Johnny."

Johnny carefully chewed the last bit of apple, and he swallowed so slowly that he thought it would be tomorrow before the apple found its way into his stomach. His grandfather sat quiet and still in his chair. He seemed to be looking up at the ceiling. "That's right," Elgin said. "You eat like that, and eventually you will come to know what an apple truly is."

Johnny looked at the apple core in his hand, examined it with a touch of his imagination, wondering what that apple really meant in the big picture, but he quickly let go of that thought. "You still haven't answered me," Johnny said, looking again at the apple core, no longer knowing what to do with it, where to put it now that he was done eating the apple. Any other day, he would just drop it in the garbage, but today Johnny felt lost. "What happened last night?" Johnny asked. He put the apple core into a pocket of his jeans, wiped his hand on his jeans, and stared at his grandfather's eyes.

Elgin looked toward the space of Johnny's voice. If he had been able to see, he would have been looking directly into his eyes, returning his stare, for the first time since that night of the rains when Lehuong died. Elgin still saw that night, that rain, those puddles. He still saw Johnny walking down Dinwiddie Street to the house. Dribbling his basketball like he would live forever. Walking like nothing in the world would ever change. And he saw himself standing on the sidewalk waiting for Johnny to come home, his foot bleeding from a piece of glass he stepped on when he ran, barefoot, out the door into the rain. His eyes confused and tired. Elgin did not have to answer Johnny's question. Johnny knew then, as he saw his grandfather look at him, that his grandfather was blind. He pulled his own gaze away from staring into his grandfather's used-up eyes and turned his back to his grandfather. "You need anything before I go?"

"Coffee."

"You going to be all right?"

"You didn't rearrange the house, did you? Bathroom's still in the same place? Kitchen sink still right here in the kitchen, right?" Elgin asked. "Nothing's all that different, Johnny. You only think it is. I'll be fine."

He poured his grandfather a cup of coffee, set it down in front of him on the table. "I'll be back." And he walked out the door.

Elgin reached across the table to the cup, found the handle and rested. He counted to ten. Counting was still the same. That hadn't changed. But he was still left with the consequences of having seen, of having lived for so many long years in a world that forced everyone to always be looking. Never a moment's rest from looking, until now. He wondered if that would ever change. Elgin's thoughts began moving too fast, and he felt dizzy. His thoughts always ran away from him, jumping from one place to another.

Elgin took a sip of his coffee, rested his thoughts, his body, in the quiet of the morning, sitting alone at the kitchen table, like a moon nobody sees. He waited the morning away; at least he thought the morning was disappearing. Time came from somewhere else now, and it moved differently. Time had abandoned clocks and lights and could no longer be truly measured. He felt time lodged between his ribs. Stuck in his muscles. Settled in his joints.

Elgin shook off those thoughts, rose from his kitchen chair, and shuffled up to his bedroom to dress for the day. He would stay home. "Stay put," his mother told him when he was a child, after she placed him in a chair. "Don't move. Don't blink an eye." Now, he was doing this to himself, for himself, staying put, slowing down.

He reached for the book he had been reading the night before, the book he would never finish. He thought of taking it downstairs and out onto the porch with him. He opened the book and ran his hand over the print the way he had seen blind people do. Nothing. The page had swallowed the words, or at least no words made their way to his fingertips. He knew the words were still there. That they had not escaped. He tried remembering the last sentence he read. Something about some boy walking street after street, not searching for anything, just walking. Something about a river that had gone dry. What happens to a river when it isn't there anymore, when it's just dirt and wind? What do you call such a thing that has gone away or worn out its usefulness? When God makes other plans for it? Elgin pressed his thumb deeper into the page. He tried to rub out the words, or perhaps he was trying to rub through the page, or trying to get to the beneath of the page. What's under words that can't be seen? There has to be something beneath words. Waiting. Maybe that was the place of truth. A stillness under the breath of words.

He tossed the book onto his bed and went back down the stairs to the front porch. In his blindness, he expected to stub a toe, slam his foot into something, smash his shin into a table, trip, or fall down. But nothing happened. He simply made his way to the screen door, paused just long enough to breathe in that rich scent from the Monongahela River, then he walked out onto the porch and sat on the swing. He looked out onto the street. He looked. You can't punish a blind man for looking.

CHAPTER 5

After Debra told Fred that Lucas had disappeared, she began praying in the bathroom. In this perfect stillness, in the darkest of the dark night, she spoke to God, listening to the faucet dripping, listening to Fred sleeping as if nothing was wrong. She prayed into the silence of each night, searching for the sound of her own heartbeat.

Debra feared that, because her prayers made Jesus sad, he was not granting them, so each night she began by begging the Father of Jesus, God, to forgive her for her melancholy prayers and to forgive her for her desperate pleading. She pleaded with God and with Jesus and with Mary and with so many of the saints, except for that arrogant Saint Jerome, the one who thought he could just go into the desert and read books. She pleaded for one single moment of rest. Debra prayed for her madness to slip away from her, to slip out the window, to vanish the way her innocence escaped years before she could say anything. She told Jesus and God and Mary and the saints that she would leave a window open, so that her anger could escape, be carried away in the late summer breeze, if only they would pull the madness out of her, steal her rib, if only they—all of them: Jesus, Mary, Joseph, God, and a gang of saints—would break into the house and ravish her and destroy her madness. She promised she would keep her eyes closed. "No one would ever know," she whispered, and waited. Debra promised to clench her teeth like a good girl, if only this madness would be taken from her. And every night, she offered herself to all those who made prayers come true.

Slowly, Debra's anger, her madness, began to find its way into everything, into every corner in the house, even into the water in the shower. When she showered, she felt the anger in the water falling onto her skin, little beads of madness entering her pores. She suffered the burning of her skin in this madness, suffered it, but never fully gave in to its hopelessness. She battled it with chocolate. She battled it with prayer. She battled it with promises. She battled it with gratitude. She battled it with small gifts, a giving of thanks for rain, for heat, for humidity, for fresh vegetables, for sexual desire, for Jesus dying, repeatedly, on the cross.

But this anger, this disappointment, was strong and brave. It settled into every cup of coffee she poured, into every ear of corn she shucked, into every flower she touched. It lingered around the outside of the house while haunting the interior. It found its way into the branches of the maple tree that Lucas' bicycle leaned against. It hid under the front porch and waited, warping some of the planks, rotting others. Her anger got everywhere. There was no escaping it. And she worried that her anger would draw more anger, foreign anger, to the house. And she feared the house would decay and that her skin would fade away. Debra feared this anger would cause dry rot and give birth to termites and that it would make her bones fragile and break, that her heart would stop or crack and that this anger would turn her skin too white, too pale, and she feared that, if her skin became too white, then too much would become visible, too many lies, too many memories, too much of her hunger. One morning, she sat at the kitchen table for what seemed like hours, if not days, moving each tiny circle of Cheerios around in her cereal bowl, searching for her anger in the milk, in the cereal; fearful, that if she were not attentive to her every action and desire, she would swallow more of this anger. Fred sat across from her at their kitchen table, mute. Staring.

At night, Debra rarely joined Fred in their bed. She wanted to keep this anger to herself, to protect others from being infected by it. She had also grown afraid of being touched. Fred longed for a return to some kind of intimacy, but he feared that even the most accidental touch could destroy Debra. So he gave up calling her to come to bed, begging her to allow herself to sleep, to rest. Now, he shared their bed only with phantoms. Debra fell asleep, or, more accurately, collapsed, in different places throughout the house: curled up in the bathtub, or on the sofa, spread across the floor in the hallway, or face down on the kitchen table. Some nights, she collapsed flat on her back in the backyard, legs and arms spread out offering herself—body, soul, and anger—to a God who had given up on Debra, on Fred, on stories, on the city of Pittsburgh. Or perhaps she was simply offering herself to the highest bidder, to the one who would make it go away. Or, more likely, she wanted something that no woman, no daughter, no mother, no human being should ever dare to want.

Most mornings, Fred found Debra standing at the kitchen window. Every passing moment of everyday of their lives reminded both of them of their solitude. Every street. Every alley. Every doorframe. Every window. Every time the phone rang, they became more alone, more isolated from each other, more isolated from their friends, their family. A month ago, they stopped answering their telephone. They had not planned on doing so; it simply happened. One night the phone rang, and Fred looked at Debra, and she looked at him, and they both just waited for the ringing to stop. Neither one said, "You should have answered that." Neither even thought it. They both knew that answering the telephone was as futile as opening the door when someone knocked. They both knew the ringing or the knocking would stop, and eventually they would return to being alone with what little remained of their lives.

On nights when it rained, Debra took long walks into the darkness, challenging the darkness to keep Lucas away from her. Neighbors watched her from behind curtains. Or so she thought. Her eyes were uncertain in the dark. Fearful. Searching out the blurred circles of light from the streetlamps, cursing potholes in the sidewalk or puddles that soaked her feet. Her hair wet, full of leaves. In her former life, she was a street urchin, standing outside strip joints, shoving religious tracts in the hands of everyone, and whispering tales of salvation to each man as they stared down onto the concrete of the sidewalk, before entering the club, always looking over their shoulder at little Debra. Even as a child, she felt that, if a man wanted something in the way that his eyes seemed to want something, then that man should simply say so. Now, she walked the rain-soaked streets of her neighborhood hoping to find Lucas. She walked as if the rain understood her, as if the rain listened. She did not ask anything of the rain. Did not beg the rain to return Lucas to her the way she begged God to bring Lucas back. She trusted the rain.

But most nights after praying, Debra stayed home. She locked herself inside the walls of her house and wandered through the hallways from room to room, turning on and off every light in every room three times to dispel the ghosts, then flickering each lightswitch a fourth time and leaving it on to light the room. She walked in the darkness, lighting candles, carrying flashlights, shining their narrow beams of light under beds, into corners, out into the yard, up into the tree. Most days, she did the same. Turning on lights in the middle of the afternoon. There could never be enough light.

The electric bill nearly sent them to the poorhouse. Fred worried that all this light everywhere would explode the electrical wires or set the house on fire. Everything, Fred thought, would be consumed in flames. He only wanted for the world to be forever in darkness. Night and day he sat in the darkest dark and prayed he would become part of the dark, to disappear into it. He called this darkness, which he longed for, his "godawful darkness." Debra insisted on light, insisted that light made living inside her unbearable anger possible. And when she left the house to go to the park or to go shopping, she carried flashlights and candles with her. She drove with her headlights on; often, she turned on her high beams.

Debra believed that the time between light and dark held a secret. Kept it safe and warm. A secret beyond secret, a secret that came into the world from the stories she created of his birth. She thought of this time between now and then as simply the time of Lucas' secret. Each dusk and dawn, she stopped her body, stilled her thoughts, and became quiet, as the world transitioned from light to dark or from dark to light. She did not wait; she simply paused and experienced the tension between light and dark, not as a bridge or a connection between light and dark, but as a tension, a pulling both ways at once.

And with every passing day she grew more tired, so much more tired than Fred, and so much more tired than she had ever imagined herself capable of being. The kind of tired that kills the body, the spirit, the heart. Exhausted. Worried. Anxious. A body without a soul. Debra's father had survived a war that he refused to talk about by using his wits and by not obeying every order. Her brother survived Vietnam by hiding near trees, near creeks, and by holding his breath as often as possible. One morning Bob went AWOL, walked away from the war, finding his way to another land, one without language, a land without television or radios. He said that you could never get to that land from anywhere, let alone from where you were standing at any given moment. He could only travel to this mystical world beneath the trails through the jungles of Vietnam, if he kept walking. He could never stop. He had to walk and walk. And he had to believe in the way he walked, trust each step, and never question any of it.

Her brother looked into her eyes when he told her these stories, and he asked her if it was ok to hold her hand and keep her safe. He held her hands in the way that she liked, soft and uncertain. Bob said there were trails under rivers, trails in the clouds, and he stayed there until they came to get him, to take him back, to have him help them set more villages and more forests and more creeks on fire. To burn Vietnam into a heap of ashes. Her father survived bombs and fire in some other unspeakable war. Her brother survived the bombs and the fire and the mud of Vietnam. Yet, somehow, her only begotten son seemed to have disappeared into the innocent streets of Pittsburgh.

Debra pressed her body tight against the kitchen sink, staring out the window into the morning. The steady drip of the faucet was enough to destroy anyone's sanity. She thought of Bob's stories of Chinese water torture. The steady falling drop of water on his forehead until he cracked and spoke in tongues. He told her that no drop of water was ever innocent. A single drop of water, followed slowly by another drop caused more damage than a steady stream of water.

"I'll fix it," Fred said.

"What?"

"The dripping. It needs a washer. Or maybe it just needs to be tightened."

"Oh. I thought. I thought you meant." Debra stopped her sentence. She leaned over the sink toward the window and counted to ten. She always counted to ten to measure anger, to measure disappointment, to wait for love, to pause before or after orgasm, to pour coffee. To hold herself on that ledge before releasing herself to her muscles. To find a private place for her desire to wait. While she counted, she maintained some vague desire for truth, but a fear of knowing herself, perhaps a little bit too intimately, haunted this desire. "I thought," she began again, "I thought you meant everything. I thought you wanted to fix," she rested her forehead against the window, "everything." Debra sighed the word more than spoke it. She pulled herself back upright. "I guess that's not possible, though, is it? To fix everything. To fix this anger. Us. To fix Gabriella and her eyes."

Debra did not turn away from the window. She had grown used to not seeing Fred. At times, she thought that perhaps Fred too had gone. But then came these occasions when his voice found its way to her, from behind her, from another room, or, on a rare occasion, from the porch. "Leave the dripping alone," she said, her voice torn and thin, nearly as worn out as the carpet in the living room. "It's necessary."

Fred put the *Post-Gazette* down on the table. He covered his face with his hands, stayed like that for a few minutes, trying to understand his own thoughts. "Luc." Fred started in on a sentence. He still remembered how to talk, even to Debra, but all he had were words broken down by age and sadness. Beginnings of words, a few letters that tended to get exhausted before others joined them, hints of a sentence, but nothing more. "If only." His voice quit on him again. "Maybe," he took another weak stab at a sentence; he saw Debra waiting for him to say something that would melt the world away. Her eyes softened. "That saint, the one." But Fred could not remember which one. Saint Peter of somewhere. Saint Ignatius of somewhere else, somewhere even farther away. Saint Anthony. Fred once knew all the saints, knew which ones to pray to. It had to be Saint Anthony. Dear Saint Anthony, come around; something's lost that can't be found. Fred looked down at the floor, searching for the name of the patron saint of children, then he looked around the kitchen, searching for something that would change everything that had happened. He saw bananas. He saw a toaster. He saw Lucky Charms, Cheerios, a box of doughnuts, a stack of mail. He stared long and hard at that stack of mail, but he could not think of anything. Finally, his mouth just kind of opened. "Sorry."

He stood, hands in his pockets, feet tired and weak, mouth dry with longing. He stood there in that kitchen with a nearly invisible Debra. But he also stood there with a lingering hope. He stood there until he could no longer stand there, then he quietly walked out the kitchen door and went to work. He knew how to go to work. He also knew his way home from work at the end of the day. He knew those two things, and he knew how to drink beer. And he still knew how to talk to Jim, even if most of their talk was silent. And he knew he loved Debra. And she loved him. He knew and trusted that more than he believed in a vanished son.

The screen door closed. She felt Fred leave. She did not see him leave, even though he walked past the window, before her very eyes. But her body felt him go. Every morning, Debra's body felt Fred's body leaving her, like he was some sort of dead man pushing himself up and out of her rib cage. She felt the weight of his hands pressing down on her ribs as he climbed out of her, like she was giving birth to loss, to a continual leaving. At the end of the day when he returned, she felt nothing at all. She simply knew he had returned. She only felt his presence back in the house in some abstract way that had nothing to do with her body.

Debra looked out the kitchen window at her son's bicycle. The sight of it pained her so deeply her ribs creaked. She put the dishrag down on the counter and picked up a knife. A day did not go by that Debra failed to sharpen the kitchen knives. She methodically began her ritual of knife sharpening while staring out the window, waiting for something in the world to change. An unexpected, sweet drowsiness spread through her thin muscles. Her pale and eloquent memories of Lucas seemed to be disappearing into the vapor of her daily life. She feared that a new terror, one more true to her desires, would find her if she were not careful. But Debra did not know how to be careful. She stopped sharpening the knife and looked down at her hand. She had cut her thumb. Soon, the cut would be infected. It burned into her skin; she felt her nerves near fire; before long, the infection would burn into her bones. Perhaps it would destroy her, make her flesh rot away, until she, too, disappeared into the earth. Debra knew that by taking certain precautions she could be safe. She scratched the cut, squeezed it, then poured hydro-peroxide on it and watched tiny white bubbles form.

She accepted the pain. Then she smiled.

Debra turned away from the window, settled her tired body into a chair at the kitchen table, put the tips of her fingers into the milk she had spilled earlier that morning. Her blood dripped into it. Again, she counted to ten, remembered an orgasm from her youth, one she had while locked inside a hotel room, safe and sound, with a man so old she thought he was nearly dead. She imagined her missing son walking into that hotel room, confused and uncertain of what to say or do. She imagined him walking into the kitchen disappointed with how soggy his Lucky Charms had become, but deliriously happy with the rich pink, near-red color of the milk. At the count of ten, she opened her eyes to an empty kitchen—the same kitchen she had been in when she had closed her eyes—and a near-forgotten youthful orgasm lost in the same body it had been in before she had closed her eyes.

Debra abandoned the kitchen and wandered around the house, with a vague desire for truth, no matter what the truth taught her. She walked up the stairs to Lucas' room. She screamed out his name loud enough for every living soul in the city of Pittsburgh to hear. She called his name, until the calling of his name bruised her throat and scarred her tongue. Then she stopped. She quit breathing for a moment. Exhausted, she leaned against the doorframe to Lucas' bedroom. She longed to whisper his name into his ear. "Lucas." This breath of his name soothed her burned throat. She walked into his bedroom and sat on his bed, touched his pillow.

Debra longed to confess to her son, longed to tell Lucas stories of years ago, before she began forgetting, stories of childhood and of mirrors. She whispered her memories into this empty room. Night after night and morning after morning, she confessed. She recited stories of how she behaved before she met her husband, stories of when she was a child and did not know better. One story weaving into another, until her throat got tight and became dry, a desert of hope. When Fred walked into the room, her words turned to dust. They lodged in her ribs. She wanted God to steal one rib, to lift this one rib out from her. Wanted God to make from this rib a new life for her, one without memory, one without torn flesh and muscle, one without this constant pain. One that was not a trap. Debra dreamt of fires that waited for her on the edge of town. She harbored nightmares of empty houses waiting for fire on Federal Street.

She remembered a boy who played with matches and a girl who walked a safe distance behind the boy. This girl watched the boy from behind trees, around corners, through windows. The boy who played with matches once showed the girl a condom and told her what it was used for. His voice remained steady and calm. Debra thought the boy must be waiting for the girl to blink, to look away, but the girl did not look away, did not blink. And her breathing did not change. And when he asked if she wanted to touch it, she did so with the very tips of her thumb and index finger. And the girl was careful not to change her expression. Not to smile. Not to frown. To touch as if touching did not matter, as if touching with the tips of her fingers did not affect the rest of her body.

The boy who played with matches looked familiar to Debra. She seemed to recognize him from some dream. He showed broken bottles to the girl and told her that he was never afraid, that pain only hurt until it stopped. He asked her if she ever played with paper matches? He wiped the snot running from his nose with the back of his young hand and asked her if she ever burned her fingers. The girl told the boy that she could not carry matches in her pockets because the matches burst into flames. And that, before she could change anything she had done, her thighs were on fire, and she would begin bleeding and her skin disappeared in the flames. "There's no stopping it," she said. "Fire eats fire, and that's when the madness happens. And there is no turning back. There only is a dream of water under red rocks. Fire destroys fire, but you can't drown in fire. You can only drown in water."

Debra, or the girl, remembered looking through a window into a room in a basement. A naked light bulb hung from a string or a wire. Across the street, boys smoking cigarettes in the playground stared at her. She remembered it was winter. The girl had forgotten her gloves in her locker at school, so she put her hands into her coat pockets. Police watched her out of the corner of their eyes when they drove past, but they did not stop. Those winter days, when there was no heat at home, the boy who played with the matches stayed after school talking to the janitor. And the girl, careful not to be seen, watched.

One day, after the school became empty and dark, the janitor led the boy down into a basement. There, the janitor drank dark brown liquid from a mason jar and the boy watched. The janitor looked into the boy, trying to read the boy's thoughts. And the boy looked back at the janitor as if they had already agreed on everything that could never be said, on things that could only be felt and remembered. The boy pretended that the girl was not staring through the window, that her hands were not in her pockets, that her tiny ears were not burning red from the cold wind. The boy and the janitor did everything that they had agreed on, but none of it was seen by anyone. Not by the police passing by. Not by the boys smoking cigarettes. Not by the girl standing in the snow. Not by Debra. Not even by the boy.

A few weeks later, the janitor left town. Late at night, in bed, after all the children had fallen asleep, mothers and fathers told stories to each other about the janitor, stories that they secretly hoped were true. Children stayed in their beds, but they could hear the stories seeping through the walls, they could hear the stories in the cries of their mothers and in the creaking of the bedsprings.

The boy who played with matches and the girl who followed him remained silent. The boy and the girl stayed to finish the school year, to long for summer vacation, to wish for the snow to melt. The girl continued to look at the boy with matches, pretending he could not see her looking at him. On the last day of class before summer vacation, the boy who liked to play with matches and the girl who followed him gave each other the kind of smile that people give to each other when they know a secret between them and know they were going to hold onto that secret until some undertaker laid them to rest. Debra told the boy she remembered that her secret, like all true secrets, was made of stone and drowned in the bottom of the Monongahela River.

CHAPTER 6

Johnny panicked when he saw shadows. Even when clouds covered the sun, he could not relax. Clouds only disguised shadows, making them more indeterminate. On cloudy days, shadows became uncertain of their own destiny. They seduced and they lied. They doubted God, questioned Him for bringing light into the world. Shadows reminded men and women, boys and girls, that God cannot protect them, that God had never been up to the task to begin with. Shadows reminded people of their fear that God was only a word, reminded them that other forces were at work in the world and that these forces were stronger than any word could imagine, certainly stronger than God.

Lehuong told Johnny stories about a man who had no shadow. And she told him that this man was not the only one. There were many men who escaped having shadows by living inside shadows or beneath them. Men who became shadows. Neither asleep nor awake. Patient men whose shadows disappeared when it rained and who slipped into the darkening concrete or mud. These men knew how to wait while everyone passed over them. And they never left a trace. They hungered for the grey half-light when the world became uncertain. Johnny forgot everything else about his mother's story, and not knowing the end of the story worried him the most. He feared meeting a man without a shadow or a man who became a shadow. And he remembered a distant voice, a cloaked voice, little more than a whisper, that spoke beneath his mother's true voice.

Johnny jumped off the bus on Forbes Avenue and walked among

the shadows down Liberty Avenue. They stretched out from buildings, moved alongside people on the sidewalk, evaporated into other shadows. Trying to avoid stepping on the shadows, he repeatedly bumped into people. For Johnny, it was safer to bump into people than to step on their shadows. He wound his way through the streets of Pittsburgh, across the bridge to join Chas.

When Johnny walked up to him, Chas said, simply and directly, "T.J.'s gone."

"What?"

"T.J.'s dead."

"How is that possible?"

"I don't know. He's in Rats Alley. Who knows? Who ever knows with T.J.?"

"What's he doing there?"

"Lying face down, dead. I saw him. It's him, Johnny. And he's dead."

"In Rats Alley?" Johnny took a quick look across the street at the alley, then back at Chas. "It's not like you're talking about any place. You're saying you saw T.J. in Rats Alley. His body. It makes no sense." Johnny caught his breath. "You call the police?"

"Right. That's what I did. The very first thing I did. That's what we all want. Call the police. We can wait for them. Go to the phone booth and call them. Go ahead. Then we can stand on this sidewalk, under this tree, and wait." Chas looked at the payphone on the corner, the missing receiver, shook his head. "It won't change anything. T.J.'s shoved back in the shadows. He's joined the darkness."

"We have to pull him out. We can't just leave him there. Let's just pull him out a little. Get him in the light."

Johnny looked across West North Avenue at the dark, narrow alley between The Garden Adult Theater and the Apache Lounge. A white man, in one of the shiniest polyester suits ever worn by anyone on this planet, walked, or nearly walked, past the doors to The Garden. He came to a complete stop when he saw Johnny. The polyestered man gave Johnny a long, slow look. That sweet-come-hither kind of look. Johnny attracted such looks from men along Liberty Avenue and on both ends of North Avenue. Men and women alike were willing to destroy their lives for one kiss, for one chance to touch his skin. Their hands became animated, and they joked about not knowing what to do; they asked Johnny or themselves or strangers standing nearby if there was anything that could be done. When people talked to him or simply stood near him, their hands became confused. They put their hands in their pockets, took them out of their pockets, then stared at them, turned them over, looking at them; they lifted their hands toward his face. Tenderly. Stopped themselves. Thought better of it. Blushed.

And people had no idea where to look. Where their eyes would be safe. Should they stare at Johnny's hands? At his eyes? His mouth? His shoulders? His legs? Every rule of polite society exploded when people approached Johnny. People breathed differently around him and had trouble finishing sentences as soon as they came close to him. His beauty distracted everyone in the city, and, if those who lived in the suburbs surrounding Pittsburgh had known about Johnny, they, too, would have been distracted. His beauty made time impossible. People touched their lips, trying to coax words out of their mouths, when they spoke to him. They had trouble with verbs, with wanting to say things, to do things to him that would destroy who they had come to believe they were. The trouble always began with verbs. People spoke to Johnny with every other kind of a word, but never with verbs. They feared what a verb would make them desire.

The polyestered man standing in front of the entrance to The Garden shoved his wrinkled hands deep into his pockets, kept them there for a while, and then he pulled out what appeared to be a few bills. Johnny finally caught the man's gaze. The man touched his lips with two fingers, then he held the bills up. Johnny shook his head and looked over at Chas.

"We got to figure this out."

"Nothing to figure out. Dead is dead. Maybe T.J. just quit. Ain't no shame in quitting this. Got to respect a man who has had enough and does something about it."

"It ain't like that. There's an answer."

"That is the answer, Johnny. Dead. There isn't any other answer. In this world, you don't listen for a scream. You don't look. You walk on. You sure as hell never go back. It's like the stories your grandfather tells. There's nothing to go back to. There's nothing there."

"T.J. is there, Chas. And this is different. Those people in my grandfather's stories aren't real. They're just names. We knew T.J."

"This ain't different, and those people in those stories are real. They're part of you. Where do you think your Grandma's from? You think your skin is from Pittsburgh? You're as much, probably more, from over there than you is from here. You got no true Pittsburgh in you. Face it, you're from Vietnam, Johnny. You're in those stories." Chas pointed at the polyestered man across the street still looking at Johnny like the whole world had disappeared and he was the only survivor. "Your friend got his eye on you." Johnny laughed. Chas rubbed the back of his neck, looked into Johnny's quiet eyes. "And what do you think your grandfather's screams are? You think for a minute they not real?"

"It's not the same. Not here."

"It is the same, Johnny. War is war."

Johnny looked at Chas and shook his head. "We have to pull T.J. out of those shadows. He's not safe."

"You and your shadows. They're just shadows. They're not doing anything to him. They don't do nothing to you." Chas stopped talking, looked at his own shadow, then up at Johnny, smiling, daring Johnny to look. "A black boy boiled in Vietnamese blood who hates shadows. Fears them. How you expect to go on living in this world? You're a tragedy waiting to happen." Chas turned to walk toward Cedar Avenue. "C'mon. We have to go." He took a few slow steps, looked over his shoulder. "You coming?" Johnny didn't move. He kept looking at the alley. Chas walked away, down east North Avenue. He didn't bother to look back.

Allegheny Park was nearly empty. Everybody was already at work, or they were staying locked inside their houses, trying not to move under the weight of the morning's humidity. Some sat on their stoops, too tired, too hot to move a muscle. Johnny wished he could forget that T.J. was dead, and he wanted, needed, to talk more about it, but it was clear that Chas wanted nothing to do with his death. He never much liked T.J. He thought he was always scamming. A few years ago Chas accused him of stealing ten dollars out of his sock drawer during a poker game or something. He'd been eyeing T.J. ever since. Johnny shook his head and ran after Chas. When he caught up with him, Chas smacked Johnny on the back of his head. "Your grandfather do it?"

"Yeah. Gone blind. And crazy talk about how I eat an apple."

"What are you going to do?"

"Nothing. It is what it is. It's what he wanted."

"A man with those kinds of memories probably will enjoy being blind."

"It doesn't make sense," Johnny said. "There's always something more to see. What is happening keeps happening, whether you see it happen or not."

"Like T.J.'s dead body? Like more boarded-up houses? It's seeing the same thing over and over that made him want to stop. More torn-down houses. Ruined streets. Seeing it and feeling like he can't change none of it." Once Chas got going, there was no stopping him, and Johnny sensed that Chas was just starting. "Why would your grandfather want to watch it all get torn down? Piece by piece, brick by brick. He's tired of seeing life disappear. He's got memories inside every brick in this city."

Chas stared into Johnny's eyes with a look that made Johnny uncomfortable. He believed that Chas saw something inside him that his grandfather was afraid of seeing and that Chas wanted to be sure Johnny could see him seeing, that Johnny knew for certain he was looking down into those secret places his grandfather never wanted to see and that Johnny himself did not quite know existed in him, places that maybe his grandfather feared he had been the one to put there. Those places that in the final days make you into you. He held Johnny's gaze like he was hypnotizing him, and Johnny feared to even blink. He knew there was something at stake with how he responded. Knew that this was one of those situations where there was a right answer and a wrong one. And he did not stare back at Chas so much as simply remain there, with his eyes open a bit too wide.

"It's not only buildings that they keep knocking down. They're knocking down whatever it was that your grandfather thought he had left. And what?" Chas looked over across East Street, held his breath, before releasing more words. "Dumping concrete down on what used to be homes, burying neighborhoods. Freeways built to make their escape faster, easier for them to get in and out of the city without seeing us. Now they're building condos along the rivers." Chas looked up into the heavens, shook his head. "What's a condo? It's not even a real word. Yuppie droppings. White people got words none of us would ever say, words none of us even want to say."

Chas looked back down from staring at the heavens and stared into Johnny with those hard red eyes of his, mad eyes gone crazy from basketball and drugs. "Condos? Ain't no forgiveness for that. I hope I never meet anyone who lives in one. Damn." He laughed just enough to make Johnny that much more uncomfortable. "Something more to make us forget we ever lived here. They get us to forget enough, and then we'll become ghosts walking these streets. The mills. The warehouses. You look at your grandfather's hands and see what you see."

"You're crazier than he ever will be, Chas. What are you even talking about?"

"Nothing," Chas said. "I'm talking about nothing." He stopped in front of the narrow passageway that led to Stanley's door. It was not even an alley; it was simply a space between two buildings, and it was so narrow and tight you had to squeeze in sideways to make your way to Stanley's door. "Just keep an eye out." Chas disappeared into the shadows.

CHAPTER 7

"Johnny tells me you're blind. That true?" Emmanuel hollered up at Elgin. "He said you're so blind you looked directly into his eyes and didn't blink." Emmanuel held his tongue for a moment before saying anything more. He waited, gauging Elgin's reaction. But Elgin kept to his silence. "You ever going to see again?"

Elgin remained quiet and still. He seemed to be looking out across Dinwiddie Street at the vacant lot, the place where the Tupistyn's lived. Where the Beatty's lived after them. Then the Ellises. Then those Coopers. Then family after family that never seemed to be home or only seemed able to look out through the slats in the blinds. Then, finally, that family who made noise and didn't have any kind of name, at least not one that anyone was willing to say aloud. Then one night came the fire. Nearly burned down the whole neighborhood while everyone was sleeping. People still talk about it. Still point their fingers and whisper. Then, after the fire, the burning, the flames, came nothing. Empty. A space between other houses. Hopeless weeds. Worse than an eyesore. And that emptiness gave birth to a heap of charred wood, broken bottles, rusted cans, rain-stained pages from the *Pittsburgh Post-Gazette*. Then came a few homeless men trying to make the best out of that place of nothing. Trying to survive winters by burning what they could find in metal barrels. Then even they gave up. Now that empty lot looked like the kind of place where only the saddest of animals would come to die.

Emmanuel stared deeper into Elgin's thoughts. "You there?"

He followed Elgin's stare and looked back over his shoulder at the empty lot. "Least you won't be looking at that eye sore no more." Still nothing. Elgin stared off in what seemed like a quiet prayer to some lonely yesterday. "You contemplating the past, or you fixing on seeing into the future?" Nothing. "Words, Elgin, words. You got words in you still, don't you? You got your madness in you, I'll give you that much." Still nothing. Not a word. Not a blink. Nothing. "Dammit, Elgin. This just some sort of tired-ass way for getting attention, or are you truly come to an end with seeing? And what? Now you give me the quiet treatment, like we married."

Elgin's feet rested thick and heavy on the boards of the porch. Feet so callused he no longer felt the splinters in the wood. "I hear you, old man. I hear you. Ain't no way to stop you from talking. Being blind don't end nothing, Emmanuel. The world is still out there. The world won't go anywhere because I am done with seeing." He turned his gaze toward Emmanuel's voice. "Close your eyes. Go ahead, do what I say once. Close your eyes, then open them again, real slow or real fast. It don't matter. You'll see. Thing is, the world will be out there waiting for you to return to it. The world's too big for simple blindness. Nothing stops. Nothing changes."

"It does," Emmanuel said.

"Doesn't."

"You'll never see it coming."

"What? See what coming?"

"Anything." Emmanuel put his hand in his pocket, made some rustling noises. "A baseball. This baseball I got right here in my hand. The one I'm going to throw straight at you."

"You don't have no baseball." Elgin shook his head. "I'm blind, not stupid. Like you walking around with a baseball in your pocket. When you ever have a baseball? And how a man like you gonna muster up the strength to throw one?"

"But what if I did? That's what I'm saying. What if I had a baseball or a bat?" Emmanuel looked at Elgin. He didn't seem any different. If anything, Elgin seemed more focused, more attentive. He seemed to have finally arrived someplace that he had been meaning to arrive. "How you gonna to look at those old photographs? Ain't never known no fool who likes staring into Polaroids like you do. Blind man don't see no photographs, Elgin. They don't. You've looked at those photographs every single day of your life, like they're more real than this here place. You look at them more than you've ever looked at me. It's God's truth, it is. Every damn time I come over here, you pull them out like you're just getting back from some vacation. And the way you look at them? Downright creepy. Hold them all careful like you do and look. Your fingers all gentle, like there's something in them photographs that might get broken. Like if you're not careful with your looking, them people in those photographs will up and disappear. Got to admit, it's not normal, Elgin. Admit that at least. Nothing don't mean nothing no more."

Emmanuel was right. Elgin had shoeboxes stuffed with photographs. And he had written stories, not just names and dates, on the backs of them. Tales of the before and after of the photograph. A few were in frames. Some were taped to walls. Others lay naked on tables or on windowsills. Elgin loved seeing, loved what seeing did to him, and his Kodak Instamatic or his Polaroid helped him with seeing. He told Emmanuel that a man had to train himself to see. No one was born knowing how to see. Even Adam and Eve could not see. God had to teach them a thing or two before the world became visible to them. "Parents teach their children to eat with forks and spoons, like it's dangerous for them to eat with their hands," he told Emmanuel. "But parents think it's safe to send their children into the world without knowing a lick about seeing, without warning a child about all that seeing can do to them or to the person they looking at. Plop a kid down in the world, and that kid starts seeing. Parents figure let the world teach the child. Talk about child abuse."

Elgin told Emmanuel that his cameras taught him how to see when he wasn't using a camera. He learned to be attentive to miracles, to the unsaid and the invisible by looking through his camera. So this whole going blind business of Elgin's made even less sense to Emmanuel. "Looking at photographs. Taking photographs. All that's going to change," Emmanuel went on. "Ain't no such thing as brail photographs. They're just going to be invisible in your hands. What good is a photograph if you can't see it?"

Elgin thought of what it would be like to hold one of his photographs in his hands in the way that he tried putting his fingertips on the words in that book. Even when he could see, he occasionally closed his eyes while holding a photograph, its serrated edge creating a strange, almost paradoxical blend of mourning and memory. Elgin never knew what might become visible. All of what might be there without what was there knowing it was there. A photograph never remains innocent. Just like a mirror is never innocent. A photograph sees things just like mirrors see things. And if you are awake, when you look at a photograph or into a mirror, things appear that aren't always visible. But they are there.

"People hold a mirror or a photograph in their hands like they ain't afraid of them, like they ain't worried about the shadows," Elgin said. "And I guess most shouldn't worry much of what is there, since most people got no patience for seeing." Elgin scratched at the back of his neck. "Your eyes got trouble of their own. People who truly live their lives, they hold a photograph or a mirror in their hands like an open book, and they ain't afraid of writing in it. Your eyes can't be trusted no how, Emmanuel, least not in most ways people use their eyes, but you can entertain your eyes to no end."

"What?" Emmanuel asked. "Blind and crazy all in one night." He wiped at his brow with his bare hand. "Crazier, since you always been the crazy one."

Elgin tapped his forehead. "The photographs aren't what's real. It's the memories. A photograph got nothing to do with reality. It leaves behind what ain't no longer there once you take the photograph. You think about it long and hard enough, and you realize it never really was there. None of it. And what you can't see, you can't see. It's not like," Elgin stopped, not to take a breath, not for anything. He just stopped, brought the sentence to an end, even though he was not done with it.

There were days, like this one, when Elgin's teeth hurt so much from talking, or when his mind started to wander, that he simply abandoned sentences, left them drift into silence or left them hanging in the air, waiting for his voice to come along with words to finish them. It's one of the reasons he loved photographs so much. Their pure silence. When Elgin looked at photographs, the world stopped making so much noise.

Even when he was trying not to die in that war, looking at photographs saved him. Enemies rustling leaves and branches in the bushes. Bombs dropping everywhere, exploding over and over. During the day. During the night. In Elgin's dreams. In his cereal. But the silence was worse than the noise. Something was trapped inside that silence. When Vietnam became still, everyone got on edge, everyone started waiting. That silence was never a true silence; it was a time of waiting for the next sound, the next scream, the next gunshot, but the worst noise was the sound of a single gunshot, worse even than a series of carpetbombs. You never simply heard a single gunshot; you felt it with your entire body. It came out of the darkness, out of the trees, and it went straight through you, down into your bones, even when it was miles away.

And the sounds of the women in the forest. The women who could not escape. The sounds coming from their bodies, from their mouths. Their cries. Elgin did not know what to make of what they were saying. Not then. Later, Thuy would tell him. She would teach Elgin the Vietnamese words for mother, for father, for child, for son, and for daughter. She told him stories of blindness, of wanting skin to melt. "Make me a ghost. Make me a ghost." Over and over. Father. Mother. "Make me a ghost."

Elgin did come to understand the sounds they made when they begged to die, when they prayed to him and the other soldiers to end their pain. Officers ordered him to never kill those who asked for death. He was told they had to suffer. Killing the Viet Cong was moral. It was what God wanted Americans to do. But killing them when they begged for death was like murder. Those who wanted death needed to endure the pain; they needed to learn pain, to understand the story of pain. And the only way to learn the stories of pain, the only way to somehow be forgiven, was to experience pain from beginning to end. If God wanted them dead, God would have had them die, not suffer. God needed them to suffer. It was God's will. Officers told Elgin this repeatedly. If these people, these gooks, believed in the stars or the moon or the sun or the trees or whatever they thought of as their god, then their gods would have the kindness to let them die peacefully. Such a god would not want these people to endure pain, and then to die, and then to be left in the mud and to be forgotten. Or left there to remind every gook, every one of them, that one day this will be them. Dying in the mud. Forgotten.

Elgin escaped from that noise by holding photographs and looking at them when it was light enough see their images. He carried two photographs of his grandmother, one of his father and sisters, and one of some girl. He kept one of the photographs of his grandmother in his fist while he slept. The photograph of the girl was one of a girl he wished was his girlfriend. A girl in the neighborhood gave him this photograph, but told him that it did not mean anything. The girl said, "Good luck, Elgin."

A few days later Elgin boarded a bus that took him to a dusty place in the great white South, a place with barracks and heat, unbearable heat, and, there, he was taught to kill everything in sight. And then he was shipped overseas, and he did just that. He killed and killed every living creature that crossed his path, until they finally released him, and he returned to Pittsburgh.

Elgin saw that girl, the one who had wished him good luck, walking up and down the Boulevard of the Allies between Smithfield and Wood Streets. She looked as tired, as worn down as he felt inside his soul. Her lips had turned grey. Her hands had given up on being black and were becoming white. She looked like she would never forgive Pittsburgh in the same way that Elgin would never forgive the army. She looked dead. Maybe even beyond dead, without the strength to beg for death. If she did have the strength, she looked like she would open her mouth and beg for silence, for the quiet to take her. Instead, she leaned over and looked into a window of a car. When the car door opened, she got in. A short time later, she was returned to the boulevard and got into another car and another and another. And she wiped her mouth with the back of her hand, but she could never wipe any of it away. It's all a person can do. It's no different than shooting at the ripples in a creek.

Thuy remained dead in Elgin's photographs. When he looked at these photographs, he remembered touching her, but he could not make her present. The few photographs that Thuy brought with her from Vietnam, the ones of her family, of her home, of her life before Elgin, and some of her life after meeting him, were more like wounds than like photographs. Each one torn. Each one defeated in some way, scorched by the sun, damaged by the river. One had mud on the bottom corner. She insisted that the mud stay there, that no one clean the photograph. She cared for that mud the way most people protected their photographs from other people carelessly smudging them with fingerprints. When Thuy held that photograph in the cupped palms of her hands, the way a mother holds her fragile newborn child, she seemed to be listening more than seeing. Listening in a deeper way than Elgin could ever imagine listening, hearing the stories of her ancestors who had been left behind, who had become dust, whose bones were buried in the hills. When she heard those voices and held that photograph, she experienced the kind of love that Elgin feared he could never give her, that he wanted so desperately to hand to her, to somehow put into words or into actions, to put into touch what his heart was feeling. Thuy became silent with these voices. That mud was her land staying with her, while her mother and her father and her two sisters and her brother remained in Vietnam. Lost somewhere. When she died, Elgin put this photograph in a glass box. The mud reminded him of all that he did not do, of all that he could never do for Thuy, of all that he wanted to do. That mud reminded him of each barren footstep he took through those hills in Vietnam. Each footprint in that mud.

Emmanuel stepped up onto the porch. He was familiar with Elgin's departures, the way he stopped his sentences in mid-thought, holding breath and word together in a communion of silence. Emmanuel sat down on the other rocking chair and settled into the quiet.

The two men waited for their stories and their dreams to come back to them. Both men were surprised they were still alive; surprised that they had somehow outrun the odds, the stray bullets and the true bullets, the long nights of Colt 45 and rotgut wine, the needles in the back alleys, the tired, bored women in the shadows. Emmanuel survived a wife, Rose, who wanted nothing more than to see him dead, saying to him nearly every night: "I'm going to bury your junkman's ass in that cemetery on the hill. And on the day that I bury you, I will be rewarded. God rewards those who are patient." He smiled at her and poured himself another shot. Rose died ten years ago. Her heart exploded in the midst of one of her screaming fits at the neighbors. Emmanuel thought he would smile when that day came, but he did not smile. He got quiet for a few days—rumor in the neighborhood had it that he even went so far as to say a prayer or two—and then he went on with his life, went to Red's Ibo Landing Bar and Girlle, and he drank with the same seriousness and told jokes that he had been telling for the past decade or so, and he struggled up the hill to Elgin's porch to listen to his stories, and he returned to his epic quest over the street corners looking for more tired women, and he went back to watching baseball. Things happen. People die; they pass on. But it doesn't change much. There was still beer to be drunk, there was still baseball, there were still stories to be retold.

And Elgin somehow survived Thuy's death, and then he somehow survived Lehuong's death, too. Even though his heart broke in half when Thuy died, then broke in half again when Lehuong died, so that now Elgin has four pieces of a heart broken and floating beneath his ribs, he refused to die.

"When I was young, Grandma Cece told me that God keeps count of what you look at," Elgin said this without turning away from staring toward that vacant lot across Dinwiddie, without making the effort to look over across the porch at Emmanuel. "You get to see just so many things—people, television shows, photographs, street corners, boxes of cereal, dead bodies. After you've reached the number of things you're allowed to see, you die. Death can be simple that way. The minute after my grandmother told me that, I started closing my eyes as often as possible." He let out a laugh, one of those short, soft ones that he still carried with him from childhood. "I ate with my eyes closed. I walked down hallways with my eyes shut. Fell down them old stairs in Cece's house many times, but I kept my eyes closed. Bruised up my knees and elbows. Figured it was time's way of marking my body, reminding God I had some extra days of living in me 'cause I was being careful not to waste my eyes seeing what didn't need to be seen. I read books with my eyes shut real tight; all the while, teachers screaming at me to open my eyes. I even watched television with my eyes closed. You remember that Partridge Family? I can't imagine what that show would have been like if I'd had my eyes opened. Voices themselves enough to make me quit dancing. But I liked listening to them for some reason."

"I bet you kept your eyes opened during *Soul Train*."

"I did. That I did. And I am glad for that. I didn't mind sacrificing a couple days of my life for having watched *Soul Train*. And I kept my eyes open during ballgames, too. You know I did that." Elgin chuckled another one of his old laughs, one from back when Thuy was still alive. "That one year no one thought anything of them. If only Aribba had been there in '79, too."

"If only."

They both got quiet with that. It's what happens to men in Pittsburgh when you mentioned Clemente or '79. A man of true heart. A year of wild magic. Sister Sledge blasting out of every single radio and boombox in the city from late summer to early autumn. Every man, woman, and child in the city smiling. Wasn't normal to see so much happiness in a city breaking apart at the seams, but those Pirates brought everyone in Pittsburgh together that autumn. So any time you talked about that man who played right field and made those amazing basket catches, or you spoke of '79, everyone got slow and quiet.

"I'd keep both eyes wide open to see Clemente play one more inning. Keep my eye on him for every pitch. I'd barter with God or the devil for that. Him lifting that knee and stepping into every pitch." Elgin finally looked over toward Emmanuel, smiled; then he looked down at his own hands as if he were looking for something, as if he could still see his cracked hands.

Even in high school he was careful with seeing. Careful not to waste any of it. Other kids thought him shy with looking. With girls. But it was simpler than that. He was sensitive to sight, to what it did to him, to what it might do to others. He worried over what seeing took out of him, took away from him. The way sight marked a man. He tried to find subtle ways to close his eyes.

Elgin did that careful eye-closing trick of his everywhere except in Vietnam. He never closed his eyes over there. Not once. He didn't sleep. He didn't dare to dream. He kept both eyes open, and he saw more than enough to kill him. Elgin only trusted closing his eyes when he was with Thuy. He could not even take naps unless she was near him. But when he kissed her, when she touched his face, when they made love, he kept his eyes open. Some things are worth dying for. And some things stay with you even in blindness.

79

"Maybe you still believe in your grandma's tales. Maybe that's what you're doing now," Emmanuel threw back at Elgin. "Trying to cheat death. Going blind is just a more crazy way for keeping your eyes closed."

"Maybe."

Elgin stared off at some point nowhere on this planet. Some place long ago and far away. It might not have ever been an actual place in the here and now, but he was seeing something with those blind eyes of his. And that place he was seeing was more real than the vacant lot. He looked to that place with his whole body and soul. Hard and careful. Attentive. His eyes settled there. It seemed like that place— wherever it was, whatever it was—was pulling him to it. Giving him back the stories of his ancestors. A tugging at the very heart of Elgin's being. His ribs. His lungs.

"You don't look all that blind. You look like you're looking," Emmanuel said. "Like you're seeing." He looked in the direction of Elgin's stare. Shielded his eyes from the morning sun. "It's just an empty field." Emmanuel settled back in his rocking chair and rocked. Shook his head. "Gone crazy is what you're doing. Truly it is. What's over there worth staring at, Elgin?"

"Things you can't see, Emmanuel. Things I can't see. Things I didn't see. Things I still can't see, now or before," Elgin said. "Things a man hopes for." Elgin turned his hands over, formed them into a cup like he was about to make an offering. He prayed for one moment of strength to make it all right. "For all I have done," Elgin let out. Just a whisper, if that.

"What'd you say?" Emmanuel asked.

"Nothing," Elgin replied. "Ain't said nothing." Elgin looked back down at his hands, looked deep down as if he could see the age of his hands, as if he could see his mother, his grandmother, his grandmother's mother, as if he could see the man he had become, and the man he was once long ago, in those cracked hands of his. Elgin rubbed his thumb into the creases. He rubbed into the mud that had been left behind from Vietnam, the invisible mud that stayed there in the creases of his hands. Elgin looked down at this hollow cup formed by his hands. The absent memory of touch. His hands were empty. It's what happens to your hands when you live long enough or too long, when you outlive those you want. It's what happens to your hands, to your sight, when the deep loving turns to ash.

80

CHAPTER 8

Nothing could ever be said that would change anything. Words remained just words. T.J. is dead. Shoved back in the shadows of Rats Alley. Under the shadows. Covered by shadows. Forgotten. Lost. Dead. Now and forever, amen, as Johnny's grandfather would say. Johnny felt stuck in that prehistoric place before words.

"What's Stanley been doing?"

"Nothing."

"Nothing? What do you mean, nothing? What's nothing?"

"He's fitting fleas for shoes."

Johnny looked over at Chas and shook his head. "Yeah, that makes sense. I can see Stanley's fat stubby fingers putting tiny shoes on fleas." Johnny looked down at his own fingers, imagining how small flea shoes must be. Last week, Chas came out of Stanley's place and said that Stanley told him a story, a true story, of a man he lived down the street from in Cleveland, a man who actually laughed himself to death. Someone told a joke and that man started laughing and his laughing overtook him and he could not find a way to stop laughing, so he died. "Every time you meet with Stanley you invent new bullshit." Johnny leaned his shoulder into Chas', threw him off stride a little, nearly bumped him into a parked car. Nothing.

"Fleas," Johnny said again. "I guess someone's gotta fit all the fleas in Pittsburgh for shoes. And who's better to open a flea-shoe-fitting store than Stanley? I guess those are flea shoes you're carrying in that bag? Right? Gonna set up that flea shoe store. Find tiny people with

Doug Rice

delicate fingers to work there." Johnny smiled, then he looked down the street at an abandoned police car. "What did he say about T.J.?"

"Nothing. Now let it rest."

"Seriously? Nothing? Not even, 'Oh'?"

"Not a word, Johnny, because I didn't bother Stanley with any of that."

Johnny shook his head again. "You keep shaking your head like you been doing all day and it's going to fall off, roll down the street," Chas said. "You got something that needs to be said, you go and say it. You all high and mighty."

"That's some tired bullshit." The savage sun bore down on the two of them. The air deadly, humid and still. Pure heat. The kind of summer heat that destroyed dreams.

Chas avoided Johnny's stare. "You gotta let this go, Johnny. It's nothing."

"There's a story. He didn't just die."

"He did just that. Die. And that's all he did. He lived. He died. Now drop it."

They headed over to the corner of Federal and North. When they got to Rats Alley, T.J. was gone. Evaporated. No body. No bones. No remains. Not even a scar in the cracked earth of the alley. Just the empty shadow world. "See? It never happened," Chas said. "Sometimes that's all that happens to life. It just goes away. Everything is in the past. He faded away."

The day, as exhausted and as hot as Johnny, was fading too, disappearing into dusk. A long, slow drift toward the waiting darkness. "There's a story." Johnny squeezed through the space between the hurricane fencing and the wall of The Garden and slipped into Rats Alley. He kicked at the garbage, looked for anything that might have belonged to T.J. Nothing. Just the uncomfortable scent of urine, of old beer gone flat in half-empty bottles, broken glass, needles, soiled jeans, spilled memories, underwear, discarded takeout pizza boxes. Nothing more than, and nothing different from, the debris of every other alley in the city. The refuse of night desires. Johnny kept his hands in his pockets. Kept his body tight and narrow. Afraid to touch anything. He kicked at this and he kicked at that, but touched nothing. Careful, very careful, not to touch the brick wall of The Garden

82

or of The Apache. Johnny stumbled back out of the alley onto West North Avenue.

"Told you," Chas said. "Nothing, right? Nothing is nothing. Dead is gone."

Johnny shrugged his shoulders, looked across the avenue at some girls standing near the bus stop. "There's a story."

The sun dropped down behind the buildings of Pittsburgh early that night. Day workers disappeared from the streets, climbing into buses, stepping off buses, shuffling home. Cars stopped at the traffic lights. Drivers kept their eyes locked straight ahead, no sideward glances to the corners. No lingering looks filled with quiet longing. None of the drivers wanted to risk a tap on their window. Any sign urging them to pull around the corner. Johnny kicked at the last shadows of the day. Chas had gone off running errands for Stanley.

Johnny decided to haunt the corners before heading to the South Side. He wanted to ask everyone if they'd seen T.J. He knew he needed to be careful, to keep it gentle, just a slight nudge of a question. No pressure. No second questions. "You seen T.J.?" "No." "Nah." "Watcha asking for?" "I'm just looking for him. Nothing more." "What you want with him?" "Man's got a right to his privacy." "Don't be looking at me like that. What do I look like? T.J.'s keeper? I ain't his keeper. Ain't that boy's keeper nohow. You got to back off." "Ain't seen him." "Let him be." No one had anything to say. Not a clue. Or they weren't willing to say anything aloud. The whole North Side deaf and dumb over T.J., as if last night or this morning or whenever this happened, whatever it was that did happen, never actually happened.

Still, the absolute truth was that he was not around and that wasn't normal. He always cruised past Johnny and Chas to get in a word or two about the weather, about the Pirates, about the need for something more beautiful in the world than the boring drugs he was tired of doing, about the slow deterioration of music and his desire to create a music, a rhythm, that would go straight into your body without a person needing to hear any of it. T.J. called it bone-shaking music for the deaf. He also wanted to make movies for the blind. Not braille-films, but films that, like his bone-shaking music, went straight into your body. "No need for seeing it if your body cannot resist it, and your body just takes it in. Seeing. Hearing. All that makes our bones and muscles lazy. We got to get on back to our bone home."

T.J. not coming by to rant about the voices in his head meant something. Maybe he was dead. Or maybe he just walked away, down the street into the sunset and out of the picture. And all the quiet around the neighborhood meant more than what it was saying. The Street Elder told Johnny that maybe he had had enough with his life, enough of the streets. "Look for the simplest, briefest story. In and out is what I say. Leave no witnesses," she said. "Some people aren't here for the long of it," she said. "It happens."

A car slowed down, a station wagon with fake wooden side panels, and pulled in closer to the corner. The Street Elder looked into the car, stepped toward the curb and waited for the driver to roll down the passenger-side window, but he pulled away. It looked like the car itself panicked, lurched forward and jumped back into the lane to take the driver safely home to his white wife and his white kids, and most likely to his tiny, white dog before he did something truly foolish. The Street Elder smiled. "I'da given that boy a heart attack before we even got started, and left him with a heartache he'd feel for the rest of his life." She laughed and looked back down the avenue.

Johnny waited for her to say more about T.J. She turned away from the street and walked over to Johnny. "You never stay on the streets longer than you do," she told him. "With the streets, you stay until you leave. And that's all T.J. did. And that's all you're doing. It's all I'm doing. Chas is right, there's no story, at least not much of one." She put her arm around Johnny, held him strong for a moment, pressed her fingernails into the flesh of his shoulder. "You ever try to forget something that happened to you?"

Johnny squirmed out of her awkward hug. He looked out onto West North Avenue, then back at the Street Elder. "No."

She looked at him. "No? Some bully? Some girl? You're not too young for that." Johnny leaned against the wall of The Apache. "You're asking about T.J., like knowing something is innocent. After you find what you think it is you've been looking for, the day comes when you find yourself doing all you can to forget whatever it is that you figured out, whatever it is that you felt."

The Street Elder waited for Johnny to say anything. "You pray your life away for that one love," she went on. "Then one day that love appears, it comes to you. Stands there in front of you. You see it and you move on toward it, wanting it, thinking this is what you been living for. This is what life is about. That love wants you, and you want it, so you move to it. You got no idea what you're going to learn. What all it will do to you, to all of who you is. But you want it, so you go after it. And whatever it is that happens when you experience that love you been wanting, you won't ever be able to forget. Not in a lifetime of forgetting. You find out more than you thought possible or you find out something you dream you could wish away the knowing of it. But you can't. It's what you can't know about any of this until it's too late, then, like it or not, you know it. You can't just walk away from knowing, once you decide to walk toward it."

"T.J. never did anything to me or to no one," Johnny said.

The two of them held onto their stares. Each looking for something that the other was keeping invisible. "Your mother?" She asked. "You ever try," but she stopped. Johnny's lips moved slightly, like they had been tickled. He couldn't say anything. Words aren't made for talking about mothers. Those words stay stuck in bone and heart. No breath can bring them out. "One of these days, you're going to try to forget something that someone's done to you. Especially something you felt on your skin or with your muscles, your heart. Knives. Matches. The butt of a cigarette. Love. A paper cut. Something someone left behind with their teeth. A time someone said something about loving you, about adoring you. Then leaving. The kind of leaving that keeps the memory of it in your skin."

Johnny looked up at her. Something terrible had happened to her mouth. Probably something that someone did to her years back, and, right there in front of him, her body began remembering the very night that it happened and the man or woman who did it to her. Her lips, twisted and too thin, turning grey around their edges. Her teeth wrecked by too many alleyways, too many times being pushed into brick walls, too many times being pulled into vacant doorways. "It happens when it's supposed to happen, Johnny. Not before." She looked up and down the nearly empty street, then she pushed open the red door to The Apache Lounge, took one final look at Johnny, and said, "You're the kind of friend that wants something that can't never be looked for. It can only be found. You got your mother in you." The Street Elder tripped over the doorstep into The Apache.

The night turned darker. Streetlamps flickered. A few more men squeezed their way into Rats Alley. Johnny stepped out from under the awning of The Apache toward the street corner. He stood beneath the sky, took a quick glance up and down West North Avenue across the street at the park, then stared up into that desolate night sky. The few stars he could see made no sense to him.

Stars over the city never formed dippers or bears or rams or any of those other shapes Johnny's grandfather told him about. Stories about how stars revealed to you exactly who you were, what you were made of, but those kinds of stars didn't seem to be city stars; they seemed more like jungle stars. His grandfather mixed up stories about stars in the dark nights in Vietnam with stories about lightning bugs in the backyards of Pittsburgh. Sometimes, Elgin confused the stars with the bombs. Lights falling out of the sky. Lights trailing down from the heavens. Summer evenings between dusk and nightfall, Johnny's grandfather swatted at lightning bugs, trying to save everyone from the kind of danger that appears innocent until it's too late. Other nights, he ran into the house to escape, hid in the kitchen from the fireflies lighting up the backyard. His back pressed against the wall, hands flat on the floor, eyes peeking out the window. Mouth opened, wanting to warn everyone, but too afraid to make a sound. Small explosions of light that quickly passed away. When Johnny made fun of his grandfather tripping on the steps as he ran away from those tiny exploding flies setting fire to the dark, his mother would slap him and tell him straight, not just with her words but with the red pain of her eyes and with her hands holding on to his tiny biceps, shaking him: "You know nothing of that man and of his fears. Of what light becomes in his eyes. Of fire in the night. The orange fires that burn into his dreams and skin."

And his mother was right. Johnny knew none of that; he only knew to run when his grandfather sat down on his rocking chair. Each story going to the same place. Mud and fire. Bullets. Bombs falling from the heavens. Villages burning. Footprints in dust disappearing at dawn. Footprints in mud drowning beneath rainfall and blood. Boots, lifeless, abandoned under trees. "You have to know enough to want to be awake. You can't starve yourself from your past." More than the words, Johnny hated the way his grandfather looked at him, the way his mother looked at him, the way Grandma Thuy remained in the shadow of the room without a word, barely with a breath. "The life you've been given to live is a prayer. Pray it," Johnny's grandfather told him. "Pray your life," he repeated.

Johnny pulled himself out of his thoughts and looked back down West North Avenue. Old hollow men made of rags and bones stood planted in the concrete sidewalks, trying not to melt away in the evening heat. Scents of morning, noon, and night, scents of the whole of today and of yesterday, and of the day before yesterday, and of all the days before all the other days before yesterday, soaked their skin and their clothes and their hair. Nothing but rags and bones, withered skin, and that smell. Home. His grandfather told him you smell home, you don't see it. "You close your eyes, and you breathe in deep, that air, that smell. That's home. You smell Pittsburgh on your skin." Lately, these scents from the streets of the North Side had become more of a home to Johnny than his home on Dinwiddie. These scents, and the scents of the Monongahela River over on the South Side near the Birmingham Street Bridge, had become his true home. He waited beneath the streetlights.

"You still here?" Chas called from down the avenue.

"Yeah." Johnny met Chas in front of the doors to The Garden. "You get all those shoes delivered for the fleas?"

"You're the funny boy today, isn't you?" Chas glanced over at the glow of a white man who stopped to look at him. The man held his ground, looked into Chas' eyes, didn't even blink when Chas tried to stare him down. The man, wrapped in sadness, put his hand into his pocket, gave Chas a nice long time to see his desire, before slowly walking, nearly backpedaling, into The Garden. "Lonely streets tonight." The man looked back over his shoulder at Chas. "I'm not talking to you, man." Chas turned back to Johnny. "You haven't been asking about T.J., have you?"

"I asked."

"And?"

"Nothing."

"Like I said, there isn't a story." Chas started walking away. "I'm going in The Apache. You?"

"Walking the bridges."

"You should go home, Johnny. Your grandfather's gone blind. You need to be there." With that, Chas slipped into The Apache.

Johnny backed up a few steps to look into Rats Alley one last time. Complete and utter darkness filled the alley. Only the blind could see into such darkness. Sounds of men struggling with their bodies and with the bodies of other men escaped the alley. Sounds trying to lure other men into the shadows. A constant struggle of belts and zippers. Men wrestling with their desires. Men with men with men. Johnny knew all the stories of the Helen Keller room and of the Blind Hallway inside The Garden. And he knew about the bathrooms in The Apache Lounge. Those stories were nothing compared to the legends that people told of what happened in Rats Alley. Every god man ever invented has abandoned Rats Alley. They've just given up on it. Only reckless men, who cannot imagine any other way to escape life, venture into Rats Alley, because it is the last place on earth that they can go. Men who have forgotten the names their mothers gave them when they were born go into that alley and do not come out until they have forgotten more than their names. Men who do not want to be seen and who do not want to see go there. Fingerprints left behind on each other's skin. It was said to be the only place in Pittsburgh where there were no safe words, where every movement left scars. Stories cluttered that alley, and no one walked into that alley without knowing all those stories, without wanting to become a part of those stories, without wanting to leave something of their own mysterious bodies behind for the soothsayers to turn their bodies into mythological tales. There were no accidents in Rats Alley, only desires.

Johnny stood at that opening to the alley longer than he should have. There was nothing to be seen, he knew that; nothing that could be seen; still, he tried to see, longed to see any glimmer of something that would give him hope. Even if he only saw a reflection of something that he could not name. Anything. Johnny nearly found himself being pulled into that narrow passageway, nearly found himself wanting all that he could not name. Perhaps he was hoping that T.J. would rise out of the ashes and the debris of the alley. But nothing. Nothing.

CHAPTER 9

Fred spread out a roadmap of Pennsylvania on the kitchen table. "Look." Debra turned away from the window. She looked down at the map, then up at Fred. "There," he said and pointed at the red circle of Philadelphia on the map. "And there." With a finger from his other hand he pointed at Pittsburgh. "That's how far away from you I feel when we are standing in the same room."

He looked into Debra's eyes. She felt him enter her. She felt him inside her, his eyes, his hopes, his longing, his anger or frustration, his love for her mixing with her love for him. She saw his sadness, and she saw something in his eyes that was on the verge of quitting, something about to disappear, but that was begging Debra to rescue. His eyes had already stopped being green and were now more of a disappointing grey. He looked like he had become winter. A weakness had overtaken his lips. Somehow, Fred had become frail without Debra even noticing.

"When," he started to say. He wiped sweat from his forehead, then pressed his finger harder into the red circle that was Pittsburgh on the map. "Come back," he started again, but, again, he stopped. He began folding the map, gathered what strength he could, and said: "When will you ever come back?" His voice sounded the way Debra imagined a window must sound like the moment a baseball hit the glass and shattered it. "I miss." He knew there were probably other men who could finish that sentence, really finish it, and say whatever it was that needed to be said with all their hearts, but he was not such a man. Being trapped inside this same house, with her every day and every night and to still miss her, to still want her, to still need her, the way his heart longed for her in this way, was downright painful. He could not say all there was that needed to be said.

He wanted to ask her where the life was that they had lost, but he knew she would only say Lucas' name. She would say that Lucas had carried her heart off with him into a fairy tale. Fred would have to wait until the child brought her heart back. She would say her heart was in his pocket. She would say these words, go so far as to believe them, even though both Fred and Debra knew they had been losing the life they were sharing before Debra realized that their son had gone missing.

Fred watched Debra. He waited for her to acknowledge that he had spoken. He stared into that moment, watched the movement of her ribcage. Listened to her slow breathing. She rolled up her sleeves. Outside the window, the sun was growing as old as Fred's eyes, disappearing behind the West View Cinema Dream Palace. She waited for the day to quit, to be done with them, waited for twilight to turn ashen, before speaking.

"There are voices," she said, but, like Fred, she struggled with a feeling that she had said too many words in her lifetime and that it was best to live the rest of her life without words. She wanted to find a place unfamiliar to herself. And now, even trying to speak confused Debra's mouth. Her mouth had grown accustomed to rest, to waiting. Her words felt foreign to her desire for solitude.

Debra coughed, tried to clear her throat for the words, for any word, to give to Fred, to say, for herself, a word that would clear away all this fog and this heat, all this that she feared she was forgetting, a word, one word, a single word that would make her child appear. She reached into her pocket, but there was nothing there. She had spent the day searching the house for a photograph of Lucas or for a birth certificate. Something. Anything. She only found frantic drawings and dust.

Debra walked toward the kitchen table; her thigh bumped into a chair. She moved close enough to Fred to be close without being intimate. His skin made Debra clumsy and forgetful. He tried to move closer to Debra, but her shoulder twitched, so he stopped himself. He, too, bumped into a chair, rested his hand on the back of the chair to steady himself.

An innocent silence filled the space that separated and protected Debra and Fred from all the harm that waited for them. Her dry mouth, lips and tongue, sought out words to confess all she had done and all she had failed to do. She rummaged through her body for memories that could justify all that she wanted to do with her hands to this man she had married years ago. Her body waited. His waited. When she finally did begin speaking, she knew not to look at him and she knew to release the words in a rush, so that she would not stop them from coming out of her. "There are voices inside my head, and none of them love you anymore." These were the only words she remembered how to say aloud. The other words were trapped in an unspeakable language and told her to do things to Fred, things he would not like very much, things that would change the way he looked at her and change the way that he thought about love and about desire.

She unpinned her static, broken hair. "I keep trying to hear the other voices, our old voices, but they have abandoned me." Her hair fell down over her shoulders. She lifted her skirt above her knees. The way she lifted her skirt ought to mean something. One day it did mean something; it meant so much more than either Fred or Debra could remember. The way she stared across the kitchen table at him. The way her mouth waited. Fred thought that she was beginning to remember. But she only said that she was drying her hands and that she was trying to understand how he got there. In this room. Where he had come from. "I thought I had locked the doors," she said. He looked at Debra as if he were watching someone dear to his heart disappear before his eyes.

Debra wanted to tell Fred stories about the girl she followed when she was a young girl. A desire to confess to him, the way she confessed to Bob rose up inside her, but mixed with that desire was a rage that she feared she would not control, a rage that spoke in sound and muscle, a rage made from stolen ribs, cracked ribs, a rage from beneath the soil of the earth. She wanted Fred to know this rage, so he would look at her differently. She wanted him to see her in her flesh, the flesh made in those early days of her life of hiding behind trees and of looking through windows.

Once upon a time, Debra told herself, she was a young girl, and she followed a reflection of herself along the river, to an old motel on the North Side, where a woman had let the curtains remain open a slice, a crease. Being lonely carried Debra there. It was a stupid, weak cliché, one that never would change unless she grabbed the cliché around the neck and strangled it. A cliché from old movies, from new movies, from everything everywhere. A cliché gone wild with wanting. A woman looking at her muddy palms, mistaking the mud for time, mistaking skin for something that would protect her.

The woman pulled off the man's belt and said, "We can begin with this." She held the belt before the man. He looked at it in her soft hands. She, then, handed the man his belt. He took it and dropped it onto the floor. The woman fixed her eyes on it. Like the whip used on the body of Christ, this man's belt was not innocent. Precise and simple.

Years later, Debra would ask for this from Fred. She would ask for the sound of rain falling on her soul and for the fury of dreams that she had neglected. She would ask for the kind of desolation that marks flesh. Debra would ask Fred to unleash her earliest memories of being loved, but Fred would become quiet. He would sit on the edge of their bed and say that he was a coward. She would kneel beside him and weep forgotten hopes from her childhood out of her body.

Debra watched the woman move her foot closer to the belt. Then she raised her eyes and looked at the man. The woman unbuttoned her dress. She let her dress fall onto the floor. She wore nothing beneath her dress. Just flesh. No lingerie. No memories. No desire. No bruises. Nothing. A tiny mole on her pale thigh. The woman was not even sure if this flesh was her flesh.

She laid face down on the bed, looked over her shoulder, and said something that sounded like, "Make my skin understand." She longed for her skin to mean something to the young girl in her small dress at the window. To the people that this young child, watching from the window, would stop on the streets, outside weddings, and tell this story to for years and years, until the young girl's throat would become too tired and too sore and too used up. The woman closed her eyes, buried her face in the pillow. Waited. Nearly suffocating, wanting to suffocate. And waited. And the man allowed her to wait. He picked at the hands of his wristwatch, pulled them off. The man said, "You can wait." And he sat on a chair in the far corner of the room, until the woman said she wanted to be done with waiting. The man raised his body from the chair and walked over to her. Beneath the weight of the man's footsteps, the floor made inarticulate sounds, sounds of longing and despair. The woman's breath changed. Outside the window Debra counted and waited, too. The man twisted the woman's arms behind her back, kissed the underside of her wrists. Then stopped.

The woman said she wanted to know what happened next. There are only so many words at any given moment. Debra closed her eyes, but did not look away. She parted her lips, but remained still. Silent. The man left his shoes on. She knew that much for certain. The world became blue and wet.

Even if you close your eyes, there are sins everywhere, and, if you keep your eyes closed, there is speech for the unspoken. Debra walked away from looking. She walked away from the window. She walked along the edge of the Allegheny River, followed the trail, until she found breadcrumbs and pebbles. She walked until she heard her mother's voice, her father's laughter.

But Debra could only want to tell Fred all this. This and so much more. "I want." But her throat stopped her. She raised her hand, as if there was something in her palm that would explain all this to him.

Fred looked away from Debra and opened the refrigerator, reached in to grab a beer. "Lucas isn't here in this house, our house, now." He did not know why he said it, and he was not completely sure what he even meant by it. "I think we're just supposed to wait." Words kept coming out of his mouth, falling onto the kitchen floor. He opened his beer. "We're meant to wait. It's all been done." He knocked back the first pull of his beer. "We need to believe that he is on his way home." He raised the beer to his lips, but stopped. "It's not about forgetting." Fred had no idea what he meant. Beer did that to him. Beer and wanting Debra in that physical way that happens to a man, even a man of his age when looking at his wife. "You begin listening, and you hear what you need to hear. Listening isn't giving up. Listening is listening."

Debra looked at Fred, but she continued to hold back her stories from him. She held onto all that she knew, all that she thought might be true. She refrained from telling him of her need to confess. "Forgive me, Father, for I have sinned, for I am sinning, for I will sin." Her need to be forgiven controlled her, her need for someone to speak over her skin. The desire for someone to place a thumb on her forehead. The crying. The shouting.

The stony agony of vacant hallways, empty rooms, closed windows. Her tongue dried and cracked from wanting to speak. "I want," Debra said. She twisted her hands, twisted them, trying to wring them dry of some sin, to wash the sins from her hands, or perhaps she was rubbing these sins deeper and deeper into the palms of her hands. "Find Lucas." Fred watched Debra close her mouth. Most people merely stop talking, words just quit coming out of their mouths, but Debra did more than simply stop talking, more than simply stop letting words fall out of her mouth. She brought her lips together, closed her mouth, a clamping shut. A tight locking of her thin, narrow lips. "I want Lucas." She kept stopping herself.

She thought again of the boy she had lost one day long ago, the boy who played with matches. If he came back to her now, she could follow the boy. He would lead her along the dark streets and guide her safely to basements and windows and alleys, to all those reckless places where dead men lose their bones, and she could watch until she saw what she needed to see, until she heard the nervous voices that would awaken her. Debra let out a tiny bubble of a laugh. "I can't find Lucas, Fred. But you know that." Debra started to turn back to the sink, to return to gazing outside at the maple tree, at Lucas' rusted, nearly destroyed bicycle leaning against that dying maple tree. But she stopped. "Everyone knows." She took a step toward Fred. Stopped. She looked confused, uncertain of how to move or where to go. "Is this what we are supposed to do?" she asked.

"I don't think Lucas is missing, Debra." Fred placed his empty beer bottle on the table. "I think that he got spirited away." He reached his hand out toward Debra. "Come to bed. It's late, and it just keeps getting later."

That night Fred and Debra touched each other for the first time in ages. Fred touched her. Debra touched him. They might have kissed two or three times, but certainly no more than that. "You kiss my forehead like you were kissing a gravestone, " she said. He tried to remember how to kiss her in some other way. His mouth, his lips lost on her mouth, on her lips. He seemed to remember something about his tongue and about closing his eyes. And some distant memory of his teeth and of her collarbone. He tried. Then she tried. They seemed to have left their bodies on some distant shore when they climbed into bed, and now they were waiting for everything to end, every movement to stop, every breath to become quiet.

Both feared touching the other in ways that might change something, that might create a new memory, one that neither Fred nor Debra could survive. She wanted to end this once and for all. Everything. She waited to say something to him, something that was waking inside her, but her mouth remained still. She wished they had been more patient when they were younger. She wished they lived closer to the river, to any river, and to a river more wild, a river that man dare not try to contain, a river with a soul so deep that it touched the very roots of the beginning of the world. She was glad that the dishes were all clean, that there was not one dirty dish in the whole house, except for the one glass filled to the very brim with milk beside the plate with the doughnut on the kitchen table. She was glad the Pirates were not playing tonight, glad that Fred would not be thinking about them, glad that Jim was not knocking on their kitchen door.

Debra wanted Fred to do things to her that she had witnessed men in dreams do to her, and she wanted him to say things to her like the men in her dreams said, things they truly meant to say and do, but afterwards the men in her dreams were sorry, but she did not want Fred to be sorry. She hated when the men in her dreams told her they were sorry. She wanted more than that. She wanted those men to forget about their need to be sorry when they did all those things to her, even that one thing that made tears fall from her eyes. All those things that made her remember. Debra wanted Fred to look at her without sympathy, without regret, she wanted him to look at her without caution and for him to begin there. She wanted things done. Her body was prepared for this.

Their bodies moved against each other or around each other, going this way and that way for what seemed like hours, but most likely was only minutes or seconds. Elbows. Feet. Knees. A hand here. One there. A brush of her lips or a brush of his lips across some lonely skin. Abandoned fingers digging into muscles, scratching into bone, wanting to mark, to cut, to heal. Fingers that clutched at the roots of her desire, but that worried about disturbing the universe. Debra searched for a place on Fred's body that she remembered. A place to recall a time before. She struggled beneath his weight shifting her thighs, adjusting her knees, but she clung to Fred and pulled him down on top of her, pulled and pulled and pulled. And she held him there with a mighty force.

Debra felt something unhinge, something pushing inside her. She felt something cry. A tear. A muscle. A rib. Her fingers went away from her body. Nothing Fred did or could ever do, nothing Debra did or ever could do, would ever repair her skin. Her eyes hurt. "Pull," she said, and she felt something splitting her open.

Even though both were sweating in the humidity of the September night, everywhere they touched each other was cold. Debra said she stared through windows when she was still a child and that she must have gotten frostbite one of those nights, and her fingers had never quite gotten over it. For years, she tried to warm them, to thaw them. It's what happens when a shadow crawls up and enters your heart. It's not so much the words themselves and what they might mean that break you. It's their shape. The way they fit in your mouth. The weight of the words in your body. The way a word makes your mouth feel, the taste of a well-worn word. She pulled Fred closer. She could not get close enough to him, and he could not find a way to get close enough to her. Each time they pulled themselves into each other's embrace they became more distant. Her eyes so wet, and they hurt. This pain. She put her mouth near Fred's ear and whispered. "I don't know what happens to the shadows in the dark. I don't know where our shadows are." Fred collapsed on top of Debra. "They must still be here. They can't just disappear. They must still be here."

Debra woke in the dark. Fred was asleep near the edge of their bed. He always slept there on the verge of falling off the bed onto the floor. The deep night had stolen all the light from their home. The quiet city miles away. She said she could still hear snow falling from her childhood, even though she had not seen snow fall for months, for years, for days. But Fred did not budge, did not hear her. She felt that snow from childhood on her skin, in her joints, a snow that fell all over Pittsburgh, one that buried the city in all that needed to be forgotten and forgiven. She quietly climbed out of bed, picked up her robe from the floor. His belt lay innocently beside it. She pulled on her robe, then walked out of their bedroom, down the hallway. She turned on the nightlight, and then she went from room to room turning on lights, until she fell asleep.

In the morning, Fred and Debra woke up in different places in the house. Fred made his way into the kitchen. Debra was already standing, stationed so it seemed to Fred, at the sink. Over breakfast, they tried to look at each other, tried to say something about the weather, but too much silence filled the room. Fred finished eating, and, like the day before this day and the day before that day, he went to work. Debra sat at the table until she could no longer sit there, then she washed the dishes and waited.

CHAPTER 10

Elgin woke slow and quiet. His blindness had settled into his body. He had become familiar with it and enjoyed the privacy his blindness afforded him.

The past few days, though, Emmanuel had begun going out of his way to tell Elgin about all the wonders he'd been seeing. He said Pittsburgh had never been so vibrant. He told him that there were new colors in the world, not new shades, nothing subtle like that, but whole new colors had suddenly appeared. "You're missing all this, Elgin." And when Elgin asked him the names of these new colors, he replied, "You crazy? Words can't stay up with all there is to see. Words is words. Seeing is seeing. Ain't no one can come up with new words fast enough for these colors. They colors, not words."

Emmanuel's voice had become more frantic, more shrill. Emmanuel seemed to be trying his best to convince himself that seeing was the most important thing in the world. He began every conversation, since Elgin had gone blind, with: "You should've seen what I seen today. Patricia did this with her hair in such a way that you ain't never going to believe, and there are no words to describe Patricia. You know how that is." Or: "The way Henry be looking at Jewelle. Not even disguising it no more. Man got no shame. He looking straight at her with a world of desire in his eyes."

"Next thing you'll be telling me is that the rats have gotten so big down on Forbes Avenue that they've started adopting children as pets."

"You never know, Elgin. You blind now, so how you going to

know?"

Maybe Elgin's blindness had made Emmanuel that much better at seeing. The invisible world was coming into focus for him. But Elgin knew he was fooling himself with thinking Emmanuel was capable of that. He only wanted Elgin to feel stupid for going blind, but Elgin did not even think it was so much that. It was more that Emmanuel appeared terrified of going blind, thinking he could catch his blindness or that, simply getting older and older, everyone eventually tires of seeing and goes blind in the night. Elgin reminded him that his blindness was a gift from a God who was asking Elgin to forgive Him for His sins, for His neglect.

Going blind saved Elgin from the oblivion being created by a world that was too full of things to see. It stopped him from losing what remained of the world that was worth saving. He held onto the old stories that came with seeing on the inside of his thinking. Kept them safe. Everything Elgin wanted to see was on the inside. There wasn't much left on the outside for him to look at, and most of what was out there for him to see was being torn down. The old neighborhoods were becoming invisible. Renaissance this, renaissance that. Call it what you want, to Elgin it was a stealing of stories. Memories were dying. Outside, in the world of the seeing, the past was being erased more and more. All that was true was being forgotten.

Emmanuel accused Elgin of being nostalgic. Accused him of wanting nothing to change. Freezing time. "Think of all that got torn down to create everything that you're holding onto. What got bulldozed over to make your house and these streets. It's the same thing. This used to be apple orchards or something. A forest." But Elgin did not believe him. He knew what Emmanuel was getting at, but it wasn't what Elgin was thinking. Elgin just did not seem to have the right words for any of it. A sadness came with seeing not only what wasn't there, but also seeing what was there. The remains. An architecture of forgetting.

And so much noise filled up all the silence that he was beginning to fear the loss of silence. "I wonder what kids are going to think silence is?" he asked Emmanuel. "Silence is being driven mad by noise, and seeing is being driven crazy by light. What's going to become of stars in ten years? Imagine living a whole life without seeing the dark

dark of night. I didn't know that until I went to Vietnam. It took a war to set me free to see stars. Imagine what it would be like to only see the lights of the city. You know there's a problem when light destroys light," he said. Elgin held tight to the arms of his rocking chair. "And Johnny thinks it's gone quiet when the television is turned off and when the police sirens stop for five minutes. You turn off a television, and people call that silence."

Elgin sat for a while on the edge of his old bed. He sat with the image of Thuy in her slippers, her delicate fingers on the knob of the dresser, about to pull a drawer open. He reached behind him, toward the center of their bed and rested his hand there, felt the warmth of the quilt. He looked over his shoulder, as if he were still capable of seeing when he truly wanted to see. He gazed in slow, blind misery at that one place on their bed where Thuy put her body down to sleep, to dream.

Even blind, he found himself looking toward the places where memories still lived. The thin fabric of Thuy's nightgown. The tight fearlessness of her smile. Her perfect skin. All the bombs that fell down on her family, all those bombs that fell through the trees, onto her home, near her flesh, could not destroy her skin. No man can expect to remain unchanged when he touches a woman that beautiful. She changed Elgin, and that was enough for him, the way he became this other man, even while carrying the fire of that war in him. Her beauty stole him away from those fires. And he remembered the sound that remained in her voice, her struggle to hold onto her past, to never let go of her mother and grandmother and great grandmother when she spoke English.

When Thuy was forced to learn English, she told Elgin that she would never forgive America for doing the damage that speaking English did to the shape of her mouth, the feel of her tongue inside her mouth, the pain that English brought to her lips. Words with more than one syllable posed the deepest threat to her past, so she slowed her speech nearly to a complete halt in order to pronounce each syllable separately, to protect her past from these new sounds, from the pain speaking English caused in her teeth, her tongue, her throat. "Those big words," she told Elgin, "have too much noise. My teeth nearly fall out when I say them. They dry out my lips." She feared that by speaking English she would no longer be able to smile the way her grandmother smiled. None of these words that came out of her mouth in English came from those places inside her that truly mattered. The only way to those places was to travel through her native tongue. "I only touch you in Vietnamese, not English." And she refused to say, "I love you", to Elgin in English.

She taught Lehuong Vietnamese, insisted Lehuong speak Vietnamese during every meal. She told her that Vietnamese protected the stories of their ancestors and that her ancestors would die in English. "English wants us to die. It violates our mouths, our skin. Your mouth was born to speak Vietnamese." And Thuy said that speaking in the language of their ancestors while eating was to bless the food as it nourished their bodies.

Elgin knew very little Vietnamese. It burned his mouth. He often bit his tongue attempting to say the simplest words. He was never sure if it was from the memories of the war or from the way the words shaped his mouth, exercised his tongue. And when Elgin said he wanted to learn more Vietnamese so that he could love Thuy in her language, she said, "No." Just no.

Lehuong never taught a word of Vietnamese to Johnny. "English, woman. Speak English," the man who broke her ribs shouted at her. This man told her that Vietnamese sounded like it came straight out of rice paddies and mud puddles, filthy words of earth and sky, that her words were so full of water that they nearly drowned before she could say them. "Speak human," he told her, while pressing his hand against the back of her neck. "Your father fought that war, killed those gooks, burned down those trees, so none of us would ever have to hear these sounds again, so we could forget about jungles and mud huts." He pushed Lehuong against the wall of their bedroom, and he kissed her forehead with lips so poisonous that she begged God to strike her dead, to burn down their house while they were sleeping, to not keep her soul or the soul of this man, but to disintegrate everything. She prayed for fire.

Elgin feared some of this thinking back into the past. Any man who thought too much into his past was bound to see all that he had lost. Every time Elgin told stories of loving Thuy, of seeing Lehuong running down the street, of watching Clemente in right field, he could not help but create the feeling of loss with each act of re-membering. That world was gone. Each time he took a breath, those memories scarred his heart, burned into his eyes, and made his ribs feel the sorrow of a lived life. The blood of Thuy loving him kept shaking in his heart, keeping his heart awake, open and alive. Emmanuel insisted he let it go. "I can't help you if you don't release your memory of her," he told Elgin.

Time does not heal all wounds; if a man is not careful, time erases wounds. Then what is he left with? The cold and the silence. The pain Elgin suffered from the reality of Thuy not being with him when he remembered her was a pain far more bearable than the pain that dimming her voice or letting her skin vanish from his thoughts, from his dreams, his stories, his memories, would cause. He feared that if he let go of this sorrow, he would be letting go of the joy as well. Some days the pain of missing Thuy broke into his heart and lungs and made his body nearly intolerable, and he swore he could feel a breeze blowing through the hole in him that was created the night she died, but there would be no way for him to go on living his life without her, and that meant he had to be calling up her memory. Some days his heart beat like a boot kicking against his ribs. Still, he did all he could to kindle those memories, to keep them burning, to keep them from turning into ash.

Emmanuel argued that Elgin could not go on with his life unless he put out this fire. That no one could survive such bereavement. "You got to bury it. Call on Pete to shovel dirt on that pain," he said. But Elgin refused. For most men, the memory of such loss, the living with such loss, leads to anger and disappointment in God, in fate, in something; it leads to simple bitterness with the heart, with the failed promises of love. It did that to Elgin's father, Clarence, when Ai left him, when Ai said, "I adore you," then closed her eyes and turned around and walked down Dinwiddie one last time. All living is, is memory, and then death. Elgin knew this.

He pushed his old body up off the squeaking mattress and made his way down the stairs, into the kitchen. When he walked into the kitchen, Johnny quickly swallowed the last bit of banana that was in his mouth. "I heard that, " Elgin said. "You got to slow it down, boy." He reached for his chair, pulled it out, and sat down. "You been staying with Chas?"

"No, not much. Just running. Sleeping along the Monongahela with Sylvia. Too hot inside for sleeping." Johnny reached up into a cupboard and grabbed two cups. "You hear anything about T.J.?"

"I heard all there is to hear." Johnny brought his grandfather a cup of coffee and sat with him at the table. "Heard what there was to be heard."

"What'd you hear?"

"You know what I heard. I don't need to tell you." Elgin looked at Johnny, direct and hard, like he was seeing inside that inside place of Johnny, the one Chas seemed to know so well. But Johnny held the blind man's stare. Held it. Looked back at it. "There's a reason to living. You learn it when you look at death. What is there to believe? You're dying. You just know that."

He tried to see all that his grandfather was not saying, but his grandfather kept it invisible. This new staring, direct and hard into Johnny's eyes, that Elgin could do now that he was blind, at first unnerved Johnny, but lately he had become intrigued by it. In some ways, he liked it. He felt that it was taking him and his grandfather back to a place they had not been to in quite some time.

"You be careful with Chas. You start with drugs it becomes a hard career, harder than being president," Elgin said. "You ask your guidance counselor at school about that on career day. Ask him what the career options are for doing drugs, what the chances are for advancement, and all that." Elgin grabbed hold of his breath. Over the past few days his breathing had become more of a struggle for him. The humidity or the pollen or something in the air, or maybe it had something to do with him being blind, had begun to change his breathing. "There's no end to it. You just keep looking everywhere for drugs. It's who you become. So you think deep on that, if you're thinking Chas is living the life."

Elgin said *the* in those sentences, like it had special meaning, had more to say than just what the word the normally had to say. *The* street. *The* life. *The* game. Then Elgin would go on and on about being dead before you're 21. "The true American Dream: to have all of us be dead before we turn 21. Before we have time to think too much." Elgin going on about how, if you're not careful, death just happens to you, about how in Vietnam that was the whole point. He always ended there.

That was the part of the lecture that Johnny dreaded. His grandfather's tirades about the real design behind the Vietnam War. The white truth of America's invasion. "Get us over there fighting, so white people can build malls, and their kids can rebel and grow long hair. Making peace signs on their college notebooks. Generation of love, my ass. And they became the heroes. They still haven't looked me in the eye, still haven't found the courage to walk on the same side of the street as me. You got to educate yourself, Johnny. Ain't no one going to educate yourself for you. That's on you, son."

Elgin brought his coffee cup to his lips, took a few quiet sips. He held the cup in his hands, felt the heat. "Recruitment centers everywhere like a cancer. Be all you can be. We didn't wait to get drafted; we volunteered our way out of America. That's what they called it: volunteering. That ain't volunteering. We called it, pressed up against a brick wall. We thought it'd be safer over there."

Johnny poured another cup of coffee, added the last of the pot to his grandfather's cup. Elgin nodded, then went right back into it. "Put us on a bus, take us to a camp, ship us across an ocean, put us in the jungles, offer us drugs, have us kill as many of their enemies as we could, then ship us home, throw us back in our neighborhoods, get us spending all our time looking for drugs, so we don't have time for nothing else. Only time we got is time to look for drugs or to keep an eye out for the police. No white man takes time out of his day looking out for police. Police is invisible to a white man. And white man invisible to police. Wonder if a police ever even seen a white man? What do you think? No white man in the history of being white ever wasted his time with looking down the streets to see if it's safe enough to walk to a grocery store. Be sure there are no police waiting behind corners." Elgin ran through this tirade so often that Johnny chanted it along with him.

"Don't worry, Pops. I ain't falling for any of it." Johnny got up and grabbed a box of cereal out of the cabinet, milk from the fridge, bowls and spoons. "No need for you to worry. No need. You want cereal?"

Elgin drained his cup of coffee, put it gently on the table. "Yes."

Johnny was surprised at how fluid, how certain his grandfather's actions were, almost more careful than when he was able to see. "You got a truth inside you, Johnny, and that truth is bigger than you. Bigger than the corners. Bigger than the alleys. But that truth ain't such a hard mystery. You can't fear finding it, and you can't really look for it. It just is. You let that truth be, and trust in it. It'll show itself to you when it needs to."

Johnny poured his grandfather's cereal and milk into a bowl and slid it across the table to him. He wanted to ask about T.J., wanted to tell his grandfather to stop being cryptic, wanted to ask his grandfather why he thought Chas was telling him to stay out of it. But he figured his grandfather was saying about the same thing. They ate their cereal surrounded by silence. "You know," he broke into the silence, "they cut down Clyde's tree."

"Why'd you go and tell me that for?" Elgin asked. "What good is it being blind, if everyone's telling me about all that they see? You and Emmanuel are out to destroy my blindness. It's like you reached on inside me and erased that tree out of my sight. You didn't need to do that, boy." Elgin put his spoon into the bowl of cereal, splashing milk on the table. "And you say it all innocent, like the way you eat fruit all innocent, like there's nothing to them cutting down another tree in our neighborhood. It's their way to torture us with more sun, more heat."

Johnny made a quick mental note, never to mention anything that had to do with seeing, to only talk to his grandfather about things that did not involve seeing. Only talk about the invisible and about memories.

"How long it took them?"

"Took who? What?"

"The tree. For them to cut it down."

"Don't know. Probably the entire day."

"Whole day. You say that like it's a long time. That's nothing, compared to how long it took for that tree to grow. All those years. That tree's been there before anyone, been there before God. It stood up to rain and sleet. Snow weighing down its branches. It survived fire and humidity. Stood up to Clyde fighting with wife after wife and girl after girl that he kept locked up inside that house of his until he tired of them and kicked them out, or until they tired of him and walked out that front door. It took centuries for that tree to grow. It was the only tree I could look at and simply see the tree and not all that we will never forget. And what? Gone in a day, less than a day. It shows what man is capable of when he sets his mind to something. That should worry you, Johnny. Think of the kind of soulless man that can cut down a tree without thinking much of it. Should take a man as long to cut a tree down as it took for the tree to grow."

Elgin looked toward the kitchen window, out into the backyard to that place where a small pine tree still struggled to grow. "It's the trees that make this life tolerable, that remind us of something bigger. You see an old tree, and you know that something has been here before you. You don't need to believe in God to know that. You see the tree. You don't need stories and books and graveyards telling you that. You get all that in the tree. Any ancient tree tells you in its being here that people have walked on this earth before you ever were born. And trees remind you that people are going to be here after you are gone. People climbed those trees before you arrived here, and people who ain't even been born yet are going to be climbing that tree after you depart this world. A tree is a reminder. There are trees that remind us of all that people here would rather we forget. A heritage of loss. You take heed to that, son. Of all living things, trees most clearly speak to history. You look at a young tree, one just planted, and that's a promise. That's hope. There are going to be more days to come. You look at those old trees, like Clyde's, and you get reminded that there was a yesterday. Trees are like people and their scars, but they're more beautiful." Elgin found a deep breath, pulled it in.

Part of Johnny wanted to say it was just a tree, like the apple was just an apple. Part of him wished he hadn't said anything. Another part of him stirred around, all confused. "You need to know the things you can hold onto, and then you need to hold them," Elgin said. "They can't take that." Johnny pushed back his chair, but didn't make a move to stand up.

"T.J. says we need more trees. Says trees cool people down. He says shade is different from shadows."

"I doubt he'll be saying any of that anymore." Elgin reached for his coffee cup. "You got to quit being afraid of shadows, Johnny, and see them for what they are. There's a mystery inside a shadow, and inside that mystery is a truth."

"T.J.'s dead. Is that what you heard?"

"Without death, imagine how crowded these streets would be. They're crowded as it is, with all the ghosts, all those memories haunting every street in this city. You live to be old enough, you'll see how death is needed." Elgin started to get up from the table. He wanted to walk out into the morning air, wanted to feel that morning breeze before the day heated up. But he stopped himself, thought better of it. Johnny rinsed his cup, set it in the sink. He thought of leaving, but he, too, remained in the kitchen. They both seemed to be waiting for some kind of miracle, a sudden awareness that everything that was gone from their lives was not really gone. That everything remained with them in their muscle. "Some people don't die young enough, Johnny. Maybe T.J. felt that it had gone on too long." For a moment, Elgin wished he wasn't blind, so he could see Johnny's eyes, get a sense of what was going on inside his thoughts. "Some people got to live through it all. Everything. Things they wish they hadn't seen or felt. Who knows? You only know this. Us talking. It's all that's certain."

Elgin stood up. His knees creaked, nearly cracked. Old joints just needing to be stretched out or to quit altogether. He stumbled a little, then steadied himself at the table, looked toward the sink, hoping Johnny still stood there. "Help me out to the porch."

Johnny came over to his grandfather. He knew his grandfather did not need help, that he wanted something else. He took him by the elbow and guided him out of the kitchen, down the hallway. "There's advantages to dying young," Elgin said, just a bit above a whisper. "You die young, you miss out on all the lies. You die young enough, you still think this life can be pure, still think it can be holy. You still see the magic in the first snowfall of winter and are still mystified by how silent the whole world becomes under that blanket of snow, how snow seems to cover sounds, how snow quiets the city, makes everything still, and you press your face against that frosty window to look outside and you listen, and you don't feel the cold winter at the window, you believe in the generosity of being alive, you believe the whole world is out there waiting to protect you, and that belief keeps you warm. You think any day can hold that kind of magic. You need to keep that inside you, or it's just better to die young, before all of it disappears."

Elgin stopped walking, pulled Johnny even closer. "The way faith becomes a lie, the way truth gets erased over and over again. The way your heart gets damaged with each failed promise. When that one promise, the one you most deeply need to believe in, gets broken, but you know that, even with that promise broken, you still have to go on living, anyway. Living without the dream, without the faith, without the promise. And you realize the promise was never a promise to begin with. It was just a lie covering over another dirtier lie. A failure of desire."

He released Johnny a little and started walking again. "You re-arrange enough lies and you can call anything you want the truth. The imbeciles telling tales that allowed them to live with their actions. Telling us to go into the village. Telling us not to trust our eyes. Everyone is the enemy. Shoot and do not stop shooting. It becomes hard to ever stop shooting. I didn't risk going to sleep, fearing the dreams would return. You pray there's a human being in you somewhere. You stop seeing, and you stop thinking, before you stop shooting. Truth becomes something you must keep secret. You're not protecting it. You're just keeping it secret. And when you do speak that truth, it don't matter any longer, because everyone has turned to stone. Every heart cold and alone."

Johnny reached out his hand and pushed open the screen door to the porch. Elgin pulled him in close again, close to his breath, closer to breath than to word. "Every soul has a disease and a song," Elgin said. "You have to recognize you got both in you. You have to cherish both the disease and the song, and you have to let them both out, Johnny. You can't keep them caged."

Elgin made his way over to his rocking chair and sat himself down in it. "There are places that hold onto your soul, Johnny. You got to open yourself up to them." Elgin stared into the shadows, stared into seeing what can never be seen, what God meant for no man to see or know. Elgin looked, with a deeper desire than any seeing man could ever do with his seeing, his wanting, his longing. Seeing with the gentle silence of being blind. "Your soul stays there in those places, Johnny. You got to make a pilgrimage there."

Elgin settled back into his rocking chair. Felt the early morning sun warming his face, nearly smiled just knowing the world was still there, that God had not abandoned Pittsburgh after all. "You need to believe in some kind of path, and you got to walk it like Christ did. With your wounds open. You need to toughen the soles of your feet. Get skin thick and hard over them. You walk those banks along the Monongahela River barefoot. You do that, child. Your soles too tender now, and you suffer more than you need to suffer. Pain rises up. Pain goes at you, into your heart, through the soles of your feet. It's the pains of your ancestors coming up through the earth. You listen at it."

Johnny stood beside his grandfather, gently touched his grandfather's forearm with the lightness of his fingertips. "You running off today?"

"I need to see where T.J. is," Johnny said. "Going over to the North Side. See Chas. See Sylvia."

"Nothing can be done, Johnny."

"I know." He walked over to the steps of the porch. "I know, but there's a story. You told me that. You always say, 'A man outside his story don't have no meaning.' I need that."

"I imagine. But maybe this ain't for you. Maybe it's more about silence. There are things on this earth that are forbidden to know, that exist the way they do just for that: to exist." Elgin stretched his back, put his feet up on the railing, readying himself for a morning nap. "Some things happen and forever remain just part of an inexplicable darkness."

"Yeah." Sometimes Johnny only knew to say "yeah" when his grandfather spoke. Sometimes he could not figure his grandfather's words into meaning. "I'm off." He waved goodbye, like his grandfather could still see, then ran down Dinwiddie Street. Elgin listened to Johnny's feet hitting the sidewalk until the sounds disappeared. Then he rested his body into the comfort of the chair, took in the morning air with one of his deep breaths, and allowed his eyes to close.

CHAPTER 11

More sunshine. More heat. More humidity. This is the way it is. This is the way it was. This is the way it will be.

TJ was still dead. Is still dead. Or gone. Or missing. And Chas, like every other morning since the beginning of time, stood, always stood, will forever stand, in his regular place to the right of the bus stop on the corner of West North Avenue and Federal Street, planted under the shade of that old oak tree, the one he claimed to own. The domain of Chas. And that domain of his changed only slightly as the sun moved across the sky, shifting the shade from here to there. Nothing else ever changed. Nothing could ever change. Every morning, Rats Alley remained shadowed, dark and lonely, empty. Every morning the sun chased the last of the lingering night bodies out of Rats Alley, back to their homes in the suburbs, sent those white bodies scurrying back to their lies and to their families.

Johnny jaywalked across East North Avenue toward Federal, to One-eye Pete's place, on his corner at Reddour Street. He stood there with the Street Elder, their hands hidden deep inside the sticky heat of their empty pockets, searching for all that had been taken from them, all that had disappeared in days and nights of restless street-walking, but finding only holes in their pockets, holes that let fall away all they wished they could hold onto. The eyes of both moved constantly, looking everywhere but at each other. Staying alert to the street, to the movement. Always too much to look at or too little. But always nothing to see, nothing you would want to see, nothing you would hope to see. Much of what needed to be seen on the North

Side remained invisible. You learned young to look the other way, never to see anyone, never to look in the eyes of their desires, unless you were willing to say yes to whatever saying yes meant.

The eye of One-eyed Pete and the eyes of the Street Elder, the eyes of every person who wandered the streets of the North Side, existed inside a blind longing, a waiting to see something that they hoped was about to arrive or looking for something that had just gone, fled from the scene. Like that photograph you take one moment too late or one moment too soon. You were convinced there was something there at one time, at that moment when you snapped the photograph, or you believed, in that anticipation, that there would be something there, that something would appear once the photograph was developed, but nothing appeared. No remains. No traces. It had all been left on the street. True photographs tend to remain on the streets, the story almost about to enter the edge of the frame of the snapshot or the shutter closing a moment too late, the story having just abandoned the frame.

"One-eye," Johnny said, nodding to Pete as he walked toward him and the Street Elder. Johnny felt Chas watching him from under the oak tree, staring out of the shadows across the street at Johnny's every gesture. "Elder."

"Look at me, boy." Pete reached up and grabbed the bottom of Johnny's shirt in his tiny fists and pulled Johnny down toward him. "Count them." Pete stretched up on his tiptoes to give Johnny a closer look, so that he could look directly into his eye, but Pete was so short he only could stretch up to about chin level, if that. "Two. See that? Two. One perfect eye from childhood and one glass eye from a strange man. They both eyes."

Johnny laughed. "An eye ain't no eye, if you ain't seeing with it. You only got one eye left from birth. That other one just got put inside you, and it ain't never done any seeing. It ain't marked. It's clear. Unscratched. No maps in it. That eye ain't never seen a woman's beauty, so it is lost. You the one who said an eye ain't no eye unless it has seen a woman and known her beauty."

"You ask your grandfather about eyes and about seeing. An eye's an eye if it's an eye. And there's times when one eye gets in the way and blinds the other eye." He wiped his nose, swatted at invisible flies or fleas that lingered near his skin. "Trolls collecting eyeballs under bridges, then telling a man to keep both eyes open. There's truth in that, but it don't mean to keep eyes that only appear to be seeing open. You ask your grandfather about trolls."

"He's got natural eyes. They just quit seeing." Johnny pulled back a little from old Pete. One-eye was nothing more than rags and bones, withered skin and smell.

"His seeing moved inside." Pete was more shaman than drug dealer and was the only gravedigger, according to North Side legend, who had never dug a grave, who somehow could talk someone else into digging it, but Pete liked piling on the dirt after the casket had been placed in the hole.

"There's nothing here you need to know, Johnny, only what you think you want to know. You got to understand the difference between needing and wanting. They don't work the same," the Street Elder said. "You got to respect silence."

"Someone has to save T.J.," Johnny said. "It's that simple."

"His story got no words. And even it did, the trouble with words is that you never know whose mouth they have been in, so how can you know what they truly mean? You think a word remains pure after it has been inside someone else's mouth? You say some word, then Pete says it, then you hear Chas saying that word, and you think it's the same word you said back when you said it? Word gets changed going through all that." The Street Elder slowed down, looked across the avenue. She shielded her eyes from the sun. "T.J.'s story ain't for words. It's for the quiet. Trust in that. Some stories steal something from deep in your soul. The street does that when something gets spoken that should never be spoken."

Johnny looked up at the Street Elder. The woman had story eyes that put One-eyed Pete's weary eyes to shame.

"Some truths," she continued, "won't ever make a difference, no matter what that truth reveals. A truth don't solve nothing." She closed her eyes for a moment. She seemed to want her eyes to take a nap. Johnny stared at her eyelids. The delicate way that they closed and held to the moment. Slowly, she opened her eyes again. "Do something with what you've been told," she said. "That's all you need to know." She glanced over at Chas. "You go to Chas. He's waiting.

Been waiting all morning."

"He can wait." Johnny stared across the street, made sure that Chas saw him looking at him. Johnny held his stare, even went so far as to nod. "Is T.J. dead, Pete?"

"You've been told what there is to tell," the Elder replied. "Go shape it." She and Pete shared a look. "Maybe it's you that's not hearing it. You think there's something not being said. When the truth is right there. Ain't nothing deceitful in what we say. Ain't no designs." The Elder wiped sweat from her brow. She turned to walk down West North Avenue. "You know he's dead. Let it be." She scanned the street. "Pete?" She looked across the street into Allegheny Park, looked further down the street toward the hospital, looked up at that sky. "Where'd Pete go?"

Pete had vanished. He did that often. In between his shapeshifting, he vanished, not into thin air, but more like becoming thin air. He entered and lived inside those momentary pauses between appear and disappear. Johnny and the Street Elder looked around for him. Johnny thought Pete had turned himself into a lamppost. If there had been a morning fog, he might be wrapped inside it, but there was no fog, just heat. Brutal heat. Maybe Pete had joined the heat, folded his exhausted body into the heat and disappeared. They found him standing rigid outside Joe's Pharmacy. Even though they both saw him and walked toward him, he still seemed inside a not-there place. Or perhaps Pete blended so intimately with the whole of the North Side that he was inside its very essence.

"See those people?" Pete's voice emerged from the thin air, before he came fully into focus, no longer blurred by his disappearance. He pointed at a group of people putting down a basket in the park. "Those ones putting down that blanket."

"Yeah," Johnny said.

"They're having a picnic, right? A real Kodak moment." Pete waited. The Street Elder stopped pulling at Johnny, stopped trying to drag him up the street. "I'm waiting."

"For what?" Johnny asked.

"You to say it."

"What? Say what?" Johnny looked over at the family in the park. "They're having a picnic? You need me to say that. There, I said it.

114

They're having a picnic."

"You know why your blood feels the way it does when you say, 'picnic'?" Pete kicked at Johnny's foot. "Do you? Makes your blood go cold. Empties your blood of life. You got to know why a picnic does what it does to you. It calls up a remembering. Your mind gets to forgetting, but blood never forgets. Some girl breaks your heart, and after enough time passes, you think time healed you. You don't feel all broken no more. Years later you see her on some street, maybe you smell her scent, and you feel her in your blood, because you may have been able to let her go, you may have been able to forget her, you may have been able to be with other women, you may even think you've come to love some other woman, but your blood don't ever forget that one woman, the one who pressed her forehead hard against your forehead. Her breath on your skin. Blood don't let go. It's why you feel what you feel when you see her. It's your blood remembering, reminding you what's there and what's not there no more. And it's the same with a picnic."

Johnny hated when Pete drifted into his private world of metaphor and confusion. "A picnic's a picnic."

"Shit, boy. You plain stupid with your stupid. A picnic ain't nothing more innocent than that? Like a tree is just a tree?" Pete said. "Picnic." He kicked at the sidewalk as if the sidewalk had done something evil to his shoe, angered his foot. "People got us convinced that that's all it is. Innocent eating."

"What's any of this got to do with T.J.?"

"I'm telling you. That word holds onto everything you need to know about him being here and about him not being here. About why he can't belong here. It's in the word."

"What word?"

"Picnic, son."

"What's a word got to do with T.J.?"

"Words ain't never straight, Johnny," the Street Elder said, her voice more like smoke than like sound. "You slant a story with each word, you turn it in on itself until the true story disappears under the weight of forgetting. You got to go to that place where words once were what they were, but no longer is."

She put her hand on Pete's shoulder. Her feet seemed tired. Too many hours in heels that made so little sense to her feet. "Look at my knees, Johnny." She pointed down at her knees. She had the kind of knees, promiscuous and dirty, that would make any boy uncomfortable. The kind that all the boys stared at and desired, but didn't quite know why. One or two small pebbles stuck in her knees. "Don't be staring off. You're no innocent child. Look at them. Everything that has ever marked my knees, that's who I am."

Night after night, the Street Elder worked on her knees in Rats Alley, in The Apache, in doorways, in any place that was convenient and dark. Pieces of glass. Pebbles. Dust. The marks of her work stuck in the skin of her knees. This was her eternal truth. "Whatever it is you do day and night marks you."

She exposed her hands to Johnny, turned them over palms up. "Everything I have ever touched is in my hands. The Dunkin Donut I had with my coffee. The icing. My licking the icing off the tips of my fingers. The paper from the coffee cup. It's all there. All here. This man, that man. It's in my hands. But you only see my hands, like they're like anyone else's hands. That is truth for you? That ain't truth; that's what you're looking at. And what's been seen is emptied of truth."

The Street Elder smiled. "You use your tongue for all that God had intended you to use it for, and a little bit more, and you'll understand why a tongue doesn't have any bones. Not all stories have words, Johnny." The Street Elder exposed the scars of her tongue to Johnny. Years of kissing disgruntled men in polyester suits. The Street Elder coughed a little, and said, "A bruise, like a breath, is an inquiry into desire. It's a way men have for testing a woman's endurance. What she's willing to bear."

A few people straggled past Johnny, Pete, and the Elder, already suffering and tired from the heat. Others just stood motionless in the heat. "We are all skin and bones, Johnny. Scorched. Those people at their picnic. That ain't no truth you can see. The truth is in the skin inhabited by a cry. You see a picnic, you give it a name, you put it in a sentence, and you believe it's the truth."

Pete stamped his foot like it had gotten bored with all the confused mumbling and had gone tingling and numb on him. He stamped it again. "Damn stump always wanting to dream. Like a dream can lift you out of this heat, out of these streets." The Street Elder reached for Pete's hand to take him up the hill.

"It's time we go, Pete."

Pete looked back over at the family. "Picnic ain't no word, Johnny. It's an action. You got to know where you come from. Always remind yourself of where you from and where you is now. You can't arrive without knowing that. You can't be here without being from there. You listen here on the streets, you listen to your grandfather. There's talk you got to make sense of, and there's other talk you leave silent." Pete turned away from Johnny to the Street Elder. They took a few slow steps up Federal Street. "You ask me how many times I've gone on a picnic in my life. Go ahead, boy, ask it."

Johnny knew enough to know that Pete would just wait it out, so he asked. "How many?"

"Ain't gone on one. Not a one. And it's not because of all this concrete. And it's not because there's no shade in this city, no parks. And it's not because I ain't been asked. I been asked plenty of times. It's because that word is filled with the devil's madness. The blood of your ancestors runs through the word."

Pete stopped talking just long enough to wet his lips, to catch his old breath, before pushing out the next sentence. "There are reasons we bbq. Those people picnic, not us. Every one of them ohhing and ahhing, looking up into the skies at those fireworks, like those folk looked up at that tree limb with one of your ancestors dangling lifeless from it. That's true freedom. And now we celebrate the birth of freedom in this great land with that word. Picnic. Fourth of July picnic. I hate summer."

Pete was nearly out of breath. He started kicking, angry and flushed, at the sidewalk again, stomping it down, like he wanted to send the sidewalk into some underbelly of the earth. "You got to let it burn you on the inside. And you got to kindle it, or you become an accomplice in your own destruction. It's what they're counting on. You want to know where T.J. went? What happened to him? You got to ask where T.J. was when T.J. was here."

Pete and Street Elder began their slow ascent up one of the steepest, hottest streets in Pittsburgh, a street nearly designed to destroy anyone who ever made the effort to walk up it in the middle of the day, a street designed to remind everyone who lived on top of that hill, or along that hill, exactly who they were. A street built to claim your spirit and silence your desires. Federal Street was too steep for trolleys. Buses never stopped along it; they only stopped at the very bottom and at the very top. And buses rarely ever showed up anyway. Federal Street forced a man to round his shoulders, hunch over. That street was built to make men suffer for sins they had not yet committed. Bring men to their knees and submit to the weight of each day, of each step, of each breath. That street extinguished every dream a man ever had of surviving, even the dreams he didn't have the courage to dream yet. That street killed every tree, every patch of grass that was bold enough to try to grow there. No one ever said a kind word on that street. Not out of meanness. You just could not say a kind word. The street didn't allow it. You had to walk up that street before late morning or there was no getting home until after dusk. In the afternoons, too much angry heat rose up out of the concrete. Johnny watched them walking away. Pete turned and looked over his shoulder, back down at Johnny. "I said what I meant."

Johnny stood on that corner. His grandfather always argued with his neighbors about picnics. "It's a bbq," Elgin would say. "We're barbecuing." His grandfather never told him why it mattered. Neighbors told Elgin that he'd be stuck in that house, on Dinwiddie Street, forever, if he called it a bbq. And Elgin shouted back, "There's nothing wrong with staying, with knowing. Forgetting is what does the damage to a body, to a soul, to a heart, to the children who haven't yet been brought into the world. What's it mean to get ahead, if it means not knowing what they left behind? What's left to give to your children?"

Words seemed to be disobedient to stories. Nothing was innocent. Johnny felt, at times, that he had no origins. None he knew of. He felt he had been born in the nowhere. In the empty. Johnny's origins left him stranded, orphaned him to his own skin. His father gone somewhere before he was born, then back, then gone. Back and gone. Back and gone. A bad yoyo, the kind of yoyo that slammed back up into the palm of your hand, burning it. Reminding you. Coming back to sting you. Marking your hand, red and hot, so he could never forget a father he never knew. His mother remained forever quiet on that, not a name of the father, not a picture of the father, just holes left behind in the walls of the living room, in the walls of the hallway, in the walls of the kitchen, in the walls of her bedroom. Sweet valentines. Don't forget me! Don't you ever dare forget me. Forget-me-nots. Knots. Knotted into Johnny's flesh and blood. And Johnny felt like he was the child of this evil inside those holes in the walls. The evil that filled those holes with emptiness. Like he was what was missing from his mother's heart. Nearly nameless. American skin. Divorced from the before.

"He's my son, not yours," a man's voice screamed from inside the walls of the house. "English." And then the silence. And then a small breath of a cry. And then a broken sob. And then that man's voice inside the walls: "Say that in Vietnamese. Say it." Johnny's father a dark pain in his mother's heart, making it cold in summer and hot in winter. A heart filled with shadows. His mother died so young she never finished being beautiful and never completed all the stories she had started telling Johnny. Every story almost leading him, but never quite taking him, home. Now he carried all these almost-told stories with him. He walked the streets of Pittsburgh with so many unfinished stories, so many stories on the edge of being completed, waiting.

Johnny crossed West North Avenue, walked over to Chas. He looked at the family having their picnic, at their faces, their smiles, their eyes. "You been talking to too many people, Johnny. You got to listen."

"It ain't like that, Chas."

"You've been told. Go home, Johnny. Go to the river. It's not that T.J. is dead; it's that you need to do something with knowing it."

"I want something more than what I haven't seen."

"If T.J. had time for dying words, if he had time for last rites, if someone had been there to hear those dying words, someone that cared enough to hear them and carry them out of the alley back to the living, his last words would have been to keep this all in the shadows." Chas joined Johnny's gaze and looked over toward the alley. A man walked down the street, approaching The Garden. Both Johnny and Chas shook their heads, looked back at each other. "Some men need to go into the alley when there's nothing left and the shadows are beginning to appear. When your skin has become too marked by the scars that you can't hide from anyone."

"What's T.J. ever done?"

"If you want so much, Johnny, I'll tell you, but nothing I can say, or anyone else can say, will be enough."

Johnny looked at Chas. Waited.

"T.J. walked into Rats Alley," Chas said. "It is that simple. He knew where he was going. Same as you and me knowing. You knowing that don't do T.J. any good. It only changes things for you."

Johnny looked at Chas, baffled, as if Chas had said something in a language that had never been spoken before in Pittsburgh. He started to say something, but he stopped. He looked across West North Avenue. "There's still something not here." Even after saying that, Johnny felt like he had not said anything at all.

"It's all there is," Chas said. "Enough is enough. Every story T.J. told us about inventions, about space travel. It's all any of it is. Stories. Living. Ways to find home. Sometimes you give up looking for it."

"Something's missing."

"It's the invisible, Johnny. Leave it. None of it changes anything."

"People take dried leaves, Chas, roll those dried leaves in paper." Johnny was talking like he was no longer alive, like he was reciting words from some place outside and far away from where they stood on the North Side. Like his voice was coming up out of the roots of trees. "People stick these leaves rolled-up in paper between their lips. Set it on fire. We live in that kind of world. Put leaves rolled in paper between your lips and set it on fire." Johnny seemed like he was setting out on some journey of talking out loud until he stumbled on something he needed to say. He seemed not to have heard a word of what Chas said about T.J.'s life. "My grandfather said, 'Don't you call it a picnic.' But he never told me why. My mother saying what she said about the Monongahela, never The Mon. It's like we have to live a muted life among words that mean something else. Like we can't ever be saying what we are saying. You think any of this makes sense?"

CHAPTER 12

Debra wore lipstick so red that it nearly stopped being red and was about to become another color entirely. The kind of red that comes before red, before the night becomes the darkest moment of the night. A red driven mad by its own color. And Debra did not just put this lipstick gently onto her thin, narrow lips. She wore this thick lipstick on her flesh. She smeared it all over her lips. Lipstick so disobedient that it stained her face, scarred the back of her hand. She put it on with a wild aggression, rarely known by women putting on any kind of make-up, let alone putting on something as intimate as lipstick. With a joyous surrender that bordered on the criminal, she pressed it deep into some childhood memory. Wet leaves in springtime. Soiled ears of corn abandoned in mud. She stained her teeth with it. And her lips seemed to want more, so much more than that, and she was just the kind of woman to give her lips more.

When Debra finished with her lips, she was exhausted. The child she remembered being once-upon-a-time was breathless. This is the woman that Debra had become. This is the woman the world demanded that she become. This is all that could be expected of her. This, and so much more, is what happened to Debra. She looked into the mirror, looked at her lips; for a moment, she thought of smiling. Then this woman Debra had become cried.

When she finished crying, when the sobs dried and Debra cleaned her face of the lipstick, cleaned the mirror of the lipstick, changed into a blouse that was not stained from the lipstick, when she covered her naked feet in slippers, Debra felt there was nothing left to do, so she walked into the kitchen and called the police again.

She did this every day. She called the police and told them she could not find her son. She told them her husband was out on the porch drinking beer with Jim. He stayed out there like he was not a married man. Like the night had answers. Like his wife was not inside the house looking into the mirror, peeling apples, baking. Like the silence he shared with Jim was not mysterious, was not uncomfortable, was not more than what it was meant to be. Other nights, Fred stayed on that porch all night drinking alone. Occasionally, on those nights made for lonely men like Fred, he smoked a cigar too thick for the delicate beauty of his lips. He kept himself protected from remembering too much by surrounding himself with bottles of flat, warm beer. Those long nights when Fred drank alone, he talked to himself, to Lucas' bicycle, to the stars. He talked and talked. Muttered at that maple tree in the center of their backyard. He swore he would cut the tree down. Teach it a lesson. He said stars were fire, pure fire, and he would call one down to burn into the tree and into Lucas' bicycle. Not burn down the tree, but burn into the very soul of the tree, and he said that the star would stay there as fire. "Some mornings," Debra lowered her voice to a whisper, so no one would hear her, not even the police listening on the other end of the line, "I find him asleep on the porch in wrinkled clothes or wearing only his boxer shorts. Isn't that a bad sign," she asked. "Isn't that a sign of something else?"

Debra begged them to tell her something. She said that drinking beer never changed anything in the past, that it will never change anything in the future, that money would fall out of the trees before drinking beer would do anything good for the situation. "You don't find your son by drinking beer," Debra told them. "You just don't." She waited for them to answer. She was patient that way. She knew how to wait. She hoped they would tell her she was wrong. She hoped that they would explain everything to her in ways that would help her make sense of the world one final time before it all ended. She hoped they would say drinking beer was the answer, that it would change everything. That her husband knew precisely what he was doing. Debra wanted the police to tell her to trust Fred.

But Debra knew no one could say what she needed to hear. Truth and hope seemed to be disappearing more and more. She feared the man in the moon had become cynical and that the moon hated children, hated Pittsburgh, and hated women, especially mothers. She felt the moon trying to pull away, trying to escape its orbit. She told Fred that the moon was angry, far angrier than she ever imagined it would become and said that the moon cursed its fate.

Each time Debra tried to talk about Lucas, she became more perplexed, like she was seeking out the lost thread of a dream. Less and less seemed certain. She rummaged through drawers, hunted through the attic, and dug into the dirt in the basement, seeking snapshots of Lucas. She drew pictures of Lucas and put them all through the house. She did everything she could to remind herself that she had a son. "This happened," she told herself again and again. "This really happened." She looked at her very faint—almost too faint—stretch marks. This birth mark of forgotten and lost children. She lived each day fearing that she would forget everything she wanted to remember and remember everything she wanted to forget.

When this fear of forgetting began to eat away at her heart, she called the police. They answered, but told her that she needed to stop calling. Debra thought she heard them say something about vanishing words. Perhaps her words vanished before the police could hear them. Sometimes the police hung up on her so quietly that she did not know they had hung up, so she continued talking for an hour or two or for a day or two or three, until she realized that she was talking to herself, that the buzz she heard was in the phone, a dial tone, not a lost sound in her head. She waited a few minutes, tapped her foot, cracked her knuckles, looked out the window, perhaps looked toward the television, then she dialed the phone again. They said they knew. They said they understood. They said something about bulletins and alerts. They patiently told her this; they were attentive to the tone of their voice, then they hung up, and again Debra waited. She, too, was careful about her tone, about the sound of her voice.

"I am not frantic," she reminded herself. "I never was good at putting on lipstick. People think I look frantic. How would they know? Do you think I look frantic?" But no one was there. No one. She spoke, perhaps wanting to answer herself, to hear her own words echo back at her. "My hands have never been steady, and my lips are

123

too thin."

Fred has fuller lips. She thought of how much easier it would be for Fred to put lipstick on those lips of his. She thought how lucky he was to have such full lips. And a man at that. A man with such full lips. Once she put lipstick on Fred's lips. They were young. They were laughing. Fred kissed Debra, and she felt it, felt something. She felt Fred kissing her, and she felt herself kissing Fred, and she knew that some things happen for a reason and that this was one of them. Debra imagined Jim must like looking at Fred's lips when they stood all alone on the porch as the light changed, as it got later and later and the world disappeared, and as they drank beer after beer. Debra imagined Jim looking at Fred's lips, watching his lips between beers. She would enjoy looking at Fred's lips, if she were standing on the porch drinking beers with him all night. And after so many beers, after too many beers, if she were a man and she were Fred's friend and not Fred's wife, she would not be responsible and he would not be to blame. Who could blame such a man for what God had done to him? And it would not matter to her if anyone saw what might be seen, but should never be spoken about. And things happen. It would be the same with Jim. Things would happen. Could happen. No one could blame Jim either. Sometimes things happen that way.

Debra loved looking at Fred's lips. When they first met, the very first thing she noticed about Fred, even before she noticed the delight of his voice, were his lips. She thought they promised sins. That his lips were a sin, and she wanted that sin. She wanted it to never stop. That sin. Secrets are not forever hidden in the world, and the world puts no real effort into keeping them hidden. Secrets just wait for their time to be up, then they come out into the light, or a light shines under a door or through a crack in the wall, or a light shines onto the porch, and the secret quits being mysterious and fearful. And in that moment you feel it for the first time. All of it. The secret. The years of wanting. The years of being afraid. All those years flee, the secret trembles, and the fear weakens. That secret touches off something in you, sets it off in your mouth, in your eyes, in the tips of your fingers. You quit keeping it secret, and you feel that secret moving all through you. You look into that secret for what it truly is; you see it as it is, as something that you cannot understand. That's the truest secret. Not the lie that you bury inside of you that you call a secret, but the wilderness that you never understood. We all have that inside us. The forest of not understanding. You mistake it for a secret. Or it confuses you so much that you never see it for what it is. So you keep it anonymous. You don't speak a name for it, because there is no language. Until the secret travels through you, and the secret becomes you. At some point in our lives, we all become that secret we kept.

When Fred crawled into bed after drinking and drinking and being silent with Jim, Debra whispered: "You can tell me. I would tell you. If you touch me while you're telling me, I will think it is something else. I'm mostly asleep," she said. "I'll think I dreamt it. Your answer. Your lips. I want you to be safe. I want to hear it. I want you to say it. I think you would want to say it." But it made no difference what she thought. Fred told her that. He told her, "I am your husband. That is all I need and all you need to know." Then he turned his back to her, and he slept so deeply that the world disappeared for both of them.

Debra looked at the phone on the wall. At the chord of the phone. She lifted the receiver and stared at it, trying to remember what it was used for. Then she dialed it. The woman at the police station sounded as tired as Debra felt. "What is it like to feel so exhausted," Debra asked her. "To have your body want so much to be surrounded by water?" The woman on the other end of the line was quiet. Her breath measured. This time, it was the woman who waited. Debra held onto the phone, gripped the phone tight in her hand, and she shared in this waiting. Debra's breathing slowed. Her breath began to leave her there on the phone all alone.

"I'm sorry," the woman on the other end of the phone finally whispered, or maybe she only let out a tiny tiny breath that expressed more truth than any word could. Debra wanted the woman to say something that would end everything. She wanted to know something she did not already know. But the woman could not speak.

This time, Debra hung up. She thought that, maybe, if she hung up then everything would change. But when she hung up, Debra did not lift her hand from the receiver. She rested her hand on top of the receiver as it hung there on the wall. Later that night, she let go of the phone, or perhaps she had stood there for days like that, with her hand on the receiver, with her knees becoming weaker, with her feet becoming sore, with her body wanting food.

The next day, or perhaps days later, she returned to the phone. She lifted the receiver and dialed. She called and called, until a blister formed on her dialing finger, and then she dialed more and more, until a callous formed over her blister. She tried to wipe the lipstick from her lips. She worried that Lucas had come home and did not recognize her because of all the lipstick everywhere. It was even on the mouthpiece of the phone, on every coffee cup and glass in the house.

As the voice on the other end of the telephone told Debra that she was sorry, very sorry, Debra watched what was happening on the television. The woman told Debra that she would always be sorry, but that being sorry would not change anything. Debra asked the woman if she knew that there were people on television tearing off their clothes. They were putting their hands all over each other's bodies. Kissing. Touching. Making the kinds of sounds that should only be made in locked rooms, in the dark, late in the night, not now, not in the middle of the day. There was too much light for all this. She asked the woman on the other end of the line if she should close her windows so that no one would hear. Debra wanted to report this, too. And she wanted to look away from the television screen, but she could not look away. She did not know if it was possible to find a safe place for her eyes. So she just looked. Not much else could be done. Maybe turn the channel. Maybe turn off the television altogether. Unplug it. Beg Fred to take the television out to the garage. But Debra was so tired, it was impossible for her to concentrate. The woman on the phone said she had to hang up. She told Debra that they were doing all that could be done. Debra waited a few hours, waited while the bodies on the television had stopped tearing off their clothes, had stopped moaning and turned into cartoons. Then she called again. Waited. Then again. She continued calling, hoping one day no one would answer. But each time she called, they answered. They always answered.

And Debra wondered if this were really happening, any of it. If the people stripped naked on the television were real. If Lucas was truly missing, or if Fred drank as much, as often, as she imagined. She wondered if looking for something that she had lost was real, and she wondered what she had lost. She wondered if the voices on the phone were real. If Fred's lips were really so full, so thick, so warm, and she wondered if the little boy who played with matches lived happily ever after, and if she had ever truly been a little girl, a girl smaller, younger, than she was now, a girl who followed the boy who played with matches. She wondered if sin was still possible. She thought that perhaps it was all simply on television, all of it—Fred, Lucas, naked desires, Lucky Charms, the color red, Jim, beer, the voices—or, she thought she was inventing stories to pass the days while Fred worked, while her beauty and love broke away at the seams and spilled onto the floor.

Since the night they last touched each other in an effort to discover that deep bond of sorrow, Fred and Debra had formed some type of precarious truce over their love, over the disappearance of their son, over when to pay the bills. They spoke less and less each day. Not just to each other, but plain speaking anywhere, to the neighbors, to the butcher, to co-workers. Even speaking to Jim had become a chore for Fred. Jim had to coax words out of Fred, and Fred rarely uttered more than a word here or there, rarely ever a whole sentence. Fred and Debra had begun forgetting speech. And the less they spoke, the more they approached some final destination.

"Monday," Debra said. "Today is Monday. I am tired, Fred. You call."

Fred thought it felt like Tuesday. He ruffled the newspaper, looked up along the top edge of the corner of the *Pittsburgh Press*. Monday. Debra was right. Monday. He had gone to work. He thought he had been there for two days, not one. Days no longer made sense. "It's time we stop, you stop. The calling," Fred interrupted his own sentence, looked at Debra's mouth, her lips, still stained by the lipstick, now just barely red, more of a rubbed pink. "The calls," his mouth seemed lost. "They. What we do." The words sat there, inside his mouth with his saliva, his teeth, his tongue, waiting, but his mouth or his lips seemed to have forgotten how to release words into the world. Debra tapped her fingers on the table. Fred, as usual, tapped his foot on the floor, almost as a response to Debra's finger tapping, a dueling song of desires that could no longer be placed in words. Sounds were still possible inside their house, even if their voices had mostly disappeared. "It no longer helps," Fred began. His mouth having returned to what it knew to do. "The calls. You're just too lonely. The world is lonely now. It will stay that way."

"Don't you say that. Don't you dare say that. It's not the whole world, Fred," Debra replied. "This lonely belongs to me. Even you don't have this lonely. It's lost inside the nothing. It is this white space between words. It's that lonely. That's my lonely. Mine." Her voice cracked. Something deep inside Debra pushed at her ribs. "My lonely." She looked at Fred. Her eyes lingered on his lips. She wanted him. Debra felt the wanting, her wanting, moving inside her. In her blood. In her thoughts. Inside her mouth. But she wanted Fred in her own way, her way, the way of her wanting. She wanted him not to have a choice, but to be carried away by her wanting, and she wanted it to be raw. The kind of raw that broke your bones, that made trees grow out of a woman's skin, that made the roots of those trees grow into her muscles. The kind of raw touching that would make mud of Fred's skin when her sweat fell onto it. Mud more interesting and thicker than any mud along the Monongahela River. The kind of raw that destroyed memories. That made a woman think that whatever it was that she had done before had not been this.

And Debra wanted Fred's body to be so bruised by her naked touch, by her relentless teeth and elbows, that he would never be able to read the newspaper again, that the print, the touch of the newspaper would be foreign to him, that he would only be able to sit at the kitchen table and stare at the newspaper, wondering what it was for, what he was supposed to do with it. And she wanted it to be that way endlessly. Again and again. Not whatever it was that they did with their bodies, to their bodies, the other night. That was nothing. That was the two of them staying away from each other, staying off in their own corners of touching, staying with being lonely, inside it, creating more lonely with each touch, each movement.

Debra wanted to control her own wanting and to control his wanting. She wanted it to be something that exhausted words when words attempted to give it speech. She wanted to be the woman who drove out of Fred every single woman he had ever touched, and, in doing so, she wanted to have him experience the touch of every single person she had ever been with in her life. She wanted to make his entire body cry.

Debra looked at Fred, wondered if he could ever truly join her again and become that naked. "This lonely," she told him, "isn't any kind of lonely you've ever known. It is not the kind that I have never known before, not before this. It's the kind of lonely that does not know what to do with itself," Debra said. "And it's worse than being alone. It's worse than wanting to hear a voice." Her lips closed. She nearly allowed her eyes to shut. She was that close to finally resting.

Her body looked lost for a moment. She wanted to grab Fred, to take Fred, to show him something that would make him feel with his body what she meant. She wanted him to feel this urge that was moving through her muscles, turning her blood into fire. She wanted him to feel it with his body. Not to feel her with his heart. She wanted to open her skin. She nearly said it aloud, "I urge you," or "I urge to you." Debra had no idea how to say it, where to put the words in the sentence. The words themselves resisted Debra's desire to say them. She knew what she wanted could only be said by her body. She wanted to take Fred's hand, say nothing, pull his hand to her heart and press his hand against her heart, into her heart, break her ribs, if necessary, until Fred felt it, until he felt the urging beneath her heart, the deep wanting to be naked and to expose everything.

Debra tried to hold back, but she did not want to hold back. Her body twisted in too many directions. Almost too much wanting. Flooded. Like a river finding its way home by flooding the banks, returning to origins, places of birth and travel. Like the Johnstown flood back in 1889 or the flood in Pittsburgh in 1936, the one her grandmother survived. Debra felt that moving inside her. Something was waking up inside her.

CHAPTER 13

Daylight rushed at Johnny so furiously that he nearly forgot to untie Sylvia. His fingers twitched. The early morning sun about to set
his skin on fire. His mouth dry and wanting. Shadows stretched out
from the trunks of the trees along the riverbank. A touch of anxiety
crept into Johnny's hands and into his feet. Even untied, she seemed
to have forgotten how to move, and she asked him, softly, to do it
one more time. She promised him that she would not cry; she would
never cry. Not now. Not later. She had never cried before. This time
would be no different.

Sylvia grew quiet with Johnny's body so close to hers, and she
waited. Every muscle in her body relaxed, and she released a soft
breath. She seemed to have fallen back into her dream world, her
river sleep. He leaned over her body, hesitated. Carefully, afraid he
would awaken something, he took a deep breath. He had done this
often. Johnny took the rope in his beautiful hands.

"Your mother will never know."

The bottoms of her naked feet covered in mud, her knees filthy
and older than any other part of her body. Her mouth tortured beyond hope. Her hair tangled in branches, in twigs, in roots, in leaves.
Memory mixed with silence. Water and earth. A communion of flesh
and dreams. She desired to stay, to be forever here with Johnny in
this make-believe world where they would never grew old. She and
Johnny only feared her uncertain movements at night. They feared
that she would wander away, that she would sleepwalk and fall into
the river. Drown. They slept close to the river. Each night a little

closer. Some mornings, they woke with wet feet. Moist mud between their toes. Dried, grey mud caked on the soles of their naked feet. He tried to remember if this was tenderness or habit. He did not need to see her face to know that she had closed her eyes. She trusted him that much. Eyes closed. There are many different ways to disappear. There are many different forms of invisibility.

"It's not like that," Sylvia said, then she told Johnny her eye itched. Perhaps a gnat or a flea tickled her eyelash or her eyebrow. She remained still. A disciplined experience of the desire that goes unfulfilled. Waiting without thought. Her body tensed from the light itch. Only her breathing changed slightly, a subtle movement of her rib cage. The rest of her body did not move.

Faint morning light fell through the branches of the trees, touched her forehead. Sylvia's skin seemed to change color, becoming an even lighter shade of white, a white that nearly made her body disappear. Shadows settled on her thigh. Even though they never left a stain or a trace, Johnny feared they did something to him when his fingers moved over skin or bricks covered by a shadow. He wondered if skin remained naked beneath shadows. He wondered how skin survived shadows, and he feared what lifting a shadow from skin might reveal.

When Johnny was a young boy, he napped beside his mother, wrapped inside her shadow. He wanted to remember being that small and that close to his mother. He remembered this same river. The Monongahela. "Too many Pittsburghers call it The Mon," she said. "Don't you ever do that. They call it that so that they can forge their own memories, so that what came before them remains dead and doesn't get in their way. And don't you dare let your grandfather hear you call it The Mon." His mother's sharp, narrow fingers dug into Johnny's shoulders, held him tight. "I won't be able to protect you."

And Johnny remembered holes that a man had punched in the walls before leaving. A man who fled before Johnny was born. And he remembered something about a broken rib or a stolen rib or a missing rib. The holes in the walls were there when he was born, waiting for him. Lehuong's rib had healed and was never spoken of. She looked at those holes every day, but Johnny was not allowed to touch them. "You put your fingers into evil, and you become the evil," his mother said. "There's no way to escape it and no way to escape the evil in this city. Not unless you disappear from your skin. You got to sacrifice skin." Lehuong touched her son's heart, his rib cage. "Skin comes from there, Johnny."

Lehuong never covered those holes in the wall. Some days she spat at them. Other days she stood before them, stared at them, and cried. Many nights, she touched the edge of the holes gently with the tips of her fingers. Held her delicate touch there, as if she were about to enter something, remembering a pain mixed with a longing that she dare not forget. Johnny grabbed onto his mother's thigh, onto her hands, onto her fingers. Squeezed her fingers with all his little-boy strength.

Her hands looked so much older than the rest of her body, yet they felt so much younger. Her touch, so soft. The years had only scarred her skin, but had not scarred her touch. Her caress remained sacred. The lines in his mother's hand had been chiseled there by stories of some distant past. She told Johnny the lines in her hands formed a treasure map that someday they would understand and that they would follow the trails of that map over rivers, up mountains, across oceans, to live forever in wonder, to wrench a piece of hurt and beauty out of their lives and turn it into a world that had no beginning, no ending. But then she died, and he went to live with his grandfather. And that was the end of something and the beginning of something else.

And Johnny remembered a man covered by darkness, a man propped against a tree across the street from their house, a man endlessly waiting in shadows. A man who had destroyed his own name in some burning bush in a desert or in an alley. A man whose name was nothing more than a heap of broken letters.

Johnny's mother had mistaken this man's silence for love. She had mistaken a broken rib for love. She had mistaken this man on top of her, pushing inside her, for love. His balled fists in the pillow. His fists pounding the headboard, the walls. She had mistaken carrying this man's child, her child, her wanting this child to be her child and for this man to leave, for love. She had mistaken giving birth to his passion, to his pain, to his desire, for love. She had mistaken being told that silence was golden, for love.

Sylvia's foot moved. Johnny grabbed her ankle to remind her that he was beside her. Goose bumps rose on her skin. Butterflies waking. The tiniest of angels dancing to the surface of her skin. Sylvia held onto this stillness every morning. Her stillness, before waking, made her mysterious to him. The way she hesitated the first night that Johnny asked her to follow him to the riverbank, the way she refused to say anything to him except to say, "No", when they were about to take their first steps down the muddy trail toward the river. He told her not to be afraid, told her there was nothing to fear, that the broken glass was too dull to cut into her naked skin. Sylvia still only said no.

She remained planted where she stood. Feet in mud. Remained with her simple, "No," her refusal to follow. Johnny told her he would never be a thief of her innocence. His mother talked about thieves and innocence in such a way, her voice filled with pain and longing all at once. She had told Johnny's grandfather that it was the years of subtle whoring that was killing her, destroying every little bit of her innocence and of her dreams. "Men should pay if they are going to look at a woman the way that they do. The way they look with their eyes, saying what their mothers would never allow them to say, but them saying it with the silence of their eyes instead of with words. Too afraid to be true, to say it straight. No, they said it without saying. But they saying it, and no one's mother caring as long as it wasn't in words. Saying it in how they sit and look at the unwashed dishes, or how they sit and wait for their dinner, or how they look at a woman when a woman steps out of the shadows. What God ever gave them that right?"

Lehuong pulled Johnny closer to her, put her hands over his ears. Elgin sat on the rotting steps of her porch, stared off at the sunlight falling down on Sarah Street. Back then, after Thuy's death, Elgin devoted most of his days to studying sunlight. He looked into sunlight with a hard, steady gaze, like there was something to know by seeing it, by sitting down with it and contemplating it. Sat and stared into it the way a scientist squints into a microscope at the unseeable world, the invisible world that forms our lives. "The sunlight is aging," he said. "It's been aging for years. And now, as each day goes on, sunlight gets that much older. It dies quick and fast this time of year. It turns itself into ash and shadows. It hides itself from us in the wilderness. It deserts us." Elgin looked away from the sunlight into Lehuong's eyes.

"It's not a riddle, Dad. I'd rather be on the streets, leaning into the shadows. At least, there, I know what's being taken." Lehuong squatted down and put her hands on Johnny's shoulders. Stared into his eyes. "It's what those eyes take, what those hands take, what those words take, each and every word takes without even asking. It's that taking that's the everyday life of subtle whoring. No laws against that kind of taking. Their eyes keeping me silent in my bones. Reminding me to bury every breath of my own life inside darkness. Their eyes and their silence, and they stand there melting me into a shadow and expecting me to be quiet and thankful."

Johnny swore to Sylvia that he only wanted to keep her safe. But she knew what he could never imagine. She knew her innocence had already been ruined. A man, now long dead and buried in a dusty town outside of Phoenix, had, night after night, come through her bedroom window, or perhaps he had slipped under her bedroom door or had squeezed through the keyhole, or perhaps the man had crawled out from under her bed. This man waited until the world was silent, then he softly stepped into her room, lifted her out of her bed, and carried her away into the lost night to a place he called safe. In this place, he scratched away at her skin and threatened to destroy her tongue if she ever told anyone what had happened to her, what had to happen to her.

Sylvia's heart balled and knotted. A tangle of wanting. She knew this man, knew his hands, knew the scent from the chewing gum he stuck behind his right ear. She knew his voice. His calm assurance, reminding her, "You are safe," while he kept her trapped like a rare butterfly delicately pinned beneath glass. Years drained out of her. She wished that skin had roots, so that it did not simply fall off her bones onto the cold sheets. Sylvia woke every morning, her fingers buried in some memory of this man, of some man, telling her to confess, to say her prayers, to ask for forgiveness. His voice felt like the sound of poison slowly entering her veins while something precious struggled to find a place to hide.

There are things, this man said, that girls are compelled to experience. He told her that the Lord was taking her soul in her sleep. He told her that she was dreaming and told her to hold her breath. "All this will go away one day," he whispered. This man told her that her mother did not want to know any of this, that her mother needed to have secrets kept from her, so that she could go on living, so that she could go on loving her daughter. "Some things are done to daughters," the man said, "that mothers should never know." He was saving her, so that she would one day know better.

Now Sylvia dreams that this man is no longer inside her. She dreams that she can open her mouth or spread her legs and that he would fly out of her and vanish into the night. And she dreams of forgetting that night she came home, that night her mother sat on the porch waiting for her with her father's thick leather belt in her hand. That night her mother said, "Do not say a word."

As long as pain never becomes pain, pain is a beautiful idea. The longing that pain creates and nurtures in the shadows. To welcome the kind of pain that takes your body elsewhere. Sylvia became acutely aware of her hunger for this pain. A pain that would grow old on her body and never die. "Now you will know you are alive," her mother said quietly, so that the neighbors would not hear. Her mother taught her what it felt like to be alive, and her father taught her what it was like to die.

Sylvia's tongue stuck in her mouth. She thought of soap bubbles the moment before they burst and became part of the bathwater again. Her skin endured that precise moment of the soap bubble breaking. When her mother finished, Sylvia listened to her mother's heavy footsteps climbing the stairs to her bedroom. She listened to her mother closing the door. Then she walked back down the steps of the front porch, down Federal Street to West North Avenue until a car slowed and pulled over and a window opened and then a door. It was winter, so Sylvia got into the car. The man in the car called her "My pretty," and asked her if she liked his car. And she said, "Yes," because it was a word she had been taught to say, a word she knew to say. She asked the man if he were afraid that his car might turn into a pumpkin at midnight. She felt a hand on her thigh, and then she felt fingers squeeze her flesh above her knees and heard herself saying, "Yes, I will, yes." And she thought it must be this man doing this, and she told herself to close her eyes, because often it is better to be blind, even though that does not change anything. And she whispered, "Yes", one final time before she said she never did a thing like that before, and her eyes remained closed, so she would not see.

Johnny told Sylvia, once again, that she would be safe, because his skin was not broken. She could close her eyes, and it would not mean anything. It would only mean that she was tired. And he told her he would never tell anyone. Not a soul. Johnny said he knew better, had heard enough stories, standing on corners, to know better than to tell anyone about the stories along the riverbanks of Pittsburgh. Sylvia looked at Johnny with a strange sense of yearning for things lost and never had.

Days passed. Nights drifted. Sylvia returned often to the place that Johnny had shown her, where the path seemed to vanish, but also seemed to wait. She wanted to shut her eyes and watch the world disappear and to be done with remembering. She wanted to forgive life and to discover ways for beauty to be born out of her sorrow. She longed to remember that man's name and say it one final time. To release his name into the streets, into the rivers, into the trees. To carve that man's name onto a plaque and nail that plaque and his name on the front door of her mother's house. Sylvia wanted to write the story of his agitated hands and fingers, the story of his insane breath, onto tiny slips of papers and to place these slips of paper into children's books all over the city of Pittsburgh, in every Carnegie Library, in every bookstore. She wanted to crouch down to eye level when she met a child on the streets of Pittsburgh, to smile at the child, to tell the child how cute they were, and then to casually slip the story of this man into the palm of the child's hand. And she wanted to draw pirate maps, so that every child in Pittsburgh would know how to travel. Even though she was a girl, she wanted to be king of the pirates. Sylvia wanted to rid herself of the roots that this man, that man after man, had planted inside her. She wanted to swallow without feeling the pain from the bruises inside her throat.

One night, after walking street after street, getting into car after car, alone, Sylvia stepped between the blackberry bushes and onto the trail that Johnny had shown her. She followed the narrow path. She knew not to look over her shoulder. The path disappeared behind her. Johnny slept on a blanket spread out near the very edge of the Monongahela. She quietly sat down beside his sleeping body and watched him dream. Along the riverbank, the urban landscape became mystical. What was once fearful became sacred. There are ways to tell stories that change everything. There are words that rescue drowning boys and drowning girls from the undertow. There are bewitched places where city lights go dark and disappear and moonstruck stars are reflected on the surface of the river.

Sylvia lightly touched Johnny's shoulder. He looked up at her. "I need you to tie me up."

CHAPTER 14

The Pittsburgh sun wreaked chaos on a man's desires. His dreams caught on fire and, beneath such heat, a man's skin longed for the bone-cold of winter. His tongue became dusty, dried up, and cracked. Even when a man is doing what he thinks he is doing, what he is doing doesn't feel right to him, and it doesn't look right to others. On this day, the heat went in even deeper than normal. It crept into the soul of every living and breathing man, woman, and child in the city, eating into their memories. It made men want to peel off their skin, get naked beneath naked.

This heat, even in the early morning, turned itself into the kind of heat that made the most faithful of men question their religion and doubt their wives and mothers. Fathers locked their daughters behind doors, nailed shut their bedroom windows, chased them into the attic, keeping them out of reach of boys driven mad. Fathers told their daughters, and the boys clamoring about on the porch, to sweat the pain out of their desire. This kind of heat sent men out searching for salvation, but these men mostly wanted to find a drop or two of the blood of Christ, instead of any of that salvation promised by a man dead on the cross. Salvation in the form of beer, not wine.

Beer is never a choice in such heat; beer is a need. Pittsburgh heat demanded of a man that he drink beer. A man was not a man in Pittsburgh in late summer unless he held a beer in his hand. Not caressing it. Men don't caress a beer bottle. Men drink beer. And in heat such as this day was bringing down onto the city, a man needed a serious beer. Not that twist-off-the-cap beer. And none of that City of Brotherly Love beer. No, a man needed a true beer. One you had to do a little work for, so your sweat mixed in with the beer. Staggering men, bumping into other bodies and into corners of buildings as they stumbled along the sidewalks up Fifth Avenue, were forgiven for their own foolishness in such heat, were forgiven for drinking so many beers that numbers evaporated and that rent money lost its importance, and they were forgiven for saying out loud what their eyes said in silence all those times a beautiful woman walked past them, raising their impotent desires.

And Elgin was no different from any other man in Pittsburgh. Elgin, like all self-respecting men in the city of Pittsburgh, needed beer. And he needed more than to simply wet his whistle; he needed to drink beer after beer, swallow beer into the hidden depths of his body, to put out those fires the sun was burning into him before his memories turned into ashes. Elgin stared, the way only a blind man can stare, into his empty and tired refrigerator; both his stare and the refrigerator itself were exhausted by years of working so hard to keep so little, at best, slightly chilled or slightly remembered. Elgin searched as best he could for one, final bottle of beer. He knocked over a Heinz ketchup bottle and a milk carton. His hand floated helplessly here and there with wanting, encountered this and that, touched this and that.

Frustrated by his failed holiest-of-grail searches, he grabbed onto the top of the refrigerator door, pulled himself up from kneeling, straightened his back, and took one last blind look, before closing the door. Elgin kicked at the bottom of that beaten-down refrigerator until he heard something break loose and fall onto the floor. Tired and hot, a bit forlorn, Elgin leaned his forehead against that rusted door. It was all that there seemed left to do. A man lives long enough and these simple disappointments pile up, start eating away at his insides. Elgin feared these disappointments would take over and control his very existence. Every day, he felt it fall apart, one little piece at a time. He wondered if he ever would be able to put any of it back together again, if there was even any point to putting it all back together.

"Some things can't be mended with a needle, no matter how sharp the needle is," Elgin's great-grandmother once told him. "Some things you leave broken on the floor. You just look at it for what it is." She touched Elgin on his cheek or shoulder when she spoke to him. Touched him with fingers that had survived many lives. A light touch to remind Elgin to listen with his body, not his ears. Or perhaps her touch was a way of mending Elgin, of sewing together what he himself did not know needed to be mended. "Some things," she told him, "just tear open at the seams." And some things, Elgin thought to himself, tear you open at the seams, and where's the needle for that? What can you do when the pieces themselves are all cracked? When each piece needs mending?

Elgin's damp shirt clung to his skin. His feet wanted out of his shoes. His tongue desired the cold truth hidden in beer. This old, blind man, who wanted nothing more extravagant than a cold beer, pulled a hankerchief out of his pocket and wiped the beads of perspiration from his forehead, each bead a syllable of his memory of loving Thuy. A sad beginning to Elgin's day, a sorry-assed way for him to confront the humidity, the pale sun burning into the concrete of those angry sidewalks of Pittsburgh. And that morning heat was just getting started, driving innocent, kind children insane with laughter and filling them with a desire to uncap fire hydrants and beg for popsicles. The God-fearing collapsed to their knees under its weight, and old folks sat, quiet and still, in their swings on their porches, near tears, unable for the life of them to get up. Whiling the day away. Wanting to cry, or something of the sort, but too dried out to make tears, just old folks staring at the stems of flowers gone limp.

Children shouted across streets to each other, but the heat from the sun melted the sounds of their voices, and the mothers of these shouting children were too tired to tell their children to stop it with the screaming, to tell their children to walk on over across the street and talk. "Listen at you. Don't you be screaming when we all need more of the quiet to come," mothers up and down Dream Street and Fifth Avenue and Pride and Dinwiddie Streets, and all through the alleys, up and down the alleys, preached to their children. "The Lord whispers when he got something to say. You killing up the silence with all your shouting. How you gonna hear the whispers?" But these mothers themselves were too tired to work up a beating, too tired, too hot to teach the Lord's lessons, to whip those lessons into the flesh of their children. To mark their children with lessons of love and kindness.

Elgin stepped out of his house, directly into that early afternoon heat, on his quest for beer. His first breath was pure, dry fire. A tiny whisper of a breeze scorched his skin. His lips and his throat blistered. Elgin still knew how to walk, still knew, would always know, had been born knowing, the exact number of steps from his front door down to Red's Ibo Landing Bar and Girlle.

Red never fixed the spelling of Grill. He felt it added a necessary confusion to the place and told everyone those misplaced letters were not a mistake at all. They were a reckoning. "We all got someone who is dead inside us," Red would say. "A dead child holding out a hand to each of us in silence, that child just holding out his hand wanting us to grab hold of its fingertips, just wanting. Hoping." Red believed that, when the time was right, the *r* would trade places with the *i* and each letter would journey back to where they belonged, a homecoming. Until then, everything was suspended, waiting for that migration home.

Elgin walked slow and careful to the gate. He paused for a weary moment, put his hand on one of the spikes of the wrought iron fence, wrapped his fingers around it, held tight. Sweating. His old, muscled body wished for winter, for those gritty winds that blew over the Monongahela, frozen winds with just the tiniest filaments of snow, not even flakes, just slivers of ice. Elgin wanted one of those cold February days to interrupt this summer day, this heat. The only time anyone in Pittsburgh ever wanted it to be February was when it was September. In February, Pittsburghers felt that winter would never end. Hopeless ice and slush. Everyone sunk into winter coats that were never thick enough, their necks wrapped in scarves that did nothing but irritate their skin, and, with each frozen breath, they all wondered what happened to the heat of summer. Where had all that heat had gone off to? They wondered why God did what He did to them. In winter, everyone wondered where all the yellowjackets disappeared to, and how they ever managed to find their way back. And in summer, everyone wondered the same thing about winter. Boys searched the freezer for snowballs that they had hidden back in January and that their mothers had pulled out and allowed to melt in the sink. Men searched the alleys for the cold of winter. Looking for it in the eyes of some near-dead poet, homeless, crumpled down on the hot sidewalk, back pressed hard against the concrete of a building, or they searched for it in the eyes of a startled child too hot to cry, or in the lost smile of a woman in broken heels leaning against a lamppost, longing for one air-conditioned trick in the night.

Elgin closed the gate behind him and set off on his journey to Red's. One burning step after the other. Heat rising from the concrete was more dangerous than the heat bearing down from the sun. Concrete heat entered at the soles of a man's feet and became part of his whole sense of self. Elgin made his way with that heat moving through him, slow and hesitant, down the sidewalk among the people of sight. Everybody suffering too much to lift their heads. They cast their eyes downward at their shoes, too hot to put any effort into lifting their feet to walk along the dusty sidewalks. Mindless drifters occasionally bumped into Elgin as he moved among the seeing, like a sage trying to read their thoughts, trying to get a sense of what the world was becoming. He had left his walking cane back at the house. He wanted to descend to Red's in pure blindness.

Elgin's tired and quiet feet—aged and blistered by weather and war—hurt inside his worn shoes. The movement of a man's feet revealed his story more honestly than his own voice ever could. Elgin knew this much was certain in life. Knew it from his grandmother's tales, knew it from those broken footprints in Vietnam, knew it from the way the ghost of his father guarded the footprints he left behind in the river mud along the Monongahela. The sidewalk burned through the bottom of Elgin's shoes into the soles of his feet. His footsteps left the smell of smoke, the ash of his memories, rising from the sidewalk.

"It don't matter," Walter was saying as Elgin pushed through the door into Red's Ibo Landing Bar and Girlle. The front door to Red's was like an open wound. "I know where I am when I say Red's," he said. "Danicka knows where I am when I say Red's. Everyone in the city knows where I am. I ain't nowhere else."

"You don't know what you need to know to be where you is right now," Red shouted down the bar. He tapped the sign above the cash register. "You can't tell me this ain't a sign. Clear as day it is. A true sign." And Red, as he did nearly every day of his life, launched into the stories of how the true Ibo Landing was in the basement of his bar. He started into the stories of bound men and women, of shackled children. Red told the stories of those who drowned. He named their names, the men and women who disappeared into the dark depths of the unforgiving waters. Named each one of them and named their families, named where they had come from and who they had descended from, and he named the children they had brought into the world. Skin prayers. A litany of what must be remembered, of what must be prayed over in daily conversations.

"I just want a beer," Walter cried. "A beer." But the women hidden in the shadows in the booths urged Red on. His voice did more than any man's touch had ever done to any of those women, and they wanted more of his voice. When he did this naming of each name, the names became tiny poems inside his mouth. Delicate poems released into the world from between his lips. When Red started the naming, women, girls, boys, even men, gathered around and listened to the tenderness in his voice, felt the touch of his voice on their bodies. Experienced that voice of Red's in a way that made them feel truly alive and truly marked. They sat caressed by it.

Elgin slowly made his way through the darkness, over to the bar. He excused himself for accidentally brushing against someone's shoulders, then found an empty bar stool and sat down.

"People stupid with being stupid. Especially Walter," Red said to Elgin when he sat down, then he turned his attention back to Walter. "Some things you can't never wash out of you. You keep trying to, but you can't, and that's why you suffer the way you do, Walter."

"You the one making me suffer. Tell him to get me a beer, Elgin."

"Do what the man say and you get one. You know that."

"Dammit, Red. It's just words."

"They ain't just words. They're a calling back to our ancestors and they in you. And you can't rub them out. Things like these names, you try rubbing them gone, and all you do is rub them deeper into your skin and that rubbing stays."

The more Red spoke, the more quiet the bar, if not the entire city of Pittsburgh, became. Women weakened in their knees with their listening to his voice. They all wondered what else a man, with such a voice that did what it did with names, could do to them, what that voice of Red's could do to their hearts, to their muscles, to their breathing, to all that they kept tucked inside. Young women lost their virginity to Red's voice. And if young men were capable of admitting that they had a virginity that was waiting to be lost, then they too would have given it up to the voice of Red, to the sound of the names.

"Beer, just beer, Red," Walter said. "I'm not trying to rub that word, or any other word, out. And it don't matter if I'm in Ibo this or Ibo that. I'm in a bar. Your grandmother never made a man wait on a beer when she stood back there."

"You say my grandmother's name proper, and, if you do, I'll give you a beer on the house. Won't even make you say the name of the bar. All you got to do is say her name proper."

"Shit, ain't no one alive can say that woman's name. It got letters all over the place in it."

"And why you think that, fool? Huh? You ever give that any nevermind?" Red wiped the counter of the bar. "Name only difficult for a man to say, because the man ain't living right. You not patient and true enough to say such a name. You want to say a name fast and easy like if you say the name of a person you somehow know that person. Just like you wanting your beer so fast."

"I ain't looking to get to know my beer, ain't looking to take it out for a night at Crawford's," Walter interrupted. "I'm just looking to drink it. And you don't see no one giving beer names that a man can't say. Hard enough to say my own name once I start drinking, if you ever get me a beer, so I can get back to my drinking."

"Women given those old names to make it difficult on a man, like you, who wants to rush past the saying of their name, rush past the touch of her name in his throat, on his tongue, between his lips. Saying is more than saying. Man wants to hurry along a woman's name 'cause he wants to get to something else. If a man can't be patient enough to be saying your name, then he's not a man. He's just careless."

"A beer, Red, just a beer."

"You started it, Walter," Elgin muttered. "We all got to suffer now."

Red ignored both of them and kept talking. "It takes courage to be with a woman's name, like it takes courage to be true. You're not so old that you can't go and learn this, Walter. There's still hope, even for a fool like you." Red poured Elgin another beer. "You learn to slow down. And you don't go and say a woman's name like it's any other word; you summon a woman's name, each syllable, each letter of her name, and she know you respect her. You don't say a name to be done saying it. You say a name to be with saying the name."

Everyone in the bar knew what came next. Red called the names that had become nearly impossible to say, because time had erased too much, because time said to go fast instead of to slow down. "It's the silence beneath these names that is the true matter, the secret you do not want to face, but the one that is there, always there. A woman's old name is a wound of what's been lost and what's missing. You got to uncage the story in a woman's name."

Mothers gave their daughters such names as talismans to protect them. The names of those who walked over the waters. The names of those who stepped into the waters and drowned. And Red told the stories beneath the names. And when he finished, he looked at his hands like they belonged to someone else or like he had never realized that he had hands before, then he rubbed them together, trying to make visible what every day was becoming more lost. Red trusted his words, had faith that his words possessed the power of creation in them, trusted that there were words that had not been harmed and stolen by men with desires to own the flesh of his ancestors, the heart beating inside his ribs.

"You become those words you speak, Walter. It's who you is," Red said. "You born yourself through your stories. No escaping that." He wet his rusty lips. He rubbed together his palms, gone grey and scarred with years of living. "Forgetting is more than simply forgetting," Red said more to himself than to Elgin or Walter or anyone else in the bar, "more than losing your keys, or forgetting the name of one girl when you with another girl. Forgetting is watching a memory go away when you can't do nothing to save it." Red continued staring down at his hands while he talked. "When you lose a kite, that moment you realize that you are trapped on earth watching that kite go up in the sky stays with you. Watching it, when there's nothing for you to do. Just longing to grab that piece of string, pull that kite back to you, but that kite is gone. Gone for good. You're not careful, the same happens

146

to memories when someone dies. You see their stories floating off, and you left wanting to tug on the string, pull them memories back to you, but you can't be doing nothing about it. Stories just getting more and more quiet, until they ain't there no more."

Elgin had the same fears of forgetting put into him. Tales of the forgetting tree that his ancestors were forced to stand under to forget their past and destroy their desire to return. "You protect yourself from that tree. You go on and devote a sentence a day to one of your ancestors," his mother told him. "You wake each morning and tell a story about one of your kin that's passed on, and then the evening before bed you tell another story of a different kin." Elgin sat at the kitchen table listening. "You have plenty of time to talk about baseball. Remember, you are going to die someday, boy. You need to remember this. Remind yourself of it. We all gonna die. Tell the stories that matter. Keep them alive."

Red wiped something, like a tear or the tiniest of forgotten memories, or perhaps something like a gnat, from his eye. He wiped this something from his eye in such a gentle way that it seemed like he wanted to protect it from being damaged. And it seemed like Elgin had seen this and he, too, wiped something from his eye. Something that did not belong there, but something that he hoped would never be destroyed.

"You are born with the memory already inside you before you take your first breath," Red called out. "No one has to say a word for you to know it. It's burned into you. Your body can't never explain what came before you was born." He stopped. His hands trembled a bit. "Stories got as much soul as any of us got," Red said somewhat louder. "A soul grows, Walter. Even yours. It's put in you at birth like some child is put inside a woman, like a seed. And like a seed, a soul got to grow. You hear the soul growing in the moan of a man or a woman's voice. In a woman opening up her lungs and singing. Her singing, her laughing is the soul crying out. A soul digs itself into you. And that's just what a story does."

"A story is a story. A story ain't never here," Walter said. "All I need is a beer. So, pour me a draft, Red, and keep all that you want to say about anything else to your own poor self. I'm here for beer. I ain't got no intention in talking. Man comes to a bar to drink, not talk. When you gonna figure that out, Red?"

"Ain't doing nothing of the sort, unless you say it like it is meant to be said. Show respect for where you is when you in here. If I'da meant for it to be just Red's, you think I would have gone to the expense of all those other letters? You think?" Red asked.

Red would rather lose a dollar than serve a beer without due respect paid to the name of his bar. He asked everyone the same question: "Where is you?" And the simple answer never changed: Red's Ibo Landing Bar and Girlle. Anyone who shortened it or corrected the spelling or just looked at Red and told him to pour, Red would ignore.

"You really blind?" Red asked.

Elgin nodded. "A long time coming, my brother." Elgin felt the warm sweat of the glass, lifted the narrow glass to his lips.

"You'll be walking on the water before anyone knows it."

From down the far end of the bar, Walter called out, "Red's Ibo Landing Bar and Girlle."

"There you go. Ain't so hard, now, is it?" Red moved to the tap and poured beer for Walter, then walked it down the bar to him. "Keep your money. We'll call it even, for all the suffering I caused in you."

Walter slapped money down on the bar. "Keep it." He disappeared with his beer into the darkest corner.

"You back, Red?"

"Yeah. I thought that being blind made you sharp with hearing and smelling. All your other senses making up for you not being able to see."

"Hasn't been working much that way for me. I smell the weather. I can tell you rain is coming today. Smell it over the hills. And I can hear the darkness. Nothing else has changed. No superpowers," Elgin chuckled. "Every once in a while, I get an idea, but I can't never make any sense come of it. I still see Thuy with every breath. I can't imagine that changing." Elgin stopped his sentence, raised his glass, held it there for a moment, thinking. Quiet with thought and desire, then he downed the last of his beer.

"Thuy's a shadow in you, Elgin, but she's a shadow that wants light." Red wiped the bar where Elgin had spilled a few drops of his beer. He picked up his empty glass and poured him another one. "You feared too much losing her from the moment you began saving her, and you weren't saving her to begin with. She only let you think that was true, because she thought you needed to believe it. Memories end, Elgin. They end. Every explanation you got for anything ends somewhere. You must still got suffering that you need to do. Once you gone and exhausted all that suffering, maybe you can let go. Get some rest for your soul and for your tired old black feet."

"Memories disappear into words, Red," he said. "Some words defy gravity and take flight; other words suffer from gravity, words that can't do much more than return to the earth. Words that just fall from grace. You can't control it much."

"I fear that a day will come when words and memories had expiration dates," Red said. "One day I wake up, and they just gone. I wonder how the world would change if that were true. Or how the world we thought we were living in would change, if we were only permitted to use a word a certain number of times, then were forced to find other words."

"I imagine you'd be bound to be more careful with what you say," Elgin replied. "You'd be quiet more. But I can't imagine you being quiet for long."

Red laughed. "I can see people standing on corners selling words instead of drugs. People so comfortable with their words, their habits, they'd pay top price for words to keep everything the same, instead of thinking more careful before saying love or hate or beautiful. Imagine if you only able to say love six times in your lifetime, then the word vanished." Red looked hard into Elgin when he said this. "You think on that," Red said to Elgin. They both knew what was being said. They both knew what was not being said. They both knew.

Once Thuy asked Elgin if he wore his heart on his sleeve. Asked him that straight out of the blue one morning, while they were having coffee. She said she heard someone say that on the television, had heard about a man who wore his heart on his sleeve, and she wanted to know what it meant. She wanted to know how anyone could do that. Elgin remembered his father saying the same thing. Saying that Ai had asked him if he wore his heart on his sleeve. She said she could not believe he could say love to her in the way he did, with his eyes, his mouth, his lips, his fingers, his teeth. She wondered if this was it. "Love." She asked Clarence how it was possible for a man to fall in love with her in the way that he had fallen for her. He just looked at her and told Ai it was her. Told her that he thought his heart had quit on him until he met her. She made his heart appear, that he did not wear it on his sleeve, open to anyone, that she had pulled his heart out of hiding. "You unshadowed my heart, Ai. It's that simple." Love does that. It unshadows a man's heart; it unshadows his soul. His love for Ai brought his soul out from the shadows and gave it light, and he came to know something he never imagined he could know. "That's what loving you makes possible," he whispered in close to Ai, "a knowing of my soul."

He told her that he thought he had lost his heart for good, then she woke it from its hibernation. He told her that, if he did know anything about love, it was because of her, because of the way she kissed him, because of the way she talked to him, because of the way her eyes did what they did to him when she just looked at him. Ai taught Clarence love, and now he knew something of what love might be, if only the world would allow for it, for the kind of love they gave each other. She smiled at him when he said that. Her lips parted as if she were readying herself to say something, but she remained silent. Her quiet eyes. Her breath.

She took his right hand and pulled it toward her, placed it on her left pelvic bone, pressed it into her bone there. She said, "Your love for me is a pulse that is deep in me, Clarence. Desire and love ain't hiding away from you. It's there inside me. You put it in me like you did. A pulse. A steady, flaring pulse that catches in my throat. And now you tug it out of me." They both smiled, then Ai went back to stirring whatever it was she was fixing for them to eat.

Before Elgin could say anything, Thuy said that she hoped he didn't wear his heart on his sleeve. She said it was too cold in Pittsburgh for anyone to wear their heart on their sleeve, and she did not want a cold heart loving her.

"I know what can get lost and how it can get itself lost, Red. You don't have to remind me of it," Elgin said. "I know."

Not even Red's Ibo Landing Bar and Girlle could cure a man burdened by memories that he chose to carry with him, no matter how much pain they caused.

"Only time to break silence is when you're speaking so you can heal something that is gone," Red said. Then he grabbed Elgin's glass and asked him if he needed another beer.

"In this heat, a man always needs another beer, Red."

CHAPTER 15

"My son. Your son. Our son." Debra chanted more than spoke. A clumsy fury of words that tripped over each other trying to escape her mouth. A faithful perseverance that prayer could transform what was real. Sacramental words that meant something long ago, but now just seemed like a dried-out memory. Her voice reminded Fred of straw. Hopeless and prolonged. Then Debra ended her chant by whispering, more breath than word, the name she had given their son, "Lucas."

After releasing this name from her body, she paused to allow her words to go deep into Fred's sense of just who the hell he thought he was and what God Fred thought had given him the right to drink beer while their son was no longer safe and warm. She allowed her words to settle there, for Fred to hold her words, the pain, the madness, the anguish, there, on his insides, and for Fred to feel her words trembling, chilling his skin, rotting his soul; then, she returned to the beginning of her chant, and, once again, she slowly let go of each mournful and confused syllable, each desperate letter of each word, words she wished she did not need to say. Debra chanted like this while standing rigid at the kitchen screen door, peering out at Fred and Jim, peering into Fred's back. She did this night after night after night.

On the other side of that screen door, Fred and Jim stood perfectly still and longed for Debra's voice to wear itself out. They held their breath tight beneath their skin and waited to hear Debra's footsteps retreating from the screen door, to hear her feet carrying her deeper and deeper, through the fingerprinted hallways down into the cold, narrow nooks and crannies of their dusty house.

Some nights, she stood at that door chanting those seven words until morning. When she opened her mouth to speak, the air around Fred and Jim filled with the sound that locusts make when they first awake from their nap. Some evenings, before she got too far along with her chanting, before the sound of her voice damaged Jim's sense of well-being, Jim would give up any hope of enjoying a peaceful, drunken night and would nod farewell to Fred; sometimes he did so in mid-sentence, then headed back up the hill to his house, leaving Fred alone, gripping white-knuckled-tight to the railing of the porch, quietly cursing his nearly dead belief in God and his longing for a return to the youthful innocence of sex, gently dreaming of a return to his long-ago-destroyed desire for peace on earth, goodwill to men, and softly holding back his anger at every thrown-away, forgotten, spoiled milk carton scarred by a photograph of a missing child and a silent plea to find the stolen child.

Other nights, they patiently waited out her chanting. They stood, remained still, and waited, while Debra continued her endless, repetitive chant. Every night the same ritual. All Fred or Jim ever did any more was wait; they would have prayed for her to stop, had either of them been able to remember the words, the rhythms of prayers. They listened, but dared not glance over their shoulder at her, dared not allow a single nerve or muscle to twitch, dared not make a sound or move in any way, to lead Debra to believe that they might still be alive.

As they did every night, they stared straight ahead, across Fred's desolate backyard. Lucas' bicycle had disappeared long ago; perhaps Lucas—clandestine, invisible boy that he was known to be—had returned and taken the bicycle, had ridden it off on it into the sunset; perhaps the blackberry bushes had strangled it and Lucas' dreams along with it, and pulled that old bicycle and those wild dreams into the earth; perhaps they simply refused to see it, refused to admit that a bicycle could mean so much, that so much could possibly depend on something so broken and glazed with rain water, beside the barren maple tree.

Fred and Jim, lonely men in shortsleeve shirts leaning on the railing of a rotting porch outside of Pittsburgh, remained quiet and still, thoughts filled with beer and baseball, thoughts that no longer seemed to be thoughts. They hoped, beyond reason, for the chanting to come to one final end. They waited and listened in much the same way that Fred and Debra waited and listened and hoped. Days seemed to pass, but the way that time had of disappearing had become normal to Fred and Debra, and to Jim as well. Trees dropped their leaves, then picked them back up again, without anyone noticing. More often than not, Fred found himself staring at leaves or blossoms on trees and wondering when they had returned to the trees or how it was suddenly opening day of baseball season again. Moons waxed, waned, disappeared, reappeared, became full, disappeared again, became crescents. Fred's hair began thinning out. Jim put on weight. Debra's eyes changed color, and her voice seemed to become thicker, stronger, as her youth slipped away. Two or three families moved out of the neighborhood. New families moved in. The children in the neighborhood were angrier than before. They seemed ready for anything. They seemed to be preparing for something that the adults in the neighborhood did not understand. Fred had quit wearing his watch. He left it, unwound, on his dresser. He insisted that Jim take off his watch when they were together. Fred wished time would grow tired and quit. Just stop. And they all struggled in their own private ways to forget time, forget its passing, but the marks of its disappearance seemed to be everywhere. And the more they watched time disappearing, the more they felt it trapping them.

At long last, Debra's voice dried up, and the woman, Fred's wife, stopped chanting. Fred and Jim listened to Debra escape into that deeper darkness of the nearly empty house. The light in the kitchen went out. The wooden floors creaked under her weight, beneath the pressure of her tiny footsteps. The moon, or what was left of it, slipped behind clouds. Stars expired. The world became darker and quieter. Fred stared down at the nearly dead maple tree. He rubbed his eyes, trying to clear away the years of seeing. "I can't understand what Debra has done with Lucas or what she wants me to do or say." Fred spoke gently and softly, still a bit uncertain of Debra's departure, worried that his voice would break the night into fragments. The porch light drew mosquitoes and moths. Both Fred and Jim slowly relaxed their muscles. "You go to sleep and life changes. You don't expect it to. You don't want it to, but it does. Something happens, and you can't seem to think straight." Fred looked over at Jim, but Jim held his stare out across that empty backyard, waiting for summer's dry lightning to light up the horizon. "You think sleep isn't going to change anything. Not a thing. You can't believe sleeping can do such a thing as that, that sleeping has such a power."

Jim did not turn to look over at Fred; he held his gaze out away from all this, so Fred directed his gaze back out and over the yard where for years he imagined Lucas playing. "What harm can a little sleep do? A man needs his sleep. You think sleep is sleep. Nothing more than that. Nothing to worry over. You go to sleep and in the morning you wake up refreshed. That's all there is to it. That's all you want sleep to do." Fred picked at some chipped paint on the railing, pulled out a splinter, held it up near his eyes, and looked at it. He believed there was always something to see if you looked, something more than the naked eye was capable of seeing. He felt you had to make what you were looking at naked, in order to see it. You had to brush away the residue clothing it. "But things happen that you can't plan for or that you can't explain. You know that as well as anyone else, Jim. I know it too, but I always seem to forget it. A man wakes from a dream, and life is different from all he thought that it was or that it ever could be. I think maybe I'd just gotten too used to waking up and having life be the same. You get used to what you think will always be there. You think that's your world. Turns out to be an empty belief. And all you can think of is that you want an eye for an eye."

Fred pushed back from the railing, kicked at the floor of the porch, looked up at the sky, searching for what remained of the moon. "You wake up each morning your whole life expecting everything to be in its place, right where you left it. You wake up seeing what you see, and you find yourself wishing you didn't wake up. You wake up wanting it to go back to being what it was."

"Hard not to," Jim replied. He stretched his spine, rolled his neck. Jim put his arm across Fred's shoulders, then clumsily patted Fred on his back. Awkward as he felt, when need be, even Jim knew how to nurture a friend in need of something beyond words. "All kinds of things happen, Fred. Most often we don't see any of it coming." Jim squeezed Fred's shoulder, patted him on his back one more time, maybe two times, rested his hand on his shoulder. Jim did not know what to do next, so he just let his hand drop to his side.

"We should go."

"It's not like there's some place to go, Fred." Jim shoved both his hands into his pockets. He seemed to fear what they might do, worried they might shake Fred by his shoulders to wake him out of whatever dream he had entered, or maybe his hands would try to comfort Fred more than words could ever do, make Fred feel that everything was going to be all right, that it was just a matter of time. Jim had a sudden fear that he might do something with those hands of his that no man in Pittsburgh should ever do to another man, could ever do with another man; at least not do and still be a man in Pittsburgh. Some things you just can't ever do, so you keep your hands in your pockets, afraid you might disturb the universe or bring down the walls of Jericho. And, for some reason, Jim feared looking at Fred, feared that even a casual glance might turn him into salt. He stared out over Fred's backyard, out away from Fred's full lips. Something was breaking apart inside of Fred, and Jim worried that once that something broke, whatever it was, that there would be no way back. "You said Lucas would be back when Debra brought him back. You said she was in control. Called it destiny. You always said it was more about waiting than about seeking. You trust. You believe. Then it happens right in front of you. You quit believing in all that?"

"Like Lazarus?" Fred asked. "Like faith? Maybe we shouldn't have given up on the habit of prayer." He grabbed a few empties off the railing and put them in the beer case. "It's been too long, Jim. Waiting isn't working. Waiting has failed us. It has failed Lucas. And I think it has destroyed Debra. We need to go looking." Jim helped Fred clean the porch. He grabbed more empty bottles, returning them to the beer case as well, then picked up the stray pieces of labels the two of them had peeled off the bottles, and put them in the trash.

"How do you look for a story?" Jim asked.

"Bob will help," Fred said. "He knows more about what it means to go into shadows than anyone." Jim looked at Fred. Neither of them said the obvious; neither Fred nor Jim said what they knew was true.

Fred still believed in fairy tales, still believed in moments of spirit and pixie dust, and, when he drank enough, he still found himself believing in Santa Claus, leaving out milk and cookies, while Debra shook her head in disbelief. So, simply waiting day after day made sense, but Fred seemed to be believing more than waiting, and it now seemed like they had been waiting too long, and his belief was falling away. Belief had more to do with things that he could not see, and hope had more to do with those things that just were not there yet. He tried as best he could to hold onto hope.

"You think that belief can erase belief?" Fred asked Jim. "Can it?" Fred stopped picking up the bottles, looked hard into Jim's eyes. "It's what I feel happening, belief erasing belief. There's nothing there. No faith. Nothing. And hope? I want hope, wish for it, do whatever I can to keep it in me, but the nights get shorter, and the dawn comes like it never left, and the dawn forgets to bring light with it, so the morning stays dark." Fred wiped at his eyes again, before a tear had a chance to fall. "Belief erasing belief. It's not right when that begins to happen."

Jim tried to say something. He parted his lips, but looked away, down at his hands, as if he were about to do something with those hands of his, or as if he felt the answer was written there in his hands, then he quietly returned to picking up the remaining beer bottles.

They finished cleaning the porch, took a final look around, like they were criminals checking to be certain that they had not left any fingerprints. Satisfied that they were not leaving any traces of their having ever been there, Fred said, "Let's go." The two modestly drunk men, for the first time in what seemed like years, decades, centuries, or perhaps it was only a day or two, stepped off the porch, down the wooden stairs, and walked out into the empty backyard.

They walked, slow, deliberate, uncertain of exactly what they were doing. Their movement across the stone pathway through the yard was like a prayer. Each step slower than the step before. An untrained eye would think that they were standing still. A more attentive eye would recognize something else going on, that they were doing more than simply walking away from a porch. Something was at stake in ways that would surprise the two men, but not surprise Debra so much. She knew things happened that could never be explained. She knew there were things in the world—actions, desires, hopes, casual glances, and inadvertent touches—that were not meant to be understood.

Fred and Jim felt deep in their souls that they were leaving something behind on that porch. They knew they were losing something that neither one of them had strength or knowledge enough to say. And what they were losing or leaving back there on that porch might never be found again. They sank deep down into the knowing of that. Some things had to be lost, had to be abandoned, to clear a space, for whatever it was that they were about to come to know. So the two men left the porch, careful not to read each other's minds, careful not even to read their own minds, for that matter. They walked, empty of thinking, quiet of talking, careful not to look the other in the eye. In this way, they embarked on their pilgrimage.

Even in the presence of each other, the two men felt that they had entered into a strange solitude. Their cracked hands were confused by not having bottles of beer to hold onto. Their voices uncomfortable with so much more silence than the silence they had grown accustomed to, the familiar quiet of not talking. This silence was becoming something else. It was not just that they were not talking. Inside this silence, a stillness began erasing something. Before pushing the gate open to leave the yard and step out into the alley, they looked back at the porch, then up at the tiny light shining through the second-floor bedroom window. They stood like that, staring at something that seemed to flicker in the shadows. Then, whatever it was that the two men had left back there flickering on that abandoned porch, vanished.

In the alley, they returned to walking more like the men they were meant to be, and Fred broke their silence the moment his shoe crunched down into the first bits of gravel. "Bob will know. If anyone knows the invisible places, it's Bob."

Debra's brother Bob was darker than the blackest of the blackest sheep in any family; he was the lost soul of the Schmidt clan, some said the most lost soul in all of Pittsburgh. A few years ago, a man took a photograph of Bob while he was walking down Grant Avenue and that photograph trapped his soul inside it. Fingerprints now covered Bob's soul. He was the only man who had left Pittsburgh and never returned, even though his body seemed to still be in the city, walking the streets, tripping into and out of bars, cleaning gutters and shoveling snow, and petting every single mangy cat that wandered through the night shadows and crossed his path.

Bob had spent years in Vietnam, volunteering again and again to re-up. He told everyone that he had a madness that needed fuel, and that Vietnam had that fuel in the trees, in the mud, in the tunnels. The bullets flying through the air in Vietnam behaved differently than they did in America, and those bullets did something to his thinking. They got inside his blood and spoke to him. Bullets seemed smarter there. They had a conscience. Ancestral voices and desires possessed them. He spoke, slow and careful, to the bullets. Held deep conversations with them about time and space. He knew those bullets could distinguish right from wrong in ways that baffled human beings. "For thine is the kingdom," the bullets whispered as they flew through the air, and Bob whispered back to the bullets in prayer, "the glory forever and ever." And he asked not to be led into temptation, and he begged forgiveness for each trespass, and the bullets answered.

Many, many nights, after trying to understand the bullets, he wrote home about his skin being boiled, about his skin changing colors, from white to grey to orange to white to ashen to orange to white. He wrote about blisters burning his tongue, about eyes that could no longer see during the day, eyes that could only see into the night. He wrote letter after letter about footprints, naked footprints that had something of a dead man's departed soul in them, something twisted and unspeakable, but present and waiting. Something beyond beautiful. Something beyond love. A promise that had been broken in a life that had come before this one.

And when he wasn't writing home about all that, he was learning from the bullets, about all the ways that the bullets were changing his understanding of how things worked in the world, about boots tied to tree trunks, about footprints that refused to go away, about pain that felt new and more playful than any pain he had ever experienced before, and when Bob wasn't writing home to dear, dear mommie and daddy and sister and his few, so very few childhood friends, about all that, he wrote home about the women of Vietnam.

These women showed Bob their water skin. They showed him the bruises that marked the earth and showed him the pained roots of trees so ancient and strong that the trees defied the bombs falling one after another from the sky. They showed him places where the earth opened and where the light came through. One woman taught him to fly, in only seven days.

There were rumors that Bob had died four or five times over there. One story was of Debra and Bob's mother carrying a body bag full of his mangled remains off a plane, lugging it up over her shoulder and carrying it all the way home from Washington International Airport to Pittsburgh, then dropping his body in the Allegheny River. Dumping him there and not telling anyone about it until months later. But that story could not be true, because Bob did eventually come home, and because he is still alive. When he finally came marching home, or however it was that he made his way up to the front door of his parent's house, he came home crippled, trapped in a wheelchair, and unable to speak more than five or six words at any given stretch, but some miracle, one that baffled every doctor in Pittsburgh and beyond, cured Bob, and he started walking again. He stood up and said, "Fuck it all. I'm from Pittsburgh." He looked his physical therapist in her eyes and walked down the hallway and out the door. He walked until he got to where he wanted to go. And once he got there, he stayed. "Too much nonsense in my body," he told Debra.

And then the voices started. They came through the walls. They seeped through his clothes. They came through the shower and through the telephone wires. They rained down on him from the ceiling, from the skies, from the moon. He told Debra that the moon was raining dust on his head, and the skies were raining stars down on him, and it hurt. It hurt like hell. These voices came at him from every direction. And they wanted Bob more than any woman had ever wanted him. They teased him. They seduced him into going into corners and alleys where no man should ever go. They destroyed whatever was left of peace on earth, just like the bombs that were dropped through the hills of Vietnam destroyed women and children, destroyed their bones, their stories, their homes, their villages, destroyed everything about who the people of Vietnam thought they were and destroyed everything they thought they valued, so that every one of them would eventually shut up and become Americans. Those voices cut into his flesh, into his heart, turned his soul orange with surrender, and all he could do was scratch and scratch and scratch at his skin, tear away at the rashes left by the voices on his skin.

The insides of Bob's eyelids turned orange with remembering more than what was necessary to remember. His eyes quit being so beautiful and became wild. He saw angels pissing white urine in the corners of bombed-out churches and temples. He spoke to these angels, these visions of loveliness, but they ignored him. These angels spoke in tongues and wore clothes that drove Bob mad with desire. He saw this, but wished he had never seen any of it. He saw weeping dogs sleeping on porches of abandoned houses. His heart hurt like a broken window. He heard voices that he dare not meet in dreams. Roots that clutched. Trees that grew out of stony rubbish. He did not know that death had undone so many. The green of Vietnam burned away. Bob bled orange blood. His fingertips turned orange or green or some other color. His words became colors. Eventually, he learned to live with the voices the same way that he learned to fly.

And that was when Bob began writing letters. He could not stop himself. He feared the letters he wrote were not true; he feared that he was not actually writing them. He stopped people on the streets and asked them if they had received letters from him. He wrote to Debra asking her to be honest, asking her if his letters made sense and if she could deliver other letters for him, secret letters to boys and girls who did not quite yet know better. He asked her if orange was still a color, that, if only she could buy an orange crayon for him, everything would make so much more sense. He did not want a whole pack of crayons. There were too many colors in an entire pack. He just wanted orange, only orange. He felt there was too much blue in the world, that the planet was making poor decisions about color and weather.

He told Debra he wanted to call her, but that he had to be careful, that there were reasons telephones carried voices. He asked her if they were on to him. Them. They. If they knew more than they needed to know. He asked if it was safe to watch television. He thought television was a bad idea, had always been a bad idea. Most televisions knew more about him than they had a right to know. "What makes you think," he asked Debra, "that a television is not watching you? What makes you think you can ever really turn off a television and be certain that it is off?" He hated the way that televisions waited everywhere, in hotel rooms, in waiting rooms, in bedrooms, in living rooms, in bars. They were everywhere, and, when they were not turned on, they were waiting and watching.

Bob told Debra he would rather live in the darkness. In a cave. He wanted her to join him. He drew a map for her and told her that Mary Shelley wrote Frankenstein in a cave or in a bed or in a dream. He knew a cave had something to do with it. He hoped to meet Mary Shelley in a cave. He thought it would be interesting. He thought they would have a lot to talk about. He looked for Mary Shelley in The Hang Son Doong. He whispered her name in those caves, whispered her name into the walls of the caves. He begged her not to be jealous, that nothing came of it. Bob asked Debra if she was disappointed in him. If she was too old or if he was too young for any of this. Or if she worried because he was her brother and she was his sister and that things had happened before they were born and told her that none of that was their fault. Things like that just happen. They could not do anything about any of that. He liked how rain looked on her skin. How, when her hair got wet, things were bound to happen.

Then he asked Debra if the world had let her down. He feared living in a cave would change what people thought of him. He tried to wipe the voices off his skin the way Debra scrubbed away her acne. Nothing invisible is ever invisible for long. Everything that appeared to be invisible was just waiting. He dreamed of writing letters that would make people happy without them knowing why they were so happy. He said that sometimes you just have to give into it all.

At first his letters were innocent enough, the kind you could read in public, on a bus, the kind you could show to your mother. They were polite and were written with a grammatical finesse that was rare for someone who had grown up in Pittsburgh. And they were pleasant and did not mention anything that might disturb an impressionable mind. Then he started writing long, eloquent, delirious love letters, insanely erotic letters, to Marcia Brady, the actual character, not the actress. Not that Maureen McCormick, Bob never wrote to her. Maureen McCormick was nobody; she was just a shadow of Marcia Brady, a stand-in for the real thing. And Bob decided he wanted to marry Marcia Brady, of that he was certain. He had convinced himself of his love for her. He wanted to marry her on the Brady Bunch television show itself, in some exotic location. Hawaii or Guam. He promised to do more than love, honor and obey her. He promised to show her what a cloud could feel like on her tongue, he promised to take her to the hiding place of the true moon, the one that God kept hidden in the jungle, the one the woman showed him when she taught him to fly. He promised to open his heart and show it to her. To give it to her, to say, "Here, Marcia, this is yours. You can have it." He promised to do things to her, things that were better left unsaid for now, things he would tell her about over coffee.

Bob waited for Marcia Brady to reply. He waited for her to call. Vietnam taught him patience. He waited for her to say something one night on the show, to let his name slip out from between her innocent lips. Lips so innocent they were not yet any color. He promised to teach Marcia to fly.

Bob loved Marcia Brady, loved her even more deeply than he loved the Eartha Kitt Catwoman. When she refused to write to him, Bob became suspicious of her stepfather. He felt that Mr. Brady knew nothing about Vietnam. That he was living in his nice comfortable two storey house, tossing a football with his sons, pretending there was no war, pretending the war never happened, pretending Bob did not exist. He thought Mr. Brady was capable of more harm than good. He wrote letters warning Marcia, suggesting it was best if they eloped. They could meet in Ohio, near that river or lake that was always catching on fire.

He loved her in ways that were deeply troubling to everyone in his family, except Debra. He loved her in ways that disturbed everyone in the neighborhood. He loved her in ways that made everyone suspicious of what else a man capable of loving Marcia Brady might be capable of wanting. If he wanted Marcia Brady in the ways that he wanted her, imagine how he would want your daughter and what he might do to your daughter and how that would change everything.

Fred and Jim knocked on the door that led into the house where

Bob lived. They stood quiet, perhaps listening for those voices that haunted Bob to seep out of the walls and infect the two of them with Bob's madness. They waited under the glow of Bob's piss-yellow porch light, like two orphans waiting outside the door of a family who had promised to take them in, but had moved away to some other town or who were simply refusing to answer the door.

"You still believe in any of this?" Jim asked.

"Any of what?" Fred replied, and knocked again.

"Waiting. That there can ever be an end to waiting?"

Fred eyed Jim like he had broken a sacred promise. He shook his head, balled his fingers into a fist. "Wish I could just punch a hole in all this waiting. Stop it that way. With my fist." Fred unclenched his fist. "Something's changed in all we've been doing or not doing, Jim. The waiting has become something else, something I never meant for it to be. I'm not sure how waiting can escape like that." Fred knocked again.

"That's not possible, Fred. Can't be. Waiting can't hide or go away or change. Waiting is not like that. It's just the space that opens between wanting something and that day that comes when you have the thing itself. It's not hiding. Debra got Lucas lost. We've been standing on that porch and Debra has not changed any of what she is saying. And the waiting has been just the space and time keeping our desire separate from Lucas. It is that simple. Nothing more. Waiting is different from hoping. So what is this?" Jim asked. His lips were tired and old, so much older than they were yesterday, so much older, rougher, more in darkness than in light.

"We can end it now," Fred said. "The waiting. I believe that, Jim. I think we have begun it already, leaving the porch put an end to it. Maybe we're the ones that have escaped waiting." He knocked again, looked at his knuckles. "I think we got settled with waiting, not disturbing anything. You live with something long enough, you tend to get used to it, comfortable with it. Debra's pacing. Her chanting. Her long silences. Drinking eight, ten beers a night. Picking paint chips off the porch railing, instead of sanding it down."

While they were still trying to figure out what it meant to wait and what it meant now to no longer wait, Bob emerged from behind the darkness. He just stepped out from inside the shadows the way the river ghosts along the Monongahela appear out of the fog. He seemed to be pulling some of the darkest shadows with him as he walked around the sharp corner of his house toward Fred and Jim. "Quit your knocking. I'm not in there," Bob said. He walked up to the bottom of the porch steps. "Can't sleep in this heat. Want sleep, but can't have it. Better this way, I guess. Dreaming in this heat doesn't do anyone any good." He shielded his eyes from the darkness the way most men shield their eyes from the sun. "It's brutal. The darkness. Too much of it isn't so good for anyone, not even me." He squinted up at Fred and Jim, wiped darkness or sweat or some invisible threat away from his forehead. "You two out roaming the night? Up to no good? Grown tired of the safe neighborhoods, that sanctuary of that porch of yours, and want some trouble? You look for it in the right places, you are bound to find it. Trouble knows where to wait."

"Lucas," Fred said. "We want to put an end to this, Bob."

"Thought you were going to just endure it."

"It's no longer the right thing to do."

"My sister know you're here?"

"Debra never sleeps, not even for five minutes. There is no peace. She says she can never die in the way that she wants to die. You know what she means? What she wants?" Fred searched Bob's eyes, his mouth, for some sign that he understood what Fred himself could not understand about Debra. He hoped there was something in the brother-sister bond that could make everything clear.

"Looking is as painful as waiting, Fred. You need to know that before we stir any of this up. Looking won't take any of the pain away. It won't distract you. It might even deepen the pain. Sometimes looking takes you closer to that one cry, the one neither you nor Debra ever let out, the cry that none of us has cried. None of you have cried your own cry yet, the cry that is personal. It's an ancient cry, and once you cry it, it doesn't ever go away. Your body re-members it. It's a cry for your own pain that comes when you realize you have to live the rest of your life with this loss, with what's no longer ever going to be there again."

Bob walked up onto the porch, put his hand on Fred's shoulder. "It's safer to wait. You wait, you might never have to let that cry out of you. You might be able to bury that cry inside of what you call your hope." Bob pulled open the screen door. "Go on. Get in." Fred and Jim walked into Bob's house. Bob looked back out at the night as if he expected a ghost to be following him, then he walked into the house.

CHAPTER 16

Up and down the avenue, in and out of the shadows, walked the girls—the true-to-life girls, the would-be girls, the if-only girls, the once-upon-a-time-I-was-that-young girls. The elderly, the nearly too youthful, the girls who clearly knew better. Boys walked the avenue, too, or they leaned against streetlamps. Beautiful boys. Fair and tender boys. They made their way into and out of cars. All night long, deep into the early morning. Everything imaginable was permitted along the backstreets or in the side streets of the North Side. More than everything imaginable was permitted in the alleys. A tragic end awaited nearly every one of these girls and boys, and every girl and boy was aware of it. Felt it near to their skin.

Sylvia wanted to escape such an ending. She felt that she knew more about how to control her body than most other girls. She did not so much work the street as simply walk it, moving her feet from here to there. She knew she did not mean anything by any of what she did in those lonely front or backseats of those cars smelling of cigarettes, fast food, and beer. She hid nothing beneath or inside her movements. Each touch was simply and precisely that, a touch. Each word was merely that, a word. Nothing more. Nothing less. She held back her unspoken dreams of a place where she could love what she chose to love, in whatever ways she needed.

Every desire has some relation to madness. Desires invent new desires, and Sylvia believed the worst desire of all was the desire to be loved. The more anyone believed in their desire, the more they thought it real, the more it forbade them from ever coming to know it. Sylvia thought love forbade you from ever being loved. She knew that you could never go out looking for love, that love was something that broke into you. Love tore down your walls, broke bones, paralyzed you. It knocked you off your feet. Made you beg some unknown god to help you begin breathing again. Love didn't just penetrate you; it got inside you and it stayed. It tugged and yanked at you. You became it.

Sylvia never risked revealing any of those beliefs or any of her other beliefs to anyone. Even when men asked her to tell them her dreams. She only told them what they had convinced themselves they wanted to hear. She gave them their own secrets back to them, without them even knowing she was doing that. She would tell them, "Beg." She would say: "Suffer." She would say, "Yes"; unless she felt they needed to hear her say, "No." She would say, "Touch me here and there and here again. Yes." And she would say, "Again." And her voice would be soft. And her eyes would close almost as if she had done nothing to close them. And the men would go about finishing what they thought they had started.

Sylvia told those men she had to leave home. She made a little sad face and nearly cried when she told this story of fleeing a home damaged by parents. She told them that she was a runaway and that she felt she was too innocent to be doing any of this, but that she would do this for them, for them she would do what needed to be done. Sylvia told these men that one night her father sat down in a chair in the kitchen to have a cup of tea and the chair gave in and shattered into a million tiny pieces, and her mother said simply, with her tired mouth, that now they would have to kill one of the children. Sad as that thought was to her mother, there was no other way. What else could be done? There was not enough money, and, now, there would never be enough chairs at the table. Where would they all sit? Her mother sounded so sad, and Sylvia's little sister would have cried, if she could understand what she was hearing her mother say. So, Sylvia told these men, "I had to leave home." And, even though those men had lived so many more years than Sylvia had lived, she knew what none of these men dared to know: that there was nothing to lose. Nothing. Not misery. Not joy. Not love. Nothing. She knew that everything these men feared losing the most, they had already lost.

Sylvia's father told her that she had nothing to fear, not in this life. He told her this nightly. Hush little baby, don't say a word. Ever. Don't you ever say a word, little baby. Poppa's gonna this, Poppa's gonna that. And you'll still be the sweetest little baby in Pittsburgh. Good night, baby, sweet dreams. And this man told Sylvia that there were no mysteries anywhere, not in her heart, not in a man's words, not in the quiet of night. He told her that even this was not a mystery. Her father taught her that perhaps the only mystery was that there is no mystery, that there never was a mystery. She held onto her father's cynical wisdom, but did not give her trust to it. She was convinced that mysteries were everywhere. From the bottom of the staircase, her mother would scream: "Say your prayers, Sylvia. Pray the Lord your soul to keep." And her father would whisper, "Don't cry."

Sylvia never meant anything when she got into car after car after car. She knew what she was doing; she just did not mean anything by any of it. And, like she knew there were no mysteries locked inside her father's bedtime stories, she knew there were no mysteries in any of those cars. Men rolled down a window, a door opened, and Sylvia simply stepped in. The door closed. She rode down the avenue in the man's car, then up a side street. Later, they drove back to the avenue, the door of the car opened, and she stepped back out into the night. The car itself sped away, off on an important mission to be elsewhere. She did all this night after night, because she wanted to escape the cold in winter or because she wanted to escape the heat in summer. It was truly that simple.

Sylvia wanted someone to take her where she would never hear her parents calling her name, never hear them calling her for dinner, calling her for Christmas morning, or calling her simply for the sake of calling her. To not hear her mother call her the spitting image of all that broke her heart, to not hear her father call her the child who would never, not in this lifetime, ever know any better. To not hear her father tell her that he saw in her the spitting image of his own diseased heart. She no longer wanted to be anyone's spitting image. And she did not want to hear her father say that no girl should look like her. What kind of girl goes around looking like her? With those eyes and those hands? Those eyes? What kind of girl, her father asked, what kind of daughter would dare to have eyes like hers? She wanted to be away from a father who told her that there are things in life that can never be taught; they can only be learned in the darkest corners of the earth, and learning is never simple. "You have to lose something in order to learn something," he told her. "What are you willing to lose?" He asked her, and he moved so close to her that she could feel her father inside her.

Sylvia hoped to someday be far, far away from that house where her mother knitted sweaters and scarves for babies who would never be born, where her mother smashed pink hearts and yellow moons and orange stars and green clovers with a hammer, because she hated that leprechaun more than she hated that man, her father, the man who stole her mother's car and her mother's savings and her mother's heart and her mother's trust of country and western love songs, and fled across the wide open spaces of America to Arizona or some other godforsaken place, surrounded by women with knees and elbows that seemed to be in the wrong place. Sylvia wanted to flee that place where that woman mourned that man with impossibly high cheekbones. "Like you, Sylvia. Like you. He had cheekbones like yours. I see him in you," her mother sang to her daily, each morning waking Sylvia with that little song, to remind her whose daughter she was, so she would know what she descended from.

And Sylvia knew her father would never die. She knew the man was immortal. She knew that he would just leave for good someday, just walk out the front door, carrying rabbit ears from the television set and maybe a suit or two swung over his shoulder, get in that beat-up Chevy Impala, and drive. But he would never die. She knew he would be even more alive to them, to her mother, to her own desires, once he left for good. Sylvia longed to escape, if just for a night, from that place where her mother broke coffee mugs because there were too many coffee mugs in the world, and the world needed more space. So she walked along the streets and bridges of Pittsburgh and slept along the Monongahela River with Johnny and became an orphan with a secret hideaway that felt like a home in ways that orphans never seemed to experience.

And none of this getting in and out of cars, and doing this and that, counted as anything other than what it was, so long as she never asked any man his name and so long as she never told them her real name, or so long as she did not close her eyes and think any of it had anything at all to do with love, or so long as she did not mistake any of these men for that man, that night, those nights, when she heard her father slip off his slippers and breathe so fast that she thought this is what a heart attack sounds like up close, or that this is how a train that is about to jump off its tracks sounds. So long as she did all this and so long as she could remember her name in the morning, none of it made her anything more than a young girl.

Sylvia's callused feet hurt from her standing for hours in her battered tennis shoes, which looked like they had been tied by a distracted child about to rush out the door at the sound of the ice-cream truck. Her fingertips were cold in the winter; her palms sweaty in the summer. Her knees, her ankles, nearly every joint in her body already arthritic and swollen with pain. Strange for someone so young. And the men always said that. They said, "You look too young to be out so late."

Perhaps these men knew a mathematical equation to configure a woman's age with how late in the day she could stroll down North Avenue or East Ohio Street or Liberty Avenue. "You're awfully young," they said to her. "How old are you?" Then, each man waited in his own way for her to answer. The way they waited told Sylvia a lot about them. The way their hands moved on the steering wheel or the way they reached over the car seat toward her body, her shoulders, the back of her neck. The way they used their eyes on her. She enjoyed how quiet the car became, silent and still, even locked inside those cars where music was playing or a talk show was playing on the radio; the car itself became quiet.

But the men rarely ever looked at her face while they waited, and they never looked her into her eyes. Instead, they looked down at her lap, at her knees or at their own hands or straight ahead through the windshield. Sylvia would move her skirt, adjust it just enough to create a deeper curiosity, just enough to show them that she controlled their eyes. She could make them move their eyes wherever she wanted them to, simply by breathing or by moving her fingers, or by crossing or uncrossing her legs. She knew men were trapped by their eyes, condemned by how they moved their eyes, as much as by

Doug Rice

what they looked at, what they wanted to see, by what they wished they could see. The promise that there would be more to see. Later.

Sylvia felt a practically childish power in moving a man's eyes from here to there and back again. Men hurt themselves with looking at her, and she knew that this little power she had was not so little. When a woman forces a man's eyes to look, and she holds that look there and convinces a man that what he was looking at will never change, then a woman owns that desire.

"All looking is preceded by a dream." Johnny told her. He said his grandfather preached it. All looking begins on the inside, before you open your eyes. Your insides determine what you see, before you even open your eyes. Sylvia liked telling men the things that Johnny's grandfather said. She liked watching how they looked at her after she said these things.

Some asked Sylvia if what she said was a veiled threat. They then looked at her like they wanted to frisk her; some actually did, checking beneath her clothes for knives, for guns, for razorblades, for puppies, for God-knows-what-else. Some told her that a girl like her needed to know her place, needed men like them to put her in her place. A girl like her was too young to say such things. Pretty lips like hers weren't made by God to frighten men. But Sylvia knew better. She knew exactly why God did what He did to her lips.

Those men who searched Sylvia never found anything unexpected beneath her clothes or beneath her words or beneath any of the places and things they went looking beneath. They only left their fingerprints where there should never be fingerprints. Then these men returned to clinging to what they thought they knew. Even though they found nothing there, nothing beneath, nothing but what it was that Sylvia was saying to begin with, these men continued to hold onto their belief in things unseen. They believed more deeply than before in hidden, invisible meanings that they thought had been written carefully between the lines and tenderly placed on the underside of the words; these men continued to believe more in what was not there than in what was there in her direct words and actions. And Sylvia could tell that these men were more curious about that meaning than about the simple, actual meaning of her.

When men said they wanted to tickle her, that they liked the innocence of a young girl's laughter, she warned them not to. Once she started laughing, she told them, her body became unpredictable, and her voice grew strong and loud. She screamed out her pleasure. And her screaming and her pleasure went on for days. It shook walls. Broke windows. Disturbed small animals. Books fell from shelves. Her laughter disrupted public transportation, changed the weather, and upset that old Mrs. Thornberry down the street while she watered her garden. It made Mrs. Thornberry blush and retreat back into her house, lock her doors and close her windows. Sylvia's laughter woke the dead, killed the living, and confused the undead. She truly was terribly ticklish. And she knew she needed to be careful. Unexpected bursts of laughter changed her, and no one wanted that, least of all these men living discrete lives in suburban homes with lawns and pets and wives and children.

Her father told her that it wasn't right for a girl to be so ticklish, to abandon her body in that way. "You shouldn't let that happen. You shouldn't do that to your body and to those around you." He told her that her laughter disturbed him, made him feel foolish and inadequate, that it gave her mother nightmares.

Sylvia's feet, callused as they were, remained ticklish. A tenderness rested beneath the thick skin covering the bottoms of her naked feet. She refused to let anyone touch her feet, and, at the end of a long day of strolling the avenue, she herself was afraid of rubbing her own feet, afraid of tickling herself. Even Johnny had to be careful when he tied her to the tree. Her shoulder bones were more ticklish than the bottoms of her feet. She told every man before anything started, and told them again while they were doing whatever it was that they were doing to her, to never put their mouth near her shoulder. It was not safe.

Tickling Sylvia led to more than fits of laughter. Her body became uncontrollable. Knees, elbows, hands, fingers, thumb, teeth became reckless and did things they would never do in other situations. And the tickling that unleashed her laughter also unleashed words that she never would think to say aloud. Sylvia felt blessed by being ticklish. She felt it was a gift and believed that girls who were not ticklish were more easily threatened, more easily controlled, by things being done to their bodies. Ticklish girls knew where they were threatened; they understood boundaries and knew what was fully at risk with moving beyond those boundaries. When she grew up, she wanted to start a tickling academy for girls who were not ticklish, for girls who could not laugh or who had forgotten how to laugh.

Once a man squeezed Sylvia's knee, then moved his hand up her thigh, and squeezed there, wanting to tickle her. She told him that he needed to stop that, that it would be better for both of them if he stopped. But he said that tickling her would excite him. "It's not about you," she told him. "It is not even about me. It is bigger than us sitting here in your car, wanting February to end so that we can say we survived another winter in Pittsburgh." The man's hand moved to Sylvia's waist. Squeezed her there. She was barely breathing. Her body tensed. Her right hand searched for the handle of the car door. "It is simply too dangerous." She looked into his eyes. "I need to go."

The man smiled an impish smile and pulled a feather out of his pocket. He acted like he was a magician pulling a rabbit from a hat. He even said, "Ta-da!" He expected Sylvia to laugh, he expected her to give in and let him, perhaps even beg him, to use the feather on her.

She told him there were clichés everywhere in America: in his car, in his bedroom, in his garden, along the avenue, up and down aisles in the grocery store, above him in the night sky. His dreams were drowning in clichés. She told him that he had never kissed a girl with his own lips, that his lips were drenched in clichés and subtle forms of sadness. Clichés waited inside doorways, alleyways, bathrooms, underneath carpets and rugs, in basements, even in basements lit by a single light bulb hanging from a string. Every American carried clichés in their bones. They had replaced sex and love and a good cup of coffee. They waited for men like him, assaulted men like him on a daily basis, laughed at men like him. Sylvia told this man that he should pick one of those clichés, instead of wanting to tickle a young girl in his car after midnight, while the freezing rain muffled her laughter.

"You would not know what you were getting yourself into, and, once it got started, there would never be any way to turn back." She looked at the feather in the man's hand. "My laughter is not meant for the likes of you. You can't buy it." Sylvia echoed the words of the Street Elder. She told him the night was getting late and that some things were better left unknown. He brushed her lips with the feather.

He was about to chuckle, a sweet, innocent daddy-like chuckle, the kind that happens in such a situation, before everything that could have been interesting turns into a cliché and is stopped from becoming pure and innocent before it even has the chance to begin. Before his lips could even form the very beginning of the chuckle, Sylvia changed. Her eyes. Her breathing. Muscles formed around her lips.

"True fairy tales catch on fire at the end, immediately before you can say 'happily ever after,'" Sylvia said. "What do you want?" She asked him, but she knew that he would never know what he wanted, that he could never know again what he wanted, that all that he ever thought he wanted was no longer possible. "True desires are private affairs. A true desire wants you to beg forgiveness."

The two of them sat still for a while. Sylvia listened to the rain; the man appeared to no longer be able to hear. She watched the rain form droplets on the window. She enjoyed the little rain bubbles on windows. "Wanting to tickle me is a metaphor for something else. What is it that you want to do to me, to yourself? You want me to know something that you can't know." She continued to look out the window, not at the man. "Be honest."

Sylvia knew how to make an offering. She felt offerings were important. She continued watching the rainfall, continued looking past the man, out the window into the night. The man slowly put the feather back in his pocket, unbuckled his seat belt, reached for the door handle, opened the door of his car, and climbed out. He walked down the street into the night rain, getting wetter and wetter and wetter. She watched him. She shivered. The car must have gotten colder with him gone, or maybe she shivered, thinking of how cold that man who wanted so much to tickle her must be in the rain. She watched him until he stopped beneath a streetlamp. He stood there hoping the light from the streetlamp would protect him from the rain, but the man seemed to dissolve into the rain.

Sylvia waited for the rain to let up before leaving the car. She walked away from the man's car, glancing over her shoulder occasionally, to look after the man, fragile and alone, under the streetlamp, waiting for something to change. She walked until the man disappeared, walked until another car slowed down and another man rolled down his window and smiled and said something about the weather, about the night, about broken dreams, walked until she stopped walking and followed another man's voice out of the cold rain and into another warm car.

She waited near the door, while the man moved aside whatever papers needed to be moved aside from the seat of his car. "Here, let me make room for you." The nice ones all wanted to make room for her in their cars. And this man or any other man would look at her and say, "You look so young, too young to be so alone." Every one of these men would almost let out this uncomfortable laugh from between lips too narrow and thin to be the lips of a human when they said it. And she would imagine these men, with barely enough skin in some places of their body and far too much flesh rolling over other places, teaching in a stuffy classroom in the suburbs, their bellies hanging over the belted waist of their slacks, their teeth going a little more yellow each day, their eyes a little less sympathetic, their breath a little more intoxicated by the simple evil of living their lives. And she would imagine boys and girls suffering in those rooms where these men patrolled the hallways, where they paced up and down the aisles of the classrooms, where these men never forgave any one of the boys or girls for being boys or girls. Nobody, not the boys, not the girls, not these men, nobody wanted to be in those rooms, but there was no other place to go, so everyone stayed in their assigned places, saying their assigned words. The boys and girls remained locked in those rooms with these men who thought Sylvia was too young to be so alone.

"Yes," Sylvia would say, "Yes, I am young, too young to know better, and too young to even know how young I am." Then she waited for their reaction. They wanted her to giggle, so she was careful to giggle, to hide her life from them and to give into their desire for the warm safety of the clichés that they were convinced were their own choices, their own fantasies, their own dreams, their own lives. They wanted her to be innocent, and they insisted she did not need to forgive them. They said, almost with the way they touched her or with the way they stopped their car to let her get out and return to the night, that they forgave her. Some actually went so far as to tell her. To say, "I can forgive you." But she knew something that none of these men knew, that most of them would die not knowing.

"Can I take you somewhere?"

"Yes. Anything is possible," Sylvia replied. She looked into their eyes. They looked like they had figured out every truth there was to figure out, the kinds of truths that would destroy a young girl if she knew them, the kinds of truths that would stop a young girl or boy dead in their tracks if they believed in them, truths that would break the hearts of boys and girls in such a way that they would not have the strength to go on, but Sylvia knew these men had gotten the truths wrong. That their truths were necessary lies they were telling themselves and telling each other and trying to tell their children, so that they could go on with their lives.

"Yes, take me to somewhere," she replied. "Yes." They usually simply took her around the corner to Dream Alley. Sometimes up Federal Street to the top of Perry Hilltop, where the view of the Golden Triangle was "majestic." A man once said that to her. He told her to get out of the car and "take a look at this view." She brushed off her skirt and wiped her mouth with the back of her hand, then joined the man looking down at the city.

He squeezed her shoulders together, tight, just like the cliché he thought he was escaping demanded that he should. "It's majestic," he said. "It truly is." He gently patted Sylvia on her back, not in that father-daughter sort of way, but more in that buddy or father-son sort of way. "Majestic." Sylvia remembers his hand. She thought it was easier for her to have pebbles cutting into her tired knees than to have a man pat her on her back. It never felt like tenderness; it felt more like he was being condescending. "When I was a young boy, there weren't so many lights down there," he said. "Too much soot from the mills. Now that's all gone, and you get this." He stopped patting her back. He placed his hand behind her neck and massaged her neck, occasionally squeezing it, sometimes squeezing it a little too hard. "You know what you know, little girl," the man said. "You can't erase any of it."

Sylvia wiped her mouth with the back of her hand again. The man released her neck. All that was wild came to the surface of her skin. Marked her. She rubbed the back of her neck where the man had been squeezing. She knew this moment was part of forever. She knew what eternity meant. Every night she knew it. Every man she met took her there, but they always brought her back. None of them were able to destroy what they so desperately tried to destroy.

The scars they left behind—the one on the underside of her left wrist, the one on her left ankle, a purple line that cut through skin and muscle into her bone, the one on her side, the scar of a terrible fingerprint on her skin that seemed to somehow move around her body—reminded her that her past was real, that it had happened, that it was continuing to happen to her everyday. She did not need some man, who thought he knew something about some truth, telling her that each man who touched her can't be made to go away. Every man is forever.

The man turned his back to the city and walked toward his car. "I have to go up north, away from the city, " he said. "You'll find your way." He drove off. Sylvia looked at the place where the car had been. For a moment she felt frail, then she turned back to the city and began her descent down Federal Street.

CHAPTER 17

Seeing a ghost along the banks of the Monongahela was not as rare as folks might think if they were unfamiliar with the stories that traveled from mouth to mouth. Often ghosts were seen walking through the fog lifting off the river, shaking off the river water, wiping river mist from their eyes, shrugging the cold off their skin. So, when Johnny first noticed a small white boy under that old, thick willow tree along the river, he thought for certain he was seeing his first ghost.

Johnny's great-grandfather, Clarence, wandered along the shores of the Monongahela trying to find a dry passage across the river, seeking a secret tunnel carved under the bed of the river, or looking for a boat cloaked in fog to ferry him across. "Water traps the ghosts of all our ancestors," Elgin told Johnny. "Water confuses their desire to return. Too much water between Pittsburgh and that place we want to think of as home, so we've been trying to find home here. These streets. These rhythms. It's why our skin is what our skin is. It's what this city does. Wailing for that long-lost dry land across the water, while standing at the edge of water."

Johnny's grandfather told these stories every chance he got, so there would never be a forgetting. The deeper skin truth. So that when the last person to know an ancestor died, the story stayed in breath, inside muscle, in memory. Death could claim the body, but not the story. To turn each story, each memory of each ancestor, into a phenomenology of breathing.

179

"Our great mother crying on the bank," Elgin told his grandson. "Imagine the stories lost in those tears falling into the sand, dying on that beach at the edge of the ocean, as men pulled her sons away from her, pulled them out of her sight. Her eyes quit seeing the day they took her sons. Those men stole her sons from her sight, from her embrace. They took the names of her sons from her lips. Her sons shackled. So she stood at the edge of water and became a shadow. Not without hope. Not fearful. Standing for all eternity on that beach, a faithful reminder to live this life. Her hands emptied. Life is not promised. You got to live what life you got."

In those stories, Johnny's great-grandfather Clarence sought some way to be forgiven for all that he had done with his voice, with his heart, with his hands, with his fists, with his pain, with his hunger, with every word that he ever uttered and soiled the world with. He needed to be forgiven so that he could cross the river and, if not find his way home, at least join the comfort of death.

Elgin warned Johnny to be careful around ghosts that wanted to find a way to cross the Monongahela. Ghosts promising gifts, ghosts whose words bore holes into your heart. He told Johnny to only befriend those ghosts who watched over the river. The ghosts who quietly stood in the mud of the river, who kept a careful eye on the river and kept their lips still. The ones who asked for nothing. Those ghosts carried the history of his ancestors, the stories necessary for living. They were the ones to listen to, if only to listen to their breathing, or to their feet moving over the earth. The ghosts walking near to the edge of water held home inside them, had truth in their decaying bones. They knew they were where they needed to be. Stayed without wanting to be going to some other place.

Clarence, like the other ghosts seeking a way to cross the river, had damaged the world, so he was condemned to stay locked inside the kind of world that he himself was responsible for having created. Death possessed an anger toward these men who had borne so much pain into the world. Such men needed to stay between death and life, to take on all the pain that they had created while they were alive. The afterlife locked Clarence inside this world that he himself, while alive, had created for Sula, his wife, and for his son and his daughters, Joie, Ruby, and Rosie. There was no forgiveness, not for his sins.

He would endure this world of being neither here nor there for eternity; he would trip over the rocks and skin his knees; he would cut his thighs on the barbed wire of this world; he would slit his tongue on the rough edges of his words.

Each time Clarence spoke a single syllable, he bruised his tongue. His lips and tongue turned more and more purple with every word he uttered. Blisters formed on the insides of his mouth and down into his throat. His saliva burned into these raw blisters. When these blisters scabbed over, came near to healing, something deep inside Clarence compelled him to speak, and the syllables lifted the scabs, opened the wounds. And he was forced to hear the noises of his own creation—the screams, the prayers, the sounds of his fist on flesh—all the sounds that he had brought into the world turned against him and attacked his body. He was condemned to never experience silence again. The tiniest sounds, the sound of a gnat flapping its wings, would attack him, attach the noise of its whirring wings to his skin and bones. Those sounds settled there. Irritated him. Forever and ever.

Clarence haunted the riverbanks of the Monongahela. Silent and cold. Dry and thirsty. Each word of each sin lodged in his joints. A nomadic soul wanting a rest that he would never attain. Coughing dry dust from between cracked lips, wanting water but never able to touch water. Even when rain fell down on the earth and covered the riverbanks in wet, dark mud, Clarence kicked up dirt, dried earth.

Elgin insisted that Johnny understand how deeply rooted these stories were in his own skin. "They make you into what you can't know you are," he said. "It's the sound of my father's voice inside your breathing, inside your talk. He is you as much as you is him. Your story began before you ever began. Before your mother cried her first tear. Before I kissed your grandmother. Before. That's when words begin making you. In the before. Words take over the story and appear in the breath that came after. My father was and always will be the beginning of the before. But he's not just there. He's here." Elgin pounded Johnny's heart. "He's in there. Part of you being you."

Before marrying Sula, Clarence had fallen in love with Ai. He was older than Ai. Much older. Years broken, like dried-out twigs of a dead tree, separated Ai from him. The years between those two were brittle like that. Still, she let herself go, and he let himself go. They became reckless with loving each other, reckless with words, reckless with throwing their bodies against each other. Sheets torn to shreds. Bodies covered in the marks of their desire. Bodies weak and exhausted every morning, every night. They pushed language out of the way, elbowed words into the forgotten places, and let out their true breath from rivers, from mountains, from skies, from moons, from trees. Mud-promises, those kinds of promises brought out by the spring rains that then dried up in the summertime heat.

Ai pulled Clarence inside her, not just his body, but his life's blood, his past, all of him. "I want to feel you breathing your breath out of me, from inside of me. I want to feel your breath inside my lungs." And he did what she asked of him. And he asked her to ask for more, to ask for the moon, to ask for his name, to ask for what she was most afraid of asking for in all the world, to ask for what she wanted to ask for, not what she needed, not what she thought he wanted or needed, but what she herself wanted. He wanted Ai to want, and he was willing to somehow disappear from all those places where he had been scarred and battered and to travel into the inside of her wanting.

Clarence liked knots, and he liked being uncertain and lost with what he thought he knew. He felt such knowing held something truer in it than what could be said in words. He believed all that he needed to know, all that he had forgotten or had forsaken or lost along those three rivers surrounding and coming to a point in the city, and all that he had come to know in the alleys on the North Side and off Liberty Avenue, was inside Ai.

She had strong blood. Stronger eyes. And she penetrated him as much as he penetrated her. She said his name so often it scarred her throat, dried out her mouth. Her lips bled from saying his sweet name. She feared she would wear away her tonsils. And she wanted Clarence. Not only did she want him, she loved wanting him. That act of wanting him drove her mad with desire. His breath doing all that it did to her skin. Love, like what she felt when Clarence touched her, was fragile like an egg, so he knew to touch her slow and patient, the way rain touches skin, the way frost melts from tiny blades of grass. He touched her in this way with his roughened fingertips, worn down by working in the mills, callused from pulling out vegetables, fingertips worn to the bone with years of living in a city of dust and heat. In this way, he carried Ai off, the way she carried him off to some other place neither had ever known before.

All the blood and all the sorrows of all those yesterdays washed away when she looked into his deep, old eyes. And she told him that. She told him straight what he did to her. How he woke up what needed to be awake in her. All of it. And she told him how she never wanted to go back to sleep. Not ever. That she was done with sleeping. She told him that she felt her name was safe inside his mouth. "The way you say it," Ai said, "The way you release my name into the world. You keep my name warm. My name's at home inside your mouth." Then she asked him to say it, to say her name.

One night, she took his hand and this woman, with those young eyes looking at his old flesh, taught him more about touch than a lifetime of women and of working in the mills had ever come close to teaching him. She turned him inside out that night. It was as if she made him a virgin again, made it seem to Clarence like he had never touched any other woman before in his life. She taught him that you have to dismantle a heart to truly see what a heart can know. "It's like opening your eyes in the morning and wondering where the night went," she said.

And Clarence came to learn that you should never touch any woman the same way twice and never touch one woman in the same way that you touched some other woman. Doing so is downright careless. "How can you expect to see a woman's true smile, that is only possible when she sees you, if you touch her like you touched some other woman? How can you hear a woman's soul laughing, if you are asleep with your touch when you touch her?" she asked Clarence this. Then she took his hand and guided it to the most fragile place of her body. He touched her as if he were a boy without a way for knowing what touch could do. Her lips quivered. And her moans that night would have broken the darkness inside any man. She taught him to use his hands, the tips of his fingers, to flirt with the impossible. She did this to him, and as they slowed down, as their breathing became quiet and the rain fell against the window of Ai's bedroom, she said, "Listen."

And when she wasn't busy saying she wanted him, Ai was busy saying other things to him, telling him all that she desired when she closed her eyes and stayed awake, more awake than she had ever been before in all her life. That kind of being awake that made the rust on her soul disappear. "Do that thing to my bone, there, that bone, do that thing that you do with your mouth, with your hands, with your teeth to that bone. There." And, like he was finding a way to say a true prayer, he did. And she would say, "Yes." Her mouth wild with laughter. Her throat soul-deep with the songs of ancient rivers. And then she would stop breathing for a while, not long enough to die, only long enough to come close to dying, long enough to see into some other life that no woman had ever given herself the right to see into before. A life that no man had ever given himself such a right to see into, either. She told Clarence to do this, to do that. And he did. And her breath would get stuck in her throat and stay there until she remembered how to breathe. A quiet longing that took her into the memory of the time before she had bones and flesh, a time when she was pure of words. And then Ai would say, again, she would say, again and again and again, your teeth. Just that. Your teeth. And her skin would wait, because her desire was so deep, and his touch would wait, because waiting was as much like touching as touching was.

And Ai began speaking in the original language, the one that had been left behind after the Tower of Babel had fallen. Her voice, her body, her mouth discovered that language, those first words, and she opened herself to them, and she screamed those words out near Clarence's body. She bit so hard into his collarbone she drew blood. Ai scratched into his back, dug her fingernails into his flesh. Left scars. Ruined him for any other woman. No woman could ever break into his skin again. Not ever. She infected him with her past, with all that she had done, all that had been done to her, all that she had taken on. She gave him this fever of all she had ever known, all that had crossed her path, all that had torn into her skin. She pressed her mouth against his ear and mumbled words that were like a breeze across a desert, lifting sand but making no sound, leaving behind no trace of a sound. Words that destroyed everything Clarence thought he knew about himself and changed him down in the very root of his knowing.

But never in public. Never in those places for others to see. Never for others to know. She wanted to keep all this away from everyone. She called it their secret. Flesh and screams locked inside a narrow bedroom. "Do not let anyone see us." She would lock the windows, lower the blinds, close the curtains, turn off the lights. She hid under blankets and covered her mouth when she was about to let out screams so raw that they even frightened her. And then one night she pulled Clarence in close and she said it. Those words just came out of her mouth like they were true and natural, like it was all that was left to say. She said she was falling in love with Clarence. She sat on top of him with him inside her, with sweat falling from her forehead and said, "I fear I am falling in love with you."

But Clarence worried she said it because she wanted it to stop. She wanted her loving like this to go away. He felt that maybe she had scared her heart with loving him. And he thought that by saying it aloud, Ai wanted to release it from her heart, that by getting it out of her body, love could not work its magic on her. In her voice, in her body, he felt this fear Ai had of falling in love with him. He wished she would let it go. He wished she would not fall in love with him, and that he could protect his own heart from falling in love with her, he wished Ai would just stay, would realize that words were stories that connected nothing with nothing.

His heart burned into his ribs like those purgatorial flames he had been warned about by his mother. He had not known such destruction before and began forgetting who he was. Ai said her parents would take her out back if they found out. Her father would unlock the shed in the far back corner of the yard and take her out to this shed and wait with her in the darkness until the neighbors had gone. Then he would beat sense into her. Her mother would wail, until the moon fell out of the sky and drowned in the river. Her father would mark her skin with failed poems, failed promises, failed prayers, failed love, failed promotions at work, and her father would mark her until she gave up the ghost of loving Clarence and came to her senses. She said he needed to understand this.

Clarence stood on the corner of Pride and Colwell Streets listening to Ai's voice, looking into her dark eyes. He felt his hands wanting to do something. His feet longing to walk, to make a getaway.

He felt something happening to his lungs. He felt a scar forming in his eyes that would never heal. And he heard a voice inside urging him to clear his throat of his desire for Ai, and to find other stories, other women, other bodies. But her beauty paralyzed Clarence. The dark skin of her elbows and the even darker skin of her knees, the insane beauty of her thin feet, her toes, her hands. He could not imagine ever seeing beauty comparable to the beauty resting in the palms of her hands. If he could have imagined such beauty anywhere else in the world, perhaps then he could have walked down Colwell Street to that other place where there was beauty close to Ai's beauty, maybe down Dinwiddie Street to Fifth Avenue to Red's. But those delicate, strong lines in the skin of her palms, lines that cut deep into her memory, into her heart, into her desire, kept him standing there. He would never again see beauty near her beauty. Her beauty cut into Clarence. The way her name felt in his mouth. All this paralyzed Clarence.

When he lay beside her, when he felt the girl weight of her body on his body, the pain of every heartbreak he had ever experienced in his life, the pain of every bone that had ever been broken in his life, the pain of losing his parents, the pain of nearly dying from starvation, lifted and disappeared into thin air, as if none of it, as if nothing bad, had ever happened to him. Ai gave this to Clarence.

So Clarence stood before her and waited, unsure of what he was waiting for, of what there was left in the world for a man like him to see.

While loving Ai, his world became pure light. He worked harder than he had ever worked before. Loving her, being loved by her, did this to him. He was more and more inspired with each breath. He swallowed all his fear, all his shame. The way he walked the streets changed. He poured coffee in new ways. Magical ways. He astonished friends, neighbors, and strangers with the way he poured coffee from the kettle to the cup.

Clarence returned to being a woodworker, not a carpenter, but a man who worked with wood until a shape appeared. He covered his floor with woodshavings, with dust, with joy. He created furniture that seemed to come straight out of his dreams. Furniture so beautiful no one knew what to do with it. And he did this every day with each hour, each minute of every moment of being alive. The world had never seen anyone so alive. And on weekends he drove his car down roads, across highways, over mountains, across bridges, wanting to make love with Ai. Wanting to hear her voice. Wanting to bite into her dark skin.

Clarence wanted only to taste Ai, to taste the way she lived her life. To taste not just her life, but to taste the very actions of her living her life, the way every moment of each day stayed on her skin, to taste this on her fingertips, on her lips, on her toes, on her neck, on her lower back. To place his mouth there and to wait. He could wait with his mouth there on her skin, tasting her scent, until the end of the world. He could wait that long. Longer if need be. With Ai, the memory of every other woman that Clarence had ever known faded.

And she wanted him even more deeply. She dreamed of him. Fantasized about him. Obsessed over him. Created worlds of joyful celebrations in her imagination, in which they had children, beautiful children with high cheekbones and eyes that startled every passerby, children with long, strong legs and nappy hair that astonished their ancestors. Children so poetic and so intelligent that they never learned to walk. They danced. They refused the mundane movements of walking. So they danced. And their way for understanding the world could only be spoken in dance. These children of Ai's dreams cherished her and Clarence. In her dreams, they lived beneath stars in a secret garden near a river. And she loved and loved and loved Clarence. And he loved and loved and loved her more deeply than the deepest deep of any river. They carved their initials in rocks, in the river, in the bark of trees, in each other's skin, in their dreams, in the walls of abandoned buildings, in sidewalks.

Then Ai left.

She woke one morning and did not call. And did not return his call. Then, in the evening, Ai called and said: "I adore you. I want you. But I can't be with you." And there was silence. Everything in the universe that could make a sound stopped. And Clarence could not breathe, let alone speak. When she said, "goodbye," he felt the weight of every single day that he had ever lived in his whole entire life fall on him. He felt the many years of his life break every bone in his body. In the distance, he swore he could feel a child dying on some highway in the night. His body turned cold, his heart quit; he felt his flesh covered by February snow in an alley on the North Side. A cold breeze cut through Clarence's broken heart. His heart cracked, and a winter fell on him like no other winter had ever fallen on him before. Then, an emptiness formed inside him, like his heart had been lifted out of him.

And Clarence became cold. Colder than that February winter that had fallen on him. He stood at the edge of the Monongahela River and cursed his heart, his foolishness, his grandmother, his ancestors. For more than a year, he wandered the streets of Pittsburgh unwilling to talk to anyone. He had given up on what words could do, on words carrying any meaning with them. Words, for Clarence, only erased what was there and true. And every time rain fell, he still heard Ai's voice saying, "listen."

Then Clarence met Sula. He told her he loved her. He said that to her. Those words. "I love you." Words. He said words to Sula. But that was all he said, all he did. Words. He courted her in threadbare clothes. In one-syllable words. In language and breath bereft of poetry and hope. They walked along the rivers, mostly in silence. They met each other's families and had very little to say, very little that could be said. When they ran out of things to do and places to do them, they got married. Sula said, "I do"; Clarence said, "I do". Later that night, they had sex.

Clarence put his name inside Sula. Put his name deep into the beneath of her skin. Deeper than a branding. And he told her to keep it there. To never forget how deep in her he could put his name whenever the urge came over him. And he told her to like it. He told her to tell him and all the neighbors how much she liked it. Wanted it. Begged for it. To beg him to give her his name. To beg for it in front of neighbors and family. To beg for him to turn her inside out with his name. And he never said he was sorry. Not for breaking dishes, not for the way he looked at her, not for the way he kissed her, not for anything that he did. And he did things no man should ever do, things no husband should ever do to his wife. And he did these things without explaining any of it to Sula. And he told her to be quiet, to sit still, to sit perfectly still.

Then Sula became pregnant from all that she did with Clarence, from all of it, not just from their bodies sweating in the dark bedroom, but from all of everything they did and said. Every bit of their life went into making these children come into the world. And their children—one son, Elgin, and three daughters, Joie, Ruby, and Rosie—were strong with seeing more than a child should see.

When Clarence looked at his children, he saw the children that were not there, the children Ai dreamt of. He saw only that, a burning hole of what was not there, and it set fire to his heart. Burning what he feared to forget and feared to remember. He put all his suffering into Sula. Put it in her, like she was nothing more than a sponge to soak up his sadness. He didn't know what else to do with the cracked and windblown pain that ate away at his heart, so he put it inside this woman who was not responsible for any of his old and tired greyness. And his putting it there was a greater sin than all the other sins he had committed in his lifetime.

Then he began tearing her apart with his drinking, with his mad lust, with his terror of being alone, with his wanting to punish Sula's body for being so beautiful, but not so beautiful in the way that Ai was beautiful. He told Sula that Ai's skin was so much darker than hers, lips so much fuller, and eyebrows so much higher, and flesh more delicate. And he made Sula repeat this back to him, to say that she was not beautiful in the way that Ai was beautiful. And he made her tell Elgin and their daughters that, if only Ai were their mother, they would be so much more beautiful. And he forced her to say all this out loud nearly every day. For her to remind herself of this, to remind their children of this. And the children—Elgin, Joie, Ruby and Rosie—sat with their tiny hands folded in their laps, with their eyes looking at their hands and hoping there was something there waiting for them in the cup of the palms of their hands. And their father, the man who did all this, saying no one would ever be so beautiful as Ai and saying it wasn't him to blame; it was this one woman who destroyed him, who stopped him from ever being able to love another human being again.

And for this sin of saying he loved a woman in words, when his heart remained closed, frozen, broken, for Clarence to say to Sula in words, "I love you", and then for him to do all he could to destroy her, and for him to never accept the gift of Ai coming into his life and of

Ai devoting time to being with him, and for him to not accept what all that it was that Sula gave him day and night and morning and evening, year after year—for these sins, he was condemned to walk in dust along the Monongahela River for all eternity and to never be able to cross the river to the other side. He would never rest. He would never be able to quench his thirst. He would never die. He would live eternally experiencing the weight of the words that he burned into Sula's skin, that he burdened Sula's heart with.

CHAPTER 18

Years before Bob returned from Vietnam, the Compson house caught on fire and burned completely to the ground. Nothing remained of the house or of the family, aside from stories, ashes, and a few scattered rumors. The house itself disappeared from the earth. This fire that put an end to the Compsons was the kind of fire that burns fire. It burned so hot that the local firefighters thought it would destroy the entire neighborhood, but through divine intervention, or something else holy and unspeakable, or perhaps through something unholy and most likely too evil for words, only the Compson house burned and burned and burned.

Neighbors say the fire burned for years. Some say it is still burning, that it will always burn and that nothing will ever be settled. The flames leapt up into the night sky, seeking enlightenment or redemption. The houses on either side were left unharmed. Children watched the flames reaching out of the earth toward those heavens. Their parents told them to be careful, to not get too close to the flames; in even softer voices, they told their children to pray and to be thankful. "God is good. God is kind. There are lessons to be learned."

When all that fire grew tired of being fire and quit burning, only a scorched hole in the earth and a small pile of ashes remained. Nothing else. No charred wood. Not a refrigerator or a stove. Not sad, abandoned mementos. Nothing. The house and everything in it had been reduced to a single pile of ashes. Everything that everyone wished could be forgotten, but that would never truly be forgotten, rested in those ashes. The Compson family was missing. They still are. Years later, a new house was built where the Compson house once was, and Bob bought that new house when he returned from the war.

With that Compson house burned down into the earth, no one in the neighborhood held onto any sort of belief. The words had burned out of the Bibles in every house for miles around, and the souls of all those who lived nearby were eaten by those flames. The faith of everyone living in the Compson neighborhood perished. More than any other kind of faith, these people had lost their faith in the possibility of enchantment. And that did something to each of them. It changed them in ways that made them doubt their children and made them think twice before taking God at His word.

Nearly every day, the oldest of Bob's neighbors, Mr. Fenneston, pointed all that out to Bob. "You can rebuild a house," he shouted over at Bob, while he was trimming his rosebushes, "but you can't ever get belief back. Lumber and bricks isn't belief. You can't make faith and trust appear out of thin air. You can't." The old man turned red in the face with anger. He nearly spit the words across the street at Bob. Drool dripped from the corner of his mouth. "You can't rescue what's already been gone, Bob. What has been taken is taken." He wiped drool off his chin with the back of his hand. "Every burning is a burning forever."

Mr. Fenneston shook his clippers at Bob with such rigor that they fell out of his hand to the ground. "It takes more than wood and nails and shingles and paint. More than all that," he said as he bent over to retrieve the fallen clippers. "More than anything you can imagine, Bob. You're not man enough to even begin imagining what needs to be imagined to get done what needs to be done. There's no resurrection, no rising from dead ashes." The old man spit at the ground. "You ruined it for us." He turned his back to Bob and cut into the stem of one of the rose bushes like he wanted to destroy the bush, kill it, send it back somewhere.

Bob tried to explain that he was not to blame. That it was true that he had done other things, bad things in that war, but that he was not the one who rebuilt the Compson house. Investors bought the plot of land and built this new house. He was not the one who started the fire. He had never seen the old Compson house, did not even know what it looked like, never met the Compsons. He was in Vietnam when all this happened. He just wanted to live as close to his sister as he could without causing problems.

On the day he moved into the modest two-bedroom house, Mrs. Drucker brought him an apple pie, one with a crust that literally melted in his mouth. "Why'd they even try to rebuild the Compsons' house? It makes no sense," she said. "What with all that happened and all that could happen, all that seemed to be waiting to happen." Mrs. Drucker appeared to be gazing in slow misery beyond the house that stood before her very eyes, off into the past, into a shadowy vision of those Compson windows that had burned away. "You have that same look in your eyes. Compson eyes. Like you left something you needed to do back in the past, and you still want to do it. The Compsons kept too much under their floorboards. Hidden cries."

"Those parents trying to heal their children of whatever it was they thought was wrong," she continued. "Giving them both, boy and girl, the same name, like there was no difference, not in name, not in flesh. Old man Compson had stories of his own, dark ones. And he had to tell them, like something was forcing him to. He carried them with him from his own past, up from Mississippi, in his bones and in his feet, carried them wet and lonely from other rivers. Angry rivers that flood too often. Stories that became a part of you once you heard them. Some say that's what did it, that's what caused it all to happen so quick." Mrs. Drucker told all this to Bob while his friends carried his scant belongings into the house. "Sorry as I am to say it aloud to you, I'd rather remember that house, their family, than see this. See the Compsons' two Quentins in the yard playing, mirror-like, as near to being identical twins as you can get without being true twins. Mistaking the boy for the girl and the girl for the boy. Likely there was not much of a difference when it came down to it. The past doesn't die just because it's not here any longer. You can't rid yourself of it. It stays with you in the worst of ways. What has burned has burned."

Mrs. Drucker looked at Bob with a tenderness that he had not seen before. He nearly blushed. He stared down at the pie, then he looked back up at Mrs. Drucker, nodded his head without fully understanding what he was agreeing with. The two stood in the quiet. Nothing much happened. They simply stood beside each other. Bob cleared his throat, tried to chase the quiet away. He thanked Mrs. Drucker for the pie and told her he had to get back to moving everything in the house. He told her that he did not want his sister becoming upset with him.

"You be careful with all that," Mrs. Drucker told Bob. "Be careful beneath the eyes of God, and you be careful with …" a light breeze carried off her voice. "Careful." Then Mrs. Drucker walked away. Bob watched her disappear across the street, watched other neighbors hide themselves behind their curtains, behind their blinds. When Mrs. Drucker arrived safely on the other side of the street, Bob turned around and walked up the steps to his house. And when he did, he felt all those neighbors staring back at him again, peeking through their curtains and blinds. A war does that to a man, makes him more aware than he need be, makes a man feel things in his neck, his spine, things that eventually break a man's heart.

The shadows falling from Bob's house lied. They had minds of their own, wandering souls searching for bodies. The pain that the Compsons could not take with them into the afterlife waited in those shadows. When shadows extended out from Bob's house onto the sidewalk, neighbors tiptoed around the edges of them, so as not to step on them or in them or, worse yet, to fall down into them. They feared it was possible to become lost, to become forgetful, to drown in those shadows, and they feared what that drowning might do to them. When the shadows disappeared at night, the neighbors became more troubled. In the light of day they could see where they marked the sidewalk, the lawn, their bodies. At night, shadows continued to mark the earth, but they disappeared into the dark beneath the dark. The night cannot form shadows; the night can only hide them and make them that much more dangerous. The way the past shadows your heart. There and not there.

Some mornings, faint wisps of smoke came up out of the ground in Bob's front yard. The earth itself was still burning from the Compson fire, and it seemed angry. Bob told himself the smoke was just fog drifting off the river, or morning dew turning into mist from the heat of the early sun, and rising off the grass. But in his heart he knew better; he knew the smoke was smoke. He smelled it, and, when he touched the ground where it was coming from, the ground was hot—not just warm but hot, hotter than when the orange smoke spread across the beaches in 'Nam.

Bob loved his house. Spoke to it. Touched the walls with his fingertips, almost could feel what would have been there if whatever was there in the beginning would have stayed. On the interior walls of his house, he wrote stories backwards, trying to discover where they began and why their beginnings mattered. Sentences never made much sense to him unless they caused more trouble than they solved. And he did not trust sentences. A sentence never cured anything; at best, a sentence was a thrilling misunderstanding of what you desired to say with your touch. He believed that each sentence had a shadow sentence, one more powerful than the physical sentence itself.

In his front yard, he carved his dreams into the trees. Not his hopes for a future, but his dreams that haunted his sleep. He carved the words of his dreams into the trunk of the trees and into their limbs, in handwriting so small that his dreams were nearly invisible. He was careful not to harm the trees. He wanted his dreams to live with the trees. He felt it important to have his dreams become a part of time, of weather—rain, sun, snow—and part of the seasons—blossoms, leaves, the falling of the leaves. His front yard was a green world. Bob casually dropped seeds on the ground and they flowered. Most mornings, he sat on his porch with his dreams in the trees and with flowers sprouting in the most unexpected places.

In his back yard, he spit onto the dry earth, hoping something would grow. But the dirt resisted. Nothing grew. God had made that patch of yard for keeping the dead dead. His backyard remained barren even when it rained. Without trees. Without grass. Without flowers. Without shrubs. The dirt itself refused to turn to mud. It stayed dry, hard, cracked. All nature of things broken beyond repair, things broken beyond recognition, things that could only truthfully be called things littered Bob's backyard. Some days, around high noon, darkness fell around the back of Bob's house, shrouded the yard in it, turned shadows into ice, even in summer, created the kind of cold that hurts a man's skin, that forces a man to remember the forgotten. The cold that comes before the burning.

Fred and Jim made their way into Bob's kitchen and sat down at the table. Jim held back the temptation to ask what time it was. He knew better than to ask about time around Fred, and, in a house like Bob's house, the question of time appeared naïve if not downright insane.

Bob pulled three beers out of the refrigerator, snapped them open with a bottle opener. He handed one to Fred and one to Jim. No glasses. Bob, like every other true Pittsburgher, believed it disrespectful to pour a beer from its bottle into a glass, and Fred and Jim felt the same. Bob believed in the purity of beer, and pouring beer from bottle to glass disturbed the essence of beer.

"This kind of heat is likely as anything else, more likely, to kill a man if he isn't careful with what he does and why he's doing it. Might even convince you to kill someone if it doesn't kill you first," Bob said. "In Vietnam, this kind of heat did more than any cease-fire agreed upon by men far away in air-conditioned offices. You best sit still in this heat. Dream of moving, but you don't go and fall for it. You remain quiet and still, careful not to disturb anything. The delicate balance. The mermaids in the distance speak to me. But I'm not going anywhere. Not yet. Not in this heat. They'll have to wait."

Bob looked from Jim over to Fred. Jim and Fred looked at each other, shook their heads. "Cheers, boys." Bob lifted his beer to his lips and drank. He watched for what might appear in Fred's or Jim's eyes, looked for something that might reveal a truth, the kind of deep truth that can only be expressed outside of language. He waited for the others to rest their bottles on the table. "Lucas has become a whisper," Bob said. "That's what you think?"

Fred looked up from his beer, wiped his lips with the back of his hand. "Lucas has been gone too long, Bob, and I'm worn out." He took a pull from his beer and tried to look Bob in his eyes, but Fred was never able to truly do that. The eyes of Bob nearly hurt Fred's eyes, so he looked away from Bob or shielded his eyes in the same way that he did when he looked too long, too directly, into the sun.

"Talk is worn out, too, Bob. There's holes in my words. Gaps in my sentences." Fred glanced over at Jim. "I can't complete anything. Barely able to finish my beers. And now Lucas has gotten lost among

Debra's words." Fred set his bottle on the table, kept his eyes on it. "Is there something you haven't told anyone, Bob? Something you've been holding back? Debra just mumbles. She just repeats herself."

"If you're not more careful, Fred, you'll end up submitting to your own myths. Lucas is finally where he needs to be. Trust that. You risk disturbing what needs to be left alone."

"We do this, and Debra will get to rest. Your sister would sleep again. Lucas would be where he belongs."

"We do this, and Lucas will only be where you think he belongs for Debra, Fred. It would solve that. And only that. And what would that do to my sister?" Bob took another sip of beer. Looked at Fred, then at Jim. Bob watched again for what was in their eyes, for what might slip through. "And Debra doesn't know you're here?"

"She would not want to know. She hurts. There's pain all through her. Everywhere. Her eyes. Her knuckles. Her joints. Her voice. She just hurts and hurts and hurts. It doesn't stop. She can't walk without it coming up out of her."

"Pain is part of it. Makes you remember that you are not the only one who knows pain. But if you want to do this, I guess we can."

"Take us to the places that don't make any sense, Bob."

Bob saw something uncomfortable in Fred's eyes. He glanced over at Jim, waited for him to say something, but he looked away. "I'm going to tell you two, again," Bob said. "You want to live inside a fairy tale. You want to believe everyone comes home. You think 'happily ever after' is the only way for a story to end. You've forgotten the fairy tales that turned ugly. You think Hansel and Gretel is about finding a house made out of candy hidden away in a forest. You have to remember parents did that. Parents are capable of doing that— abandoning kids in forests." Bob looked at Fred. "Parents do that."

Fred gripped his beer tighter, thinking that somehow the world would return to being the way he needed it to be, the way he wanted it to be.

"We can go out into the night, if you think this is necessary. Stir up the ashes. Wake sleeping dogs and all that other nonsense." Bob shook his head. He took a quick glance over at Fred, then finished his beer, pushed back his chair, and rose to his feet. "I've done this before. I've stirred up ashes, saw more than I thought was possible.

Couldn't give any of it a name. Just stared at it and felt my bones breaking."

Bob walked over to the wall and put his fingers on the words that he had written there. "You can't ever really know where any of it comes from." He spoke directly into the wall. "What it is. Or if it will ever go away. You end up finding what you never wanted to find. Some of what you find you realize you have been carrying inside you without knowing that it was there. You find places where the light falls through and other places where the light turns into darkness. A child burned beyond innocence in a field. It's seeing the impossible that makes you want to stop looking." Bob turned away from the wall. "You have to come to terms with that. You look and you might stumble over something that can never be forgotten. It happens, and when it does, you get scarred in ways you can't ever understand."

Bob stared down into his bottle of beer like he was accusing it of every disappointment he had ever experienced in his life. "You think you might believe in something, so you do all you can to see it. Force it to come out of hiding. Some things are hidden for a reason, Fred. You shouldn't question that. Evil, true evil, the kind that can't be seen until it's too late, waits at the gates, leans up against the skin. Evil understands more about waiting than love ever will. People hurry love. Evil knows not to do that. Evil knows to be patient." Bob tossed his empty beer bottle into the garbage can. "Beer is like every other thing in this world. Eventually it melts into air. You go on living with the memory of it and not much else. Maybe a certain feeling."

Bob walked past Fred and Jim and pushed open the screen door leading to the back porch. He turned and looked at the two men who seemed to be stuck in their chairs, quiet, and staring into all that had gone away. "You can't get to where you want to be going if you stay in those chairs." Bob flicked the lightswitch for the back porch three times to scare off any ghosts. "It's all we know to do to calm down the night. Turn on lights, carry flashlights, burn candles, do all we can to push the darkness back. God sits in a tree laughing at our sad efforts to change all He made."

Bob limped out onto the porch. Every now and then his feet did a kind of stutter when he walked. He'd tell those who laughed at him that his toes had a lisp when it came to walking in the heat. But the truth was, Bob walked that way because it was the only way he knew to walk, if he was going to save his soul. He took each step of the old wooden stairs one at a time, until he had made his way into his dry and dusty backyard, into a godless land that had been abandoned.

He stood there, under the faint glow the few stars strong enough to survive the hum of the city lights. He jammed his fists deep and tight into his pockets and let out a cry or a howl from so deep inside his lungs that it sounded like it rose up from some other world. Bob's burnt, green-yellow eyes watered up with tears and his heart slammed against his ribcage like it wanted to escape. Bob stood like that and waited for Fred and Jim to follow his path.

Pockets of grey smoke rose from the dirt. Burning. The earth hot beneath Bob's feet. His knees weakened, and he collapsed into a dark, murderous fit of prayer. Fred and Jim stood in the half-light of the doorway, staring. "None of it. None of what you do is innocent." He seemed to be talking directly into the earth. Jim glanced over at Fred. They both shrugged and released a small, embarrassed laugh. Bob's mouth still carried the ashes of that war, and he spit those ashes out of his mouth as if they were words. Any man who lives inside fire, the way he seemed to do, had no fear of Heaven or of Hell. A mangled and confused look of wonder and religious desperation took hold of Bob, like he was praying to see something that more than likely would never appear. He pulled himself out of his trance and looked up at Fred and Jim through eyes that had been ravaged by war and by love, by hunger and by thirst. "C'mon, we got a problem to solve."

The three men walked around the side of the house and out into the empty street. They directed their bodies in silence toward the heart of the city. As always, Bob led the way. A trinity of bewildered men who had known each other since kindergarten. Years of creating secrets and of keeping them. Each secret deepened their bond to each other, but each secret also filled them with fear of talking too much, or of talking too late into the night, or of talking too freely after having too many beers. A fear of simply knowing too much of what should never be known and could never be revealed about another person. Years filled with a silence that tightened and tightened. When they got together, Bob was the one who did most of the talking; that is, if you can call what he did with words talking. He never had much control over his mouth; the fractured syllables he put into the world crawled out from beneath his memory, from inside the crack of a broken rib, from the depths of the Mekong River, words or pieces of words bloodied and crippled by memories. The words that remained with Bob were ones he brought home with him from Vietnam. Words often tongued with fire.

Fred rarely visited Bob since Bob's crippled return from the war. But the wearing away of their deeper bond to each other began immediately after Fred married Bob's sister. You can't look at a man the same way after he does such a thing to your sister. Even with all those secrets between them, Fred went ahead and married Debra. A man marries someone's sister, he can't look at the brother in the same way again, and the brother can't ever look at his friend the same way again, either. You stop yourself from talking too often, and you pray more for ways to forget than for ways to forgive or to be forgiven. But none of any of that mattered to Debra. Even after she married Fred, she continued to visit Bob once a week, usually more often than that. Neighbors whispered about her visits. They feared the fires would come back. Fred kept silent about Debra and Bob, about how they looked into each other. Fred knew better than to try to understand any of it.

"All we have done," Bob said to himself. The universe remained undisturbed. Bob stopped walking, waiting for Fred and Jim to catch up. When they got to within hearing distance, Bob repeated again as much to himself as to the other two men: "All we have done." Fred and Jim did not seem to hear him, or, if they did, they ignored him. They looked like two old men, a broken hero and his hobbled sidekick, trying to find a way to escape from an old, faded Western, one that seemed bent on exhausting them. With Fred on one side and Jim on the other, Bob continued staring straight ahead and muttered: "All we have failed to do." The three men stared into the night. The darkness had buried Federal Street. They looked into the distance, at the lights of the city, down at the narrow street that snaked its way through Perry Hilltop. Never worry about the houses covered in darkness. Everyone sleeping tight in those houses even with all those bedbugs biting. Only worry over houses with lights on. There was something violent about a light coming out of a window setting

God's darkness on fire. The world began and ended here, at the top of Federal Street, or at least the world became something different here. All three men knew that things would never be changed once they were done. Some choices marked you and stayed with you like a stain on the chastity of desire. They knew walking down Federal Street on this night was one such decision.

CHAPTER 19

Debra's mother said that Debra suffered from a weakness in blood by having too much of her father inside her, fighting to get out. "That man must be turning you inside out with pain and longing," her mother said. "You got none of me in you. It's all your father's blood. Cursing you. His curses will set fire to the forests and will dry rivers of their water. They will rot your teeth. Your breath will be filthy with his blood, stink of it. And those curses of your father's will make you long for that which no girl should ever want."

But Debra did not feel cursed. She enjoyed her father's blood, enjoyed how it felt running through her, curing her of a past that clung to her, but she also felt her mother's blood, wanting her to bleed to death. The blood of her mother battled the blood of her father. Her mother's failed dreams left scars on Debra's pale, freckled skin, to remind her of the invisible scars left in her by her father. Debra often asked Fred to bring his eyes down to her skin to see if he could see the marks of her mother, but Fred did not understand what she wanted, could not understand her in the ways that Bob could, so she could only confess to her brother, not her husband.

Every day she sat on Bob's bed and confessed all her desires that survived from childhood. She wanted to grow up and write stories everywhere. She wanted to write them inside other people's books. She wanted to fill in all the white spaces in books of poetry with the stories that frightened the poets, the ones the poets turned away from and left empty. She wanted to write stories on bathroom walls;

to paint stories on the brick walls in the alleys of Pittsburgh; to write stories in chalk on the sidewalk on the corner of Fifth Avenue and Smithfield Street, directly below the Kaufman's clock; she wanted to put them into bottles and float them down the Allegheny and Monongahela Rivers; to write them on the bathroom mirror to men she loved and for men who loved her, the men who stared directly into her soul, the ones who could see under her skin. Debra wanted to write story after story on the inseams of the pants and on the insides of the collars of the shirts of the men she loved and who loved her; she wanted to write stories under the pillows of her lovers, on boxes of cereal, beneath tables in restaurants. She wanted to write stories on the skin of lonely women who were about to give up on love, so that they did not become bitter, so that they could know love, real love, not romantic love. She wanted to write tiny, fragile stories on the lips of women or men the day after their lover said goodbye to them and left them, just left them, abandoned them because they did not have courage to stay.

This woman, who told everyone in the neighborhood that she was the mother of a missing boy, wanted to write without metaphors, without symbols. She wanted to write straight onto the page and wanted nothing to be cryptic. She wanted to write tight, narrow sentences on money, sentences that made people stop dead in their tracks, so they could feel their spirit breaking when they bought something, anything. When she was young, she was given detention in high school for a month and her parents had to pay a huge fine to the school, because she had torn pages out of all the books that angered her. She had destroyed nearly every Hemingway novel, had crossed out words, torn out pages, had taped her stories over those of that cigar-smoking maniac. She changed all the pronouns in all of Hemmingway's novels from he to she. And it worked. She told neighborhood children that Hemmingway destroyed verbs, and there was no going back. Where could one go after such misery, she asked. She told young boys that she imagined a world without Hemingway and the rest of them, the rest of those miserable souls preying on a woman's hope, on her dreams.

Debra dreamed of love, not of falling in love, but of being in love, of being with love. There is a connection between love and being lost. Girls, even those hiding along the riverbanks, need to be brave enough to lose their way. Love was only possible without maps. Debra dreamed of a child, and of loving this child with all her heart. She dreamed she was still following that boy who liked matches, the one who disappeared when she grew up. And she wanted to cure the sorrowful voices she heard along the streets of the North Side. She told her brother of a man who appeared in the shadows whose touch could silence nightmares and migraines.

But dreams fade. Children, when they are not vigilant, fall into puddles, drown, become adults. They give up the ghosts of their own childhood and fade away from themselves. They begin trusting the stories told by their friends, by their parents, by their teachers. When children were not careful, they became lost to themselves, and eventually such children are forced to die inside their own skin, living out the rest of their days and nights in borrowed skin. "The world is bent on destroying girls. It's busy digging a grave for all children, every time the world tells you a story, every time the television is turned on, every time you listen to a song, every time you go shopping. The world is haunted by dream stealers," she whispered. "Do not go gentle."

"I dream the women I watched through basement windows in the abandoned steel mills along the Monongahela River were not real women and that what was happening to them was not happening to them and could never happen to them and would never happen to me and could never happen to my children," she said, while wrapped in her brother's arms. "I gave birth to daughters who were not afraid of my disapproval; I still dream I have these daughters inside me, but Fred just looks away. He looks out windows. Dreams are the only place left in this world where we never lie. I find the very root of wanting, and I taste this root, this stain that we carry." Bob rocked his sister in his arms. "We were not meant for this."

"I want to tell Lucas that I am sorry," Debra whispered while sitting at the kitchen table drinking a cup of coffee and wondering where Fred had gone. Debra wished God would turn her into Rip van Winkle, and she could fall asleep forever and ever beneath the maple tree in the backyard. She had heard rumors of people who did not know how to wake up. She wanted to join those people. But

Debra knew better than to allow herself to fall asleep until the beginning or the end of time. She was no fool. She knew to be wary of the promises of some dreams. She heard of dreams that seduced girls, dreams that made girls walk down hallways barefooted, down narrow corridors and out into the streets, through alleys, across dangerous intersections, and down muddy trails toward forgotten rivers. She knew to be careful around those dreams that wanted to keep a girl asleep.

CHAPTER 20

Sylvia pointed her toes toward the moon. Her naked feet tired and wanting to rest, the way Elgin's eyes had begun to rest. Her skin damp. Her ankles nearly broken. The exhaustion of climbing in and out of cars, of stepping up and down broken curbs. "Look at me."

Johnny looked at her, but there was part of him that had no idea what he was doing or what he was supposed to be doing. His eyes became shy. When he did look at her, he saw rashes on her pale arms and legs. Knees covered in dirt. Scratched knees that revealed more than a religious commitment to kneeling.

"The ropes," Sylvia said. Johnny looked. "My body tied flat to the earth."

Johnny felt that he no longer belonged there. He felt that she was too innocent and that he stole something from her when he looked at her, but he didn't know any of this; he only felt it. He waited while this feeling died the natural death of all sensations that have no words and that go silent and stay in your heart.

"See?"

He began seeing what he thought she wanted him to see, what he should be seeing. The visible that had no meaning. The visible that was simply visible. A beggar's callused palm holding coins. Johnny saw the burns from the ropes on her wrists and ankles. The mud on the ropes. He saw what so many men had done, all that they had left behind on her skin.

"Come closer."

Doug Rice

Johnny still did not know what she was asking him to do. "It was our idea. The ropes. The way the ropes hold me back from the edge of the river when my body wants to walk in my sleep." Sylvia stopped and looked into his eyes. "What would your mother see?" He shrugged. "Nothing," he replied. "She'd see nothing. A girl tied to a tree sleeping in the mud of the riverbank."

"You act like tying a girl to a tree is innocent." Sylvia turned her head to the left, stretched her neck. "Your mother would see so much more than there is to see. And none of it is here in these ropes. Everything she would see is locked up inside her own thoughts and fears. The Street Elder says that anything anyone says is nothing more than a mirror of what is already inside them, right?"

"Something like that," Johnny said. He looked at Sylvia, looked near her lips, then he quickly looked over at a leaf by her ear.

Sylvia watched his eyes. He did all he could not to simply close his eyelids. She could see that he did not want to see what might be waiting for him. She saw him looking near the edges of anything that might become visible on her skin; hesitant, but perhaps looking to see a conjured truth, instead of what there was there for him to see. "If you live your life, you have no control over what's happening. You give yourself over to the Divine Providence of the man in the car that shuts the door, as the Street Elder says. But when you tell a story, you have complete control over it. You take the story to where it is safe for you."

Sylvia watched Johnny's eyes, waited for them to go quiet. "There are so many stories buried here, in seeing me like this, and seeing you beside me. Stories waiting to be told." She arched her back. "My father, your father, any father, would see everything they wanted, everything they have longed for. Fathers would see all that they wished for, but were afraid to admit, to say, or to do. A father would want to rescue me. A damsel in distress waiting for her Prince Charming. Or he would want to change places with you. Maybe rub his hands together, thinking all of his dreams had just come true. Making up stories for what he was involved with seeing. He'd see his stories and would see nothing of what is before his eyes to see."

Sylvia laughed a little. "There's nothing for us to see here, because we see what there is to see, and that is all we see. Everyone else sees with their dreams or with their past. Those men in those cars can only see what they have names for. They only do the things that they want to do to me, because it's what they can say." She nudged Johnny with her knee.

She looked at the tender beauty of Johnny's eyes, the subtle beauty of his skin. Everyone—men, women; boys, girls; angels, demons; even the gods—adored the beauty of Johnny. The color of Johnny's skin cast a spell on everyone. Were it possible to fall in love with a color, everyone would simply give his or her heart to this color. Everything anyone ever thought they knew about color was changed by a glimpse of his skin. It was the color of passion, if passion were a color. Skin about to become darker, on the edge of a darkness even more beautiful and more powerful or seductive, or simply more lovely, than the color of his skin now at this moment that flees. His skin made the deeper fires of his memories, of his mother's memories, of Grandmother Thuy's memories and of his grandfather's stories became visible. The fires of these stories burned into his bones through his skin, marking his skin on their way to his bones. And Johnny's true task was to learn this language of his skin, so he would know the pain that needs to be remembered, because, once pain is forgotten, all that is part of the pain is forgotten as well, and pain becomes just that: pain, not history.

The olive lightness of his mother's skin lightly touched and transformed the strong blackness of his never-known father's skin, and somehow the two colors transformed the color of his skin into a color between colors, a color without words. A color beyond what anyone could ever know. The color of Johnny's skin made God blush, forced Him to realize that He had not thought of everything there was to think of, that God Himself had no control over true beauty. The color of his skin nearly paused, waiting to become some other color, and it was at this moment of stillness that his skin created this beauty, a beauty that troubled language and desire. Still, Johnny's mother warned him to be careful. "Skin imprisons a man, Johnny," Lehuong told her son. "Especially in this city."

Sylvia let out a soft cry, nearly a tear of the simplest happiness that she recalled from childhood, from infancy, a happiness she had felt in her body, when, as a small child, she touched her toes for the first time, the moment she found her toes and pulled them toward her mouth. She felt that kind of safe happiness when she lay down, tied to the willow tree along the banks of the river with Johnny. "Tighter, Johnny. Just tighter."

He started untying the knot, so he could tie it tighter for Sylvia, so he could give her what she needed. What she wanted. What she waited for. He smiled at her and watched her eyes staring up at the sky, searching for stars or for a glimmer of the crescent moon. Like Johnny, Sylvia felt more at home beneath the moon. The moon caressed her.

Sylvia held Johnny's gaze. "Do you know what tighter can do?" Even when Johnny tried to look away from Sylvia, she continued to look at his eyes. He pulled the rope tighter, tighter and tighter, and, when he sensed her breathing change, when he felt her drifting away from the river, dreaming her way out of her body, he pulled the rope even tighter. "Tighter is just a word until you do something with it," Sylvia said. She closed her eyes. "No one knows this," she whispered. "No one can." She coughed. Her eyes watered.

Johnny did not understand much of what she was saying. He looked down at Sylvia's perfect stillness and thought of asking her about T.J. He felt she held some knowledge beneath her eyelids. Some truth. He wanted to ask Sylvia if she walked in her sleep when she was a child and wanted to know if she had to be told that she walked in her sleep or if she just woke up one day in a different place than the place where she had gone to sleep. He wanted to know if sleepwalkers all knew each other, if they shared the same language, the same movement at night. T.J. told Johnny that each night he wandered out of his bed, barefoot and cold, and down streets of the North Side, until he found places so dark that God could not see into them. Places where he could disappear from God. In those empty places filled with the darkest shadows, T.J. quit being scared. He let his body relax, and nothing frightened him. He said that walking in his sleep protected him from everything that he ever feared. Johnny watched Sylvia's body relax as she neared the very edge of sleep, and he stopped himself from asking her anything.

Johnny knew Sylvia wanted him, perhaps needed him, to protect her from her own desires, to protect her from those nights when she suffered the dreams that nearly woke her, the ones that made her body, her lungs, make a sound like that of a neighing horse. Johnny somehow knew how to pull her out from those nightmares, to quiet her. He felt all that he experienced when he was near her had something to do with love that is love without expectations, without wanting. Just the love that comes with loving, the love of being near to and with the person you give the love to. Sylvia became more quiet.

"You want to see those ghosts?" She kept her eyes closed while she spoke. "Just wait for them. You wait." Her words softened, became breath. Her breathing shifted into the rhythms of sleep. Her ribs rising slowly, falling slowly. She whispered something that came near to being a word, but Johnny could not make out what she said, then she fell asleep.

He waited for her body to become perfectly still. He looked out at the Monongahela River. The water reflected the bright moon and a few stars. Johnny stood up, brushed the dirt from his clothes and walked to the edge of the river. He closed his mouth, took a breath through his nose, held it, then released it. Did it again. And again. He hoped to catch the scent of a ghost. Nothing. He stood. Quiet. Waiting. Closed his eyes. Waited a bit longer, then he knelt in the dry earth. He looked for the footprints of ghosts, carefully feeling for them with his hands.

The stories of all ghosts are written on the soles of their feet, and each step a ghost takes imprints their stories into the earth. Each footstep contains words and images that reveal a truth that speaking only touches lightly. Deeper truths are in the silence of the footsteps, the weight of their bodies on the earth.

While fighting in Vietnam, Elgin had taken photographs of footprints. At first, he did not understand why footprints were everywhere, why so many soldiers were walking through the jungle barefoot, until he looked closer and saw that they were the footprints of ghosts, that each footprint was a story. Story after story after story. So many lost dreams, cryptic hopes. So much death. He told Johnny: "You need to learn how to read footprints." But he also warned him about the power of ghost stories. They became different once they got inside you.

But he did not fear his Grandfather's warnings. He wanted to know Clarence's stories directly from those footprints. Words disappear truth, and memory forgets what most needs to be remembered; the true of the true gets remembered in skin, not words, and that truth remains there. The true is that stain. The marking. People call it a birthmark, and that is as close as you can get to giving it a name. A mark that you bring into the world with you. Other times, that mark is bigger than all that. It becomes fire, and it burns your skin, leaves its trace in pigment. You can't erase such a stain. You can't make a shadow disappear, not once the shadow of the story of a ghost covers your skin. Johnny's skin burned with these wordless stories that spoke of oceans, of the middle passage, of hysterical whips, of lanterns and barbed-wire fences, of jungles and chants. Only stories that live without putting words to them can ever be true. There is no escaping. You do not remember this past, not in your conscious living of your everyday life; you carry that past with you. A story may begin with words, with sounds, but it ends with skin.

He started sleeping along the riverbanks of the Monongahela after his grandfather told him all this. After Elgin told him that Clarence was trapped along the river, locked inside the in-between: not dead, not alive; not awake, not sleeping. Trapped by the passage from dry land to dry land over wet fear. The hulls of a ship. Wet. Hell waits beneath the water. Damaged by all the sins he brought into the world, Clarence was condemned to this place of fear and aimless nightwalking.

Johnny wanted to find the footprinted stories Clarence left behind. These forlorn ghost footprints were only visible at night, in moonlight. They disappeared at the break of dawn. Sunlight burned these footprints back into the earth; sunlight erased their stories. So, most nights, after tying Sylvia to the small tree, Johnny haunted the riverbanks, seeking his great-grandfather's stories, hoping he would somehow recognize his footprints.

CHAPTER 21

"There's no first sentence for what we are about to do, for what we have begun. No sentence can begin something that started so long back," Bob said. "You think that is the beginning of something. Beginnings are hidden." His voice sounded bruised, like he had swallowed something years ago that his throat could never forgive him for. He stared down Federal Street, not acknowledging in the least that Jim and Fred were standing beside him. "If there is a sentence for any of this, it's gone off elsewhere."

Bob had a way of refusing to say what needed to be said, like the tour guide whose true intention was to get you more lost than more oriented in a foreign city. "You know there is something amiss with the world when a father feels it is necessary to go looking for his child. Who is more lost, Fred? You? Debra? That child you've been talking about for years?" He turned to Fred. "It's the world we live in." He touched Fred lightly on his shoulder. "The world has gone haywire. It has. You think telling the truth of a story will change any of that?"

Fred shook off Bob's hand. "No," he said. "Yes. I mean, the world is one thing, and stories are another."

Bob wiped night sweat from his brow, then, once again, he shielded his eyes from the dark. "The night will do more to blind you than the sun, Fred." Bob looked down Federal Street, waited for Fred to say something. "If there is ever a fire in this city, this will be the first street to burn. Debra feared this street. Feared all that she might remember. The moon does that. Gets you to remember what could be easily forgotten or confused with some other life you once thought you lived. She never seemed to know better." Fred looked at Bob when he said that, but Bob kept staring straight ahead at the lights in the city, looking at time past, at a time before Debra knew Fred, at a time before she knew her innocence would decay. The time before Bob disappeared into the jungles of Vietnam.

Fred and Jim rarely knew what to make of what Bob said. They trusted his understanding of shadows and of mysteries, but could not put meaning to his words. The three men became quiet as they continued on their journey toward Pittsburgh. "I don't like what happened any more than you do, Fred."

As night slipped away and the morning opened, Pittsburgh became vaguely erotic and sinister. The three men reached the corner of Federal Street and North Avenue. The North Side, to Fred and Jim, had become nothing more than a heap of broken images. People tripped over roots that grew out of the stony rubbish of the cracked concrete of the sidewalks. Near Reddour Street, One-eye Pete practiced his street-corner theology. In the uncertain light of the early sunrise burning into the city, he seemed almost blessed by his madness. Most people have trouble being a saint in the city, but not Pete. Across North Avenue, Chas leaned against a tree, his tree. He appeared to be a touch desperate. The Street Elder walked slow and easy, stronger, more beautiful than any Pittsburgher had words for. Her beauty was fearless and came from living her own life, the one she created each day, and by allowing her skin, with each mark, each scar, and each wrinkle, to remember and make visible this life she lived. A few young people struggled up and down the avenue, back and forth, under the weight of the humidity. Old men and women, so white they had become grey with years of living in Pittsburgh, leaned out windows, slapping at gnats or flies or mosquitoes.

Johnny was home with his grandfather or on the banks of the Monongahela waiting for Sylvia. T.J., like Lucas, was missing. Disappeared. Sylvia climbed into a car. Her shoe fell off. The car pulled away before she had even closed the door. The shoe stayed on the curb about to fall onto the street. The Street Elder walked over and picked it up, put it into her purse. Some desires wear a woman down, erode her touch, and thicken the calluses on her skin. The Street Elder knew she was fast approaching the day when she would need to press her finger into broken glass to recall what touch felt like. She watched the car carrying Sylvia away turn up Arch Street.

Bob stopped in front of the Apache Lounge and waited for Fred and Jim. "Only true bar remaining in Pittsburgh," he said. "No one talks. You only do what a bar has been put on this earth for: You drink. If you talk, the bartender tosses you out onto the street. The true purpose of a bar is to create a place for men to drink in quiet solitude. A place to remember and to forget. Silently. In the dark. The trouble with you two is that you talk too much when you drink. Talk dilutes the drinking. And a true bar only has one beer on tap. Keeps life simple. You go in, sit at the bar, and ask for a beer. The bartender knows exactly what you mean. No more talk is necessary."

The three men took a few more steps, then Bob, like a retired tour guide, pointed out Rats Alley. "God does not exist in that alley. Remember that, boys. Be careful looking into it or questioning why God had to abandon it. And if you decide to walk through there, know what you are getting yourself into, know you are responsible, and realize that, when you wake up the next day, nothing will be the same. Breakfast will taste different. The texture of your skin will change. Your mouth and hands will suffer. Most likely, your heart will be damaged, not lightly damaged, but truly damaged, probably beyond repair. There are actions in this world, in this life, that can never be undone. You will never be able to look any woman—your wife, your sister, a stranger, your mother—in the eyes again. You will always look at the floor, at her feet." Bob walked on ahead of Fred and Jim.

Fred and Jim stopped at the entrance to Rats Alley. Sharp sounds, cuts in the fabric of silence, came from the alley. Sounds that these two men had protected themselves from while standing on Fred's porch drinking. The two men glanced down the narrow passageway but saw nothing that could be seen. The alley held onto its darkness, even as the sun rose. Fred thought that the darkness of Rats Alley was the dark dark that he had been seeking. A dark that killed light.

A woman's voice, making a mess out of a Tina Turner song, floated out a window. Another woman danced with her shadow while looking into a dusty window. Damp strands of her hair flew in the morning light. A handful of men, leftover from a night walking the tight corridors of the peepshows, or exhausted by the muscles and desires of the alley, wearing ruby-red slippers, looking like someone had pushed them off some cloud, moved from shadow to shadow. Occasionally, they clicked their heels together, trying to find their way back to Oz.

The same men and women crowded these streets every evening. Men waiting for night, then waiting for morning. Men and women in the habit of whispering until the sun rose and burned away their voices. Some man, wrecked by divorce after divorce, then by desperate woman after desperate woman, stood down West North Avenue. He leaned against an old lamppost. Drunk, deep drunk, soul drunk, angry, with a light touch of joy, the kind of serious drunk that happens to a man once a decade or so. Some white woman with a broken arm and a sad face tried to smile at what the man was saying. The man made a sincere effort to kiss her pale neck, but mostly he just missed and kissed only air.

Madame Rosie, the North Side's only remaining toughened, unpredictable clairvoyant, sat in a nearly impenetrable loneliness at her window, cloaked in the misery that had become her life. Her sign, promising divination, flickered, nearly sighed with desperation. Her eyes, over the years, had taken on the characteristics of the paranoid more than those of the mystic. Not one human being on this avenue thought that it was better to have loved and lost than not to have loved at all. Everyone on this street, every minute of their lives, felt that the small touches of love that existed in their lives, or that they had experienced in their youth, were star-crossed. A few prayed. Even though they knew beyond any shadow of any doubt that prayer would fail, knew they were sending words to an empty sky.

Fred and Jim kept their hands in their pockets. They walked slow and childlike, careful not to step in anything, careful not to look too long at anyone. Bob walked the way that only he could walk. The way of Bob. He stepped in whatever he stepped in, and doing so did not change a thing. He looked as long as he wanted to, at whomever he wanted to, and the people he looked at grew more uncomfortable than he ever would. He watched some boy down the street playing with string. Laughing like he was some cartoon hyena. He remembered once being that high, being alone in a hallway of icicles that kept melting or in a tunnel beneath a war that never ended, even when they all came quietly home.

"You remember when reckless behavior was still possible?" he yelled back at Fred and Jim, pointing at the delirious joy of the boy in the shadows. "Sometimes memories are part of your soul."

He waited for Fred and Jim to catch up to him. Bob pulled Fred close to him. "You're not meant to know all that you think it is that you want to know," he whispered so low that it seemed he intentionally did not want either Fred or Jim to hear his words. "Or that you think you need to know." He released his grasp of Fred and said a bit louder, "Debra is confused, and she has brought you into her confusion."

"It's been years, Bob. Decades. Days. Hours. It's been," Fred tried to explain to himself, to Bob, to Jim, but the more he tried to explain how long it had been, the more time broke, numbers fell to the sidewalk. "Debra has given up what she believed." Fred stared at his fingers. He counted each one again. "No one knows."

"It's meant to be that way. You are trying to count something, stop something, that cannot be counted, that cannot be stopped," Bob replied. "Look at this street." He pointed up and down the avenue. "This street. This here. These people walking along these sidewalks. This is what eternity is. Eternity is not some abstract concept. It is not the death of time. It is a place. It is here. And not everything about eternity is pretty. It is not all that we want it to be. Some of it is a silence so quiet and still, so full of loneliness, that there is no name for it."

Bob reached into his pants pocket, searching for something, pulled it back out, looked in the center of the palm of his hand. Nothing. A speck of emptiness. "No one on this street wears a watch. They never have. There's no reason to wear a watch. And they are not escaping anything. They are in it. Those people over there," Bob pointed out a few people standing at a bus stop, "They're not waiting. They're living and breathing. People like us? Well, we're always looking at our watches. We devote most of our lives to waiting for death to show up. We may call it by other names. We may call it standing

217

in line at the bank or the grocery store, or we may call it being stuck in traffic, but we are merely waiting for time to run out."

Fred wanted to show Bob his naked wrist, to show him that he no longer cared about what time was doing, what time was up to, but Fred knew he had not fully gotten rid of time. He still tried to remember what month or day it was. He still believed that mattered.

"Goats," Bob leaned in close to Fred's ear so no one else, not even Jim, could hear him. "Goats can stand still for what seems like hours, staring at you, without judgment. Not a dog. A dog jumps at you, humps your leg. Barking. Panting. Dogs have no sense of boundaries. No patience. While the dog is doing all that, the goat is standing still. Indifferent. It's why we keep dogs as pets and not goats. Dogs distract us. Goats make us uncomfortable with what we say we know, because they make us think too much. You can't truly know what time is until you stare into the eyes of a goat." Bob slapped Fred on his back. Jim looked at Fred, and Fred said: "Don't even ask."

The trio continued down the avenue. Off in the blurry distance, at the far end of North Avenue, where the avenue disappeared into nowhere, where the locals say the city of Pittsburgh fell off the earth and disappeared into some other world that could only be lost, the place some say that the bridge to nowhere actually connects here with there, in the humid morning haze of such a faraway place, stood One-eye Pete leaning against a building, talking to the Street Elder.

His voice carried down the avenue to Bob, to Fred, to Jim. Bob believed that demons created some words to confuse the senses, not to deepen them, words that intoxicated the skin, the muscles, the lungs, and the blood. Words that harmed memory, instead of aiding it. Bob also believed that Pete was fully aware of this from his earliest childhood and that he protected himself from such words. The gods had stolen Pete's one eye because he knew the truth of words and whittled words down to the very core, peeled away everything that got in the way of a word being direct, of words revealing their ancestry and their desires. Pete believed words were impure and that their impurity was not to be trusted, and he felt that words had to be stretched into meaning. "You can't just let a word come out of your mouth, after it has been sitting around, and expect the word to have meaning."

Pete doubted tongues and all they could do to truth. "A tongue can lie. It usually does. Tongues give us false memories. Complicate the simple, but skin, muscle, sweat, they can't lie. Sweat tells the story of the body, lets you know what the body has been up to. Sweat has no choice. It's involuntary. Tongues? People go around using their tongue to say what they will. It's the man wanting something behind the tongue that is the soul corrupter."

Pete watched Bob walk up to him. He glanced at Fred and Jim, two men he had never seen before, looked the whitest of them, Fred, in the eye, and finished what he had begun before those three arrived. "The actions you do in the world makes your skin into the skin you got covering your body." The stars, the moon, all that remained of the night, quit, began to darken and disappear into the light of the morning. Street Elder helped Sylvia climb out of one final car, handed Sylvia her shoe, her broken slipper. "Cinderella returns too late," Sylvia said, and laughed.

Street Elder put her arm around Sylvia's bony shoulders, held the young girl tight to her body. The rest of North Avenue began their ritual of waking to the day. Tired men in wrinkled shirts and slacks, looking like they had not slept a wink in ages, crept out onto the stoops, plopped their bodies down. They opened the *Post-Gazette* and waited. The morning sun evaporated the men and boys who had wasted the night away lingering on the corners, the ones who had gone from shadow to shadow. Nothing and no one, not even one final exhausted body, remained in Rats Alley. Aside from one or two men who had fallen asleep, The Garden Theater was empty. The man at the ticket window sat reading a paperback novel. The doors to the Apache Lounge were shut tight. Locked. Exhausted by her wisdom, Madame Rosie had fallen asleep, her forehead pressed against the window of her parlor. Chas remained posted under his sycamore tree. Pete wet his lips, ready to say anything, even if it did not need to be said. Fred and Jim knew what they were doing was not right, the way they looked at Pete, at his glass eye. Even the way they looked away from him did not feel right.

"This here's Fred, Pete." Bob pointed at Fred. "He's the one who married Debra." Pete stared up at Fred's chin. "You know how that goes. One man marries another man's sister."

Pete chuckled. "Sometimes there's no way to stop such a thing. Sooner or later one man does all kinds of things to another man's sister. Unspeakable what can happen," he said. "Lots of women got brothers. Lots of men got sisters. Things like that go on all over the place. What's done is done. No undoing it." Pete kept shaking his head the whole time he was talking, "You just have to decide how you're going to live with knowing what you know."

"Yeah, I guess we're trying to do just that," Bob replied, then turned to Jim. "And this here's Jim." Pete nodded at Jim. "Debra says her boy is missing."

"We've lost our children, Bob. All of them. Been going on for years. We got to accept that, accept children for what they is, and let them be." Sylvia and the Street Elder made their way over to Pete. "Most problems arise 'cause people think children are innocent. They're not. Least not in the way we want them to be. A child hears voices, wanders into traffic, has dreams he can't control. A child gets scrapes and bruises, nosebleeds. They know something is going on in other rooms of the house. A child is living just like you and me is living, so how can they be innocent?"

Fred looked uneasy. His feet had grown weary of being in his shoes. "That worry you, Fred?" Pete asked. "There's nothing inside it but what the truth might be, if you look hard enough. Truth can't exist without imagination."

Pete waited for Fred to admit to something, but he remained silent, so Pete went on. "And a child is more unpredictable. Child got his own logic. You think back to how your sister was when she went wandering off. Coming back home with dirty shoes and her hands shaking like they been some place they not supposed to have gone. And all that water in her eyes. Not tears. Just water."

Pete again waited for Fred to confess what needed to be confessed, or at least what Pete thought needed to get said. Pete looked from Fred to Bob, then he continued, "A child hasn't learned to fashion themselves to fit in with what we're telling them to be. Or they haven't been convinced yet that it is all that important. You can't warn a child about sins. They already know about them. They see them. Sins in all their glory. Sins ain't all the evil that people make them out to be. Sins are complications. We need them. Need the temptation. Only a fool wants to rid the world of sin. Sins are the actions a child is about to do, that will make him who he is. It's who you are now, Fred. You're no different than that boy Debra talks about. He's not much different from you. Maybe that's why he's gone. The sins on your flesh. Your skin covers the sins you're carrying. Covers and reveals. You try to hide your scars like you want to camouflage your life. God's watching that more than the other stuff you're doing. You think you can disappear that from God? Be truthful with your sins. Show them to God, to us. You show them. They're there. They're in you. None of that 'Forgive me, Father, for I have sinned.' No, sir. No. You roll up your sleeves, and you show your sins. You say here are my sins, they're part of me. Then see what happens."

Pete's mouth had gone dry. Dust and ashes. Gravedigger breath. Even shamans get thirsty in Pittsburgh. "You can't tell a child to be meek or tell them that they bound for glory because they're blessed, and they're going to inherit this or that. Ain't truth in it unless they're living what they're living. A child got stories of their own. You need to leave them be."

Pete wiped a strain of saliva from the corner of his mouth. He looked up at the clear sky. Heat already moving in, taking over the city streets. "You tell Fred here, Crystal." Only Pete called the Street Elder by her name. "Tell him what happened to his child that he thinks is lost."

Fred saw the tired in her eyes. He saw that that small and breakable thing that we all carry within us had not been broken in her, that she kept it alive. "Most dangerous thing a child can do is dance," the Street Elder said, looking directly at Fred, directly into his heart, which seemed to be breaking the longer this night and this morning went on. "We fear such freedom. Opening a body up like that. A child dances, that child is showing an adult they got their own way about them, that they know they have a body, and it's made of flesh and blood and hope and desire, and they're showing that their body got sin inside it just waiting to get out, wanting to get out, needing to get out, and there ain't no adult that can cage that. That's why you're so scared, Fred. That child with her dancing threatens all that you convinced yourself is true. But it ain't true, is it? No, it ain't. None of it's true after all. It's just what you did to yourself to protect yourself from love, from pain, from scars."

The Street Elder leaned down close to Pete's ear and whispered something. Pete shook it off. "It's getting hot. We need to be going." The Street Elder lightly put her hand back on Pete's shoulder. "Any child is doing all they can not to die. To find that truth of how a child dies, you got to look at the ugly that is inside you. A child sees that in you. And once a child sees that, they can't never forgive you."

The Street Elder and Pete had to make their own journey back up Federal Street, before the heat of the day bore down on Pittsburgh. Pete looked back over at Fred. "You got to know how a child is lost, before you can find a child."

CHAPTER 22

The unseen power of words remained locked inside Elgin's memory and created the deepest fear in his heart. The half-stripped trees of winter. Those floating chunks of ice in the Monongahela River in February. Streetlamps illuminating nothing. Men crumpled down on the sidewalk, their backs pressed against the brick wall of a boarded-up building, their frail hands reaching out from beneath a torn sweatshirt and coat for a dream that long ago disappeared. Some woman refusing to cry, standing alone, waiting for a Greyhound bus to Cleveland, to Youngstown, to Grove City, to some place that was no longer Pittsburgh, any place where memory would stop, where she could forget the first time that man of her dreams kissed her outside Crawford's, where she could forget all that the two of them had promised to each other and what that man had done with those promises and how she had waited night after night, sitting at their kitchen table praying for forgiveness, waiting for him to come home and punish her for waiting. Wishing her heart would break, so she could pack as much as she could into one suitcase and be gone before he returned.

Streets and neglected buildings made of memory, made of flesh, made of passion, buildings and streets desperate to remain with the living, but chipped and crumbling at their very edges. Roofs collapsed or collapsing. Windows broken. The longer you live, the more you die. Buildings vanish. Men grow tired of their wives. Wives become more silent. Children disappear. Men like Elgin were all living with dead fathers, dead mothers.

Men everywhere, not just on these streets of Pittsburgh, carry too many dead people with them. The very idea of pleasure has rotted away. Rivers weaken, become tranquil, as if they had outlived their usefulness. Ghosts haunt the streets, the alleys. Words replace people. Names. Only their names remain in the world. You say the names of those people who have gone, thinking that saying their name can make them appear. Praying that a name had some magic in it. The word made flesh. So you say their name until your voice wears thin. Most times, a word never becomes more than a shape to fill a lack.

Elgin misses Thuy's body lying beside him in bed. He misses her in that place where words fail. Where light disappears. Elgin whispers Thuy's name to give a shape to her disappearance, to give a sound to the loneliness. But no word—no matter how many trees Elgin carved that word into, no matter how many times he tattooed that word into his skin, no matter how many times he said that word, her name, aloud—could make Thuy appear. Saying a word does not change anything. Giving breath to a word does not make present that which has gone away. A word cannot stop the longing a man feels. A word is just a bigger hole. A man has to come to accept that.

Language is borne out of absence. A man tells stories for the not-here, for those who have vanished, for the emotions that have been destroyed. A man says the word love like that word is more than that, more than a hole, more than something that's not here any longer. Love is a gift. Too often a man gives a gift, especially love, wanting something in return, as if the woman owes him something. A man gives a woman love, then waits like he knows exactly how she is supposed to give it back to him. Like he knows exactly how it is going to feel. Love doesn't work that way. No gift does. A gift is something to be given. There cannot be any expectations or demands that go with it. The beauty of giving someone a gift is watching what that person does with what you have given them, watching what a woman creates out of the love you give her.

Clarence could not understand this. He repeated his story of loss again and again. He accused Ai of taking something from him, instead of thanking her for giving something to him. He could not bring himself to be happy that she stepped into his life. He could only suffer because she left. He burned his soul with telling that story of her leaving him. In his mind, she sentenced him to an eternity of solitude by leaving. His stories died inside him, rotted into his heart, his soul, his muscle. A man like Clarence is incapable of telling such a story of loss without experiencing that loss over and over. He damaged his heart more by remembering than by forgetting. And, while his son felt a similar loss each time he let Thuy's name out, Elgin also experienced the joy of having had Thuy in his life. And Elgin held onto a childish, near-innocent faith. Each time he spoke her name, he thought that somehow this time would be different; this time would be the true magic, the time that the word, his voice, brought her back. But he knew deep down his voice held no such magic.

There is love in the world that is only meant to appear for a short time, then it is meant to disappear. Gone before it fully blossoms. Sometimes love does that. It needs to. Sometimes it is what a man needs without him knowing he needs it. A man doesn't need to understand everything that he lives through. That's what a man's skin is for. Love that comes into a man's life, but leaves before the man thinks he is done with it, can't be understood. Love that gets abandoned on the streets or in the rain or leaves you sitting, waiting, beside some dim lamp in a room that seems emptier than it is, is for a man's skin or for his soul to understand, not his mind.

A few years back, before Thuy died, Elgin saw a wedding ring, lightly covered in dust, in the window of North Side Pawnshop. He could not shake away what seeing it did to him. "You see a wedding ring in the window of a pawnshop," he told Red later that night, "and it changes how you tell a woman you love her; it changes what you feel you're capable of promising to a woman. After seeing that ring, I went back home and tried to say something to Thuy, like any normal man talks to his wife, but all my words had gone and left me, so I just looked at her. She called me foolish. Told me the heat must be getting under my skin. I still couldn't say nothing."

Elgin lifted his beer glass to his lips and drank a moment of quiet into himself. Red stood silent, cleaning a glass. "You got to give a woman more than words, Red," Elgin said. He looked down the bar at the street girls resting their feet, their lonely ankles, trying to cool down their skin. Summer in Pittsburgh had a way of hating you, had a way of beating you down, getting into your bones and thoughts. Only the strongest survived the humidity of Pittsburgh summers, until winter came on and brought with it a test of a different sort, to see who was strong enough to make it to summer. All weather in Pittsburgh had an attitude, forced you to submit to it. Dared you to survive.

"And a man got to do more than hear a woman when she speaks," Elgin said. "A man got to listen down into a woman, and he got to learn to be patient enough to be silent. But how's a man born in this city do that?" He emptied his beer and waited while Red poured him another. He looked into the mystery of that beer, stared at it, the color, all that it offered, all that perhaps any man in Pittsburgh wished it could offer. He was one of many men in Pittsburgh who believed that beer was not simply beer, not simply something a man drank in the dark or while sitting on a sofa watching a ball game. No, beer was more than that. There was more to it.

"You know," Elgin said without lifting his eyes away from the magic of his beer, "I went into that pawnshop before coming over here, and I asked to see that ring." He shook his head, let out a short laugh. "Maybe Thuy's right. The heat is making me into a fool. I held that wedding ring in my hand, turned it over looking at it, feeling the weight of it. It felt heavy, like it was holding onto and letting go of all the years of what that man and woman promised to each other and all the years of all that those two, husband and wife, did to each other. You know, Red," he looked up at Red, "holding that ring scarred my heart that much deeper. Then, fool that I am, I read the inscription on the inside of that wedding band, like reading it wouldn't do anything to me."

One of the street girls from the other end of the bar called to Red for another drink. Red nodded, held his hand up to Elgin, and walked down to the street girls. Elgin sat alone and quiet. He could not stop twisting his own wedding band on his finger, twisting it like he wanted to make that ring part of his skin, like he wanted to be sure that this ring never left his finger. "Man should be buried with his wedding band where it belongs," he said to himself, then finished the last of his beer.

When Red returned, Elgin slid his glass toward him for another. Red poured, remained silent. "There are words in this world that ain't never meant to be seen by anyone other than the one who the words been written for," Elgin said. "Reading that man's words saddened me in ways that no other story ever saddened me before, and I've taken on that sadness. I got that sadness in me now, what that man had written on that ring for that woman. That man's sadness. It burned my fingertips, marked the palm of my hand as soon as I touched it. Can't do nothing about it now. I'm going to live the rest of my life knowing his sadness, a sadness that I should not know. Ain't right for me to know it. No one but them two should ever know what I know, and now I'm going to know it when I drink my morning coffee, know it when I kiss Thuy, know it when I'm drinking these beers."

Elgin stopped. He looked at his beer. He knew it was still only beer, but there were days and nights, days like this one, when he hoped maybe beer could be more than that. He brought the glass to his lips, drained the glass in one long gulp. "I'm bound to live with that sadness when I fall asleep. Live with it when I'm at a ball game and some mosquito is biting into my skin. People go to movies and cry over some made-up story of failed romance. These same people walk by that wedding ring in that pawnshop on East Ohio Street and don't feel a damn thing, not a thing, and you want to know what's wrong with this world?" Something broke inside him that day, and he still carries that pain with him today. He still thinks of that day when he is drinking at Red's.

The door to Red's Ibo Landing Bar and Girlle squeaked open. Summer heat and light fell into the darkness of the bar. Elgin turned, always the instinct, the desire to see even when blind.

"See anything?" Red asked.

"Blue shadows. All there is for me now. They kind of pretty, though."

"But you hear them feet."

"Them feet I hear. In my darkest dreams I hear them. Footsteps in mud, in empty hallways, down dark streets before the sunrise. But those aren't ghost feet. Ghosts got too much pride to walk like that. Ghosts got too much at stake with leaving footprints. Got to be

Emmanuel. Walking like he's already half past dead. Man gone and forgot what he's living for. Carrying too much with him and most of what he's carrying he don't even know. Maybe he's dragging a ghost with him from the river." Red and Elgin both laughed.

"You walk too slow, Emmanuel," Red called out. "Can't even call what you're doing walking. You put walking to shame, moving your feet like you do, like you ain't got truth in you no more. You older than old is old, and you still not the father of your own feet," Red laughed, and Elgin's laughter quickly followed.

"Look who's talking at me. The way you leaning on that bar like you got no spine. And I'm going to be straight with you, Elgin, a blind man shouldn't be laughing at no old man walking slow. You be stumbling, tripping, making a mess of the world with how you walk."

"Pick up them feet of yours, Manny. It's that simple, then maybe we'll call what you doing walking," Elgin said. "It's shameful what you do with your feet. Embarrassing. Not even one foot in front of the other. It's more like one foot beside the other. Heard them feet of yours as soon as you gone and walked off your porch. Heard you coming all the way down from Kirkpatrick and Centre. And not because my hearing got better since I went blind. Crazy the way you move. Weakens my heart and saddens my soul."

"You're jealous and cranky, both of you is," Emmanuel said. "I do the purest of shuffles when I walk. Smooth and easy, the way the lords of Harlem, back in the day, intended for a man to walk. They know me when I walk down the avenue, and they know my feet got music, just subtle is all. And what do you know, anyway?"

"Listen at that," Red said to Elgin. "Back in the day, shit. Old man saying 'Harlem' like he knows where that is. Ain't even the Pittsburgh shuffle. More like, you crossed the state line and went on into Ohio, and now you don't know how to walk no more. I've seen it happen to men braver than you, Emmanuel. Man crosses over to Ohio, no telling what might become of him." Red started pouring a draft for Emmanuel. "Man don't walk that way in this city. It's like you given up on whatever it is you been doing with your life all these years. Elgin right about that. He's a prophet now that he's blind. You best be listening when he descends from Dinwiddie and graces us with his presence." Elgin laughed at that with the kind of joy most men have lost, the old joy of being young and not knowing more than they needed to know. One of the street girls raised her glass and shouted a toast down the bar to the prophet of the Hill District. "Should be a sin the way you walk over to my bar. Should charge you for wearing down the floor."

"I should take my money across town," Emmanuel replied.

"You do that. You go. See if you don't wear the skin off your fool feet walking all the way over there. Probably wear away what's left of the sidewalks, too."

Emmanuel dragged a stool back from the bar and pulled his body—raggedy bones and all—up on it, and sat beside Elgin. He thanked Red for the beer, wrapped his hand around the glass and leaned in close to Red, like he was about to reveal the mystery of the Holy Grail. But all Emmanuel said was that Red did not have words beautiful enough to describe the way he walked. "My walk makes all the poets go quiet." Emmanuel said that. He did. Then he sat back in his stool and took his first cold sip of beer, to soften the heat burning through his body.

Elgin turned toward him, shook his head. "Why'd you go and say that for? It's like you lost your fool mind."

"I know what I'm saying when I say it, and I know who I say it to, and I know it's the truth. Rest of you fools thinking truth got something to do with what you're saying and not with what I got to see." he replied. "My feet know the truth, too."

"Truth ain't what you got in you," Red said. "If you did, you wouldn't know it. Ain't no one can know they got the truth. Don't work that way. Truth takes possession of you. Truth is what truth is, and it does the talking, and when truth possesses you, it confuses you. Man who thinks he knows truth only believes lies. Whatever it is that he knows, ain't truth. It's just something he's saying. Truth does something to a man. If he tries to speak what he knows, it comes out all messy. His mouth and his tongue start bleeding all over the place with him trying to say it. Your mouth not bleeding, is it, Emmanuel? No, it's not. I didn't think so. Your mouth not bleeding, because what you saying is not truth."

"Hardest thing a man do, besides love right, is accept what he sees and what he says he sees is not truth," Elgin said. "Truth ain't like math." Elgin lifted his glass, but, before drinking the rest of his beer, he finished what he had to say. "Man only can see what he can see."

"But you still go on and on about Thuy. Like all you say about her beauty is true," Emmanuel interrupted Elgin. "You're no different than us."

"You right. You right. It took time. Seeing Thuy and not simply seeing what I wanted to her to be," Elgin said, and finished another beer. "Sometimes any man can only see a woman like he seen every other woman." Elgin tapped the bar, letting Red know he wanted another draft. "And when we think we got a woman all to ourselves, it ain't truth." Elgin took a sip of his beer. He put the glass down on the bar, ran his hand over his bald scalp.

"It's easy enough to get a woman naked in her flesh. Her clothes on the floor. Her hair damp." Elgin laughed. "That's easy, right, Red? You never had no trouble. Women just falling down all over Forbes Avenue for you. And most of our fool lives that's all we ever wanted, if we're honest about it. But a woman naked in her flesh is not who the woman is. That's only who she thinks some man wants her to be. But you get a woman to be naked in her thoughts with you. That's different. She decides to give you that, she's inviting you into her soul. That woman's not afraid to be vulnerable. She got the kind of beauty that goes untouched in this world. You be grateful if you ever meet such a woman. She's a light, and she will burn into you like you've been lost your whole life, and now you've been found. She don't care where you been, she only cares that you're here now. Such a woman only comes into your life once, though. That's all. One time. And a woman like that, she only stays if you strong enough to be naked with your own thoughts and with giving them to her. That woman says, 'Look at me,' and she means something that confuses most men. When a woman becomes naked in her thoughts, she's taking you to a secret place, and when she takes you there, she wants you to see her in the way she wants to be seen and not that simple way a man has for seeing a woman. A woman ever take you there, she blinds you to seeing any other woman. Brings a man to his knees the way a new religion does—ain't no words for it. A woman reveals that kind of beauty to you, it bewilders you. You get stupid trying to talk about it. But what'd you expect? You think you going to see something you already knew? You think everything would stay the same? Beauty don't work that way. Ain't nothing simple about a woman's beauty."

Elgin looked down at the street girls. "They know. They're as careful with it as any other woman. Careful with how they get naked for a man. Careful with what they're naked with," Elgin said. He rubbed the back of his neck. Red returned to cleaning glasses. Emmanuel drank his beer, drank it the way most men in Pittsburgh drank a beer. He drank knowing it could be his very last beer he ever drank, not fearing that he might die—no man in Pittsburgh feared that—but fearing that perhaps a day would come when there would be no more beer, when the world would go dry of beer.

"A man grows tired, Emmanuel. It happens," Elgin said. "Ain't no shame in that. Even you, Red. One day, even you are going to be tired." Elgin laughed lightly. "I think your feet gone tired on you, Emmanuel. It's why you can't lift them. Your feet afraid you ain't being true. Your feet gone and become like my eyes. You live your life wanting to find some mystery in it, and you hope, inside there, inside that mystery, is a truth, at least some kind of truth, and you hope that truth helps you make sense of all this. At least you hope it helps you wake up in the morning and pull your old body out of bed. But it's not there. Most of what you think you're trying to discover, what you think you need to know, you already got inside you. It's all in what we know without knowing we know it. That's why you can't be saying it." Elgin drank more of his beer. He enjoyed beer. It gave him the kind of happiness that, like truth, did not need words. "You just can't betray yourself, even when you think that's all that's left to do or all that you can do."

"You're both crazy," Emmanuel said. "I walk in here for a beer and quiet conversation with my boys, maybe rest my eyes on some sweet woman, and glance up at the television now and then, watch some of the ball game. And here you come at me about how I'm stepping down the street. How I walk is how I walk. Words got nothing to say of how I walk. Same with beer. You don't talk about beer. You drink it."

Red put his dishrag down. "World needs fools like you to do what it's doing and get away with it," Red said. "A man got to refuse to be nothing. Got to refuse to let them put their words on your skin.

Words are shackles no man can see, but they're there. They're always there. In the air. In your own mouth. That's the beauty of how words work on you, how they take control of what you can say or feel. They're everywhere, and that's why they're so effective." Red swatted a fly away that had been troubling his eyes. "But you believe words don't own you. You believe that?"

Red looked straight into Emmanuel's eyes. Emmanuel did not blink, did not look away. "You're mad, old man. Words do the talking for you. They replace you. You want to take control of a man? You take power over the way he talks about his body, about how his body moves. You gather up all the verbs a man ever used in his lifetime, and you gather up the ways he used them, and you burn all of his verbs. Then, what's a man to do? He can't go nowhere. He can't fight you. He can't move. He's got no verbs. How can a man move with no verbs?"

Emmanuel laughed. Elgin came close to letting out a laugh as well, but he knew better and held it back. "That's right, Emmanuel," Red said. "You laugh. You think it's funny to take a man's verbs. Steal the only way he knows how his body moves. What's left of him? He becomes a shell of himself. A man gets emptied out when his verbs don't work with how he moves. Ain't right. Change a man's verbs and you change the way a man wants a woman, the way he walks up to her, the way he holds a woman when he dances. You give up on using your own way for talking about how you move and next thing you know you can't move no more like your grandfather moved. Your body all out of rhythm."

Red walked down the bar to grab two empty glasses. Emmanuel looked at Elgin and said, "Words. Words. Words."

When Red returned, he put the glasses in the sink and said, "I heard that, Emmanuel. Words ain't never been innocent. You born innocent, but you best remember this, words waiting for you out in the world before you born. They already in the world, and all kinds of things were being done with them before you were even a moment of lust in your father's eye. Who's that coming out of your mouth when you're talking? Them words ain't never just from you. And no word ever the same word. A word only looks and sounds the same. That should worry you more than it does. Each time a man puts a word into his mouth, he's leaving his prints on it. His saliva. People worry about leaving behind their fingerprints, but they don't worry about how they put their prints on words. That's the true crime scene. What a man does with words. Any man that puts poison in his words is going to burn another man's soul away." Red became still, waited for a fly to stop buzzing around and land on the bar, then he swatted at it. "A man goes invisible on his own self. Where's that man at? Where'd he go? Underground, that's where. Invisible. And you think it funny. You think I'm the one that gone crazy with it. And now you sitting at my bar saying it don't matter?"

"It don't. Least not if you remain true behind it," Emmanuel replied.

"There you go. True this and true that," Red said. "Like it's simple." Red picked up his bar rag and again walked down to the other end of the bar. The street girls were leaving. "How are you gonna survive?" Red shouted back at Emmanuel. One of the girls touched Red's hand and smiled as he wiped the bar. Red smiled back and turned toward Emmanuel. "Them putting this and that word on top of who you are, beating you down soft and gentle with words. Damn fool is what you is." Red grabbed the glasses and carried them back down to where Emmanuel and Elgin sat. "You think a word is just a sound? That all you think a word is? You think a word just something you say that disappears once you let it out of your mouth? How you get to be so old? Words on the inside of you making you who you is. You can't forget that. And words got souls just as much as you do. Words change when you say them, the way your soul changes when the right woman touches you. Same with a photograph. You ask Elgin. They got souls. You look into a photograph too long, too hard, and you steal the very soul of the photograph. You erase what's truly in the photograph," Elgin nodded along with Red's words. "And the photograph itself begins forgetting. Got nothing more to say. Nothing more can be said. Photograph and everything in it becomes quiet. You brought death to it. Even though there's something that appears to be still visible in the photograph, it ain't the truth of it no more. You condemn yourself to seeing only the myth of the photograph. The soul is gone, taken away by all your careless staring. It's why beauty becomes so fragile and vulnerable in a photograph.

It's why Elgin is so careful when he looks at those photographs. He knows he can lose more than he bargained for, and what's he going to do when that's gone?"

One of the street girls leaned over the bar on her way out and whispered into Red's ear. Smiled. They both smiled. The street girl held onto Red's hand and held his stare. "I got work I gotta do, Ali," he said. "The boys need me." The street girl frowned and turned to join the other girls outside in the heat of Pittsburgh.

Elgin and Emmanuel looked at each other. Smiled. "You yield to the violence of a woman's beauty, you got to be willing to live with what that does to you," Elgin said. Red shook his head. "I'm serious. It don't never go away once you truly yield to it." He raised his glass to his lips and finished the last of his beer. He wiped his lips with the back of his hand and told Red he thought one more beer would do it. One more beer and that walk up Dinwiddie would not seem so threatening, that empty bed waiting for Elgin, that quiet kitchen.

"Why you think we the ones who are still here?" Red asked.

"I got money. And you, Red, you got more beer, right? So it's simple, my friend. Life truly is simple that way," Emmanuel said. "No place else left up here to be going to. You still got the best bar in the Hill. Caliban's is filled to the rafters with so many people talking a man can't hear who he is. And they're mostly talking in tongues. Like they hate English. Voices breaking against the mirrors behind the bar. Talking so loud that a man can't drink his beer with all the due respect that a man should give to his beer. And Aces just don't have the girls you got coming in here, Red. And Larry's. Make no sense to even call that place a bar no more."

Red looked at Emmanuel. "Ain't what I meant," he said. "All these ghosts. All those footprints. We the ones still alive. Why that?"

"Not for us to know," Elgin said. "Things are meant to be done. We just do the things we know to do. Hope they the right things. Can't know."

"Got to be some reason, Elgin, even if it's a small one," Red said.

"Someone got some master plan, and we just living that plan?" Emmanuel asked.

"Something," Red replied. "Something we were told at birth or something we marked by at birth. Something burned into us or buried beneath everything else we think we know. Something to direct us. Like we got to hunt it down and then live it. Each of us born with something we got to live out."

"Not like that," Elgin said. "It's not about being directed. And it's not about you having to know. Knowing too much spoils all you don't know."

Red and Emmanuel nodded. "Books teach you what books know. It's all they can do to you," Red said. "You not careful, you disappear from your own self."

The door opened again. Less light filtered into the bar when the street girls had walked out. The day was growing old. The sun was nearly done beating down on the city, nearly done burning into the skin of the people walking the streets. Light footsteps and dust entered Red's Ibo Landing. The slightest breeze followed Johnny and Sylvia into the bar, a breeze that promised rain, at least the hope for rain, but all such a summer breeze in Pittsburgh, especially in the Hill District, ever amounted to was just that, a promise, one that failed. "Pops," Johnny said as he approached his grandfather. "Mr. Elgin," Sylvia called out. Elgin felt something in her voice that was about to break and blossom. Her voice somehow managed to mix the scarred with the sacred. She came up behind Elgin and wrapped her arms around him, rested her cheek on the back of his shoulder. Johnny pulled out a bar stool beside his grandfather. "Your feet so quiet it's like you're not even here, and now Sylvia's feet have gone quiet, too. What you so afraid of?" Elgin asked.

"You heard my feet carrying me across the floor. You heard that." Johnny said. "I'm not afraid."

"You're afraid of shadows. And you got as much fear in your steps as Emmanuel here got slow misery in his," Elgin said. "Old terrors. Young memories. It's all in your steps. Footsteps don't lie. Unhurried lust that you can't yourself justify having in your heart. You can't even know about that kind of lust yet. Innocent lust, deliberate and tireless. You be careful near that, Sylvia." Elgin turned his head around and smiled at her, and she smiled over at Johnny.

"Don't you worry," she whispered into Elgin's ear.

Elgin smiled his old smile. That smile came out often around Sylvia. He put his hand over her hand that rested on his shoulder.

He patted it, then simply rested his hand on hers. He felt her scars. Elgin squeezed her fingers, trying to pull the pain out of her. He went to whisper something to her, but stopped. He turned toward Johnny. "Not everyone is wounded, Johnny. But you do got some old wounds in you, and you're going to give them to people when you touch them. Your wounds never stay yours alone." Elgin reached for his beer. He wet his lips a little, purifying them for the beer, took a sip almost as if he were uncertain about what whether or not he should drink any of the beer. He looked slightly confused. "You become what you become when," Elgin stopped. His words seemed to break.

"When what? This? This is our destiny?" Emmanuel asked. Still startled by his beer, or by something so deep inside him that even he did not know what it was or where it was from, Elgin ignored Emmanuel's question.

"We're all sitting here. That's true. But how'd we all get here. I'm not talking about walking down from up the hill. I'm talking about the other passages. Got to look back to see how we got to be here," Red replied. "Got to be a reason."

"Maybe there is. And maybe it's innocent," Elgin said. "But none of it is for us to know. All the while we're going through this life we only think we know our purpose. Mystery's a good thing." Elgin finished the last of his beer. His final beer of the night, and asked Red to pour him one more final beer of the night. The final beer of any night at Red's tended to be more than one final beer. A few more people entered the bar, and Red walked down to get their drinks.

"How do we know anything?" Elgin asked. "One day a man gets out of bed and he goes across the ocean and he's told to kill every single thing that moves. So that man does that. He kills nearly everything. Rivers. People. Snakes. Trees. That man kills and kills, and all the time he thinks he's right doing it. He kills nearly every living thing in that country. Leaves it dead as he can. Even the dirt." Elgin flipped a fly from his hand, turned his hand over and stared into the palm of his hand, looking for all that was lost. Staring at it like he wasn't blind. And everyone at that bar, even Johnny and Sylvia, thinking Elgin could still see, that he was not truly blind. "Even when you're staring at death, staring directly at it, a man still can't know his purpose. It ain't something to be known. Not in that way. The truth is that you don't got to know it."

Elgin drank more of his beer, rested his tired lips. Johnny mumbled something to Sylvia, and she slapped him on his back and told him to just listen for once. "You listen to an old man, and one day you become an old man. You don't listen, and you might not ever be old enough to tell these stories yourself." She told Johnny death happens. It comes and takes away what you expected to always be there. "Thing is," she whispered to him, "your grandfather is still here."

Elgin slowed down his drinking. He wanted this beer to last. He held the glass against his cheek to cool his skin, then took another sip, a small one. Sometimes Elgin did this. Sometimes he remembered that drinking was not just drinking, but putting something into his body, and that he was actually creating his flesh and blood by doing it. That eating and drinking was all part of being alive, of living your life.

"God is curious," Elgin said. "People forget that, or they think that He's just a manager. God's the only true poet there ever was. God says, 'Tree,' and a tree appears. That's poetry. That's what a poet can do: make what ain't here, be here. But God got no plan laid out for anyone. We're free. He just gives you so much time, then He sits back and watches. I'm telling you, God is curious that way. He is. He wants to see what you do with the life He gave you; otherwise, why He let you live to begin with? You make a purpose in how you're living. Those ministers stand up in their pulpits and say do this and do that, live this way, live that way, but mostly they say don't do this or don't do that. What do they know? They're people. God is not watching to see if you obey what some other man is telling you to do. He's watching you create something. Most people waste their lives away just talking about being true or talking about all they're going to do. You got to live your truth. Put it in the world. You just can't sit on some stoop here on Fifth Avenue preaching. You do that and you end up spitting more sand out of your mouth than truth."

CHAPTER 23

Debra quit. She put down the towel that she had been holding onto since the morning she awoke and told herself that Lucas had disappeared. She dumped what few crumbs remained in the cardboard Mr. Donut box into the trash. She poured the soured milk, which was as close to being butter as milk could be without actually being butter, down the drain in the kitchen sink. She stood perfectly still, listening for a sound that would make sense of everything. In the distance, or perhaps it was not in some distance at all, but rather in some other time, a time long past, a place far far away, in some other life, Debra believed she heard a child crying, a boy trapped in tales of hope and dreams. Debra knew such places existed. Places that would change what she remembered about her life. Places where the ribs of boys and those of girls became confused. Places that God had forsaken.

Debra pressed her fingers into her skin, feeling for her ribs, counting them. She had forgotten how soft her skin was, how much could be done to her skin by her, by others, if only she gave them permission. How simple it was to change the color of her skin. How easy it was to turn her skin red or to go deeper and bring the purple out of her soul and have it become visible.

Debra told Fred to do things to her skin. Even when he was uncomfortable or uncertain, Fred did these things and her skin remembered. She said, "Yes", and he did beautiful things that made her happy, but he had not done everything that she longed for. There were times when he said he had to say no. When he said he could not, he just could not. Times when he told her that some things in life are unbearable, that a man could not go on living after doing such things. Those times when Fred felt he needed to say no, needed to refuse, he became sad, and Debra was forced to comfort him, to tell him that she understood and would someday forgive him.

As she pressed into her skin, thinking of Fred's fingers, his lips, the shape of his mouth, she experienced a kind of loneliness that frightened her. She wanted to cut into her muscles, to release this loneliness, let it free to roam about the house, along the streets, along the rivers. When Bob and Debra were both very small, before he had killed anyone in Vietnam, before he had returned to Pittsburgh and begun writing on walls, and before Debra had followed the young girl, Bob went into the room where his sister slept and told her that loneliness never leaves its trace on a girl's heart or on her skin, and he told her that most girls mistake loneliness for wanting to escape what they've become, and he told her such girls were not trapped; these girls had become imprisoned by words, but they could be erased if she rubbed hard enough. Words were bruises that people put on paper, because people were afraid to live with their skin and muscles. He warned his younger sister to be careful around loneliness and despair. He rubbed his sister's feet and reminded her that she was skin and bone and muscle, not words. And loneliness was only possible because of words and for her to never mistake her body for words.

Words did nothing to skin, and sometimes, he said, when you touch yourself or when someone else touches you, a shadow from the touch remains, and, while you may think it will go away, it doesn't. When she touched her skin, she needed to remind herself that there were boys and girls in dark concrete basements. Some were playing, but some were standing perfectly still, unable to move, restrained, and near crying. Some boys and girls hid in shadows, some prayed for shadows. Bob released Debra's feet and looked up at her thin, awkward lips, her fear of smiling. He looked into her desire for something to change the way things had been happening, and Bob said nothing more than that. He stopped talking.

The brother and sister remained quiet. Bob sitting at Debra's feet, Debra sitting on the edge of her girl bed. They were unable to move, until she leaned down and touched her brother's cheek as gently as possible. She saw something in her brother's eyes of what would happen to this boy when he became a man if he were not careful, and she knew not to say anything. She knew that Bob, too, knew this. Even back then, she knew that sometimes what a girl feels can only be felt. She knew there was nothing Bob could do about it. Things like this happen to boys before they can change any of it. But that was years ago.

Debra continued pressing her fingers into her flesh until she found her missing rib, or at least until she found that place in her body where once there had been a rib, before some man stole it and carried it into a forest. She felt the wall of her skin and understood why her knuckles were bleeding and why the soles of her feet were callused. She understood more clearly that, when people looked at her, they only saw her skin. She knew there were men who enjoyed seeing her skin, and she knew there were men who did not know what to say when they were near her, but Debra could see what they wished they had the courage to say, and she knew what they wanted to say would make more sense if they had left words out of it, if they had not relied so heavily on telling stories and just done it, done what they wanted to do to her skin by doing it, instead of talking about it.

She was uncertain which kind of man she preferred, but she wanted to encounter a man who had never said one single word in his entire life. A child born incapable of speech, a boy growing up and refusing all the efforts of the adults that surrounded him, begging him to speak. A man with fingertips rubbed raw from touching, and she wanted this man to touch her. She needed for her body to experience that kind of touch. And she wanted her own fingertips to be that raw. And she told Fred this. She told him that, if she met such a man, Fred would have to be understanding about what she would need to do and that it would not change much about the two of them loving each other, touching each other.

The knife rose in her hand as she wiped her eyes. Debra feared that she would go blind one day, that her children would disappear, and that she would live each day of her life abandoned and alone. She lowered the knife and replied, "See, Fred? See how impossible it is not to speak, if you can?"

The sun fell through the slits in the blinds and the cracks in the walls of their little house. The morning bells of St. Teresa's church rang, reminding Debra of her need to confess, to walk to church, to walk down the center aisle, keeping eye contact with the statue of Jesus, dying for her sins and for the sins of all those men and women who had led her into temptation and whom she had led into temptation. Some mornings, she wanted to watch Jesus dying on that cross while his Father, angry and childish in so many ways with His grief, watched silently, refusing to lift a finger to release His son from such suffering. And she imagined meeting God along a road or in some motel, a secret hideaway, and she imagined walking up to God and slapping Him across His face for all His righteousness, for a pride that killed His only son, for a pride that continued to strike fear instead of light and joy into the hearts of His believers. The same pride that God used to destroy the sons and daughters of Job. Debra promised she would do what Job failed to do. She would remove her hand from covering her mouth, and she would tell God what Job remained silent about. She would force God to face what was true. And she would make God suffer in ways that Job was too innocent to do. If living had taught her one thing, it was that there was very little left to fear about the afterlife.

The bells of Saint Teresa themselves had become mournful and seemed to be giving up on belief, on faith, on trust in a God who claimed that He could, or someday would, emerge from beneath shadows. If God or Jesus or some other son that God had fathered, if any of them would come now, Debra would smile, but this Second Coming would not change very much, the living and the dead would be too tired, too exhausted, to care very deeply over how they were judged. The bells, too weak to make any wall collapse, sounded like some sort of tormented pain that comes with a betrayal following the loss of love. Mixed with all that she imagined, she heard her brother's chaotic voice beneath the sounds of the bells. Debra wanted to believe that her brother continued to believe in words, in speaking, when he was away from her. She wanted her brother to confess to those brave enough to listen, for him to release himself from all that he needed to release from his soul. All he had done. All he had failed to do. All that awaited him. The life of the world to come.

Debra prayed for him to silence his nightmares. Sometimes she felt like she was praying to Bob. She wished that her brother would return to Vietnam, but to do so without a gun. She wanted him to live with the people he had told her stories about, the woman who taught him to fly, the men in the tunnels who taught him to live unharmed, even when threatened. She wanted him to return the way she herself hoped some day to return and to live with the boys from her childhood, to live with those boys whom she had followed, to live inside narrow passageways.

She stared at the knives on the counter, at a stack of dirty dishes, at one banana, at a final doughnut, and at the dishrag. She opened the window, picked up the doughnut, and threw it out into the yard. Then she stepped back from the kitchen sink and looked up at the window as if knowing she would refuse to ever look out this window again. She took a few disoriented steps backwards, nearly falling over a chair, then walked away, far far away.

Debra drifted out the kitchen door onto the porch. She called her husband's name. Nothing. Fred was not sleeping on the porch or in the yard or on the steps. The world or kidnappers or desire had taken him away. His voice. His body. The stories. Vanished. The beer bottles were gone as well. Nothing remained from the day before. She thought, perhaps her husband, like her son, never existed. Fred seemed to have taken all their words with him as well, had erased what she thought she believed, stolen all the words that they had shared. She placed her fingers on the railing of the porch and called his name again, gently, not much above a whisper.

She looked out over the yard. The bicycle still leaned, heavy and rusted, against the maple tree. She looked down the alley toward Gabriella's back porch. She knew that if Fred were there, she could do nothing about it. She would have to accept it, live with it, grow old with knowing her husband was in Gabriella's home eating the food she cooked, looking into that woman's burnt, green eyes. Joe and Clarice waved from their porch, held up their coffee cups in some sort of gesture, whose meaning she had a slight, but not full enough understanding of. She began to raise her hand, but stopped there. She moved it in what, to her, felt like a wave and, smiled, but her smile was clumsy and uncertain.

Debra walked into the yard. The grass tickled her ankles, and the morning breeze lifted the leaves of the trees and turned them upside down, preparing them for rain, or at least promising rain, and she felt that breeze on her thighs, felt what it promised or threatened. She walked over to the bicycle and touched it with the same fingers she had used to touch her skin. The bicycle was as real as anything else, more real than Fred or Lucas. She called out her husband's name as carefully, as quietly, as she had said her son's name so many days or years ago.

Debra knew she could not stay in the yard. She knew there were no answers, not there, not in the yard. She knew the bicycle was real, but that did not solve anything, and she felt that so much of everything else that she believed-in seemed to be only made of words. She remembered watching television and seeing the body bags and hearing men argue about whether or not the Vietnam War was a war or a conflict. The words—war, conflict—seemed to matter more to these men in their suits than the body bags. She remembered one man screaming in the background as police carried him away, screaming that it was the American War, not the Vietnam War.

She stared at the television and said: "War, Vietnam War." And, without blinking, she said, "Conflict, Vietnam Conflict." But the body bags remained. Nothing happened. The word changed nothing. She hoped saying "conflict" would make the body bags disappear, but what could a girl sitting in Pittsburgh do to change any of that? And Bob was right, she thought, all that he had told her about words was true.

She began hating words that day, began wanting more things to be done directly to her body. And she wanted all these things to be done to her without words. And she promised that she would never tell stories of all the things that were done to her body to anyone except children. They understood that words still held something magical in them.

Debra called out her husband's name again. She waited. Then called again, this time more softly. She feared that saying his name would break something, or, perhaps, she thought it best for his name to disappear, for the thought of her husband to fall silently away. She seemed to be trying to remember the name they had given to their son. The breeze became a bit more aggressive. Goosebumps appeared on her skin. When Bob returned from Vietnam, he told her that goosebumps were angels waking up and coming to the surface to look around.

Debra was cold. Her skin. Her face. Her ankles. Cold. She folded her arms under her breasts and wondered if it was still summer. She wondered how long she had been sleeping. Her body felt older. Dreams could do that, age a woman, steal her youth. When sleep settles in a woman's bones, there is always the possibility that the woman will never truly awaken again, that the sleep will stay inside her, even though she appeared to be awake.

Debra looked up at the porch, thinking Fred might be there, that she had simply walked past him and not recognized him, but he was not there. Jim was not there either. She touched the bicycle one final time, knowing that she would never touch it again, that it would have to go, and she walked away from her house, down the alley, to Gabriella's back steps. She pulled open the screen door and knocked. When Gabriella came to the door, she was not wearing sunglasses. Her eyes were naked, vulnerable. She must walk around the house that way. Available. Ready and waiting. Wanting.

"Everybody knows," Debra said. "They all know, Gabriella. Everyone. The neighbors. They have been talking about all that they know. I think Fred knows."

"What, Debra? Knows what?" she asked.

"This. All this. All we have been saying. All that needs to be forgotten, forgiven," Debra replied. "Fred," she hesitated, looked into Gabriella's eyes and tried not to allow herself to be seduced by what she feared was most true about this woman's eyes. "Is he with you? He wasn't in bed this morning. He's not on the porch."

"No," Gabriella softly whispered. "No, he's not with me, Debra. Come inside."

Debra peeked around Gabriella into her house. "Fred?" Debra said her husband's name even more softly than Gabriella had said no. She wanted to show Gabriella that she too could speak very quietly. She nearly stepped into Gabriella's house, but her feet were not strong enough to carry her over the threshold, so she sat down on one of the chairs on the porch. She looked over at her own porch.

"You could see Fred from here, if you wanted to," she said. "From here, you would know so much."

Gabriella stepped outside. She sat. Listened to the birds. "The morning hides more than the night does," Debra said. "Fred thinks I am wrong. He thinks no one disappears in the morning. You do not inherit anything by waking in the morning. It may feel like a new day and that you are inheriting possibility and birth or rebirth, but you do not. The morning struggles. It wants to protect the terrible silence. The morning wants to keep that all hidden from us. It wants us to forget."

"Where's Fred, Debra? What happened?"

"Debra," she repeated her own name and felt a desire to say more about what she had known, what she had been told. "I believed everything. Every story." She looked out across Gabriella's rose bushes into the alley.

"What story?"

"I had a son who was too beautiful for Pittsburgh. You believe that, don't you, Gabriella? And this breeze today. You believe this? The breeze? You see what it does to your skin. You feel it. That's what makes it real. This breeze will bring rain. It will." Debra looked over at Gabriella. Her eyes were beautiful. She should forgive Fred. She understood why he wanted to stay on the porch drinking all night. She reached across to Gabriella and patted her hand. "It will be ok."

Gabriella told Debra that she was fine and asked again what she thought everyone knew and who knew what everyone seemed to know and why any of it mattered. And she asked her what would be ok. All Debra managed to say was the name of her missing son and something about how some children, even young children, are better off that way.

"Most children remained trapped," Debra said. She stopped patting Gabriella's hand and began to squeeze it. "Children hear too many stories, and we tell too many. Children listen. They always listen. And they believe, not just in Santa Claus and monsters under the bed and in Jesus Christ and in the power of their toys. Children also believe in the word made flesh. They believe. They do not need to leap over faith. They live their belief." Debra slowly released her grip on Gabriella's hand. "And they believe every story they tell is true. They have no reason not to."

Debra carefully folded her hands on her lap, rested. Gabriella crossed her legs. There was more to this woman than her eyes. She had been told stories about this woman's legs, about their mad and unruly capacity for joy. She attempted to look away from Gabriella's naked legs, her knees, her ankles. She thought a body like hers must get lonely, cold. A woman with such a body needs to do more than simply make coffee in the morning.

"We must put an end to poisoned girls waiting for kisses that are more dangerous than rotten apples." Debra continued staring down at Gabriella's feet. "There needs to be an end to orphaned girls who rise from the ashes and an end to desperate boys who still believe their sisters can save them." Debra reached for Gabriella's hand, but missed. "I thought I was old enough to face the morning. That it no longer frightened me, but the sun still punishes the sins we commit during the night. The sins that God never imagined. You will know them, Gabriella. All of them. Pray that your mother dies before this happens. You live thinking you are impervious to superstition, but the gentle, wicked voices carry you into alleys. Don't they? We had so few choices, you and I. Those voices brought us to the fire, to those places along the rivers where even water turns into fire. The stories we invent to explain what should never be explained, what we should never want to understand. And those voices put a desire in us that remains a mystery so confusing that we cannot confess it. That's why it's a sin. All a sin is is a desire that remains a mystery. And we commit ourselves to the sin for the mystery of doing it. We sin because of what we hope we will understand, even though we know we will only be further confused by it all. We end up calling this confusion guilt or remorse, when it is just our pleasure in having done the sin."

Debra continued to gaze straight ahead, refusing to blink, delicate with her voice. "Cursing God's name because of our love for ourselves. We say 'Goddamn' because we believe that God Himself is not intelligent enough to damn what needs to be damned. Creating stories because God failed. Because He never answered our prayers. Because He stole from us what He had no right to take." Debra looked at Gabriella. "None of us can sacrifice pain, Gabriella."

Gabriella tried looking more carefully into Debra's eyes, tried to look with a tenderness that was not too obvious. "You cannot covet what is not real, Debra. God fears we will create more than what He created, and we will enjoy all that we create more deeply than what He has created. God thinks our stories will replace His," Gabriella replied. She looked away from Debra's eyes. "Lucas," Gabriella began again, careful, like Debra had been earlier, so that she did not feel accused. "Stories know how to end. Nothing has changed. No one is talking. No one, Debra. You just," Gabriella hesitated. "Stories end, Debra."

Debra remained still. Her body tired. "Everyone knows, though. They do. You can know something without saying anything. The way they look at me, at our house. You never look at me like them," Debra said. "I see all the neighbors turning their heads. I hear them whispering. I hear them saying things that no mother should ever be forced to hear. Those same neighbors, Gabriella, leave blackberries go bad on the vine. They just shrivel up and die." Debra pointed across the yard at the bushes. "I think blackberry bushes are the same as the burning bush on Mount Horeb. Those blackberry bushes are testing us. And those of us who do not pick the berries are sending God a message. Joe and Clarice go to mass every Sunday, but they do not pick those berries. What do you think is more important? What do you think God cares about?" Debra leaned back in her chair. She touched her lips, then placed her hand fully over her mouth to hold back any other words.

"And don't you think I don't see how Fred looks at me. I understand what it means. What he needs," Debra said. She looked at Gabriella's bared throat, her muscled shoulders, a chastity of desire, and she wondered why Fred only noticed her eyes, she wondered what that said about him and about the way he touched her the nights they found each other in the same bed. "I can't bring myself to say what needs to be said. I never could." She wanted to surrender. She looked at her hands, turned them over, sought for the marks of all the useless things she had done with her hands. Debra longed to look into Gabriella's eyes, but she could not lift her gaze.

"Debra," Gabriella said. "Fred is gone for now. Just for now. He comes back. He always comes back." She followed Debra's gaze, looked at Debra's hands, and leaned in closer to Debra. "Fred knows.

He understands. And you know what there is to know. You know what can be known." Gabriella did not know if she should say Lucas' name, if hearing his name would help Debra to make sense of what she was beginning to understand or if saying his name would only confuse Debra more deeply. "This is yours," Gabriella said and placed her hand on Debra's shoulder. Debra felt Gabriella's breath on her skin. Her cheeks turned red, her heart sped up a little, and her own breathing became more erratic. "But there is nothing that anyone else knows. We have all suffered. We have all looked at your emptiness."

"You mean we did not see what we wanted? What was necessary?" Debra said. Her voice was close to pleading, like that of a child's voice. Debra had become an open wound that would never heal. "People say he died the way love dies between a husband and a wife. It just isn't there anymore. Love leaves you. And death is no different. It is just life leaving you. Every story suffers from the same fate. It has a beginning, and then it has a leaving. What were we thinking?"

"You think back to all those befores in your life," Gabriella replied. "Go back to the very first before. See what is there. See what the beginning is."

Debra wiped a tear from the corner of her eye and peered out over Gabriella's rose bushes, afraid to look at her. "I want to be done with yesterday. Fred always wanted to escape. Maybe he has finally done that. Escaped the yesterdays and discovered a way to move on to tomorrow. Maybe he let go. Maybe I should let go of what there is to let go of. I wonder if I changed my name, ran away. Started over. I wonder if Fred would hunt for me?"

"He would, Debra. You know he would."

But all Debra truly knew was that, sometimes, even mothers have desires and a deep-rooted urge to be honest. And sometimes a fairy tale is what happens when a woman closes her eyes to sleep and forgets who she was meant to be and dreams of a gentleness gone wrong. She stood from her chair. She told Gabriella that things were different. That Lucas could never return. Gabriella put her arms around Debra, held her. "And Fred," Debra said. "I thought he would be here. A story does not always end the way you hoped it would.

Sometimes it breaks in half and you wake up and realize it was nothing but a trap."

Debra walked down Gabriella's steps, and she returned home. She wanted to put an end to walking through the house, up and down hallways and stairs, to stop sitting in an empty bedroom and confessing to those who were no longer there. Debra waived to Pete and Clarice when she passed their yard. She decided not to look at the bicycle leaning against the maple tree. She did not need to see it one more time. The porch remained empty. The kitchen table was still clean. Fred and Debra's bed remained barren, sheets tucked tight, and quilt unmoved, unwrinkled. She lay on top of the quilt. She thought one dream is as good as another. Anything that happens could as easily happen to anyone else.

CHAPTER 24

"You think T.J. was too young to die?" Pete asked. "No one is ever too young to die." Pete coughed something dry and dusty from his throat, a few years of dirt and river, some pain from a war across the ocean, and a woman who hurt the old man when he was 54 years old, a woman who crushed what might have been his heart. She was the only woman in his life that Pete came close to marrying. He told everyone he never married because he never wanted to be jealous of the freedom of birds. He said that would not sit right with him. "He's dead. Gone. No one looked for him. Not the police. Not the newspapers. No one. Only you, Johnny. That's what you got to remember." Pete looked at Johnny. "You understand what I'm saying? Last night, three white men come looking for a boy that ain't even gone. The police. Milk cartons. Neighbors. It's a sin. But who's looking for T.J.? You. And no one. That's the world we live in." Pete pulled Johnny by the elbow and pointed up and down the street. "You look around any of these streets and you see there's more not here than what's here," Pete said. "Lookit over there." Pete pointed down East Ohio Street.

"What?"

"That." Pete kept pointing at the overpass. "What do you see?"

"Nothing."

"You can't see nothing, Johnny. It ain't possible." Pete slapped Johnny on his back. "Look again. See what's been washed away." Pete stared up at Johnny, then looked back down East Ohio Street. "Now, what'd you see?"

Doug Rice

"Concrete. The highway," Johnny said. Pete looked away from Johnny and over at Chas. He elbowed Chas, mumbled something, and the two of them laughed light and easy. "Like you see anything different, Chas." Johnny turned back to Pete and asked, "What do you want me to see?"

"I want you to see what ain't there no more. That road there. It's not making you wonder at all? Trouble with trying to see what's in front of your very eyes is that too much is covering over it. What's not there?"

"Can't see what's not there, old fool."

"Exactly." Pete laughed and wiped that Pittsburgh morning sweat from his forehead, the kind of sweat that burned into your skin, that made a man think seriously about suicide and even more seriously about beer. Pete had his street-corner-shaman look in his good eye. "What was there, ain't there now. They took it."

"You're crazier than my grandfather. Heat and old age must be tearing you up."

Pete shook his head again, kicked at a stone. He was always kicking at stones, trying to wake the dead or the river ghosts. The purest of all enigmas is that of memory, of time that seemed to have gone away and taken people, homes, and desires with it, time that seemed to have become past, to have murdered itself. The most direct, most intimate, form of suicide is the loss of memory. Such a suicide becomes a death that keeps a man living while all that is of what that man has become dies.

The fate of all memory is that it only seems to disappear and only seems to take the pain away with it. But memory can never be erased, not even by new love. Memory simply goes into hiding, cloaked in forgetfulness. It remains lodged inside muscle and bone. And memory haunts the present. All of it done in silence, and, once done, no one can escape. It's done. Anything that you think is dead, that you think you have forgotten, when you bring it back to life, it is bound to pain you. Like a scar. Like the mark of a needle. Like the rib that gets broken by loving too much. Memory is the one true agony carried in the body. And there isn't any way to heal what the past has done to the present, what the past is about to do to a man's future, or what a man, uncertain of his own memory, does to what he

252

makes his past into. There is no true past for any man, not even the past locked inside Elgin's photographs or on the tip of Red's tongue, in the thicket of Red's words. The past that was is less real than the past that was not. And any man is just as likely, more likely, to hold onto the past that was not than to hold onto the past that was. Even rain cannot wash away that kind of memory, that kind of belief, once it takes hold of a man.

"What they took was our neighborhood, Johnny, our homes. That's what's not there," Pete said. "Those floods from back in the day could not wash away those neighborhoods, but man could take our neighborhoods down with little more than a thought or two. Ten years from now, who will know that people used to live where that road is? And who is going to care, if you don't care? Everyone will think that road been there since the beginning of time, like time began when they begin remembering." Pete brushed a fly or gnat or some buried fantasy away from his eye with his hand. He inhaled more of that Pittsburgh heat, the kind of heat that is unkind, not so much malevolent as simply unkind, to a man's skin.

"What's done is done," Johnny said.

Pete wiped more sweat from his brow, wiped a little of the saliva dribbling down from the corner of his mouth. He stared at Johnny, then back at the freeway. Dreams seemed to be dying, and Pete looked sadder than he did that day those people were having that picnic. Trapped by the kind of sadness that offered no hope. He looked like he was going to be that way for the rest of his life. Johnny knew he was seeing a man coming to know that he was done with it, all of it, the way his grandfather was done with seeing.

Pete rubbed at his good eye, squinted, rubbed it again, trying to wipe a lifetime of memories away or maybe just trying to wipe a tear away before anyone could see it. "Gone in a month, like it never there to begin with. Just scars left on the hillside, old bricks too stubborn to be moved away. They tore down kitchens where people huddled around stoves to stay warm and tell stories. Drove bulldozers over front porches. One day those ghosts are going to walk again. They going to come back. Mark my word."

Pete kicked his toe into the concrete of the sidewalk like he had given up on waking the ghosts gently with his voice. These ghosts could not be coaxed into coming back to life. They had to be kicked and kicked, to pull them out of their stubborn state of being numb to all that had happened, all that still was happening. Pete looked at Johnny in the same way he looked at the sidewalk while he was kicking at it.

Pete stared silently at Johnny looking over at the freeway. Johnny was dreaming his life away, traveling that freeway, going some place that would make all that he remembered of his childhood disappear. Pete saw that look in most young people around the North Side, like forgetting was better than remembering, like forgetting made living safe. "T.J. will be the same kind of gone, if you're not careful," Pete said. "Your mother, Johnny. Your grandmother. They all be gone if you don't keep them here. These are our stories, and they stay alive on the stoops, but the stoops are disappearing, so once they gone, where the stories go? You see them ghosts walking the streets, the ones that have woken from their fevered sleep, they got winter in their hearts 'cause of all they lost. They carry what they lost. It's what makes a ghost a ghost. And you can't talk lightly of all the savage pain they hold from some ancient loss. A ghost possesses a rage and a euphoria. And ghosts don't believe in time no more, so they never tire of walking. But we're as responsible for them being here as they themselves is. That's how it is. They more tormented and tired than we ever will be. Sometime it's downright cruel what we do to the past. How we create terror out of it. Ghosts are more sinned against than sinning."

Pete looked at Johnny. "You be careful with what you think is gone."

Pete, Johnny, and Chas became quiet and stared down East Ohio Street, across East Street at the freeway, hoping the freeway would collapse or disappear, hoping that houses would grow back, the way weeds were persistent in growing back, in refusing to die. But staring at something will not change it. What was there was there, and what was not there now was no longer there. Words. Stories that drifted. One day, none of it would be there. Even Johnny would be gone. He knew that, at least he knew that in some part of himself. Rats Alley would be gone and The Garden and the Apache. All that would survive would be nostalgic moments of longing, of old men trying to convince young boys that back in the day it was better.

Johnny was the first to walk away, to say goodbye and walk down East Ohio Street to find Sylvia. To find some way to lose himself. Before rounding the corner at Cedar, he turned to look back at Pete and Chas. They stood looking off at what was no longer there. Neither one had moved, most likely neither had even blinked.

Johnny turned away and walked down Cedar and across the 9th Street Bridge into the city. His life nearly ended that morning, when he crossed Liberty Avenue. A car came out of the shadows into the light when he stepped cautiously into the street. Johnny froze and thought this is what fate feels like. This is how life ends. I have discovered my destiny. Sooner or later this is what happens. Pete told Johnny that you only get what belongs to you. And nothing, not even love, can save you from what needs to happen. But the car missed Johnny. Johnny stepped back up onto the sidewalk. He placed his hand over his frightened heart and felt shame mixed with fear rising in his cheeks. He remained still and silent for a moment, staring straight ahead, waiting for the light to turn green.

Johnny's grandfather once told him there was no such thing as blind destiny. If there were, not one soldier would ever have made it home from Vietnam, not even in body bags. "It's the doing that makes the done," Elgin said. "You can't turn your back on all that you done. It's done, and once you done it, you realize you have done it, and when you realize what you done and you agree to be accountable for it, that is the moment when you come to know who you are and who you been."

No deed goes unpunished, Johnny thought to himself, and no shadow is pure. No man goes out seeking his destiny. They just tell themselves they are doing that. They cross oceans, they grab onto the golden locks of some woman imprisoned in a deserted castle and climb straight up that wall to rescue her, they slay dragons, they cross streets. A man makes all sorts of sacrifices that he feels he needs to, even though the future remains unknown.

The light turned green, and Johnny safely walked across Liberty Avenue. His heart slowed, his shame no longer marked his cheeks. The shadows faded.

CHAPTER 25

Fred, Jim and Bob walked into the White Castle, sat at the counter, and released a collective three-man sigh, something rare for even one man to do in Pittsburgh. But the men did just that. They sighed. Once they had completed their sigh, a thin waitress looked up from her *Post-Gazette* and walked over. She saw their empty eyes and immediately poured them coffee. She knew the men wanted coffee, needed it. She also knew not to get them cream or sugar. No man with any respect for his manhood put anything in his coffee, not in Pittsburgh.

Like beer was beer in Pittsburgh, coffee was coffee, and, in the White Castle, coffee was angrier and more bitter than any coffee on this planet. This coffee also seemed disappointed in itself. Coffee burned beyond being coffee any longer. This coffee knew all the dreams and promises people had faith in were lies, and it knew something that escaped most people in Pittsburgh, and it seemed intent on burning what it knew onto the insides of anyone brave enough to actually drink it.

The waitress returned to where she was before the three men entered. She stood, as she had been standing for decades at this time every morning of every day, at the door between the kitchen and the counter, smoking a cigarette and talking to the cook.

"How real do you think any of this is?" Bob asked.

"What?" Fred replied. "The White Castle? This coffee?"

"Yeah, I guess we can start with that. For all we know, this place might be a spaceship left here by aliens," Bob said. "How did this place get sandwiched in between these other buildings?"

Fred glanced at Bob. "What are you saying?" Fred asked. "We're sitting here, right? I can touch you, poke you." Fred jabbed his finger into Bob's shoulder. "We can find a mirror, hold it up, and see if it reflects us. Most of what we allow ourselves to see in a mirror is better off not thought much about."

Fred blew across his coffee in a vain attempt to cool coffee that can never be cooled. White Castle coffee remained hot forever. It wanted to burn the tongue of anyone insane enough to drink it. Blister their lips, scorch their throats, so that they would have a deeper experience of what was involved with speaking.

"We're talking," Fred continued. "There's not much more real out there in the world than these words." Jim remained quiet beside his friend. He stared into his coffee. Jim seemed incapable of moving, of picking up the cup and bringing it to his lips, or he seemed to have forgotten how to do such a thing as drink his morning coffee or wake up, truly wake up to the day.

"That's what you believe, Fred? Words? Telling stories. Looking into mirrors. Leaving footprints. I'm not asking you about your faith in the world. I mean trust." Bob looked at Fred, but Fred was careful not to flinch, not to let him know what his words were doing to him. "I mean," Bob stopped for a moment, looked out the window of the White Castle. "This, Fred. I mean this reality. The one that isn't going anywhere. What else is there?" he asked. "How real do you think everything has been lately?"

Bob kept stopping himself. He knew what he needed to do; he just did not know how to say it or the kind of harm that could be caused by him saying what needed to be said. He knew what truth still remained in the world was better left unsaid. Jim cleared his throat as if he were going to say something, to talk in the presence of Bob, something Jim rarely ever did. Bob looked over at Jim. But perhaps Jim was simply issuing a warning, reminding Bob that this was not the kind of thing a man can talk about in public.

Bob stared back down at his coffee. He dared not lift his eyes, but spoke directly to the coffee more than to Fred or Jim. "We gave that son of yours an awful birth, Fred. We did. All of us." Bob seemed to have fallen inside the cup of coffee. "You think Lucas has a shadow? You think the world you live in would allow such a child to have a shadow? You ever see the child in a mirror? My son," Bob tried to understand what he needed to say about his son before he said it. "He . . . I saw him in mirrors. He never really escaped mirrors. Always in them. Even now. You ever watch what a child does to a mirror when they are looking into it? What they do with their hands, their fingers? A child never only looks."

Bob lifted his coffee cup to his lips, drank a little, burned the inside of his mouth, burned his throat, burned a hole into his stomach. The truth of White Castle coffee is that there is no way to stop the pain once it gets started. One sip most likely takes three days off a man's life.

Bob hoped Fred would say something, would admit that he remembered his son and what remembering his son did to Fred's soul, but he just stared straight ahead. There are sons that should never be spoken of with the man who married your sister. Sons who should never have been given a name. Sons who were lost before they were born. Bob wanted Fred to look at him, he wanted him to remember the night when they were teenagers, the night he asked Fred if he ever had a sister. "Did you?" Bob asked that night. "Did you ever have a sister?"

Bob's heart turned to ash that night. Right there in his parents' backyard. The moon burned a hole in the night sky. Stars dropped out of the sky. They simply died and fell down from the sky. Rivers went dry. That night Bob realized that sins were never forgiven and that they were never punished, either. Sins were sins. And no miracle could save any of them—not Bob, not Fred, not Debra, not Jim—from what had happened, and no human mercy could understand any of it in a way that would allow anyone to bring forgiveness. And Bob's heart stayed in the ravaged dust of that yard. Barren and dry. And he knew he could never judge the innocence of a child after that. He knew that such a desire was foolish and that no one, at least no adult, could understand that kind of innocence. The innocence of a child would always be misunderstood, and any attempt to understand it would make the child's innocence filthy with regret. The blood of such a love that troubles a man's heart would trouble his soul, too, if he had a soul.

All that had been done to daughters and sisters. The true terror was not just in all that had been done to daughters and sisters, but in a man knowing those things had been done and knowing where he was when such things were done and knowing he did nothing about any of it, knowing he was as responsible as any other man. Only sorrow could come to a brother who knew such things. And the month after Bob came to know more than a man could possibly dream of knowing, more than a brother should ever admit to knowing, he left for a war that seemed to kill as many men as it saved. And Bob went into those fields killing as many men as he could kill, because he was told doing so would save the world from enemies who could not be seen. And he killed as many of these unknown, invisible enemies as he could, until the day he found himself lost in the forest and taken away by the women whose skin was made of rain.

"How long have you and Debra been talking about Lucas?" Bob asked. "Telling story after story?" Fred shrugged his shoulders. "How long have you and Jim stood on that porch of yours drinking and looking at that bicycle, with my sister locked inside the house wandering from room to room?" Fred did not even bother answering him. He just shrugged off the question. "How did that bicycle get there? You remember? I can't."

Bob sipped his coffee, tasted the bitter madness of all that that White Castle coffee had endured, or perhaps what Bob actually tasted was his own bitterness, his own loss of faith, his own disappointment in himself for not telling Debra what he knew and what he understood about himself, now that he knew what he had done. And he knew how difficult it was for any man born and raised in Pittsburgh, and who had gone off to Vietnam, to sit and talk about sins and not ask for forgiveness. "Has all that we have said made any of this real? Anything? All these years talking about what is not here and not once talking about what is here. What was done."

Fred touched the handle of his coffee cup. He knew he had to be delicate. He had to be careful. Fred knew the simplest thing to do was to concentrate on drinking his coffee. He knew that was why they had stopped at the White Castle. And he knew, once they had all finished their coffee, perhaps ordered eggs and eaten them, the three men could be on their way. He hoped that, if he simply did not say a word, then all of what Bob was saying would be forgotten. A man has no right to remember all that another man's sister has done in her life, even if that man is married to the other man's sister. Men should remain quiet. Knowing is strange enough. There is no need to say anything. A man has to accept what he needs to accept and that is enough. A woman, a sister, has her right to her past, to her privacy, and a man needs to accept that.

"Be mindful," Bob whispered.

Fred feared what was now possible. He looked at Jim, seemingly, for guidance. "We're in the White Castle on Cedar Avenue," Fred whispered. "This is coffee. Pittsburgh is Pittsburgh. Debra is sleeping at home. Lucas is only as safe as the stories we tell." Fred thought simple words spoken aloud becoming reality. "Debra and I have a son, and I am the boy's father," Fred spoke softly. He kept his head down. His chin tight in his chest. The day this all began, Debra told Fred, "You and I have a son. You are the child's father." Debra looked into her husband's eyes. She touched his cheek. "Nothing else has happened." Fred still did not move. "Don't complicate anything," she said. "He is a boy. Our boy. You are a father." She showed him a paper with his name, her name, and the boy's name on it. "Sign this." She then handed Fred a paper with a tiny footprint drawn on it. "And this. Words prove more than any of us are likely to admit." Fred drained his coffee cup.

"We've done everything we could, Fred," Bob said. "More than what could be expected of us. More than I ever thought was possible. Doing all we did, day after day for years, hasn't really done much, though, has it? There are people in the world—boys, girls, prostitutes, women in the foothills throughout Vietnam, men left behind in tunnels—who do not need stories. And there are others who only exist in stories. It's the stories that we tell that make them real. You can say what you want about Lucas, Fred. Say what you feel you need to say for Debra's sake, for your own sake. Hide away what you feel you need to hide away to be safe. Words will let you do just about anything. Words are flexible that way. Most everything in life may begin with a story, but, sooner or later, a boy becomes flesh and blood or he doesn't ever become anything but words."

"If the stories are the lies, and if the mirrors or the shadows thrown down on the sidewalk are the truth, then what?" Fred asked. "How is it possible for any of us?"

"Go home, Fred. Nothing is waiting for you in the city. You know that. Pittsburgh is empty. At least, empty of what you need to find. You know that what you tell yourself you are looking for is not here. It can't be. What has been lost is lost. That's what happens when the past disappears or when the story exhausts itself. The son you hope to find, the one you want to return, the calm you want and the calm you dream of giving to Debra, all of what you've been believing in for so long, is not to be found in the city. Not in any alley. Not in some basement."

Bob finished his coffee, put the cup down loud enough for the waitress to hear. She ignored him and kept talking to the cook, hoping the three men would simply leave the diner without wanting anything else. Bob tried for eye contact with her but failed. "You go be with Debra, Fred. You two need to see what you have been keeping yourself from understanding. Clean out that boy's room, so you can see something that you are afraid to see. Both of you. And do the cleaning without telling any stories. And everything you touch, you think of what you are truly touching."

Again, Bob tried to get the waitress's attention. Again, she ignored him. Frustrated, he looked down at his hands, rubbed them together. He nearly felt the pain of all the years, all he had done with these hands. He counted his fingers, a habit he had picked up from his father. Every day when his father came home from working in the mills, when he sat at the dinner table, the first thing he did was count his fingers. Bob still had ten, five on each hand. He was amazed by that, by how a man living the life he lived could possibly have all his fingers. The skin at the very tips of his fingers was wearing away, eroding. He figured it would be gone soon.

"You ever think about how much you touch in one day? All that your hands go through in one day?" Bob looked up at Fred and Jim, then back down into his hands. "Just here at breakfast, think of all we touched. Think of all that we did with our hands. We touch so much that you would think that the skin on our hands would just wear away. And we do it all without thinking much about any of it." Bob shook his head. "And not only what we touch just in a day, but how we touch all the things we touch. Every day of our lives we touch things. People. Day after day. Do you think it is possible to go a whole day without touching something?"

Fred and Jim looked at Bob. They knew he was off in his world. Fred usually became uncomfortable around him because of it. He thought, when Bob drifted like this, that too much opened up, too much became uncertain, that he might say more than what in all honesty could be said or trusted. "I doubt it, Bob," Fred replied. "I can't imagine doing that. We touch as much by accident as we do with intention."

"So much hides away in the small things," Bob wiped his mouth with the back of his hand. "There I go touching again." He laughed. "What do you think all this touching is doing? You think it's possible to do all this and somehow remain innocent?" Bob waited for Fred or Jim to reply, even though he knew they would have nothing to say or they would be too afraid to say anything.

The waitress finally walked over, refilled their cups, and asked them if they wanted breakfast. They each ordered, and she took their orders over to the cook, who did not seem very pleased about having to do his job. Bob picked up his cup, blew across the coffee, a hopeless ritual.

"I think when you touch something that it stays with you. It may seem like it disappears, that it is gone from you, but it stays. I think you touch some other person and that stays even deeper." Bob put his cup down, looked at the tips of his fingers. "You ever think of why God gave us hands to begin with? The devil roams the earth looking for boys with idle hands, so he can put them to work doing his bidding, instead of doing God's desire. Everything a man does with his hands, his body, his mouth, he's doing to the people in his life. A man's wife or children experiences it all, even though they were not with him when he did any of it. Hands reveal more than words. You understand that? Maybe you need to ask Debra that, Fred. Just ask her about all the things her hands have done. Have her tell you the story of her hands, and maybe you can make sense of why Lucas matters so much to her."

The waitress brought their food. She looked at the three men with that nearly dead gaze a doll gives you, a woman too tired to be furious with living and with too little left of her imagination to do anything about it. The woman's lips seemed haunted by those dried-up desires that more and more people on the North Side had begun carrying with them and continued to carry with them until they found a way to give up and die. The waitress opened her mouth to say what she says every day at this moment, after placing the plates in front of hung-over men or men just waking to their day, but this time nothing came out. No words. She just walked away, leaving the men to their breakfast. They ate their eggs and toast and their home fries, wrapped in the cloak of their silence. An end to all the betrayals.

"Too much clutter," Bob said between bites. "You and Debra have gone and crowded yourself with too much. Words. Things. You clean up that room, Fred, and you are bound to find something you did not know was there. You think you are just cleaning. The same is true of your memory. Sometimes I feel like I am deliberately losing stuff in my stories, doing it so I can find them later, when I go back to the memory."

Bob looked down at his plate. He tried to bring himself to eat some of the potatoes. "If the coffee doesn't do you in, these potatoes will," he said, then looked back at Fred. "You need to stop waiting. I've told Debra this every afternoon when she snuck into my house. Every time she walked through my door and closed it behind her, and we sat at my kitchen table or on the floor in the livingroom or went upstairs, and she rested her forehead on my shoulder. Sweating. She wants to keep hiding away." Bob looked over at Fred. He waited. "No one can tell a man what he does not want to know, Fred. It isn't possible. Certainly can't convince a man that any of it is true."

"Eleven years, Bob." Fred said. He put his fork on his plate and wiped his mouth with the napkin. "A man can believe in all kinds of stories. Even stories he has never told. I sat on the edge of our bed, and I listened to Debra leaving. I listened to the story she told, and I watched her disappear that day."

"It was never about you saving her from what she did or what was done to her, Fred." He placed his hand on Fred's shoulder, squeezed it. Few men in Pittsburgh were as comfortable touching another man as Bob was. He paid it no mind. He knew exactly what he was doing

when he touched another man, even a man with lips as beautiful as
Fred's. No harm comes from touching another man, or a woman
for that matter, so long as you know what it is that you are doing.
"A woman does all she does and it makes her who she is. And this
woman is my sister, Fred. She'll always be my sister. You marrying
her didn't change that."

Something about the understanding that the three men had all
agreed on years ago crumbled a little. Jim experienced it first, knew
how close Bob was coming to saying what should never be said. He
stood up, put a few bills on the counter, and said he had to be going.
Now. He had to leave now. This very minute. Not many men could
handle the deterioration of such agreements, the worry of what it
would lead to, and Jim knew enough about himself, about what he
could and could not handle, that he knew he needed to leave. He said
goodbye to Fred and Bob and walked out.

Once outside, Jim nearly bumped into a boy whose skin was so
beautiful that Jim doubted his own innocence. He watched the boy
walk down the street. He knew what he was feeling, knew it had a
name, and knew that it was one of those names a man should never admit to himself. He felt an urge to follow the boy, or, perhaps,
at least run after the boy to apologize, but instead he turned away
from the boy with his eyes and with what little touch of desire that
had survived in him from the life he had lived, and he looked back
through the window of the diner, at the backs of his two friends, at
Bob's fingers squeezing into Fred's shoulder.

Jim came close to reciting a litany of sins, ones he had committed, ones he desired to commit, sins that, if he had world enough and
time, he would commit with the boy who bumped into him, then he
did what he had done most of his life, he turned away from the diner
and quietly walked up Cedar toward East North Avenue. He walked
away, knowing that men like him, men who remained as quiet as
he did, some day perished. Men like him never died, they perished.
And Jim felt like he was walking away from more than the diner. He
felt he was walking away from the stories, from all that had been said
and done, from all that had been promised, from all that he once
hoped was true.

"I just listened, Bob. I sat and listened, and each word Debra uttered carried her away. It's a difficult thing to do. To sit and watch your wife escape. And she never looked at me the whole time. She just told me what she wanted me to know. I never needed to hear all that she said. But she said it. I had thought it, but then, when she said it, I came to know it in a way that was different than thinking it. And you weren't there then, Bob. You were still in Vietnam. You were missing in action. The letters had stopped. The military told us you died. Then they said you were AWOL. They concocted some story about you falling through the earth, to the center of the earth, and you had started a commune of refugees there, and you were plotting crimes against nature and God and the United States. Then once again they told us you were dead and in a body bag and would be home any day. Then they told us you had done your tour of duty, and you were coming home. Then they said they lost your paperwork. They were no longer certain that they knew what happened. All the places you had gone. And they asked us if we were certain you had joined the army."

"They began accusing Debra of seeing things, of unnatural desires." Fred laughed, pushed his plate away from him. "Your sister. You say she is your sister because you need to forget. You say that other woman was your wife and that you had a son. And that son of yours went to Vietnam, too. Father and son fighting for America, like super heroes. You say a sister is no different than a daughter and that a sister is more than a woman. But your parents died and that put an end to it. Death will do that. And there comes a time when you have to realize that every word you ever spoke has not changed a thing. Just like all the stories we have told about Lucas, all the birthdays, all of it, has not changed anything. And that bicycle leaning against that tree is no different from some other bicycle in anyone else's yard."

Fred looked out the window, hoping to see Jim still standing there, staring in at them. "Jim sees a fear of truth every time he looks at that bicycle. He sees a reckoning. The rapture. Lilacs blooming one final time. Jim told me all the lilacs would die before rust took care of that bicycle. He told me that. Just goes to show you what happens to a man's mind when he goes and takes all those poetry classes. Rust is no metaphor. It's what happens in the world. Rust kills poetry."

Fred shrugged Bob's hand from his shoulder and reached for his coffee cup. The coffee had gotten as cold as it ever would get in the White Castle. He drank that coffee in almost the same way that he drank his beer. "Jim said we should give that bicycle a name, the way people name dogs and cats. We should call it Rosebud, Jim said." Fred laughed. "Rosebud. Or Ishmael. Jim, and his books."

"Doesn't matter what name you give it," Bob said, "You just have to ask the right questions."

"Jim said the right name helps all that. Guides the journey, the questions. He says we have to give it a name before we can begin," Fred replied. "What do you think we are most forbidden to see? To say? Maybe those are the only questions worth the effort of asking."

"Maybe it's more about what keeps you from asking what you're afraid to ask?"

"We both know where we've been. What we've done."

"And all that happened when we were children? None of it needs to be forgiven or remembered. It's inside us. That's enough."

"You forget what happened. You forget it because we were children. There are no other ways to look back and to understand now what happened then. You can't understand it once you are no longer a child."

"So we should sit down with some child and tell all the stories to the child, and the child will explain everything." Now it seemed like Bob was the one who was afraid. He kept his stare locked on his coffee.

"Debra confessed and confessed in that room," Fred said. "It did not change anything. It did not help her. Day and night she confessed, and when I walked into that room she stopped talking and looked at me as if I had just killed everything that she trusted."

"You can't truly believe in much more than what you can imagine, Fred. Old words that have been worn out by saying them too often."

"The words are not that old, Bob, and none of them are very worn down, let alone worn out. We said what needed to be said. Those words are untouched."

"The way a boy dies says a lot about his father, Fred. The stories we tell. The ones we don't." Bob held up his coffee cup in a heroic effort to get the waitress's attention. She ignored him. "I've got nothing to do with them. And I don't want anything to do with them anymore. I am done with them, but you need to be straight with them. And Debra," Bob stopped himself again. "She has to be willing to survive."

"Like that red wheelbarrow."

Bob looked at Fred as if he were the one that suddenly had become less sane, like he was the one who had come home from Vietnam about as close to being in a body bag as a man can get, while still escaping it. "Like the bicycle, Fred. The bicycle. It's that simple. No more. That bicycle never belonged in your yard. Never."

"Moving it will not change much."

"You know it will, Fred. It is why the bicycle is still there. The bicycle does not stand for hope. It is not a prayer. It is a bicycle. You have to undo what you have done, what Debra has done."

"But not you. You are going to hold to everything as it has been. No sacrifice from you."

Bob looked again at the waitress and gestured with his cup. The woman finally decided to make her way over, as if it were the most complicated decision she had made in her entire life. She poured another cup for Bob, but stopped before reaching the top. She looked at Fred, and he nodded. She emptied the rest of the pot into his cup. "Coffee does not grow on trees, you know," she said, then walked back to the cook, mumbled something out of earshot of Fred and Bob, and the cook looked over at Fred and Bob and laughed.

"I did all I did. You know that. Debra knows it."

"And now?"

"Now it is out of my hands. It never was in my hands. You and Debra are the ones that started it all. I did not bring Lucas into the world. I did nothing to take him out of the world."

"And you just go on writing on walls? Playing with matches? Kicking at dirt?"

"It's not dirt. It's the earth." Bob looked at Fred to be certain Fred understood exactly what he meant. "Nothing is ever the same once you have done it. The next day, Debra was not the same. When I came back from Vietnam, she was not the same. Married to you the whole time I was over there. What that must have done to both of you. And now? You do what you are doing because you think it is right. You think it makes sense, and you think it will not really change much. Then you do it. Sometimes it takes years to settle in. Even then, sometimes it never really settles. It keeps moving. You still want to believe in it."

"And you're the one telling me to go home. Clean the room. Empty it?"

"I'm not psychic, Fred. I only know that it seems right. If not right, it certainly is necessary. But what will come of it all? Jacob's Ladder for all I can know. Tower of Babel. Who am I to know?"

"You shouldn't have done it, Bob."

"Children get born in all sorts of ways, Fred," Bob replied. "You and Debra. You need to start believing in what you tell yourself you know and sort it out from what is no longer true, what you and Debra have been inventing. Children come into this world in ways that remain mysterious. It's as much about desire as it is about anything else. But if you think long enough about it, you come to realize it's more about death than about anything else, shoring fragments against a ruin that you cannot save yourself from. Death wins out. Sooner or later you will find yourself standing in the ruins. It doesn't matter what you do about bringing children into the world or how you do it. The truth is, a child is born and a child dies. We die. Once we were children, and once we believed everything what our parents told us. We believed in sons dying for our sins. We believed in going to bed early and eating Wonder Bread. We believed our parents when they told us that they were our mothers and fathers, and we thought that would never change, could never change. We believed that Hansel and Gretel would find their way home. Debra believed that a prince came into her bedroom and woke her from her sleep." Bob shook his head. "Now look at us."

"Yeah, look at us."

"Go home, Fred. There was nothing to find. You can tell Debra another story, or you two can sit in that room and quietly clean up everything. Get a camera and take photographs of all the places that we searched, if you think that would help."

Fred looked at Bob. "I wish some of what you had done," Fred started. He wiped his hands on his jeans, then he tried to start again, "Some of what we caused to happen, even in our sleep." Fred noticed the waitress looking in their direction, staring at them. Fred slowly finished his coffee. He spoke softer. "I wish you had not done some of it, Bob. It never seemed right to me. Even at the time. There was no way to protect Debra. And then you left without telling anyone, without even saying goodbye to anyone. And when you were away writing letters home, Debra never could understand what had happened. I don't think she wanted to believe any of it, at least I tell myself that she did not want to believe it. Maybe she did. Maybe she wanted it to happen the way it did."

"The longer you live, the more believing breaks down, Fred. It all stops. You wake up one Sunday morning and realize there's no reason to go to mass. You realize that that priest standing up there is just as human as you are. And it's not so much that you decided to turn away from God, as it is that you begin to understand what God is truly capable of doing. You realize that what happened to Job was not a testament of his faith, but the revelation of the terrible truth of God. You look at that, at Job's daughters under a pile of stones, and you realize God did that. He let that happen. In most ways, when you get right down to it, God made it happen. And while you are cutting your way through the jungles in Vietnam, the whole time you know God is doing this. God is watching this. God set this in motion. You're going to kill the enemy, because we trust in God. It says so. Printed on money, so we never forget whom to trust. Then you spend the rest of your life, night after night on that porch drinking beer, wishing the story you've been telling yourself and Debra and everyone around was not true. Wishing you could lay your hands on God and teach God that pain is not simple. Teach God a lesson, because you have come to realize that God, not you, is the one in need of a lesson. A lesson God will never forget. You get to the place where you realize you never had to fear God. You realize that, and, when you do, you realize what you have done is not so evil."

"That is what makes you able to sleep? Live with what all that has been done? All that you have done?"

"It's not about that. It's not. Years ago, Debra and I were brother and sister. Now you and I are sitting here. Time passes."

"Nothing gets healed, Bob. The wound is lurking beneath what you can know or what you can admit to yourself is possible." Fred stood up. "And there is no way to forgive what you cannot forget. That never happens." Fred put his hand on Bob's shoulder. "I'm tired. You are right. We looked. We walked down Federal Street. We walked along the North Side. I know what I have known all along. And that's enough. More than enough."

Bob stood up. The two men put money on the counter. The waitress smiled at them, but did not move. Bob doubted that she would ever move again. They walked out the door into a morning fragrant with that scent that comes the moment before a summer rain. Bob looked up into the clouds. "Rain is in the air," Bob said. "Find your way home, Fred. It's not the same as it was. The way home. You promise not to talk. You make that your vow. You touch Debra and see what that does to her skin. See if you burn it or if her skin turns cold. See if her shadow disappears or turns to ice. A lot that gets said with what a body does when touched."

Bob and Fred walked away from the White Castle and headed back up Federal Street, slower and older than the night before. Their tired bodies found their way over the top of the hill, down Center Avenue, around Horseshoe Bend, until they arrived at Bob's small house.

The two men stopped at the gate to Bob's house. "You take what you need with you, Fred." They stared into each other's eyes, held their gaze a bit, as the summer rain fell gentle and warm on their skin. "The right laughter mixed with summer rain cleanses the world of all its sins," Bob said. "All of them. You just need to trust that what's been done is done."

Fred smiled, nodded. He turned to walk down the street, but before he managed to get even a few steps away, Bob called after him. Fred stopped. "Dead in my tracks," he thought to himself. "I'm stopping dead in my tracks." He looked back at Bob.

"There was never anything we could do. Nothing," Bob said. "It's difficult to find a boy who isn't truly lost." Fred said he knew that. He had known it all along. He just thought maybe something would appear and put an end to the sadness. He hoped that Debra could forget everything, put it all aside, as easily as they had.

Fred then turned away and headed up the small hill into the alley, across the gravel, and to his house. Home. To his wife. To all the

271

stories he had left behind. He walked into the yard, grabbed that bicycle by the handlebars, and yanked it out of the blackberry bushes and dragged it to the garage. He didn't bother to put it inside. He simply leaned it against the doors. Should someone want it and take it, that would be as good as anything else he could think of. Fred watched rain fall on the bicycle. He thought of more rust forming on the bicycle. He tried to see the rust forming, but laughed at himself. He wondered what happened to skin when rain fell on it. If rain could do what it did to metal, then he wondered what it might do to skin. He wiped rain from his forehead, looked at his fingertips, half expecting to find rust there, and walked toward the back porch. The light was on in the kitchen. Debra was sitting at the table.

Neither Fred nor Debra could bring themselves to say anything. There's a silence that goes deeper when it is between two people. When only one person is silent, it is more quiet than silent. This moment in the kitchen was a true silence. Year after year of having coffee together, having sex with each other, dreaming beside each other, lay beneath this silence. Buried. Even though Fred was standing perfectly still and Debra was sitting even more still, they could hear the floor creaking, like some memory tearing open at the seams. What begins with family eventually finds its way into your soul. It settles there. Once that happens, there's not much anyone can do to change it.

CHAPTER 26

The ghost of Clarence sat quietly on a rock near the edge of the Monongahela River. He feared walking. Feared leaving footprints. Worried that someone would stumble upon them and read the final story of him and Ai, the story he protected from the world. With each footstep, he imprinted that story into the earth, exposed it, made it vulnerable to someone stealing it from his memory.

All of Clarence's other stories of Ai were gone. He told them to protect himself from loving Sula, his children, or anyone else ever again. He knew, by making his skin thicker and thicker, he would never be vulnerable and would never risk losing anyone. He used those stories about Ai as a way to possess her. He put her inside his stories and condemned her to them. Made her the woman he needed her to be. Every day, from the day she left him, he said her name aloud at least once and told at least one person a story about his life with Ai. His friends told him to let her go. They were frightened by the way Clarence talked about loving that woman, frightened by the sound of his voice, by what happened to the muscles in his face when he said her name.

Even while Ai and Clarence were together, his friends worried. "Love like you got for that woman got no mercy in it," Earl said. "It's a love that turns you foolish with wanting more than a man got any right to." Clarence shook off every word his friends said about the dangers of loving Ai. "You need to love only a little," Phyllis told him one night. "You protect a part of you, keep a part of who you are, so if she do break you heart, your heart still got something in it, so your heart don't turn to ashes, so you can go and give some love to someone else who come along."

Every night the same drift of voices. Every night he refused to listen. His friends said loving a woman in the ways that he loved Ai was bound to end in disillusion. "It's what happens when your life revolves around loving a woman," Earl told him. "The love itself destroys what is in front of your eyes. It blinds you, Clarence. That kind of love imprisons you. You got no place to breathe. You suffocate yourself, and you suffocate the love itself. You strangle it. Choke it."

Even an innocent word can be an act of violence, when a man loves a woman beyond reason. Earl warned Clarence about how words do things to a woman that no man can understand, and when she did finally leave for good, and Clarence kept going on and on about her, his friends said that it wasn't right for him to be doing that. They told him that he was going to wear his tongue out. A woman has a right to leave a man. A man has a right to get angry, to drink himself over the edge and into foolishness, to punch walls. Then a man needs to accept it. That woman was gone, they told him. Gone. No coming back. And talking about her was hollowing out his heart. Blinding him. No good could come from it. "You wanted that woman too much, Clarence. Ain't right. Never was. What did you expect?" Earl asked. "No woman can survive such desire. You burned her bones gone, just turned her bones to ashes and dust. She nearly turned herself invisible on herself. Like she couldn't see her own self no more. And it weren't love, Clarence. It weren't. It was desire. You didn't love her; she didn't love you. It was the two of you choking the you out of each other. "

Clarence only told everyone that it was love. It was. He called his friends fools. "You all drowning in a damn fear of touching a woman with your own naked truth. You touch a woman like you scared. A man can't fear going into the unknown. That's what love is. The unknown. If it's already known, why you go there? You touch a woman, and it wakens you. If you fear that, you will never know anything worth knowing," he told them. "You fools, too frightened by life. Thinking that if you live your life you might lose it. Well, you will. That's a promise. You all are going to lose your life. You losing it now, in what you call living. You are all gonna die when the day comes for it to happen. Ain't none of you can stop that from happening. Might as well be going there with all you got."

His friends shook their heads at the old man, took him by his shoulders, shook him hard and wild, told him to wake his fool self up out of his dream world. They told him that all this talk of Ai would only kill what life he had left in him. "A real man got to live the life he's been given," his mother said. "The Lord don't care much for those wasting away their lives with being past to the present. You get on with what life you now got. What life you had, you had, now be grateful with this here."

But Clarence refused to listen. He turned Ai into a myth. He wrapped her up inside these stories and kept her there.

Now, in death, all the other stories were gone. He only held onto one memory. One. A kiss. In life, he punished everyone for not being Ai. In life, he strangled her freedom by holding onto this memory. In death, he continued to protect it, to hold it. But love is not meant to be owned like this, and when Ai tried to steal herself back from him, that day she told him she needed to go, that she wanted to stay but had to go, Clarence felt her running off with his very soul, and he surrendered himself to a nearly inexplicable aura of loneliness.

Any love can only bear to be touched so often, then it erodes, and when a man is not careful, each time he touches a woman she begins to disappear more and more. Ai becamed scarred by Clarence's touch, even though it was Ai herself who had taken his hand that one night in the rainstorm and taught him to touch her in those ways that now frightened her. They put their love for each other on their skin, burned their love into each other. His touch shocked her, and the way she went about touching him made her think she had never known anything about herself before this. She wondered who she was before touching Clarence, and she began wondering who she would become by touching him in those ways. Then she became fearful with her wanting, her wanting too much, so much. She grieved for his touch when he was away. Those fingers. Those lips. That deep voice of his. Clarence left the ashes of his touch on her skin, and she came to know a love that she never thought was possible. But for Ai, it was too soon. It was too much. She could not catch her breath, so she let go.

There are words for everything imaginable in the entire universe. There are words for animals and plants that have become extinct. There are words for things that you cannot see with your naked eye. There is even a word for eternity. But there is no word for this, not for what Ai was feeling, for what her muscles were experiencing, for what her heart was doing to her thoughts as she told Clarence she needed to leave, that she did not know what else to do. For this, there are no words. Ai started to say what would become her final words to Clarence, but her voice stopped. She simply raised her fingers to her lips and placed them there, gently. Her slight gesture carried with it the look of sacrifice.

Johnny stood along the Monongahela, keeping his eyes fixed on the trails winding through the blackberry bushes. He listened to the breeze. Even though he'd been told that ghosts don't make any sounds, he still thought that perhaps a clumsy ghost would rustle leaves or branches, would wake the living. He waited in this way every night. Near morning, he would untie Sylvia, then run across the bridge to check in with his grandfather before making his way over to the North Side. Most nights, Johnny hoped for rain. He thought rain would make better soil for footprints. In summer, dust became too thick for clear footprints. They all blurred together, drifted over each other. Stories mixing with stories. The breeze practically erased each footprint before any could be read.

For all those nights of patient waiting, attentive watching, Johnny only found footprints of the living. Dull footprints of people coming to the river to escape the city streets. No ghost footprints. No stories. No words. Just plain footprints. But Johnny believed that he would find his great-grandfather's footprints. So he inspected each footprint, and he was careful with his breathing when he crouched down near a footprint, in case it was the footprint of a ghost. Careful with each breath, so as not to disturb a single word, a single mark left behind in the footprint. Reading the footprinted stories of ghosts required touch as much as sight. The living lifted the stories of the ghosts from their footprints onto the palms of their hands. Many of the stories in the footprints confused him. Most, he simply could not read, let alone make sense of. Fragmented moments of a story opened in a few of the footprints, but Johnny became more lost by reading them.

Elgin had shown Johnny such stories carved into the palms of his own hands, stories he had brought back from Vietnam. Stories he himself could not make sense of, but that he now carried. Stories of dead soldiers, of small children burned beyond their innocence, and of men and women trying to dig roots out of soil ruined by American bombs. Tales of destroyed families bombed into tiny pieces of flesh. Each line in the palm of his grandfather's hands was a story; each wrinkle a memory.

The night Johnny saw the grey figure of a man near the edge of the river, he thought that he was hallucinating. This nearly invisible man teased the river, something that few ghosts had the courage to do. His grey skin blurred into the night fog. He felt that he was seeing through the man, rather than looking at him.

Johnny crouched down and leaned against a tree, keeping his own body hidden from the gaze of the grey man. He'd been told that ghosts carried their life scent with them. Those who smoked smelled of smoke; those who lived in the heart of the city smelled of that humid heat, the scent of that steam that rose out of manhole covers. Johnny sniffed the night air, but smelled only the mud of the riverbank. The old age of the river. Then he recognized something else. A scent of what rust would smell like, if God ever decided to set it on fire. Anger. He caught a distinct whiff of anger burning into the river, into the night air, into the riverbank. And even more than anger, he smelled loss. Broken flowers. The kind of loss that has no beginning. The kind of loss that will have no end. The story of a hole that Clarence had been born with already eating away at him. A hole that, for a time, Ai filled.

Elgin told Johnny that Clarence lived every day, after Ai left, locked inside a sense of loss. He sacrificed beauty that day. From that day forth, he only saw all the ugliness and all the misery that existed in Pittsburgh. And he took it all into him, and Clarence, himself, became ugly.

"It's true, Johnny," Elgin said. "My father was not only turning ugly as sin, his ugly was becoming our sins." Clarence could never truly see his wife nor see his children. They, and everything and everyone else around him, remained invisible. He could not experience what Ai had given to him; he only felt what she had taken from him when she left. His breath and skin smelled of this abandonment. This loss weighed heavy inside every word that he spoke. It crowded his eyes, turned his pupils red and yellow, made the white disappear straight out of them. His sweat stank of it. Holding on to this loss burned into his very being, draining his skin of its deep beauty, and, after he died, the house still carried that scent. It sunk into the carpets, the wallpaper, the pipes, the water. Everything. Sula wanted to burn down the house. She feared that she would carry that scent on her skin, that her children would live a life burned by the scent of Clarence's loss. And now Johnny smelled it.

He knew this grey man had to be his great-grandfather. This apparition. Johnny was clearly not looking at a living man. An innocent man. He was seeing nothing, seeing everything that was not there, that could no longer be there, and what must not have been there when the apparition was alive. He was breathing loss. Pure and simple loss. And all there was to see of this scent of loss was a shadow. The grey shadow of this nearly disappeared man slid from the rock onto the trail, leaving footprints in the wet earth. Imprinting words, drawings, images of his life into the earth.

Johnny quietly made his way along the path behind the shadow man. He held back a bit and waited for the man to completely disappear into the shadows before approaching the footprints. He knelt on the ground and felt something deep inside telling him this would stain him. He thought of leaving, of walking away from whatever this was, but he was drawn to this desire to know something forbidden. He moved closer to the footprint and brought his hand near to the edges of it. He leaned close and held his breath.

He saw images of Clarence's hands. His fingers. The tips of his fingers. Tiny scars like thin paper cuts. It was the footprint of the day Ai left. The day she called Clarence and told him she needed to say goodbye, that she needed to breathe, to find her own life, that he had already lived his life. Ai told Clarence that he had lived those days and made his life from those days, and now she needed to live these days, to make her life from these days.

That day Clarence accidentally cut the tip of his index finger on the edge of a piece of paper. The sting of this cut stayed with him, reminded him of this moment. The next morning, while slicing into an orange, the juice stung this cut. He never allowed it to heal. He died with this paper cut still in the tip of his finger. Each morning, Clarence irritated the slender slit at the tip of his finger; some mornings, he added a cut to another finger. He rubbed salt into these cuts. Every time he touched a woman he felt this pain.

Clarence thought of adding cuts to his lips, small, thin slices. He kept these cuts open and available to pain. The salt from Sula's sweat seeped into the cuts, reminding him to never let go of the pain, to never find any pleasure in Sula's body, in her touch. He feared that if he did not feel pain when he touched Sula, he would fall in love with her, and, in falling in love with Sula, he would forget Ai. He feared forgetting Ai more than he feared death.

Johnny followed the trail of Clarence's footprints. Each footprint scarred Johnny's skin. Wrinkled his young skin. Story after story he had heard before, stories that his grandfather had told him of his great-grandfather's life. Johnny thought of the scars on the Street Elder's tongue. Her knees. The rivers of memories that lined her tongue, her lips. He feared what all the stories in these footprints would do to his skin, to the palms of his hands. Words never seemed to look like the things that they were about; they never sounded like the things people were talking about, their feelings or their desires. The desperate longing to say something true. Elgin told Johnny that he wished he could write Thuy's name on a piece of paper and have the writing of her name somehow feel like her touch or to have her name written on paper look like her, instead of just those four letters resting on a piece of paper, marking her absence, reminding him that she was no longer there.

One day, after having lunch and taking a walk along Chestnut Street, Ai kissed Clarence gently on his lips, then stepped out of his car to return to work. Clarence stopped her. He called her name, and she turned around. Waited. On this day, in the middle of a spring afternoon, with the sun warm enough, but not too warm, as he walked over toward Ai, she asked, "What?"

Later, she would tell him that she thought he had stopped her because she had left something in the car, and he was giving it to her before he drove the miles, mile after mile, home. He said nothing. He took her into his arms and kissed her. One. Single. Time. He kissed her so deep down into her soul that nothing would ever be the same again. Nothing. They kissed so deeply, they both forgot their names. Clarence's lips on Ai's lips. Her lips on his. Their mouths opened. Every clock on the planet stopped. Time waited. The most faithful beer drinkers in Pittsburgh held their breath, but had no idea why they were unable to drink their beers. Pittsburgh would never be the same. Clarence's right hand pressed into the small of Ai's back, pulling her toward him. His left hand was lost somewhere. He never could quite remember where his left hand had gone. He thought his left hand must have been holding onto Ai's right shoulder. It had to be somewhere. A hand doesn't just disappear.

Ai embraced Clarence. Her hands clung to his shoulders. Her knees buckled, and she nearly collapsed. For one moment in time, she looked at Clarence in complete astonishment, not realizing what had just happened. To her. To him. To the rest of their lives. To Pittsburgh. To rivers. She felt something break and heal in her at the same time. She felt this is what it is like to drown. And Clarence felt the same. It was that kind of kiss. "So this is what a kiss is," Clarence thought to himself. "This is how your soul feels when it awakens. This is what a woman's body does, what a woman's body feels like when you kiss her."

He felt like it was the very first time in his life he ever kissed a woman. He let Ai go. She stumbled out of his embrace, never taking her eyes off him. Just staring at him. She took a few of the strangest backward steps Clarence had ever seen a woman take. She stopped, nearly fell down. Then she did. She fell. Right there. Down onto the sidewalk. And she looked like she would never rise from that sidewalk again. She looked like her life had begun and ended in the same instant. She looked like she understood something that had been lost by every human being since the invention of time and since the loss of innocent desires.

Clarence started walking toward her, but Ai waved him off. After days had passed, or perhaps after only a few seconds, she slowly pulled her body, her heart, up off the sidewalk. She brushed off her skirt, turned to walk into the building where she worked, but then turned back to look at Clarence. She raised her hand to wave good-bye to him, but it seemed that just as she was about to wave, her hand became confused or terrified, and just kind of flopped back down to her side. Her mouth began to form a smile, to form a word, but it could not quite do any of that; her mouth seemed too confused.

Clarence would never forget that moment. No one had ever looked at him like that. No one had ever seen him like this. He felt that, at last, after all his years of wandering around city streets, walking into dusty bars, finally a woman, a woman nearly young enough to be his daughter, looked at him, that a woman finally slowed down everything in her life enough to see him. He felt alive. In this moment of her eyes looking into him, he felt that she had given him life. This is what God meant by seeing, by giving humans sight, by giving them eyes. This is what seeing makes possible. Her eyes slowly closed. For a moment she put her hand across her eyes as if to rejoin time, to make an effort to return to the sidewalk and continue on her way to work, to continue living her life here in Pittsburgh.

Like Ai, Clarence did not know all that he was seeing, all that he was feeling. He watched her walk to the door of the building where she worked. He did not take his eyes off her. After she entered the building, he stood there staring at that door for minutes, perhaps for hours. In part, he did this because he no longer remembered how to move, how his body worked, his muscles, his joints, his legs. He wanted to have an inconsolable memory of Ai, one that forever escaped time, one that would become like the Monongahela River. There. Always astonished. River-deep. A shadow that stayed on his skin like a stain. A stain that became visible, remained visible, even on the darkest of skin.

Johnny looked up from the footprint. The grey apparition of Clarence stood in the distance. Lost. Uncertain. "I never once feared my dreams when I lay down beside Ai." Telling a memory betrays it. Soils it. What Clarence felt. What Ai felt. What she saw in her mysterious way for seeing. What Clarence thought he saw. It must remain unspoken. Telling the story of that kiss is to diminish it, to transform it, to break it into tiny pieces. Johnny knelt at the footprint telling this story, unfaithful to the moment between appear and disappear.

Clarence took a step down the path toward Johnny, wanting to travel back in time, thinking that going back down the trail would change everything. Johnny watched him forget Ai. He watched the story fade from Clarence and felt it become a part of him. Clarence turned more grey. "You found what you were looking for, or at least what you think you were looking for," Johnny expected someone to say, but no voices filled the air. A new sense of a different kind of loss. Johnny had never seen anything as dark as that trail along the Monongahela River after Clarence disappeared from it. Clarence had taken not just all the light with him, but had taken all the hope for light with him as well. Just gone. And Johnny looked like a young schoolboy afraid of a dark room.

CHAPTER 27

Morning light fell through the branches, stirring Sylvia out of her dreams. The heels of her feet rubbed into the mud of the riverbank, and her breathing became more rapid. Johnny knelt beside her and gently untied the rope around her delicate wrists.

Sylvia lived mostly in the night, moving from shadow to shadow, car to car, wiping her mouth, her lips, with the back of her hand, with the palms of her hands, with tissue. Wiping at stains and scars that never faded. Johnny stared at the red marks on her wrists, the dried blood. Her endless struggle with this life-long affliction of wandering down narrow hallways with billowing white curtains, along desolate roads and riverbanks, into unlocked rooms with broken windows, down rabbit holes, and into cracked mirrors. Her years of doing battle with these dreams that haunted her and stained her flesh. Her confused desire for men who bewitched her and dragged her by her hair into blackberry bushes. Her eyes closed, but these dreams did not stop. Her eyes opened, but these dreams did not stop. She dreamed of everything her body might go through one day, even if she was careful. And she recalled in flesh, not in thought, not in words, not in song or dance, but in flesh.

Over the past few months, Johnny watched her skin so carefully while she slept that he thought it had become part of his soul. He wiped the palms of his hands on his jeans, purifying them as best he could, before doing what needed to be done. He looked up the trail toward the sounds of the morning and then along the river. No one.

He slowly touched the rope that held Sylvia perfectly still and quiet. He was careful not to disturb her girl skin, careful not to accidentally awaken her, to rush her into the morning too quickly. He undid the knots, and her hand fell gently onto the earth. He touched the tips of her fingers, and she moved slightly.

Johnny paused, waited for her body to become quiet again. He watched for that sudden appearance of her father on her skin, for all that that man had left behind. He watched for it to rise to the surface of her skin, to startle Sylvia's childish breathing. Her father had taken her into back rooms, into garages, into sheds and basements, and into attics, so that she could learn about all the meanness in the world. Johnny waited for the ruins of that man, who had disappeared years ago, the one who vanished into the shadows, the man who, while wearing a pale blue leisure suit and humming "Wichita Lineman," climbed into his maroon Chevy Impala, locked all the doors of the car, and backed out of their gravel driveway. This father waved to his daughter, staring out her bedroom window, and to his wife, standing on the porch, as if nothing out of the ordinary was happening, and he drove away from Pittsburgh, across the state line to Ohio.

He drove on and on, day and night, until he arrived in California. Along the way, this father, who had whispered bedtime stories to Sylvia in a voice that she had mistaken for sugarplums and fairies, picked up as many girls with tainted blood as he could get away with. He drove lonesome highways, laughing with these girls in the front seat of his car, tickling their tight naked thighs and squeezing their fleshy cheeks, opening doors to highway motels for them and sweeping them off their feet across the threshold and plopping them down on worn-out beds; until this man, Sylvia's father, grew tired of these young girls and abandoned them, one by one, in motels or alongside the interstate, here and there across the Midwest. Her father slapped the steering wheel of his car, keeping rhythm to every song that blared out of the radio, and that man drove as far west as his car could go, drove to where the sun fell into the ocean, to where women cried every time he touched them, every time he pressed into their flesh with too much desire, every time he told them exactly what he thought of them, before telling them to leave, telling them they had to leave, to get out. That he was from the east coast and that he had no time for this, not for this, not for how they were acting, that he only had time for what he had time for.

Sylvia's father drove to the edge of the known world, to the place where all men eventually drown from their misplaced desires. Like so many men, her father would die there, be forever captured by his past, tamed by it, trapped. God had an incredible knack for creating the desires of lost men, then creating prisons for such desires, and then punishing men for having such desires. God was creative, seductive. He had a sense of humor.

At least the rumors have it that Sylvia's father died there, exploded. The coroner said that the heart of her father exploded, actually wrote that on the death certificate. Cause of death: Exploded heart. Shards of his heart were found stuck in the wall, in the carpet, and in the windows, and that was the end of him. Cocaine and beer were on the night table. Sheets and comforter were rumpled and pulled off the side of the bed. Country-and-western songs still played on the radio when the motel manager unlocked the door. A few coins scattered across the carpet. Not many. A quarter, four nickels, a dime, a handful of pennies. Clean underwear, pressed and folded, in the chest of drawers, with five or six twenty-dollar bills hidden beneath them. Shirts, pants, and suit coats hung neatly in the closet. A near-naked corpse of Sylvia's father on the bathroom floor, all the dreams and hopes, the youthful innocence, the promises of a bright future, the love he had for beer, all of it washed away from his face. His dark tan had disappeared. He had become white. Too white. A few hundred photographs of Sylvia lay scattered about the motel room, on the floor beside the bed, under the bed sheets, a few shoved between the mattresses, more in the bathroom sink, in drawers. Another couple hundred were scattered in his car, in the glove compartment, in the trunk, on the floor, on the back seat, taped to the mirror. A half-written, illegible letter that appeared to be addressed to some woman, perhaps to that woman, who walked around a house in Pittsburgh, destroying coffee cups and Lucky Charms and claiming to be Sylvia's mother? One stamp. Two or three 8-track tapes. One of Andy Williams' *Moon River*, another of *Christmas with Johnny Mathis*, and a third one whose label had been peeled off and whose tape had been pulled out of its case. A box of newspaper clippings and other knick-knacks that, at some moment in that man's life, must have meant something to someone. Another box taped shut and marked: For the girl you call my daughter.

The coroner's office mailed a death certificate to Sylvia's mother, and, after the woman opened it and stared at it for a few days, she finally read it. This woman, the wife of Sylvia's father, broke more coffee cups that day, broke every coffee cup in the house. Then she went to the Goodwill on East Ohio Street and bought more cups, a boxful of them. When Sylvia came home, her mother pressed her father's death certificate against her face. "Love so wild it proves you have flesh," her mother said. She pushed Sylvia to the floor, knelt over her daughter, and looked into her daughter's beautiful eyes. "I can't live like this. A bundle of joy. They said that to me. A bundle of joy. I remember hearing them say it. I remember believing it, trusting them. They called you that. The doctors, the nurses, everyone. You did not sleep for two years. They said it was colic, but I knew the truth."

Sylvia's mother looked away from her daughter, around the room, trying to remember what was missing or where Sylvia's father had gone or what she was about to say. She looked back down at Sylvia. "Don't you dare ever speak to God again, Sylvia. He wants nothing to do with you. He has other things on his mind, other girls that need his attention. Girls like you belong in hell. Girls like you. Girls. Say it. Say it to me. And you have it coming to you. It is waiting for you."

Sylvia listened to her mother. She ached for her and wanted nothing more than to take her in her arms and quiet her heart. She lay flat on her back on the floor, her mother's hands pressing down on her shoulders, holding her there, pinned and wriggling. Sylvia smelled the coffee on her mother's breath. "Do you know what mercy is, Sylvia?"

But Sylvia would have nothing to do with her father's death. She claimed she was not fooled by it. "Anyone can say they are dead, if they want you to believe they are dead," she said. "But no one dies. And of all the men who walk this earth, fathers are the ones who never die. Not truly. No father ever dies. Fathers, and all they do and say, are immortal. There is no death to the imagination. The imagination is deeper, more secretive, than what God can know. And every father who claims he is dead, or promises to die, even those who whisper it into your ear while their hearts are beating, about to explode or break or leap out of their rib cage and into you, is just trying to get a woman to relax. He is only distracting her. All girls know this. They know that any man who can destroy a girl's illusion is like that wind that violently blows out the flame of a candle. Such a man is a beast, a force without love, a shadow that remains, even when the lights are turned out. Girls know men, fathers, even those who claim to have died, are only waiting for girls to fall asleep on unmade beds with their shoes on. And girls know that unmade beds are just as dangerous as open windows."

But a girl who holds those memories too long—the memories of a dead father, of a father who paced back and forth in hallways and drank beer in basements, the pain of those memories, the loss of a father who never quite understood the word "father" or how to use the word in a sentence—is bound to die from the emptiness or from the longing for a father she once imagined was possible in some far off land. Every deed a father commits is impervious to time and cannot be escaped by any daughter. "The colossal wave." Sylvia had underlined that phrase in a book when she was too young to fully understand what it meant. She underlined it in pencil, then pen, then crayon. She thought, if she underlined it in crayon, the phrase would go away and everything that was being done to her body would follow. Now there is only a hole in the book. The page is torn. Her flesh falls off her bones onto the dirt. She wants water. And no other man, no other father of some other daughter or son, no son of some father, no orphaned child, no man in the moon, will ever be able to lift that stain out of a girl. And all the girl wants back is the time before flesh, before locking doors, before falling out of a crib, before beds, before a man holding a knife meant anything, before knowing the word "throat."

Sylvia not only told Johnny all that her father did, all that he failed to do, every hug after every mass, she also told him all her father said to her. Every single word. She even told him the words her father whispered that appeared innocent. Words that said no more than what they were meant to say. Words that could be said while shaking the hand of Father Boyle after mass. Even those words became soiled in the mouth of Sylvia's father.

She said her father repeated the word silence. "Silence!" He said "silence," and he smiled a wicked, deviant smile that typically led to other problems, that eventually destroyed silence and made Sylvia cautious of her own behavior, her own words, her bare feet on the carpet. The word itself made no sense. It was the most dysfunctional word in the English language, and Sylvia felt that the word did more harm than good. Every time Sylvia heard her father say that word, and every time she hears the word today, she cries, just a little.

Her father taught her how dangerous letters could be, how misleading they could be, how every letter could eventually lead to a slip of the tongue or a split lip. He said words did more to a person's lips than fingers ever could. He told her to say, "Purple." She did, then her father said, "See." Once Sylvia's father handed her a book of poetry. He put his hand gently around her throat and squeezed just tight enough to let her know what she needed to know. He told her to pick a poem and read it aloud. She did. Her lips moved. Her tongue. Her throat. She felt something happen to the inside of her stomach, and she felt her ribs wanting to break through her skin, and she had to remind herself to breathe, whether she truly wanted to or not.

"Words are more than sounds," he said. "Words make the body do things." He released his daughter's throat and she let out a tiny gasp and begged to be given permission to go to her room. "Alone," she said. "Alone." The air around Sylvia and her father became thin. Murderous. She imagined her life without a father, without a mother. But there is a terror that comes with such wishes.

Johnny thought he was immune to fathers, to what fathers had to say to their sons, to what they did, to the floors covered in broken glass, to the holes fathers punched into walls before disappearing into shadows, to their voices that came out of these shadows that they had disappeared into, to the bruises fathers left behind on the biceps and thighs of the mothers of their sons. He told Sylvia his father never said a word to him, never looked at him. And he never saw his father. Never. He only sensed a shadow of him, and a voice he heard tangled in the branches of trees, scratching at windowpanes. Sylvia looked at Johnny and said, simply, that a father is a rage that can never be stopped and can never stop.

Slowly, Sylvia opened her eyes. Beneath her eyelids, in this moment between dreaming and waking, Johnny recognized all that she had said to him, all that she carried with her of what her father had said and done to her during those childhood nights, all of the silence of her mother, all of what her mother had blamed her for doing. While she lingered in that dream state, the dust of her father appeared in her eyes. The fear that darkens a heart. Blood and stone. A whip abandoned on a side street. You wish you had God with you, but He is not there, not in the place you most need Him.

When a girl grows too big to hide under the bed, then she knows she has grown out of being able to hide from fearing what will happen to her anyway, so she gives in to it. She sees it before it happens, she sees it when it is happening, and she sees it after it happens. A girl like that wears her past, even when she is naked. Her skin is covered with it. Not even rain can change that. Her eyes watered, something deeper than crying. Memory. Like falling in a dream.

She yawned, began pulling herself from the haunted places. Her eyes, on waking in the morning before her dreams completely escaped her body, were transformed into more of a map than into a window to her soul. Red lines formed a treasure map, like those used by pirates. But these maps promised an escape rather than a treasure. Escape—not gold, not possession—for pirate girls, was the true treasure. These maps promised Sylvia that she could live in wonder. Maps and mazes of desires that she was only beginning to understand.

Johnny wanted to lightly touch her eyelids. She smiled, then she laughed and coughed worn out desire from her lungs. "Water." She tried to sit up, only to realize her one wrist was still tied. He untied it and handed a plastic bottle filled with water to her.

Sylvia looked at him with the slow breath of waking, the slow breathing of the river, the brittle morning air. Something was missing. "Your mouth," she said slowly. "A girl knows, Johnny. Even a girl as tired as me." She took another sip of water. "Your eyes. Something waking. Something falling asleep. Something borrowed. Something blue." She smiled again at how he held onto his silence, his quiet. She liked his quiet. "You look like you have become fragile."

"No," he replied. "No," he repeated a second time, as if he doubted it the first time and needed to confirm to himself, as much as to

Sylvia, that he was not fragile.

Johnny looked up through the trees at the sunlight. He feared that the sun would burn away his memories of the night before. "I saw," Johnny stopped himself. He looked down at Sylvia's naked knees. He knew where those knees had been, and he knew what awaited those knees. They both knew. Everyone knew. She stretched her legs, pointed her toes toward the sky. He watched her muscles, the gentle movement of her body. "I'm tired," he said.

"You saw?"

"Nothing." Johnny knew it was not for him to say. "Nothing."

"You saw nothing?" Sylvia asked.

"Just darkness. There was nothing there." He stared across the Monogahela. "I thought I saw something, but when I looked it wasn't there. Nothing."

"It happens."

"It's the shadows," he said. He stood up, brushed the dirt from his knees, and went behind a tree for a minute. "I'm going home," he shouted back toward Sylvia. "You?"

"Another day waiting for the night. Looking for more fathers, letting them find me, so I can save their daughters." She smiled. "I can almost believe what I say when I say it to you, Johnny." She had stopped being afraid years ago, and now she walked the streets in Pittsburgh daring the universe to take her. She looked at Johnny, and he looked at her. They shared a simple trust when they looked at each other. They knew they could be seen by each other, and they could see each other, and they knew that what came of such seeing would remain silent.

Sylvia hated mornings. The way the sun rose. The way her mouth felt. The way people looked at her, not wanting to see her, not wanting to admit that girls like her existed and that girls like her knew they existed and enjoyed being in their flesh, enjoyed the thoughts that carried them through the day. People did not want to know that girls like Sylvia slept more peacefully along the riverbanks than they did in their narrow beds at home, that these girls slept near the river, while they slept at home in terror in the suburbs. She dug money out of her pockets, looked at it, counted it, and put it back into her pocket. "You never belonged here, Johnny. Did you?"

"Guess not." Johnny stared down at Sylvia's naked feet. He imagined her walking down sidewalks without pain, without guilt. He imagined who she might be if she were to walk in such a way. He wanted Sylvia to be able to live in a world where she never needed to wear shoes, a place where naked feet would be safe and cherished. "My mother said home is where you start from. No one ever escapes that."

He looked at his own feet. The soft, nearly indefinable color of his feet. Elgin said Johnny needed to toughen them, the soles needed to be thicker. He told him that color did not wear off a man's feet or the palms of his hands. The color wore into the man, marking the inside of the man, making the man into all that he becomes. All you walk over, his grandfather told him, all you touch is on the inside.

"Pain is everywhere," Johnny said. "In the soles of your feet. In the earth. On the sidewalks. Inside cars. Everywhere. We can't outrun it. We were born into pain." Sylvia followed Johnny's gaze. She looked down at his feet, too.

"Pain isn't what makes us."

"It was out here waiting for us, though," Johnny said. "You can't doubt that. It was here inside the words before we were born. My mother wrote it in her book, too. We come from the place we come from." Johnny picked up the book his mother had given him. "I gotta go, Sylvia. Back to where I came from." Johnny laughed. "Born again. Rising. Waiting for a miracle."

"Ascension."

"What?"

"Nothing," Sylvia replied. "Stories. Stories of the dead moving boulders. Opening doors. Coming back with the stench of death mixing in with the stench of the life they lived. Maybe that's me. Us. Rising back. Call me Lazarus. Cain? I can't remember the man's name. Only that there's a way to return, as long as you refuse to look back, never look over your shoulder. You do that, you turn and look, and everything dies, turns to stone or salt."

Sylvia moved closer to Johnny, but she stopped herself. She bent over and rolled up her river blankets, put them under the willow tree. She watched Johnny pick up their rope and the chain and hide them behind the tree, bury them beneath river rocks and dead branches.

291

She slowly touched her lips with the tip of her fingers, as if she were not conscious of what she was doing or why she was doing it, then she wiped more of her dreams away from her eyes with her hands, hoping she could begin again with a new starting place, a new home.

"Life calls," she said. "Tell your grandfather I send him this." Sylvia wrapped her arms around Johnny, hugged him tight. Held him. "There's walking to be done," Sylvia whispered into Johnny's ear. "There are footprints we need to leave behind."

But she did not let go. All that had gone away, all that had drifted from her, came back to her each time she hugged Johnny. Toys she had lost when she was a child. Toys her father had hidden from her. Toys her mother had broken. Sleep. The sleep that came to her in the time before her life started. A memory of a Christmas morning when both her mother and father were laughing, and Sylvia was sitting on the floor in front of a Christmas tree opening a gift that proved to her that Santa Claus did exist, that he truly existed and that he was watching her, that he did know when she was sleeping, and that he listened to her while she whispered her secret prayers beneath the blankets, and that he understood more about her than her parents would ever understand and the tears she cried when Christmas disappeared. It all came back to her when she hugged Johnny. It is what the kind of love she felt for him can do. Love can bring back everything we have ever lost. Faith returned, not that religious faith people convince themselves that they have for unseen gods, but faith that there were places and moments and people that mattered. Trust returned. And Sylvia breathed it into her, breathed it as deeply into her body and soul as she could, before she was willing to let go.

"If only I could walk until my body dropped to the sidewalk, just dropped down to the sidewalk, so that I would never have to return again. If I could fall," Sylvia said barely above a whisper. "Just fall." She was certain Johnny had not heard what she said. She was not sure she wanted him to. She had grown tired, but she was too young to be so tired. She had become tired and old in ways that the Street Elder had never known. She resisted sleep most nights. She knew going to bed only meant that tomorrow would come. And inevitably that is what happened. Tomorrow came. The sun. The heat. The river. The cars. The men. Their anger. Their sweat burning into her eyes.

She rested her chin on Johnny's shoulder, but that did not change much. He held onto her. He knew not to pat her on her back. Not to comfort her, but to hold her.

"There are too many men in Pittsburgh," Sylvia said. She let go of Johnny. He said he was sorry. They both looked confused by what he said. "The men," he said. "There shouldn't be so many." She smiled. "Yes. It would help if there were not so many."

Johnny still seemed confused. He wanted to touch her cheek and say something, as softly as his voice would allow, but he had no idea what he should say. He watched her face, hoping to understand what it was that he was not understanding. The river lapped at the edge of the bank. The breeze moved through the branches of the trees. People had stood here before he stood here. He was not the first. People had walked these trails. Clarence still walked these trails. Perhaps no longer now, not after last night. But people had been here before him. And other boys and girls had had this exact moment of confusion.

"It's not like that," Sylvia said. "I never wanted to know all this. It's like quicksand." Johnny seemed less confused or perhaps he had begun to understand that there was nothing to be confused about. The world only seemed to work that way.

Johnny looked up through the tree branches at the clouds. "It's going to rain."

"Yes," Sylvia replied. "Rain is coming to Pittsburgh, of all places." They smiled. "It does not seem right."

"Nothing will change," Johnny said. "It will still be hot. Always hot." Johnny turned to head up the trail. "Coming?"

"Yes." They walked together until Johnny went left toward the Birmingham Bridge and Sylvia went right toward the center of the South Side. Coffee and doughnuts at O'Leary's, then over to the North Side to join the shadows, to step into the cars of missing fathers, so that she could rescue their daughters from these fathers unlatching doors and breathing in the shadows. For Sylvia to tell these men, these fathers, to say whatever they wanted to say. "Go ahead, say it," she would tell them. Then she would wait quietly until they found it in them to say what they thought they wanted to say, and then Sylvia would do it. She would do it so that she could kill the words, kill all that they said, so their daughters would not live in darkness, so they could leave the doors to their bedrooms unlocked and perhaps even opened, so these daughters would not have to climb out their windows in the middle of the night, crawl down walls and run into the forest.

Johnny crossed the bridge. The rain was light and warm on his skin. Big, round drops of rain that fell ahead of a summer downpour. He opened his mouth, catching drops of rain, and smiling. Maybe this rain had the strength to wash away what needed to be washed away. Johnny knew something needed to be washed away, even if he could not name it. He looked at the clouds coming up over the hill. They seemed to be sitting, resting at the very top of Kirkpatrick Street, deciding whether to bring rain to the city or to take it away toward Oakland.

His mother believed that rain, especially in the summer, proved there was a God and that God was watching. "Rain never simply happens," she said. "Someone has to plan rain. There must be a God behind rain. Rain is a gift."

"Evil is different," Lehuoung then said. "Evil does what it pleases when it wants. Evil has no plan. It just is." Johnny held his mother's hand. She kept looking straight ahead, away from her son, away from the places that hurt, away from promises that had failed. "No one is innocent of it. If evil comes for you, it is because you have invited it. Evil is attracted to what you have in your heart." She turned back to her son, lightly touched his heart with the very tips of her fingers, the way God brings morning dew to blades of grass.

Johnny looked down Fifth Avenue toward the corner of Fifth and Moultrie. He knew what waited for him there. He knew all that could happen to him, or to anyone, there. He hurried past that corner, and then, even more quickly, he hurried past Larry's. He kept his eyes downward, maintaining a hard and disciplined stare into the side-walk. It was the rule. Everyone in Pittsburgh knew it. If you looked up, if you looked toward Larry's, then you were asking for it, and anything that happened was your fault. He heard the voices, heard them calling to him, wanting him to lift his eyes, wanting him to stop, waiting for Johnny to, in the slightest way, acknowledge them. But Johnny knew better. He knew to be strong, to just walk. And so he did.

The rain continued to fall on his skin as he walked down Fifth Avenue. He wondered how much rain it would take to wash away the buildings and homes along Fifth, not in a flood, but in a slow, wearing away. He knew water had power, that water was strong and could erode the earth. He wondered if rain had ever done that to a building, eroded the bricks and the wood, and made the buildings vanish. And he wondered why, with all the rain over all these years, centuries of rain, why hadn't the earth simply eroded away? Johnny came up on Jumonville Street. The sounds, the voices, from Caliban's rushed out at him.

The noise was enough to raise the dead and to kill the living. Words bounced off walls at all times of the day and of the night. Words broke through the windows of Caliban's, shattering glass and spilling words and sentences and stories and beer signs out onto the street. Words blew out the electricity, not just in the bar, but up and down Fifth Avenue as well. Every time someone entered Caliban's, words came flying out the door. And nearly everyone who entered that bar stayed there until the end of their natural lives. Or so it seemed.

Inside the bar, words thumped against other words, making it impossible to know where one word ended and some other word began. Words rushed at you as soon as you crossed the threshold and stepped into the bar; even brave men ducked and prayed, hoped for the best. Words invented and obeyed their own laws in Caliban's. Neither men nor women could control their own words or the words of others. In Caliban's, words were so powerful and wild that they broke beer glasses, they broke women's heels, they gave men nosebleeds, they rubbed up against people the wrong way. Words changed what parents knew about their children and changed the way children looked at their parents at the breakfast table. Children came to know things about their parents that children should never know. Words in Caliban's made people cry tears that were more like tiny pieces of hail or slivers of glass than like tears, and when people cried, the crying hurt. And words made people laugh, raw, throttled laughter that damaged a man's throat, tore out a woman's heart. And some words waited in midair, hung there, before they went crashing to the floor or leaping to the ceiling. Words bruised parts of a man's soul that he did not even know existed.

Story after story being told, one after the other, stories being told at the same time, and no one taking a breath. Never a moment's peace. Never a moment of quiet, not even one of quiet desperation. No story began in Caliban and none ended there. The stories invented hopes and dreams, while these same stories destroyed other hopes and dreams, or exposed lies, as each story created new lies. People bumped their way up to the bar; there was no walking in Caliban's, only bumping and light swaying. These people joined the tribal moans of the sentences, most often, before they even reached the bar and had their first beer in their hand. Everyone telling everyone else to speak up. Feet stomping, hands clapping, heart stopping, and no one ever thinking to suggest that someone slow down or speak more softly.

Johnny's grandfather warned him to be careful any time he found himself walking down Fifth Avenue and getting close, too close, to Caliban's, warned him of the trickery in the stories tumbling out of Caliban's. "You be careful even walking past the front door of that bar," he told Johnny. "Better to play it safe and cross the street, plug up your ears. No telling what you might hear. The kinds of things them men and women say. And there ain't no telling what a young boy like you might be led to believe about men, about women, about the way things work. Stories so strange coming out of the mouths of those people, making beauty out of sorrow and sorrow out of beauty. Confuses a man down to his heart and soul. Red claims there's omens in them stories, if you can decipher them."

A woman stumbled out of Caliban's onto the sidewalk. It seemed like she had been pushed out or squeezed out, that the bar was too full, too many people or too crowded by too many stories, already, in the late morning. She regained her balance, stuck out her hand, palm up, and looked up at the sky. "It's raining, right?" she asked Johnny. The boy nodded. "Some days you think you found something, then you realize you haven't been where you thought you were." Her voice was rough, ravaged by the summer heat and a general disappointment with her life. She straightened out her skirt, reached down and adjusted the strap of her heel, then turned to walk up Fifth Avenue, but she stopped and looked back at Johnny. "A heart gets betrayed and those people who think they the good ones think that nothing should change," she said. "They say it's just your heart. It's not really broken. You're just sad. They say that like tomorrow will be the same as today."

The woman fingered the collar of her blouse. "It's wet." She waited for Johnny to say something. "The rain," she said. "The rain is wet." Johnny said yes, and then he mumbled that that was the way rain liked it. Wet. The woman looked at Johnny slow and careful, trying to decide if there was something wrong with him or if he was trying to say something else, something more than what a boy that young could be thinking. Johnny looked at her with about the same look. Not all people slurred their speech from alcohol; some people suffered with slurred speech because they were ghosts and were tired and dry in the mouth. The ghosts that could talk were not able to control their saliva. Johnny looked at her, trying to decide which this woman was: drunk or ghost or just lost.

"You think the one you love will always be there to love you back. It's the one thing you let yourself believe. You don't plan on death happening to them." Johnny nodded again, less sure of what he was agreeing with or to. He shoved his hands down into his pockets, thinking doing so would help him understand what he could not say.

"Don't worry, Sonny," the woman said. "Rain never harmed a great beauty. It doesn't harm no one." The woman smiled, ran her fingers through her thick dark hair. "I like being wet like this."

Johnny stood still, looking at her. His lips went to say something, almost without taking him with them, but he stopped and shook his head, smiled a little. "What do you think you're seeing?" She asked Johnny. "Lord knows what any man can see outside of his own self anymore. All the glare. You find the love unsaid, child. That's what you need to find, then you'll be all right." The woman turned and began walking away. "Go on now," she said, but she did not turn back to look at him.

He stood a while longer, staring at her walk up Fifth Avenue. More stories floated out of Caliban's. Johnny stood with his hands in his pockets, listening. They were not truly voices, they were a sound, a hum, a gentle hum that he felt with his body, as much as heard with his ears. Some man, who Johnny recognized from the Hill above Dinwiddie, crossed the street and stood for a moment in front of Caliban's. He closed his eyes, took a deep breath, held it, then pushed his way into the bar. Johnny turned away from the hum of Caliban's and walked down Fifth toward Dinwiddie.

Albert was standing, as usual, at the corner of Gist Street, shouting out all of what he most passionately believed, shouting it out like he was the one true messenger of a god that you can actually trust and have faith in without trying. Hollering up a storm in the rain, calling down thunder, complaining about what had been done to Sundays. Ranting that Sunday was not Sunday no more, that now Sunday was like any other day. "It confuses a man," he shouted. "All them stores open on Sunday, like it Friday or Wednesday or whatever day of the week."

He scratched his bald and aching head and held his Bible up to God and shouted to the heavens above Pittsburgh: "And praying ain't praying like praying is meant to be praying. A man prays to be with God. A man prays to devote time in his day to being with his Lord and Savior. That's all prayer is. Praying is sitting and being. Nothing else. It's a bringing of God into your day. That's all. Praying ain't asking. No, sir, it ain't. Asking is asking. People pray now and all they really doing is asking God for stuff. They want a better life, they want more money, they want more beer or they want the beer to taste better, they want that girl over there to fall in love with them, they want peace on earth, goodwill to men, they want to be cured of the cancer. That ain't no prayer, that's begging, and that's disrespecting God. Those people who pray like that think God stupid, think God blind. Fools is what they is. God gonna smack them upside the head when the time come, and the time will come. God's not blind. God's not stupid. He sees the life you living. Who you think give you that life, fool? He's the one who give you that life. Instead of accepting the life you been given, you're complaining. But don't you worry none, God does hear your prayer, and He is gonna do something about it. Fact is, God already doing something about it. You best stop insulting God and pray a true prayer like a man do."

Albert drank Holy Water as a child. Scooped handfuls of it right up out of the stoup in the vestibule of St. Benedict the Moor Church, any time he got thirsty. He ran into the vestibule, scooped that water, and told everyone he was holier than thou and laughed and laughed. He loved to laugh when he was a boy. He still does. Tells everyone that passes by that God gave him laughter, might as well let it out. Later, he drank vodka mixed in with his beer. "Simpler that way," he said. "Faster and simpler." In those days, it has been said that he played alongside Robert Johnson at the crossroads. Every man his age claimed they played with Johnson; if not with Johnson, men his age told stories about playing with The Bird up at Crawford's. Everyone knew none of those stories were true, but what story is? As soon as a man starts talking, he starts lying. It's the nature of words. It's what words do. Make a life into a lie. It's why, instead of talking, a man should just sing and dance when he has something to say.

"Man don't know what it's like to worship no more." Albert was on a roll. And he sang those words of his as much as he shouted them out. And no one had ever seen Albert stand still a minute, not even a second of his life. He was in constant movement. It is what a body is meant to do. "Man got a body, man got a responsibility to move with it," Albert shouted. So he danced and shouted on that corner day and night. He said, "Someone got to watch over Pittsburgh. Someone got to sing the praises and prayers of the Hill District."

Albert looked at Johnny and said: "Man don't know what it's like to slow down, to stop, to be patient. Man just go to mass, then he rush off to shop. Ain't right is what it is. Not right. Not for your soul. It corrupts your soul, prepares it for hell, instead of getting it ready for heaven. People running out of church, wanting to escape the parking lot, wanting to beat the traffic. It's like they at a baseball game and leaving in the 7th inning, so they get out before everyone else. Listen to the game on the car radio. Why they even go?"

He walked over to get closer to Johnny. He put his hand on the boy's shoulder and looked into his eyes. "That's why they go, son. That's the only reason. They go to leave. You hear me? You understand that? They go so they can say they went to mass, and then they want to get on out of that church as fast as they can, they want to get into their car and beat the traffic. Think on that. It's better to sit still in traffic after church. You get to think of what it is that been said to you during that mass. It's thinking time after you attend mass. It is. But that's not so, is it? No. People want to get away as fast as they can. They want to get to a store and buy something. Ain't right. Hell is waiting for them people, boy. It is. You can count on that. Hell's going to take them in. Devil got his arms spread wide open, and he's waiting."

Albert pointed to the sky. He let raindrops fall into his open eyes and mouth. He told Johnny to look on up there at the sky, told him to thank Jesus for the rain. "What do you believe in, boy? What? You got desire in your heart? Needles in your pocket? You got the devil in your eyes waiting to get out of you and on into the world? You going to set demons free on these streets? Pittsburgh don't need no more demons. You got them in you, you take them to Cleveland. You see the wicked in the world, that mean you got the wicked in you. Man can't see the wicked, if he don't got it in his soul to begin with. You got that? You? You?" Albert stuttered and repeated "you" so many times Johnny thought the world would end before he got the final "you" out of his mouth. Then he paused. He was not waiting for Johnny to answer. He knew Johnny had no answers. He paused because he was tired; even a street preacher has a right to being tired, to having his voice wear thin.

"It is in you, and what in you ain't going to wait much longer. I see it in you. It's in your eyes, son. You crave the miraculous, but you confuse the miraculous with looking at girls. I see it in you."

Johnny stopped and listened to Albert nearly every day when he walked from the Monongahela River up to his grandfather's house. He never made sense of his ranting, but he enjoyed the rhythms, the movements of his body, the agitation in his eyes, the sounds that came out of his mouth.

"You lookit here," Albert continued. "You listen at me like a man listens. Don't be no boy. That girl you look at when you look at her, you remember that God is watching you. He is. That's why she looks at her feet, she's not shy, she's embarrassed of what she's feeling, and knowing that God is watching her feel it, and right then and there you know something God never meant for you to know, and then that becomes part of you. It's shame and desire all mixing together. You get clumsy and stupid with your looking, standing there in front of her. You feel like you're naked." Albert pressed his finger into

Johnny's chest. "You feel that way 'cause you is naked. That girl doing to you what God did to Adam and Eve. And she knows what she's doing. You suddenly more conscious of having hands than you ever been in your whole life. And you got no idea what to do with your hands. Where to put them. You put them in your pockets. You take them out of your pockets. You don't know what you're doing. You want to wet your lips 'cause they so dry you think you in the desert, but your tongue never so afraid as it is at that moment. You know you got to do something. Stupid man walks away from such a moment, such a girl. He go home and write a poem about all he feeling. Fool is what that boy is. He's thinking words more important than touch. He don't do nothing. He writes a poem. You don't go and be that kind of fool. Smart man figure out something about who he is and who he going to be. Figure it out right at that moment, right in front of that girl, and then he gives that to that girl. He does that. Be that man. And you don't sit in church thinking when it going to end. You don't sit there thinking nothing. You sit there. You got that?"

Johnny nodded and turned to walk home. He knew this time what he was saying yes to. He knew it each time he said yes to Albert. Farther on down Fifth Avenue, Johnny saw Emmanuel heading into Red's. Johnny waved, and Emmanuel waved back and pointed up the hill, letting Johnny know his grandfather was up home. Johnny nodded back at Emmanuel. Rain was falling a little heavier now. Still, the rain felt so good to Johnny. On his skin, like how he imagined a girl's touch would feel, that girl the Preacher Man was talking about, the one he conjured up in his preaching.

He quickly made his way across Fifth Avenue, stepping hard into puddles, splashing the bottoms of his jeans, and he began his slow climb to his grandfather's house. There was not much to see anymore on Dinwiddie. Houses had burned down. Others had collapsed under the weight of the years. Trees had simply given up. Broken-down, mostly abandoned cars lined the street. Johnny tried to remember the last time he had seen a car parked on Dinwiddie that still had all four tires, that did not have a broken windshield, that could still run, that could still take someone somewhere. Cars on Dinwiddie just sat. They never moved. Some of the cars had become places for people to store bags of clothing, books. One stationwagon had become a library for the street. The doors were always unlocked. The only library in Pittsburgh open 24 hours a day, seven days a week. And no one needed a library card, just a desire to read a book or a magazine. Johnny had seen people come up to the car in the middle of the night, with flashlights, rummaging for a book. And people returned the books, and they treated the car with respect, careful to be sure the windows were up, careful to be sure the doors were closed, so that no snow or rain leaked in and damaged the books. For years, it was their neighborhood library. Theirs. And everyone along Dinwiddie cherished it. And people added to the collection. Other cars along Dinwiddie were used for other things by other people. Those cars did not fare so well, but everyone respected the library stationwagon.

Johnny looked up at his grandfather sitting in his rocking chair on the porch. A shoebox of photographs rested on his grandfather's lap. He held one photograph in his hands, staring down at it, then he looked up and across Dinwiddie at that vacant lot. "I hear you, Johnny." Elgin looked toward where Johnny was standing about to open the gate. Johnny walked up the steps to the porch, sat down on the swing.

"You can see now?" Johnny asked.

"Nah," Elgin chuckled, "but I can hear you walking, and I can dream."

"You know what's in that photograph you're holding?"

"No," Elgin laughed. "Might be nice if I could. See without eyes. See like a psychic, but I'd probably only see into the invisible past, into all that everyone wants to keep hidden. Including my own fool self. Into what was that still is. Maybe become a faith healer. Then I could join the circus and do card tricks or place my hand on foreheads and pull the past out of people. All we go telling ourselves of what was that wasn't and what wasn't that was. No memory is any better than the man trying to remember it, trying to keep it with him."

Elgin looked over toward his grandson. He had never seen his grandfather looking old before. Like his eyes were more than blind, like they had gotten emptied of something or had somehow become more secretive. Johnny's grandfather had once said that it is never

302

about what one does or did in life, it's about how a man is looked at by those around him. "People call a man crazy, he's crazy," his grandfather said. "But that's just true of living. In death it changes."

"You look tired."

"Guess I do, Johnny. Guess you right about that. You too. Your voice sounds like it tired out of itself. Been taken away from you."

"Bad dreams and mosquitoes."

"I believe you," Elgin said. "The river gets under your skin like that. The Monongahela isn't no normal river. Not like the Allegheny or the Ohio. No man can expect to sleep along that river and not be haunted by what the river is. And those dreams down at the river are just a ghost of who you is. Most ghosts we see are the imagining of our own selves, us seeing who we're becoming."

"You're right about that," Johnny said. He reached into his back pocket and pulled out the tattered book his mother had given him. Every time he touched this book, the pages, the photographs, he felt something rising up in him, something like what the root of a flower must feel when it rains. "The wilderness of your inner beauty," Lehuong whispered into her son's ear as he fell asleep each night and as he woke each morning, "will one day blossom. Burst forth. Flood Dinwiddie Street and Fifth Avenue and Sarah Street. Your beauty will wet the parched, dusty sidewalks and buildings of Pittsburgh, my little boy." Then his mother would laugh, a sweet, gentle laugh. Each morning and each night, Johnny fell asleep and woke to the sound of his mother's laughter. The entire history of a woman's soul is in her laugh, and a man who listens carefully enough can hear a woman's soul growing when she laughs.

The other sounds that surrounded Johnny—the gunshots, the sirens, the fist going through the plaster wall in the hallway, the unbearable sound of a woman softly crying, "Stop," down the hallway or out in the alley, the tenderness of Johnny's own breath those nights he could not sleep, those nights when he counted each of his breaths, the sound of the garbage truck in the morning, the sound of a train refusing to stop—those sounds broke into Johnny. Broke him down. Broke what could never be undone. All those shadows sleeping in the cradle of his heart. His mother's laugh brought hope to Johnny, helped Johnny to forget what needed to be forgotten, but that never could be forgotten. "I remember his shadow on the wall more than I can remember his body, and he had no soul. That man's soul had been nailed to the stump of a tree or drowned in a river. But his body still walks this earth. His body still does what it does to me, to you, to what will become of you."

Johnny looked across at the skin around his grandfather's eyes, skin that seemed to no longer want to be on that man's bones, skin that wanted to be forgiven, skin that wanted to forget.

"This," Johnny said. "I've been looking through mom's book, through the photographs. Reading it. Looking. There's photographs that aren't there. And there are people or something not in the photograph."

"What do you mean?"

"You never looked at this?"

"Never. It's for you. Your mother said it for you, then it for you. No cause for me to look at it."

Johnny stared at his grandfather, tried to see if anything became visible in his eyes, his mouth, his skin, anything that might reveal some other truth that he had actually looked at the book, had read it. But nothing became visible. "Some of these photographs are all white. Blank."

"They're overexposed. There's too much light in them. Your mother must have seen what she saw when she took the photograph, but it's lost now. Light ate it."

"There's photographs of streets, of Mom, of Grandma, ones of Mom and . . . " Johnny stopped. Again he looked at his grandfather, stared into him and asked him again, "You never seen any of this? She never showed you?"

"How many times a grandfather got to tell a boy the truth? You believe so little that you come at me like this? Man got to mean something when he says it. That book is for you. She said, 'I'm leaving that boy something.' She said, 'It's not like I can put kisses in a box for him to open when he needs one.' But she tried to do that, too. It didn't work. Got a small box and tried putting a kiss in it for you," Elgin laughed as best he could. Sometimes a laugh can't be what it needs to be. "Your mother showed me that tiny box, but not that book. She said the book was only for you."

"There are other photographs with someone rubbed out. Not cut out, but rubbed out, like she used an eraser, didn't want me to see."

"She wanted you to see, Johnny. It's why she rubbed it out. It's still there for you to see. You see her rubbing it. You see your mother's thumbprint, her thumb pushing into that photograph, trying to wear it away and trying to save it. And it stayed with her in her skin. She didn't use no eraser, she used her thumb. It took her time, long time, to do that kind of rubbing. And she didn't make it disappear. She put it into her skin and took it with her, so that it did not stay here, so that it's not with you. Wisdom more in the tangle of shadows than in what you see easy with your eyes."

Elgin wiped his forehead with his sleeve. He lowered his eyes back to the photograph he had been holding. "You worry too much when a shadow vanishes, Johnny. Looking for it like it still here. Your mother did what she could to take them with her." Elgin began rubbing his thumb into the photograph he was holding. Rubbing away what he was afraid he might see, even in his blindness. Or maybe it was more like he was rubbing that photograph into his skin, so the photograph could disappear, become blind, or so that the photograph could get the memory into his skin. "Imagine light without shadows, Johnny. Imagine such a light. You can't, can you? What's that tell you?"

For a moment Johnny felt like something trapped in a jar, like those fireflies he caught as a boy. More clouds came up over the hill, in the distance the sound of thunder. "You can't recognize someone's presence until they gone," Elgin said, looking away from Johnny, toward the thunder. "They here with you on the porch, in the kitchen, walking alongside you on the sidewalk. You touch them, you talk to them, but you can't recognize them being there. Most times, you don't even know they're here. Not really. It's when they gone you feel it."

Elgin's voice had grown tired, worn out, like a dog in late summer heat wandering around the empty lots of Dinwiddie, looking for shade and water. "Your mother walked into the city every day. Said she was going to grow up and there was nothing no one could do about it. All your grandmother could say was my name, like I could do something. Your mother said, 'It's what needs to happen to a girl.'

I think that journey took her farther away than even she imagined it would. She walked and walked and walked, and then her youth was gone. It just fell away, vanished into thin air."

Johnny felt a bruise rising on his skin. Lehoung gave Johnny those wounds by accident. Birth and touch. Bruises that were once hers. "I want you to be able to sleep as if you had never been born," she told her son. His mother danced with a shadow of herself, while she looked into a dusty mirror. Think of how lonely such a body must get and what must become of such a woman's soul. Those sounds that should have been kept secret. A woman frightened by all that she had come to know. An empty bed burdened by the hopelessness of desire. "Ghosts will eat your dreams," his mother told him. "They will steal what is true." His mother thought she could convert the meanest of hearts, to get those hearts to believe in love, in true love, wild, abandoned, unconditional love, but all she managed to do was discover alleys and shadows. And afterwards, nothing in her body remained sacred.

"It wasn't like that with T.J."

"No?"

"No," Johnny repeated.

Grandfather and grandson sat quiet, Johnny watching the rain form puddles that would disappear as soon as the sun came out. Elgin listened to the rain on the roof of the porch. Johnny watched the rain do something to the garden, to Elgin's roses, that it did not do to the sidewalk. He watched the rain simply fall onto the earth. And Elgin listened.

"We were picking teams one day," Johnny said. "Back in the olden days." Both Johnny and his grandfather smiled. When Johnny was tiny, he would complain to his mother about his grandfather always talking about the glory in the olden days. Always calling them the olden days, even if his grandfather was talking about something that happened a week ago. "And T.J. was, as usual, the last one picked. Any time Jasmine was not there, we were happier. We hated picking a girl before we picked T.J. We put him out in right field. He said that made him Clemente. He made that shirt. You remember that shirt?"

Johnny's grandfather nodded. "I remember what his mother did to him for ruining that shirt." They both laughed.

"He loved that shirt. T.J. took his black Magic Marker or crayon to it. Wrote number 21 on the back, then wrote The Great One's name across the top of it. Him telling everyone he was Clemente. We all had to shout 'Arriba, Arriba!' when he stepped up to the plate. He struck out nearly every single time, most times not even fouling one off. We put him out in right field 'cause no one ever hit out there. That one game he dropped three flies in a row. Lost the game. T.J. trying to do that basket catch of Clemente's, and each time that ball smacking his wrist instead of falling into his glove. T.J. dreaming that dream of becoming Roberto." Johnny waited. He knew to wait, to be quiet for a while, allow his grandfather to see it, to remember Clemente in right field making those basket catches. No one in the game caught like that. No one had that arm. And when you mentioned that man in Pittsburgh, even in passing, you stopped and let everyone around you remember.

"Yeah, everyone in Pittsburgh wanted to be Roberto," Elgin said. "And when they were at Forbes Field watching him, everyone loved him. Everyone still loves those stories. Him throwing like that. Him hitting. The Great One. Watching Clemente from those bleachers in right field, climbing the trees outside of Forbes Field just to get a look. But when that man got hurt. When his body got worn down by all that traveling. Everyone in this city called him a crybaby, saying he didn't have courage. Even Murtaugh hinting at it. Saying Clemente was faking his pain. Everyone making fun of him for being Puerto Rican. His accent. Everyday in the sports pages. Everyday. Not a day passed that someone in the newspaper, on the radio, on the television, didn't make fun of the way he talked. Calling him stupid. Saying what he doing here if he can't speak English. Like anybody in Pittsburgh speaks English. Why would any self-respecting Puerto Rican want to speak like them? Sound like them. They do all they can to kill all of us off. And what those people used to say in the streets about Roberto. It was never right. And every single white man in this city laughing at Roberto when he talked, while they all demanded his autograph on a baseball. And I will tell you this. I'll tell you what Clemente was doing here before he could speak their language. He was doing what no other man could do. He was catching fly balls that were impossible to catch. He was gunning down any fool that was mad enough to test the man's arm, and he was running those bases with more passion than any man ever. Clemente never settled. Never stopped. Never quit."

Elgin's words drifted out of him, not anger, old words, words aged by stillness and years of trauma, a suffering that had to remain silent, a suffering that went back beyond sitting on the stoops, beyond what salvation the Monongahela River could ever promise, back to stories of the before that even Red knew nothing about. Ancient shadows appeared in his grandfather's voice. Johnny's grandfather pressed his thumb against the corner of his eye, wiped a little something from it. His voice old and cracked with those years of killing men he never meant to harm, men he never saw, women and children. He wanted to scratch it off his skin, bleed it into the Monongahela.

"You say what you got to say to protect what needs to be protected. Then a man dies, a woman dies, and he becomes a saint. No white man can deal with a black man walking down the street, not in the flesh, no Puerto Rican playing right field, no black man falling in love with his daughter. Not in this city. No white man can deal with the flesh of a black man. He can only turn him inside out into a myth."

Elgin looked over at Johnny as if his sight had returned to him, as if God came down and said to Elgin, 'You need to see one last time, and you need to be brave enough to look into your grandson's eyes and not fear seeing your daughter. You need to look past your pain of seeing your daughter in your grandson's flesh and see your grandson there before you.' And Johnny felt it, too, felt himself being seen by his grandfather. And Johnny dared not look away. And Elgin didn't look away, either. And something just dropped out of the corner of his grandfather's eye. Dust. A shadow. A tear. A little speck of mud. A word that could only be seen and not said aloud. Something. Whatever it was, it fell out of Elgin's eye onto the porch. Johnny looked down at it.

"Secretly, every man has done something wrong," Elgin said, "something he shouldn't have done, and when he was doing whatever it was that he was doing, that man knew he shouldn't have been doing it. Every one of us have done it. And there was no turning back from having done it, or maybe there was a turning back, but the man missed his chance to turn around or turn away from it. And once it was done, there was no fixing it. Bricks have to fall on such a man, maybe even on his daughters. And that man has to live his life being silent with that. You feel that secret beating in your heart every day, but you can't release it. And you still got to love your heart. Got no choice about that. It's your heart. You take your heart to the river and you wet it with that water and you hope the river cleanses you of your secret. You're hoping that river can wash your heart clean. Rain didn't do it, so you tell yourself maybe the river can. You scoop together what little pieces of your heart you can, and you hold them there. You make an offering. And Roberto died in that plane crash, and everyone in this city forget how much pain they put in that man's heart. He was just a boy when he came here. Just a child. A boy, Johnny. And he came here by himself. Alone. Stories mess with people as much as these photographs mess with me. You think you're seeing what you're seeing. You think you're saying what you're saying. Messes with your sense of there and gone, dead and alive. You look at a photograph and sometimes you just believe in it. In what's there that you're not seeing, what's there that's been left there for you to not see. Them photographs your mother left you, the ones she rubbed away. They got that kind of seeing in them. That kind of marking. That's what your mother give you."

Johnny handed his grandfather one of the photographs from his mother's book. "This one. He's my father, right?"

Elgin held the photograph between his fingers. He knew what photographs could do to a man's soul if a man put his faith in them. "It's just something that happens. Like stories you start believing in without even knowing that you're believing in them. Your mother," Elgin stopped. He looked down at the photograph. A blind man may not be able to see a photograph, but he can still feel a memory rising.

"It's a fragment of what's gone. It shouldn't never have been what it was. She, your mother, she," Elgin never could find verbs to follow his daughter's name. He looked over at Johnny. "Lehuong wanted you to know something that she could never say to me or to her mother. She only took photographs of what would be lost, and those photographs themselves lost everything that was ever in them to begin with. Over time, all photographs disappear. They quit being what they were meant to be or what they ever could be. Men think a camera can do something that memory can't do. Men can be stupid that way."

Elgin handed the photograph back to his grandson. Johnny took it and moved his chair closer to his grandfather's rocking chair. "But it's my father. Against the tree. My mother's shadow is still in the photograph. She's there, too. Her shadow. I see that."

"Sometimes shadows fall between love and reality. Quiet and meaningless whispers. A violent soul that no woman wants to meet, not even in her dreams. Sometimes love becomes a sickness, Johnny," Elgin said. He ran his thumb over the chipped fingernails of his dirty fingers, picked at one of them. "Your mother only photographed what she knew would be forgotten. You ain't in none of them photographs, are you?"

"No," Johnny replied. "I'm nowhere in none of them."

"Of course you not. Now you know what you know. A photograph ain't no more than a light shining in darkness. It can't remember nothing." Elgin wiped at his eyes. "You can't photograph a kiss, not really, but you can remember that kiss."

Johnny looked up from staring at the cracks between the wood boards of the porch. He looked over at the empty lot, then up at the sky. Rain had stopped. The thunder and lightning had disappeared, drifted up behind Dinwiddie Street, gone off in another direction. The puddles were already fading away. Drying up. The sun was making its way out from behind the clouds.

For an instant Johnny almost believed he saw the shadows disappear, as if the rain had washed them all away, cleaned the world of them. He felt something close to truth fall down into the palms of his hands, and he wondered what rain would do to photographs. Johnny said, "In the end, I guess it don't matter how we go about telling T.J.'s story, but whatever story we convince ourselves to tell of him," Johnny looked over at his grandfather and smiled, "the boy was no Clemente."

Streets and neglected buildings made of memory, made of flesh, made of passion, buildings and streets desperate to remain with the living, but chipped and crumbling at their very edges. Roofs collapsed or collapsing. Windows broken. The longer you live, the more you die. Buildings vanish. Men grow tired of their wives. Wives become more silent. Children disappear. Men like Elgin were all living with dead fathers, dead mothers.

A special thank you to Iko

In Memoriam:

Kathy Acker
Whitney Houston
John C. Gardner
Edward A. Kopper
James Snead

ABOUT THE AUTHOR

Doug Rice is the author of *An Erotics of Seeing, Dream Memoirs of a Fabulist, Between Appear and Disappear, Blood of Mugwump,* and other works of fiction, photography, and theory. His work has been published in numerous journals and anthologies, including *Avant Pop: Fiction for a Daydream Nation, Kiss the Sky, The Dirty Fabulous Anthology, Alice Redux, Phanthoms of Desire, Zyzzyvya, Fiction International, Gargoyle, Discourse,* and *580 Split.* His work has been translated into five languages, and he was a recipient of a literary residency at the Akademie Schloss Solitude, Stuttgart, Germany. He has taught creative writing and film theory at Kent State University-Salem, LaRoche College, Duquesne University, and other universities.

Made in the USA
Columbia, SC
08 March 2018